A Reign of Embers

EVA CHASE

The Royal Spares - Book 4

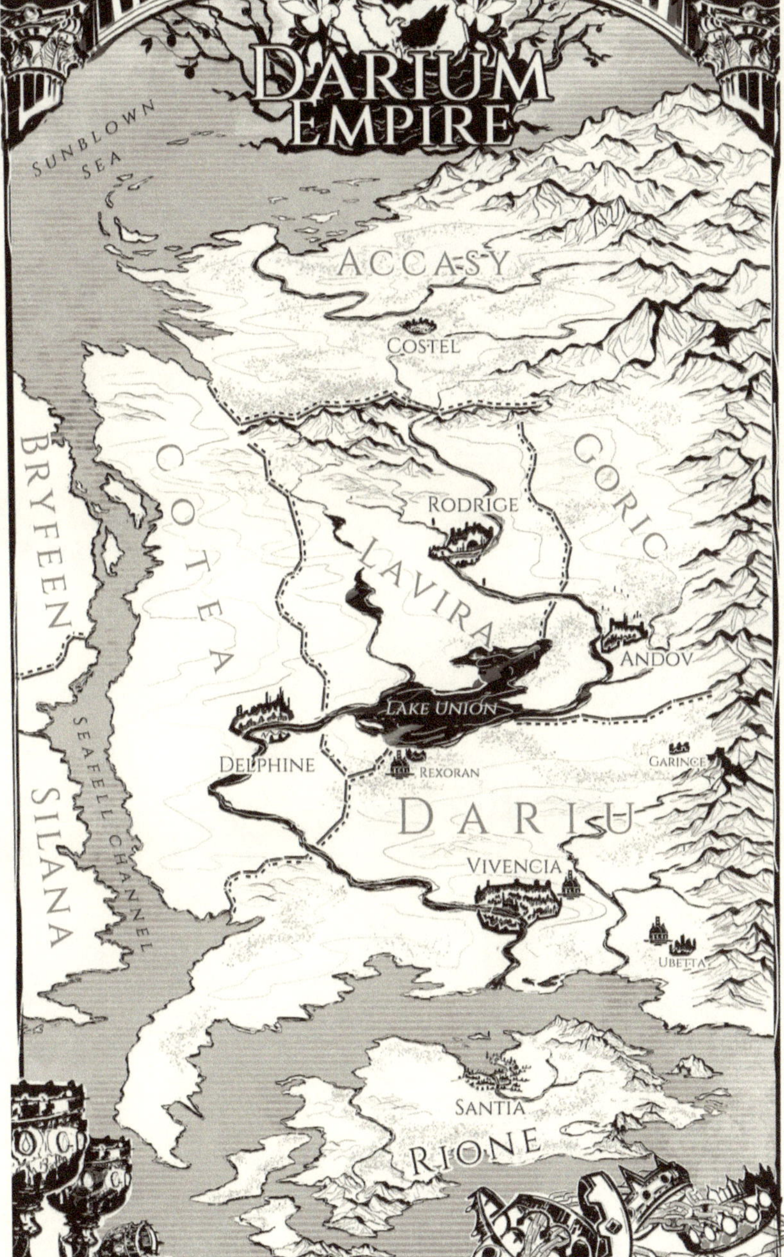

DARIUM EMPIRE
SUNBLOWN SEA
ACCASY
COSTEL
BRYFEEN
COTEA
GORIC
RODRIGE
LAVIRA
ANDOV
SEAFELL CHANNEL
SILANA
Lake Union
Delphine
Rexoran
GARINCE
D A R I U
VIVENCIA
UBETTA
SANTIA
RIONE

CHAPTER ONE

Aurelia

The smell of burnt silk lingers in the hall of the imperial apartments. I pause by one doorway, gazing toward the chambers that until very recently were mine as empress.

No more smoke wafts past the broken door, but scorch marks streak across the frame. Staff hustle out, carrying pieces of charred furniture that's beyond salvaging.

The fire started by Linus, the more insane of my twin husbands, nearly swallowed up me and my daughter forever.

My arms tighten around Coraya. Dozing against my chest, she seems unaware of all the chaos that's followed her birth.

The four guards who accompanied me from the meeting room where I was nearly murdered—*again*—have halted in a ring around me. Two of them shift to admit one of the wetnurses hired to serve the new heir to the Darium empire.

She's older than me, perhaps ten years more than my twenty-two, but she bows with all due respect for her empress. "Your Imperial Highness, I can take care of the baby while you get your much-needed rest."

A more familiar face appears just behind her: Kassun, one of my most loyal guards who's been with me from my earliest days as empress. He bobs his head in turn. "We'll make sure your daughter returns to you safely. She'll get full imperial security."

Instinctively, I tuck Coraya's tiny body even closer to my own. I'd point out that full imperial security didn't prevent one of the two men acting as my husband from turning my bedroom into an inferno, but that was only because of the authority Linus enforced, sending the guards farther away.

And he's dead now. I observed his limp body less than an hour ago, just to be sure.

The thought of letting go of my daughter sends a wrenching sensation down the middle of me, but at the same time, my legs sway. I stiffen them quickly, but my head remains in a partial daze. Despite the recent attentions of the palace medics, dull aches radiate through my pelvis and thighs.

I've only slept for a few hours since Coraya's birth and been through plenty of trauma before and after. Is she really safe with *me*? What if I sleep through her cries of hunger in my exhaustion?

I have to think of what's best for her.

"Yes," I say. "Thank you."

It still takes significant force of will to ease my arms away from my bosom and place my newborn in the wetnurse's embrace.

The woman bows to me again, beaming at me and then at Coraya with a gentle warmth that smooths the sharpest edges off my anxiety. "She'll be treasured as she deserves, Your Imperial Highness."

She steps across the hall to one of the imperial heir apartments and disappears inside with a full host of guards.

Swallowing my apprehension, I fish in the pouch at my hip for the key to my temporary new chambers, ones also meant to be used by an imperial heir. As my fingers close around the metal surface, urgent footsteps thump down the hall toward me.

"Is the empress uninjured?" a newly roughened voice demands. "It seems assassins are teeming through the palace —what are the lot of you doing about it?"

The other man who acted as emperor barges into our midst—or at least attempts to before my remaining guards move to block him. Marc's darkened eyes flash, but he draws himself up short with a flex of his jaw. His intense gaze sweeps over me.

The sight of the man who saved me, who I then saved— the man I've seen as a monster for most of our engagement and marriage but who proved to at least be less of one than his brother—sends a wobble through my pulse.

Words spill out of me. "I'm fine. The medics couldn't heal your scars?"

It's a pointless question—I can see the answer for myself. Most of Marc's golden curls were scorched steel-gray by the flames and the magical wind and shadows that battered him. A matching blotch discolors more than half of his face, rippling unevenly across the center of his forehead, nose, and chin into the natural pale skin remaining on the right side.

As far as I can tell, the strange effect hasn't been lightened at all since I first noticed it.

The uneven border of the scar makes even the shapes of his features appear different. Between that and the gravelly warping of his voice, no one in the palace now recognizes

Marc as emperor. The fact that another man appearing to be the emperor is lying dead in the palace temple would only make the true story of his identity sound more insane.

My guards have stiffened. "We protected Her Imperial Highness," one of them snaps. "She came to no harm."

Marc jerks his hand through the air. "You didn't catch the would-be murderer."

Another of the guards bares her teeth. "And you think you'd have managed it if you'd been there instead of seeing about your face? Go chase the tribune now if you're so sure of your skills. The empress needs her rest."

Marc's gaze flicks back to me. I can't read all the emotions roiling behind his tensed expression.

We haven't had any chance to speak in private since the fire. All the secrets of my crimes hang in the air between us, alongside the ways we protected each other in the end.

I need to know where I stand with him. It feels safer to have him nearby than roaming through the palace that used to be his all day, doing gods know what.

But that doesn't mean I'm going to throw caution to the wind. Just because he saved me a few hours ago doesn't mean I can count on his continued devotion.

Four more figures followed him down the hall with equal haste if more quietly. I look past my husband to the princes who played an equal part in saving my life. Three of them are the people I trust most in this world, who've defended me through so many troubles before this.

I lift my hand as if to brush a stray strand of my hair back behind my ear and make a discreet gesture. Lorenzo catches the message and gives a slight nod in answer. All four of them drift away.

Girding myself, I take on my best imperial tone. "You've all served me admirably, and I'm sure efforts are already underway to bring Tribune Valerisse to justice. For now... I must admit this morning's havoc has left me shaken. Marc did see me through the worst of it. I feel I would sleep better with him guarding my door from the inside as well as the four of you without."

Of all the things I could criticize Marc for, he's never been slow-witted. I'm sure he can realize that I'd like to speak privately.

No doubt he has plenty of things he'd like to say as well. He draws himself straighter with a hint of eager energy. "I would be honored to serve the empress so."

My other guards exchange looks, but Dariu's rulers have beaten obedience above all else into their staff. And there's no denying that I have plenty of reason for rattled nerves and to seek security in the supposed newcomer who rescued me from both a murderer and a deadly blaze.

In the silence of their acceptance, I brush my hands together. "Let us have a pallet brought first in case my rescuer needs to take his own rest. He can lay it by the door and remain on guard."

A page arrives with the requested pallet a few minutes later—all the delay I needed. I step into the chambers that still hold a trace of my husband's tart-and-smoky cologne from when these rooms belonged to him, a mere year ago. Marc enters at my heels and shuts the door behind him.

My heart thuds faster, chasing away my exhausted daze. I walk to the foot of the bed where someone has brought my two trunks—scorched but not burnt through—and sit on the lid of one.

A soft mew makes my pulse skip a beat in a much happier fashion. My tabby cat, Sprite, darts out from beneath the bed to bump her head against the side of the trunk in an appeal for a petting.

She's no longer limping. One of the medics must have healed her from the injury Linus dealt her.

As I rub her chin to her pleased purr, Marc sets down the pallet by the threshold. He approaches me, stopping when he's a few paces away.

For a moment, we simply hold there, looking at each other.

Abruptly, he reaches into his pocket and extends his hand to me. The hilt of a small knife protrudes from his fingers, held so the blade is toward him rather than pointing at me.

"You should have this back," he says in that odd combination of familiar cadence but altered timbre.

It's my knife—the one I tried to defend myself with against Linus, the one I handed Marc so he could see his scar in the reflection. The one he gave to me to begin with, back when we were first married.

The one I braced over his heart last night after I spilled every dark secret I have in an attempt to provoke his rage.

I take it from him, careful not to let my fingers brush his, and set it next to me on the trunk. I'll need to recover my belt sheath or obtain a new one if the old was consumed by the fire.

I suppose this is as good a starting point for the necessary conversation as any. "After what I told you yesterday, I'm surprised you wouldn't prefer to stab me with it."

Sprite leaps up onto the trunk and tucks herself close to me as if she's preparing for him to try. I stroke her soft fur, but my gut stays twisted.

Marc's throat bobs. "If that were my intent, I wouldn't have killed Linus to stop him from doing as much himself."

My mouth slants into a tight, wry smile. "I'm still not sure why you did that either."

"Aurelia…" He appears to grope for words, which maybe isn't surprising. He's had far more shocking revelations dumped on his head in the past day than I have, and he probably got even less sleep last night, if any at all.

His expression firms. He sinks to his knees and sits back on his heels so he's looking up at me rather than down.

"I had a lot of time to think after you left me tied up in that room," he says. "Some of those thoughts were angry. But I can't say I was angrier with you than with myself. No matter how many circles my mind runs in, I know I soured our relationship long before you ever strayed, from that first day you brought me your tea and I scoffed at it. There were things—I had reasons you might not agree with—but for a lot of it—"

He stops and seems to gather himself again, his gaze holding mine. "I've been satisfied and proud in my life, but I've never felt happiness like some of the moments I've had with you in the past several months. To stand with a partner whose wits and fortitude match my own, someone who'll talk to me as *me* not just as an heir or an emperor... And I had no idea what I really had, just how keen your mind is, just how devoted you are to the people who've earned your loyalty and how much danger you'll endure for them. As much as I wish I could have been among that number, I can see that was impossible when I'd betrayed your trust before we were even married."

I don't know what to say to all of that. A lump fills my throat, nearly choking me.

I force my voice past it. "No amount of praise is going to change where we are now. I'm not going to tell anyone who you really are—they'd probably think me mad even if I wanted to try. You're never reclaiming the throne."

Marc's gaze doesn't waver. "I know. And your daughter will never be mine, and my father will never return from the dead. The gods deal out their justice in their own ways. We'd be in a very different place if I'd valued you as you deserve from the start."

"Yes, we would." I look down at my hands and then back

at him, still grappling with confusion. "You could have discarded me this morning, consigned both me and your brother to the flames, emerged as sole emperor in a position to take a new wife and—"

Marc's voice comes out with the edge of a snarl. "I don't *want* another wife."

With those words hanging in the air, we stare at each other through a few heavy beats of my heart. Then he laughs, hollow but not as awful as the anguished sound he made after I first confessed my crimes.

"You ran through flames to win my hand in marriage," he says. "It was more than time that I did at least as much for you. I meant what I said last night. You won. You outmatched me—the empire is yours to claim. But you don't have to rule it alone. I can be here for you as I should have been before. I can—"

A snort rings out from the doorway to the bathing room. "She won't be alone no matter where you are."

As Marc jerks around, Raul stalks into the bedroom, flanked by Bastien and Lorenzo. The prince of Lavira's pale blue eyes sear like flames amid his tawny skin. His massive frame looms a few inches taller and noticeably brawnier than the former emperor even when Marc has scrambled to his feet.

"How—?" Marc's head ticks toward the walls around the bed. "You came ahead through one of the hidden passages."

I push to my feet too. "Because I asked them to, because I wanted to have someone I actually trust nearby." I glance past him to my three princely lovers. "You didn't need to step in."

Raul glowers at Marc. "I figured he'd spouted off enough pretty words trying to wheedle his way into your good graces. He's already lucky you didn't let us broil him—he should be happy enough with that."

Marc's attention ticks back to me. We never got into the reasons why *I* saved *him* from the onslaught of magic my lovers aimed at him.

"I thought there was something worth preserving," I say evenly. "It remains to be seen how much."

Bastien steps up beside Raul, his arms folded over his lean chest and his dark green gaze intent beneath his rumpled auburn hair. "He can try to pitch more of a case later, if you have to let him. You *do* need your rest. And before that, we have more important things to hash out—like what we're going to say if anyone questions how we all got to your bedroom without being seen by the guards Linus sent down the hall."

Right. We constructed our story about the fire on the spur of the moment without having any time to think the details through.

I rub my temple. "We won't want to reveal the hidden passages. They've been too useful, and the information would raise even more questions. The only other direction you could have come from… Can we say that Marclinus invited his foster brothers to his apartment to celebrate the birth of his heir, before he came to see me and her? And that he left Marc on guard when he went to check on me?"

The prince of Cotea's pale face turns pensive. "After which, we followed him when we heard a disturbance. That could work."

Raul scowls at Marc. "As long as the 'guard' doesn't dispute the story."

Marc glares back at the other man. "Any doubt in our story would likely harm my position more than yours. I can stick to the same tale."

Lorenzo moves past his foster brothers, giving Marc a wide berth, so he can slip his dark hand around my elbow. I lean into his well-muscled frame, craving the comfort.

If Marc's jaw tenses, so be it. He won't have any place here at all if he can't accept the men who've become the real loves of my life.

The tongue-less prince signs his question rather than using his illusionary voice. *Soldier attacked you. Why?*

Bastien's posture tenses. "Yes, we heard Tribune Valerisse tried to kill you. What in the realms is wrong with her?"

The memory of the high-ranking officer's remarks turns my stomach.

I close my eyes for a second to steady myself. "She blames me for the empire's struggles in the past year—she doesn't think I'm capable of guiding it until Coraya is of age. She demanded that I step aside to let someone else take the throne and said that she has Sabrelle's approval to turn the imperial army against me if I refuse. Then she lunged at me."

Marc sucks a sharp breath through his teeth. "That's ridiculous. As if Valerisse has a better claim than an imperial spouse who's proven herself more than any consort in history. That fucking traitor. When we get our hands on her—"

"It doesn't look as if we will all that quickly," Raul interrupts. "*Your* soldiers didn't manage to catch her even in the palace. It sounds like she's long gone." His scowl deepens. "Probably running back to Lavira where she's worked most closely with the army."

The thought of all the problems still ahead of us rolls over me, and my balance tilts. Lorenzo's grasp on my arm tightens. He gestures to the others.

Bastien's mouth flattens. "If Valerisse is gone, then she's no immediate threat to Aurelia. Our empress won't be able to rule anyone if she's mad with exhaustion. We can get a sense of the loyalties of the soldiers here at the palace while she sleeps."

Marc squares his shoulders. "I'm staying here, to ensure

no one makes another assassination attempt. It'd look strange for me to leave after she requested my presence."

Raul growls. "You have about as much—"

I raise my hand to stop his protest. "Marc's right. But he'll be keeping plenty of distance, over by the door, as we agreed."

My husband's eyes narrow, but he doesn't argue.

Raul draws himself even taller. "Fine. Then I'm staying too—right here in your bed, in case *he* makes any attempt. Bastien and Lorenzo don't need me to find out plenty."

"Fine!" I wave at them all to get on with their various duties before another debate breaks out. "I will be well-protected and well-supplied with information. Thank you all." I pause, and more emotion colors my voice. "For everything."

I aim a smile full of affection at Bastien and bob up to kiss Lorenzo's cheek. The prince of Rione guides me around the side of the bed and waits until I'm tucked under the covers.

Marc takes his post by the pallet at the door. Sprite curls up next to my belly, and Raul props himself at my other side, sitting on top of the blankets with his back against the headboard. He rests a reassuring hand on my shoulder.

I watch Bastien and Lorenzo slip away through the hidden panel. It's only just closing behind them when the deepest fatigue I've ever known drags me under.

Chapter Two

Bastien

I t's never been difficult for me to listen in on chatter around the palace. As far as both the nobles and staff are concerned, I'm of secondary importance compared to the Darium natives. I may have been called the emperor's foster brother, but everyone knows I'm a hostage—a powerless symbol of the empire's domination.

If they had any idea how much power I've wielded behind the scenes… But it's better that they don't, because I can still amble through the halls, pausing where I can overhear the conversations of the guards without any of them giving me a second glance.

There aren't a whole lot of those conversations to listen to. The imperial soldiers are a disciplined bunch. But I overhear a commanding officer reminding a couple of underlings to be particularly thorough in their patrol of the outer walls, and a few guards heading off-duty grumbling that the "traitor tribune" hasn't been apprehended yet.

No one makes any indication that they doubt Aurelia's claim to the throne, at least as a guardian figure until the imperial heir is old enough to rule. It sounds as though all of the palace soldiers see Tribune Valerisse as a criminal rather than a justified dissenter.

So far. If Aurelia understood her correctly and the godlen of war herself has some hand in recent events, Great God only knows how this internal rebellion will play out.

My niggling uneasiness takes me back into the palace's hidden passages. I thought to poke around in Aurelia's ruined bedroom for anything enlightening, but the repair staff are still at work. The smoky scent seeps through the walls to itch at my nose.

I linger by the closed panel for several minutes, listening to the workers, but they all sound horrified by the attempts on their empress's life too.

Finally, I tramp down to the old servant room where we held Marc last night.

There's little to inspect in that dim space. The lantern reveals the broken pieces of the chair we tied him to, lying in disarray across the floor. Nothing else looks any different than usual.

Except for something we left behind that I *should* see but don't.

As I peer at the settee where Raul tossed the gold wedding band he cut from Marc's wrist, my pulse stutters. I'd swear the severed band was lying here on the cushions, gleaming in the lanternlight, right before we left when Aurelia went into labor. Nothing remains but worn linen.

I drag my fingers along the edges of the cushions and peer beneath the furniture, but no gold band presents itself. Frowning, I straighten up again.

The broken bangle couldn't have simply disappeared. Did one of my foster brothers come back and pocket it?

If Marc took it when he escaped… will he use it to try to reclaim the throne? To prove Aurelia's crimes against him?

The oddly scarred man who's one half of our former emperor made an emphatic show of devotion when he appealed to Aurelia this morning, but I don't trust the prick farther than I could kick him.

Is it possible someone else found their way down here? Could Sabrelle have guided one of her dedicats that thoroughly?

I'm not finding any answers just staring at the space.

I return to the regular palace halls to the wafting scents of dinner. A subdued atmosphere hangs over the nobles gathering in the dining room—any spurt of laughter is quickly snuffed out. We've all donned the dark mourning clothes that last came out a year ago for Emperor Tarquin's departure.

The staff have seated all four of us foster princes together. Lorenzo nods to me with a quick gesture to say he's seen no reason for immediate worry either. Neven, who we spoke to briefly before taking up our separate investigations, fiddles with his knife.

"Everyone's acting so *sad* that Marclinus is dead," he mutters. "And they don't know— I can't believe she—"

I tap his arm to stop him. "This isn't the place to talk about it. She knew him better than any of us. She ended the worst of it, didn't she? Just as she intended."

I hold down my own misgivings about Marc's new position among us. Why didn't Aurelia let him burn while we had the chance?

Our empress can be brilliant, but she cares so deeply. She wants to believe the best of people.

If Marc betrays her benevolence, I'll gut him myself.

I'm about to say as much when a flurry of activity draws all our attention to the front of the room. Raul hurries over to join us with a crooked smile, done with his self-assigned guard duties.

Because Aurelia is entering, draped in black silk from neck to feet, with a full host of guards escorting her to the honored spot at the head table. Her mouth set in a tight smile, she dips her head to acknowledge the nobles who murmur an awkward mix of congratulations and condolences.

In the bundle of black fabric cradled in her arms, the reason for the congratulations stirs.

Aurelia stops by her throne-like chair, eases back the blanket to reveal our daughter's downy head, and gazes toward her court. Complete silence falls over the room without anyone needing to call for it.

This is the first time most of the nobles are setting eyes on the imperial heir: the baby they all think has the greatest claim on the Darium throne now that her supposed father is supposedly dead.

Watching mother and daughter together, my heart squeezes with a giddy ache like nothing I've ever experienced.

Coraya is *my* daughter. Somehow I helped create the new life now so vibrantly real in Aurelia's arms. That's the woman I love and the child I already cherish, as little time as I've gotten to spend with her so far.

But there'll never be much more time, not as long as we need all of Dariu to believe the baby is Marclinus's. I'll never get to stand beside Aurelia as her partner and father of her child. Never get to dote on our daughter as she deserves.

It's a miracle we've accomplished as much as we have. I shouldn't want more than this.

But some part of me craves it, with a burn that runs right down to my core.

Aurelia pitches her clear voice to carry through the large room. "I want to thank you all for your kind words in this time that should be so joyful but has veered into tragedy. I'll complete my husband's private funeral rites tonight, and tomorrow we will all honor Marclinus as he's due. I'm sure our daughter, Coraya, will fulfill our hopes for Dariu when she's grown. Let us do all we can to nurture that growth and protect her from whatever threats may come."

A murmuring of agreement ripples through the crowd alongside respectful applause. Most of the nobles look a bit dazed.

I suppose I can't blame them for that. None of them could have expected to lose two emperors in the course of a year or to find themselves ruled by a woman from the opposite end of the empire.

Thank all things divine that we've spent so much of that year building support for Aurelia, to the point that many might appreciate having her in charge rather than Marclinus. May our work have been enough to see her through the troubles ahead.

Her gaze sweeps over the assembled crowd again, and I manage a swift gesture of my hand in one subtle offering of affection. *I love you.*

She doesn't dare return the signal with so many looking on, but a softer smile touches her lips as she takes her seat.

I turn back to my foster brothers to start tackling the troubles I already know of. "Did any of you go down to the room on the lowest level and pick up a broken armband?"

I'm being vague just in case anyone catches my lowered voice, but my fellow princes know enough of the situation to fill in the blanks. All of them shake their heads, Raul's forehead furrowing.

"Is it gone?" he asks.

"I couldn't find it when I was down there an hour ago."

He grunts, the sound more uneasy than annoyed. "I'll take another look."

Neven's fingers tighten around his knife. "If it's missing, then there's only one person other than us who could have taken it, isn't there? What good reason could he have?"

"It wouldn't get Marc very far, I don't think," Lorenzo says, projecting his illusionary voice to us alone. *"It's a simple loop of metal—he couldn't prove it was part of Aurelia's marriage ceremony. It* wasn't, *was it? Didn't she say Linus was the twin who participated in the official rites?"*

I nod slowly. "That's true. He could have taken it on an impulse and then realized there was no use for it. But we can't discount the possible godly influence and whether Sabrelle may have encouraged someone else to meddle."

Neven's expression twitches. He sits stiffly silent as a server comes around to set the plates with the first course in front of us.

The moment the server is gone, he drops his voice to a rough whisper. "What do you mean about Sabrelle?"

He wasn't there when Aurelia mentioned Tribune Valerisse's claims. I balk automatically, so used to censoring what we discuss around the youngest of our group—but we've made the mistake of shutting out the prince of Goric too many times before.

He sided with us and with Aurelia when it mattered most. We might not have saved her from the fire without his gift of strength to bash down her apartment door.

Lorenzo picks up the thread for me, his gift letting him speak much more openly than I could with the nobles all around us. *"When Tribune Valerisse attacked Aurelia, she announced that Sabrelle is on her side—and would support the army turning against Aurelia to get her off the throne. I suppose we don't know for sure if that's even partly true rather than delusional ranting, but—"*

Neven breaks in, his tan face gone sallow. "I don't think it's just delusion. I—I should talk to Aurelia as soon as possible."

Chapter Three

Aurelia

I've never felt entirely comfortable surrounded by the Darium court, whether they were judging me for being a wild princess from the north or fawning over me to win favor with their empress.

The atmosphere in the palace has an even more unsettling energy now. Everyone feels they *should* make a gesture toward their now-sole ruler who just birthed an imperial heir and survived two assassination attempts, but I can tell nobody is quite sure what the appropriate approach would be. Their expressions waver between smiles and frowns; they halt in the middle of sentences and double-back on themselves before scurrying away.

Even Vicerine Bianca, the woman who's become the closest thing to a real friend I have despite our very rocky beginning, joins me on my way out of the dining room with unusual hesitance.

She pats the upswept locks of her shining black hair as if to make sure it's in place and tips her head with a cautious smile. "Your Imperial Highness, you've had quite the trial of a day. Is there anything you need that all these fops haven't thought of?"

My lips twitch at her irreverent phrasing even as my heart pangs that she asked at all. The last time I spoke with Bianca, I was asking her to take on a dangerous task: drugging Linus so that I could kidnap his twin. She doesn't know my true reasons, but she took up the duty without question or complaint.

Even though I can't imagine she thinks the few hours the emperor spent unconscious in her bed could have caused him to later be tossed out the window of my apartment, she's sharp enough to have some sense of plans gone awry.

I might have trusted her enough to make that risky request, but I'm not quite at the point of confessing all of my sins. I smile back at her as warmly as I'm capable of. "I've been quite fussed over, thank you. The hardest parts are those I must see to on my own."

"Of course." Her dark gaze drops to the baby in my arms, and her smile softens. "She's lovely."

The pang expands to the base of my throat. I stroke my thumb over the delicate down that shades Coraya's head and admit one thing I haven't to anyone else yet. "I'm still having trouble believing I made her."

Bianca simply laughs. "Who else could have? Look, she has your perfect composure already."

Her relaxing into our familiar rapport eases my own nerves a little. Enough for me to take her up on her offer of help after all.

I sidle a little closer and speak under my breath. "Recent events have left me rather uneasy about our company here in the palace. If you hear any hint of dissention—from the court or the staff—"

Bianca's eyes spark with understanding before I need to finish my sentence. Her smooth brown face firms. "Of course, Aurelia. I'll keep my ears pricked."

She swans off with a sway of her voluptuous hips. The other nearby nobles glance over with curiosity and perhaps a hint of disdain.

Just a few days ago, I guided Linus into banishing Bianca's husband to their estate, a punishment that wasn't extended to her. The charge was the most superficial of supposed treason, but a little of that taint may have rubbed off on her.

I'll have to hope that my favor will offset any ill-feelings I've stirred up while freeing her from that loathsome man. I'd rather see sneers aimed at her than fresh bruises on her skin... but I'm not entirely sure she'd have made the same trade.

On my way to the palace temple, Coraya wakes with a thin but demanding wail. I step into a sitting room to feed her. Once she's sated and drifting back into sleep, one of my guards has summoned a nursemaid.

I can't help balking again before I hand her over, but I'm not sure funeral rites are the best place for a baby. Would the image of the broken corpse everyone believes was her father burn itself into her brain even at this young age?

It's certainly seared into mine, however well the devouts have straightened out and dressed up Linus's body after his fall. The carefully placed cushions can't do much to disguise the caved-in portion of his skull, no matter how they've cleaned the blood from his sallow skin.

The four imperial advisors—High Commander Axius, Counsels Etta and Severo, and Cleric Pierus—join me in the temple. I follow Pierus's instructions and my memories of the rites I assisted Marclinus with after his father's death, intoning the words of respect and mourning, bowing here and dipping my head in prayer there.

By the time I've tapped my fingers down my chest in the gesture of the divinities for the final time, my spirit feels wrung out, even though I've spent most of the day dozing.

One of the palace medics has arrived while I carried out the familial rites. She walks with me back to my chambers, asking me questions about how each part of my body feels, and examines me in the privacy of my bedroom.

She steps back with a brisk nod. "You're healing well, Your Imperial Highness. Continue getting plenty of rest when you can and avoiding any significant physical strain. Our gifts can see you through the early days after birth faster than without them, but no magic can heal everything in an instant."

My mouth curves wryly. "I know, and I appreciate the help you can offer."

Sprite scampers out from under the bed and leaps up to lean her sleek body against mine. As I give her the petting she's demanding, I smile more fully at the medic. "I'm grateful to you and your colleagues for seeing to her healing as well."

The medic tips into another bow. "Of course. She was eager to be back at your side."

I'd sink back on the bed and go back to sleep with Sprite cuddled up against me, but the moment the medic has vanished into the hallway, the hidden panel in the wall whispers to the side. As I turn to face it, all four of the foster princes emerge into the room.

Bastien strides straight to me, cupping my face and drawing my mouth to his. Raul shoulders past him to sit with his arm around my shoulders. Lorenzo settles at my other side, twining his fingers with mine.

And Neven halts a few paces away, his posture rigid and his expression uncertain.

Bastien glances toward the door, the pallet next to it now vacant. "Marc's gone off to sleep in the guards' quarters?"

Raul makes a sound that's half-grunt, half-growl. "That's what he said and what it looked like when Aurelia headed to dinner. One place I couldn't easily make an excuse to follow him."

Neven's hands tighten into fists. "If he encourages the soldiers at the palace to turn against Aurelia—"

I hold up my hand to stop him. "I don't think we need to worry about that. He just needed some rest." The former emperor stayed on his feet the entire time I slept, even though he must have been equally exhausted. He couldn't justify staying in my chambers when I'm not here to guard.

Neven grimaces. "You can't trust him. We should have gotten rid of him when we had the chance, so they'd both be gone."

None of his foster brothers add their agreement, but their silence says plenty.

I swallow thickly. It's been difficult enough explaining my choice to myself. But I need all of these men completely on my side as much as I ever have.

I look down at Lorenzo's hand tucked around mine. "I've made some brutal decisions since I came to Dariu, but my goal has always been peace. The fewer people I need to hurt, the better. And Elox has sent me visions from the start warning me that I was dealing with two men in my husband rather than one… and encouraging me to embrace the better of them."

"You don't have to follow everything a godlen suggests," Raul mutters.

"I know. I thought I wasn't going to." I lift my head. "But you saw how Marc responded after I laid out all the ways I've betrayed him. Even in that first moment, he didn't lash out at me. And when he found Linus attacking me, he ran straight at his brother to protect me. He could have ensured that both Linus and I died in the fire and walked out as sole emperor without a treasonous wife, but instead he sacrificed his chance at the throne to save me."

"He couldn't have realized he was sacrificing that much," Bastien points out. "He didn't know he'd end up so scarred no one would recognize him as emperor. Once he's had more time to stew on his new situation..."

"We can't know for sure how he'll react. I realize that too. I *don't* trust him." I look around at all of my lovers before shifting my gaze to Neven. "But I believe he's earned a chance to show whether he means what he's said. His knowledge of the empire could be an incredible resource for everything I still want to accomplish—and in fending off whatever opposition Valerisse is planning. If he takes one step out of line, rain down all the vengeance you want on him. But I've seen moments of goodness in him. Any seed can grow."

Neven snorts, but then he hangs his head as if ashamed of the open display of ridicule. "I guess I can't even know... how much of Marclinus's awfulness was him and not the other one."

I pick the incident I assume will matter most to him. "It was Linus who gave your people that awful challenge with the cemetery—Linus who ordered the guards to beat you. And it was Marc who agreed to follow up that beating with a less-than-fatal punishment when I appealed to the compassion he does have, however little it's been cultivated before now."

The youngest prince shifts his weight and lets out a sigh. "All right. We'll see." His expression turns briefly fierce before he meets my eyes again. "You think Sabrelle has something to do with… everything that's gone wrong. That she's egging on Valerisse against you."

"Yes. From what Valerisse said, Sabrelle has been encouraging her to push back against any influence I have. Enough so that she felt justified attempting my assassination, both this morning and through soldiers who were following her orders while we were on our tour."

Neven's jaw works. "I think Valerisse is telling the truth. I —I've had dreams, visions… Maybe some of them really *were* just dreams, but the more that came, the harder it was to ignore them."

Lorenzo studies him solemnly. *"You mentioned the dreams before."*

"Yes. It might not sound like much of an excuse, but I really didn't know what to believe. At first there was only this sense of urgency, like everything I cared about was slipping through my fingers, like I needed to fight."

"Like you weren't doing enough," I say, remembering what he said when he shared his fears with me many months ago.

"Yes." He swipes his hand across his mouth. "But then, even when I started trying to help you with your goals … The dreams turned bloodier. More violence, more death. Most of the time, they showed you turning your back on the pain or accepting the chaos. And when I kept seeing you go along with Marclinus's challenges, barely standing up to him at all—"

When Raul makes a sound of protest, Neven cuts him off with a brusque wave.

"I realize how difficult a position you were in," he says to me. "And I had no idea how much more complicated your situation had gotten. She just seemed so *insistent*… It's difficult to ignore what feels like a divine presence in your head for weeks on end."

My voice softens. "I can understand that." Elox has never been anywhere near so forceful in his messages to me, and I still struggle with refusing to heed him.

Bastien cocks his head. "What do you think Sabrelle wanted? Did she really think Marclinus was doing a great job as emperor—did she want him terrorizing the rest of the continent? Who was going to stand up to him if *not* Aurelia?"

Neven shrugs helplessly. "You know how those kinds of visions are. The intent wasn't totally clear. The best that I could figure was that she was saying to follow the might. Side with whoever was willing to really fight, because they'd hold the empire together in the end. But I don't think she was totally against Aurelia."

He catches my gaze. "In Rodrige, when you went looking for her blessed armband—I had a vision of red light surrounding you and bringing the empire to your feet, and the sense that I needed to make sure you knew. That's why I told you to follow the signs of the gods."

My stomach drops with a sudden lurch. "Red light…"

Raul's head jerks toward me. "What?"

"I thought it was Elox guiding me—maybe I should have realized. Red isn't his color." I shake my head. "When I was pretending to search for the armband, a reddish glow caught my attention. It led me to a specific place and 'showed' me where the armband was hidden. I could have retrieved the real thing… but I didn't want to put that power in Linus's hands, and getting it would have hurt the locals too."

Bastien frowns. "Then Sabrelle was trying to manipulate even you to her own ends. The imperial family has always credited her and Creaden with the founding and expansion of the empire. She wants to see it strengthened, not broken apart."

"It sounds that way." Other memories trickle up. "A

similar glow led me to overhear a conversation between merchants in Goric who've been sending Dariu faulty goods. Maybe she hoped I'd get angry instead of sympathizing with them. And Linus mentioned that Sabrelle sent him dreams that inspired some of the trials he put his potential brides through. Even—"

I stop, caught in a sudden chill.

Raul's arm tightens around me. "Even what?"

"Marc said he'd been having violent nightmares. He mentioned it at least once during the tour. He didn't seem to think they were godlen-sent, but maybe he'd already adjusted his thinking too much for her to win him over that way."

Lorenzo's mouth twists. *"If she manages to sway him, that could be worse than Valerisse."*

I stand up abruptly. "We need to talk to him, find out exactly what she showed him. I can come up with an excuse. The rest of you, step out of view before I talk to the guards outside."

Lorenzo squeezes my hand before letting it go. With visible reluctance, the princes move to the bathing room where they won't be visible even if one of the guards steps inside. It would hardly help my reputation for the empress to be seen entertaining her late husband's foster brothers secretly in her bedroom less than a day after his death.

I ease open the door and peek out into the hall, putting on a sheepish expression. The guards posted there immediately jerk to sharper attention. "What do you need, Your Imperial Highness?"

"I find I'm too unsettled to sleep in here on my own. I keep thinking about that vile man barging into my other bedroom." I add a shudder for dramatics' sake. "I think I'd rest easier for now if Marc was watching over the doorway from the other side again. Could one of you call him here? I still have the pallet if he needs more rest—I know he'd wake if there was a commotion."

The guards hesitate for just a second before leaping to assist. "Whatever you need. It's no wonder."

One of them hustles down the hall to pass on word to a page.

In a matter of minutes, Marc arrives at the apartment doorway, his tarnished curls a little rumpled and his eyes weary but his well-built form now clothed in a proper imperial guard uniform. He steps inside, carrying a folded blanket under his arm.

As the door shuts behind him, his gaze lingers on me, appraising. "I suppose we could make this a regular assignment."

I manage half a smile. "That might serve our purposes well."

"As long as you remember to keep enough distance," Raul adds as the princes emerge to join us.

Marc takes them in before returning his attention to me. "I take it you didn't summon me only for your personal security."

"No." I fold my arms in front of me, bracing for what I suspect will be an unpleasant recounting. "I want to know about the dreams you had while we were on tour. The bloody ones that had something to do with me. Did any of them feel as if they might have divine influence?"

Marc pauses, the momentary creasing of his brow suggesting that the possibility honestly hadn't occurred to him before. "I assumed they were brought on by all Linus's aggressive ranting about you. I'd rather not— You have to believe I found them horrifying when I woke up. It was never anything I wanted."

Bastien lifts his chin toward his foster brother. "What happened in them? Spit it out."

Marc shoots him a quick glower but gathers himself. "Mostly there'd be destruction happening around Aurelia— buildings toppling or people crumpling where she walked, that sort of thing. And then I'd race in and... and slaughter her, and everything would recover."

The horror he spoke of roughens his voice even more. He swallows audibly and focuses on me again. "Why would you think there's anything divine about them?"

I don't see any reason to hide what we know. "You're already aware that Valerisse claims Sabrelle is encouraging her attempts to get rid of me. Linus mentioned being inspired by dreams she sent him. Neven has had dreams and visions he believes came from her, encouraging him to see me as a threat. And it appears that she tried to manipulate me into working toward her ends as well."

As I explain what we've experienced in more detail, Marc's jaw tenses. When I've finished, he swipes his hand over his mottled face. "In light of all that... those dreams could have been her trying to incite ill-feeling toward you. If she was urging on Linus at the same time, he undermined that strategy. It was hard to put any stock in imagery that aligned with his madness."

Raul eyes his imperial foster brother with open suspicion. "Are you still getting these murderous dreams?"

Marc shakes his head. "Not in weeks, maybe even months. I suppose Sabrelle could tell they weren't swaying me."

"If the godlen of war really is siding with Valerisse's rebellion," Neven says, "isn't that much worse for Aurelia? There've got to be tens of thousands of Sabrellian dedicats just in Dariu, and a lot of them are soldiers."

A thread of nausea winds through my gut. "If she can persuade them into seeing me as an enemy to the empire, we're going to have a difficult battle ahead. Unless..."

I trail off, overwhelmed by the thought that's struck me. The men wait for me to gather my thoughts.

Despite my own fatigue, I harden my stance. "Sabrelle reached out to me too. She gave me a chance to act in her favor. There has to be some way I can persuade *her* that my interests don't have to be at odds with hers. If I can win over her and those dedicated to her, the whole rebellion may very well fall apart."

But that requires convincing the godlen of war that a dedicat of peace is a worthy ruler of an empire… an empire I intend to disassemble.

The weight of that task stifles whatever hope flickered to life inside me. The princes' expressions darken too.

But Marc's gray eyes glint with sudden enthusiasm. "I may have something that'll help your cause."

Chapter Four

Lorenzo

I wake up into an unfamiliar sense of peace, lulled by the slow breaths rising and falling next to me on the bed. When I turn my head to gaze at Aurelia's sleeping face, the sensation expands with a swell of affection and a quiver of exhilaration.

This is the first time I've gotten to spend the whole night with her. We've never dared before. But there's no longer a brutal imperial husband who could storm into her private chambers at any moment and discover the affair.

Her delicate features look even softer in sleep. With the rest, more of her natural lively color has come back into her tanned skin, where yesterday morning it'd been leached away by stress and exhaustion.

Her rich walnut-brown hair tumbles across the pillow around her serene face. I like it so much better flowing wild

than in the upswept styles Darium custom imposes on married women. It suits the spirit of the woman I love.

A rustle by the door brings my attention in the other direction. The sort-of husband my beloved still has is getting to his feet on the pallet he spread by the entrance.

Marc jerks the jacket of his guard uniform straight and meets my gaze with the inscrutable expression that always made me nervous when he was acting as emperor. It's more unsettling combined with the gray swath of scarring that discolors more than half of his face—as if he might still be two different men, only now combined in one body.

Thank all that's holy he hasn't shown any signs of Linus's sadistic tendencies so far.

I stayed overnight mainly to protect Aurelia from *him*, though I suspect he thinks me an ineffectual defender. He doesn't know that I could summon her other guards in an instant. My gift could project an illusionary shout of warning far louder than any natural voice.

But there hasn't been anything to raise the alarm about. He didn't stir from his sleeping pallet the whole night.

A twinge in my bladder makes me grit my teeth. I sit up, debating whether I can hold out until Aurelia wakes.

Marc's darkened gray gaze assesses me as I'd imagine he might have soldiers on the battlefield, back when he got to lead the empire's army. "You can go relieve yourself. I'll stay right here."

There's a caustic note in his voice, as if he's disparaging the suspicions I haven't voiced. As if we don't have every reason to worry about how he'll treat this incredible woman after the horrors he and his twin have already put her through.

But Aurelia trusts him enough not to fear his presence. We're never going to find out just how much he's truly accepted his new situation if we're on him like jailers every second he's around her.

I tip my head in acknowledgment and pad over to the bathing room.

I keep my attention on the bedroom as I do my business, not wasting any time. After I've washed my hands, I start to stride back out and then hesitate.

Instead, I ease over to peer past the doorway, my body mostly hidden by the frame.

Marc isn't paying the bathing room any mind. He's still standing on the sleeping pallet, his hands flexing at his sides, his gaze fixed on Aurelia's sleeping form.

I can't call his expression inscrutable anymore. No, I've seen those slightly widened eyes and that strained set of the mouth before—on two of my other foster brothers. No doubt they've witnessed it on me as well.

I'm too familiar with the longing for what one can't have. Here it is again, right in front of me.

The sight sets off an uneasy pang in my gut. I don't want to sympathize with the man who's been a party to so many awful things. He doesn't *deserve* to have Aurelia—he should be thanking her generous soul that she's allowed him to live in her presence.

At the same time, I can't help remembering the moment when we had him tied up in that basement servant room, when he looked at her and told her he loved her without a trace of deceit.

He's had his entire life upended in the course of a day, but he's here anyway, serving her in the one way she's let him. I can give him a little credit for that, however reluctantly.

A rap of knuckles on the bedroom door makes both of us startle. As Aurelia stirs, one of the guards' voices carries through the wood. "Your Imperial Highness, your maids are here to get you ready for the day."

Aurelia swipes at her eyes and pushes upright. She catches my gaze with a flicker of a smile that holds enough fondness to warm me.

"Just a moment!" she calls back.

I meet her at the edge of the bed to steal a swift kiss, ignoring Marc's gaze burning into my back. As I step toward the wall's hidden panel, he clears his throat. "After breakfast, we'll meet in the room where you held me?"

We discussed last night how we'd spend the couple of spare hours before the public funeral ceremony begins. I nod and slip into the wall.

The four of us foster princes trek through the hidden passages together, the meager breakfast I forced down sitting heavy in my stomach. We emerge into the dim room at the bottom of the stairs to find the lantern already lit and Marc pushing the few furnishings to the edges of the room. The drifting dust tickles my nose.

The former emperor has heaped the broken pieces of the armchair we tied him to in the smaller room that has the sealed-off entrance from the servants' quarters. None of us comments on that.

Unsurprisingly, Raul's gaze shoots straight to the length of gleaming steel resting on the settee. He strides over, shouldering past Marc with a little more force than I expect was needed, and peers down at the sword. "So this is it. You managed to pilfer it."

Marc keeps his voice even. "I wouldn't consider it 'pilfering' when it's been my family's for generations. There hasn't been a threat intense enough in my lifetime that we've brought it out. Using it for lesser purposes would offend our godlen. I'd be surprised if many in the court even know it exists."

Another murmur of the panel brings our conversation to a halt.

Aurelia steps into the room, taking us all in with her pensive eyes. I can't shake the impression that she's checking to make sure we princes haven't mortally wounded her fallen husband or vice versa in her absence.

Marc wastes no time lifting the sword and presenting it to her with it lying across his outstretched hands.

I'm no connoisseur of weaponry, but the sword looks like an impressive piece even to me. The blade gleams with wicked sharpness; elaborate gold designs surround the steel handguard. The ruby set in the pommel sparkles around an etching of Sabrelle's sigil.

"From what I was told, a dozen Sabrellian devouts applied their gifts to bless this sword," Marc says. "You'll never find another easier to handle—as long as you're *ready* to handle it. Its blessings are tuned to the will and nerve of the swordsman. If you can wield it well, that'll be one significant step to proving your worthiness to Sabrelle."

Aurelia hums and reaches out to wrap her fingers around the leather-bound hilt. "I suppose I'd better get started then. I assume you've trained with it yourself."

Marc nods. As she hefts the weapon in the air experimentally, he touches her arm, aligning his body with hers. "To begin with, you'll want to—"

"Get your hand off her," Raul growls, shoving Marc aside. "She doesn't need your training. I've already taught her what she needed to survive your ridiculous trials—I can take it from here."

The prince of Lavira jerks his head toward Neven. "Come on, we might as well see what you picked up from those weeks in the soldiers' quarters too."

Marc's jaw clenches, but he steps to the side of the room without a word. Bastien eyes him warily as we retreat ourselves.

Raul positions himself behind Aurelia and guides her posture with a lift of her elbow and a gentle tug of her shoulder. "It's not so different from the smaller swords you've practiced with before. You'll need to compensate for the additional weight—"

Aurelia arcs the blade in a careful slice of the air. "It doesn't *feel* that much heavier. I suppose that might be part of the blessing?"

We all glance toward Marc.

He folds his arms over his chest where he's leaning against the wall. "Am I allowed to contribute now? Yes, it's magically enhanced to adapt to the wielder's body. The more confident you are with it, the easier you'll find it."

Aurelia studies the sword with a tensing of her lips. I can't say the weapon looks right in her hand.

My peaceful woman was never meant to be a warrior, however much she's been forced to act as one already. But we've all needed to bend our ideas about who we are so we can stand against the empire.

I don't think there's anything our empress *wouldn't* do if it means freeing the conquered kingdoms from Dariu's tyranny, no matter what it costs her personally.

That knowledge casts a gloom over me as I watch Raul direct Aurelia through a few basic exercises. He orders Neven to grab one of the broken chair legs to use as a makeshift weapon of his own, and the rap of steel against wood reverberates through the cramped space.

Aurelia's face sets with the determination I'm used to. She blocks Neven's jabs with a grace I doubt is entirely due to Raul's past tutoring. But when she takes the offensive, lashing out at our younger foster brother, her breath comes shorter, her arm wobbling with the strain.

She pauses, turning the sword in her hand. "It seems to shift—the way it feels. I start to think I've found my rhythm with it, and then it gets harder again."

"That's divine blessings for you," Raul mutters. "Shifty and fickle." He motions to Marc. "If you've got tips of your own, go ahead and 'contribute' them."

I might not enjoy having the former emperor among us, but Raul's caustic tone rankles me. There's no denying that Marc brought Aurelia this weapon to help her cause. He didn't have to mention it even exists.

Why is Raul heckling Marc when our old enemy is finally working toward our ends? I can't see how talking to him that way is going to make him more inclined to keep doing so.

It isn't as if I can really speak up, though, so I simply make a grimace at Raul that I don't think he even notices.

Marc steps closer, focusing only on Aurelia. "You're not fully committed yet. That makes sense—it's unlikely to happen instantly, even for a practiced fighter. The pressure of Sabrelle's influence can throw anyone off."

She lets out a dry chuckle. "And how am I supposed to become more committed? Do I need to bend down before the sword like I would a godlen?"

Marc shakes his head. "Sink into the movements. Find a place where you believe that any violence you deal out with that blade is deserved. You *can* rule the continent with a weapon like that in your hands. Keep at it until you've cut through every doubt." His voice warms with a tenderness I've never heard from my imperial foster brother before. "It might take days or weeks, but I know you have it in you."

His admiration for her itches at me almost as much as

Raul's attitude did. I bite my lip, keeping my own counsel as Aurelia faces off against Neven again.

Blade and chair leg clatter together. The tip of the sword swipes close to Neven's forehead, and Aurelia winces as much as he does.

Marc speaks up before she's even stepped back. "Don't shy from the bloodshed. If you nick him, we can heal him up. You can't hold yourself back."

Every particle of my body stiffens in rejection of that advice. It isn't about holding herself back—it's about needing to stay true to who she is at her core.

He still doesn't truly understand her.

I lift my hand to gesture to Raul—and hesitate.

How much good will it do to pass on secret messages while the man who knows the most about this weapon doesn't have a clue? That'll simply leave Aurelia with conflicted messages and even more uncertainty, all of us in a muddle rather than on the same page.

We've missed so many warning signs and toed the edge of disaster enough times because of what we didn't know, because of what we didn't dare tell Neven or him us, because Aurelia didn't dare trust in Marc's devotion over his twin's venom. Because none of us listened to Aurelia at first about what truly mattered to her.

We're never going to win the war ahead of us if even those of us standing right beside her can't properly collaborate.

Ignoring the anxious thud of my heart, I pitch my illusionary voice so everyone in the room—including Marc —can hear it. *"No. That's not the right way for her to find her footing."*

Marc flinches. His head whips toward me. "Was that— Did you—"

I stare back at him, my mouth pressed flat. *"Disagree with you? Yes. You might know a lot about that sword, but you don't know Aurelia—not well enough."*

Marc's lips part for a moment before he reels his jaw back in. "Your gift—for fuck's sake—"

Bastien touches my arm, his expression tight. "Lore, what are you doing?"

Raul has braced as if he thinks he's going to have to leap into battle right now.

I restrain a sigh. *"After the way the two of you tackled the fire, he knows there's more to both of your gifts than you ever let on. Does it really do us any good keeping mine a secret? I can support Aurelia better if I can talk as freely as I'm capable of instead of sneaking around. He can support her better if we're pooling our information and resources."*

Raul bares his teeth. "Only if this asshole actually wants to help her and isn't just looking to—"

"Enough!" Aurelia's voice breaks through his protest. She sets her hand on Raul's arm to soften the criticism. "Lorenzo's right. We have to learn how to work together, *all* of us, if we're going to have any hope of standing up to Valerisse's rebellion. Why shouldn't Sabrelle want me gone if I can't keep even four men in line."

Raul lets out a huff but has the decency to look abashed at the same time. Before he needs to say anything, Aurelia turns to me. "What are you thinking, Lorenzo? Where am I going wrong?"

Her gentle consideration wraps around me like the softest silk. *"It's not what you're doing wrong. It's how we're approaching your training. If you need to be confident and committed—I don't think you're going to get there if it means dealing out violence without direct provocation. You falter when you go on the attack. Raul and Marc should be teaching you every technique they know for diversion and defense."*

Marc opens his mouth, closes it again, and then lets out a

rough guffaw. He's still peering at me with a bewildered air. "I think my mute foster brother may have spoken well, as absurd as that sentence sounds."

I can't stop myself from glowering at him, but he turns toward Aurelia. "The important thing is being able to use the sword effectively when you need to. Sabrelle doesn't require that your strength be put toward conquest. Protecting what you have is just as valid. And that seems to be what's required of you right now as it is. We can focus on defense."

Her brow creases with thought. "Reactive strength isn't the easiest sort of commitment to show. The people need to see that I'm prepared to defend them before I actually do."

"We'll get there," Raul says. "There'll be plenty you can show them, whether it's with this sword or another. Sabrelle won't be able to dismiss you."

Our empress doesn't appear totally convinced. Her expression stays pensive through the next several exercises and her good-byes before she hurries off for the funeral rites. The rest of us depart the hidden passages through the unused bedroom that's our preferred entrance.

As Marc lopes off to rejoin the palace guard without a word to us, Bastien holds me back. "Are you sure that was a good idea?"

"How does him knowing hurt anything?" I ask. *"If he decides to start revealing all our secrets, we'll have much bigger problems."*

Raul glares in the direction Marc went. "I still don't like it." He sighs and slings his arms around my shoulders. "Come on, let's get to the bigger asshole's funeral."

Maybe I should have realized Aurelia was making more plans to prove herself behind her thoughtful eyes. When we gather on the steps in Vivencia's main city square before the pyre, there's a resolve in her posture and the set of her chin that sets off a twang through my nerves that I can't explain.

After she's finished her speech commemorating the reviled husband no one knows tried to murder her, she holds Coraya up a little higher for the watching city folk to see.

"I intend to protect our daughter, your next empress, with all the strength I have," she declares, her clear, steady voice ringing out through an amplification charm. "And so I swear on my own life that as soon as the medics declare me recovered from the birth, I'll begin my training alongside the palace's soldiers, until I can fight for her and all the people of this empire in every possible way."

As shock ripples across the watching faces alongside a rising swell of applause, my heart plummets.

She's going to spar with the hardened soldiers? Despite all their training, even they take accidental injuries in practice from time to time.

But our empress never goes back on her word.

CHAPTER FIVE

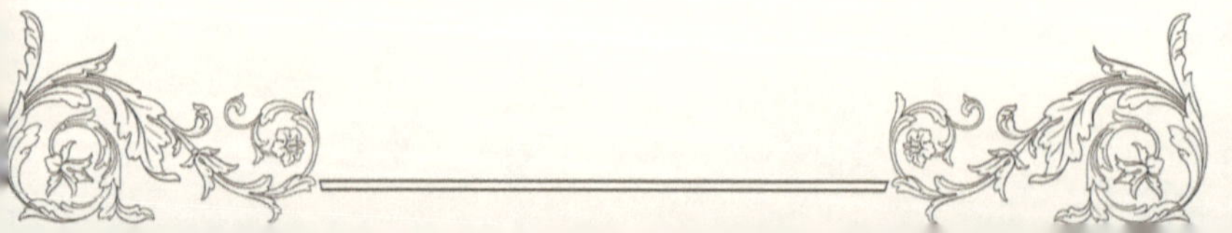

Aurelia

When I emerge from my chambers to head to the palace training room, I find Kassun among the guards currently posted outside. His gaze flicks to Marc exiting behind me, and his eyes narrow beneath his light brown curls.

He clears his throat, his expression determined though his cadence is a little awkward. "Your Imperial Highness—if I could raise a private concern with you…?"

A chill squeezes my gut. Has something gone wrong among my guards?

"Of course," I say, and motion him farther down the hall where the others can still keep watch but won't hear our conversation.

Kassun glances over my shoulder toward the others and

lowers his voice for extra caution. "This new fellow—Marc… I know he helped get you out of the fire. I'm glad he did. But he seems to be… imposing on your good will. A lot."

A softer pang runs through my chest. The guard who's proven to be so loyal despite his initial misgivings is looking out for me as he has often in the past. He can't help that he doesn't know the full story.

I offer him a genuine smile. "I promise I'd have no trouble sending him off if his presence felt like an imposition. I do actually find it comforting having him close at hand for additional protection. It's no criticism of your or anyone else's abilities. I know it's silly. But ever since Marclinus's death and the fire, it's been hard to even sleep…"

I don't like showing that shred of weakness, especially when it's false, but my last comment relaxes Kassun's shoulders. A trace of chagrin crosses his face. "I'm sorry for making you think about that awful time."

"It's all right. I appreciate your concern. Don't ever hesitate to speak to me if something is troubling *you*, no matter what it is."

His pale face brightens, and he returns with me to the rest of my entourage with more energetic strides—and less glowering at Marc.

When we come to a stop just inside the training room a few minutes later, a tang of sweat meets my nose. All of my guards tense around me with hints of uncertainty. The soldiers jerking to rigid attention don't look much more comfortable.

Even after a week and confirmation from the imperial medics of my recovery, no one's quite convinced that my latest venture is a good idea. I'll have to persuade them with actions rather than words.

I brush my hands together and tip my head to the

soldiers. "Thank you in advance for the patience and guidance I know you'll offer me! It means more than I can say to learn all I can so I'll be able to stand up to whatever forces threaten us by the most practical means. We've faced too much tragedy in Dariu already."

Most of the soldiers have been running through their exercises in a stripped-down version of their usual uniform, wearing only the loose slacks and short-sleeved shirts, no jackets or belts. A man in an officer's garb moves between them to meet me, his mouth set at an uneasy angle beneath his trim moustache.

Though he stands only a few inches taller than my five and a half feet, he's sturdily built with a clear impression of strength in his brisk strides. His features look oddly delicate in contrast, but his eyes shine with alertness beneath the short waves of his fawn-brown hair. I can't help thinking of the hunting terriers Nica's family keeps back home in Accasy.

"Captain Evando at your service, Your Imperial Highness." He dips his head with a sweep of his gaze over me. "Although I'm not sure— Our typical regimen is quite vigorous. We can do our best to adapt it to your needs—"

"Empress Aurelia can hold her own just fine," Neven pipes up from where he's just joined me. The young prince volunteered to train alongside me, saying he wanted to learn even more after the two weeks he spent consigned to the soldiers' quarters in Goric.

Kassun, who's seen the most of my previous training out of my guards, speaks up in a more respectful tone. "I don't think you'll find any reason to complain about her mettle."

A slight flush colors the captain's cheeks. "I certainly wouldn't criticize Her Imperial Highness. Is—is this the outfit you intended to train in?"

I glance down at my dress as he does. While I was waiting for my body to repair itself, I had time to commission a couple of plain frocks for this purpose. The linen gown follows the usual airy Darium style, but with no extra layers or frills.

"You might be surprised how much movement a garment like this allows," I say with a small smile. "And should I face another assassin—or, Great God help us, worse—it's unlikely I'll have time to change into proper fighting gear before taking action."

Captain Evando's flush deepens. "You're quite right. Of course. Well… Do you have an idea of where you'd like to start?"

"I'll admit my skills are relatively limited at the moment. Where would you begin with a new recruit?"

I'd imagine I have even fewer combat skills than a typical fledgling imperial soldier, but Evando appears to give the question genuine consideration. "You'll want to build up your physical strength in general and get comfortable with whatever weapon you're most likely to have on hand. We can also work in some strategies for making use of your environment. And basic combat without weapons, if you find yourself with nothing on hand at all."

A gravelly voice pushes into the conversation from behind me. "You should focus on defensive techniques. Our empress won't be risking herself rushing in to attack unnecessarily."

I don't know whether to be pleased that Marc took Lorenzo's suggestion to heart or concerned that he's forgetting his new place. The captain narrows his eyes at the supposed guard, probably peeved by the domineering tone.

The former emperor is still getting used to the idea that he isn't the top dog in every room.

"Yes, that's what I've discussed with my personal guard," I put in quickly, resisting the urge to shoot a warning glare over my shoulder. I pat the sheath on my belt. "And when it comes to weaponry, I've mostly carried a small knife, but I think it may be time I graduate to some sort of sword."

So that I can better wield the Sabrelle-blessed sword that may be my key to gaining her favor.

Evando grunts. "Why don't we start with physical conditioning and perhaps a few independent forms? We can work up to actual sparring."

I nod. "Don't go easy on me. I'll speak up if anything's too much."

Despite my words, I think the captain does hold back at first. He sends me loping around the edges of the room and then into a series of simple arm movements and lunges. But as I tackle them with all the energy I can display, enjoying the first prickling of sweat forming on my skin, his qualms seem to dwindle.

He directs me through a few rounds of sit-ups and push-ups that leave my belly and my arms wobbling and then grabs a couple of small weights from a nearby rack. "It's your arm strength you'll need to develop the most if you're going to swing a sword effectively. Core and leg endurance will keep your balance solid, so we won't neglect those areas either."

I huff a laugh. "I'm glad to hear it."

As I heft the weights, relieved to find that the captain hasn't started me on too torturous a challenge, I'm aware of Marc watching alongside my other guards. His gaze rarely veers from me. The intensity of it prickles into my skin, but I don't acknowledge him.

He'd better not decide for me that I've had enough. My personal guards aren't the only ones following my progress. More and more, the other soldiers training around me are glancing over, curious to see how Her Imperial Highness is faring. Neven, who's joined their brief sparring matches, points over at me with hushed comments I'll assume are in my favor.

By the time my shoulders and biceps are outright aching, I've gotten a few eager smiles and whoops of approval.

"That's our empress!" someone shouts from farther back in the room.

Marc stirs as if annoyed by the irreverence but thankfully keeps quiet.

The hourly bell peals faintly through the walls. I swipe my hand across my damp forehead and aim a grateful smile of my own at Captain Evando. "I think I've pushed myself far enough for my first day."

He surprises me with a chuckle and a twitch of his hand as if he was about to clap me on the shoulder like he might an underling. "It's also important to know your limits. Whenever you want another training session, Your Imperial Highness—"

"Same time tomorrow?" I suggest.

He tips his head. "It would be my honor."

I retrace my steps through the halls with my guards following. "Wait 'til they see you with a sword!" Kassun crows, and then hastily adds a respectful, "Your Imperial Highness."

My maids are waiting in my rooms—the restored empress's apartment I got to return to a few days ago. The change in wallpaper and much of the furnishings diminish the reminders of the traumatic struggle that took place here, but sometimes I think I catch a whiff of smoke that makes my pulse hitch.

While Marc takes his now-customary post right inside the door, Jinalle and Eusette usher me off to the bathing room with exclamations over my sweat-damp gown and mussed hair.

"We'll have you right as rain soon enough, Your Imperial Highness," Eusette promises in her upbeat way.

Once I've been washed and dressed in a more suitable imperial gown, my hair coiled and my face powdered, I send them off with my thanks. I'd head straight out into the palace myself to join the court at its leisure, but Marc's grim expression where he's standing by the door stops me.

I halt in the middle of the rug across from him. "What? Did I not live up to Sabrelle's standards on my first try?"

Marc blinks as if he didn't realize his dour mood was visible but then lifts his chin with a defiant air. "I'm not sure straining yourself among the common soldiers is the right way to impress her."

My eyebrows rise. "Why not? I impressed *them*, and I've barely gotten started."

"You're the empress. Why should you worry about impressing those louts? You don't want them to see you on their level and—"

"But I do," I interrupt. "I'm not going to rule like you did, acting as if the gods have raised me above all other citizens of the continent. The soldiers are *people*, just like we are, just like every noble in the court is. And they're the people who are going to be my best defense against any attempt to dethrone me."

Marc grimaces. "Then you want them to respect you, to see you as a figure worthy of all their protection."

"Why wouldn't they respect a ruler who's doing all she can to be able to protect herself and her country? I'm recognizing the work they put in and showing that I don't take their skills for granted."

"You *should* be able to take them for granted," Marc mutters. "It's their blasted job—not yours."

I wave my hand vaguely in the air. "Didn't you want me to get confident wielding a sword? It'll be a lot easier if I have all the skills leading up to swordplay. The point is to actually deserve Sabrelle's support, not to put on a sham of strength. *She's* never going to respect that. Did you consider that fact?"

My husband opens his mouth, but all he lets out is a sigh. He rubs his face. "I'm not out to undermine you. You should know that by now. But I do have years more experience in the role. I'm trying to help."

For a moment, he looks so lost that my heart squeezes. He's been displaced from so much of the world he knew and understood.

He's actually adapted rather admirably and with more patience than I'd have expected.

My voice softens. "I believe you. But my approach isn't the same as yours, as you've known for a long time. If you have practical, logistical concerns, I want to hear them. When it comes to what kind of relationship I'm going to have with the people I'm ruling over… I don't know if we're ever going to see eye to eye. You'll just have to accept it."

"I don't want to be at odds with you." He pauses, and the intensity in his eyes heightens to a smolder. "I still want to make *us* work, Aurelia. No matter what's gone on between you and my foster brothers. No matter what lies you told before. I will make up for all the wretchedness I put you through."

His tone has gone raw. Whatever words I might have said snag in my throat. I don't know how to answer the longing in his promise.

Marc doesn't move, leaving me all the space I might need, but his gaze trails over me like a stroke over my skin. "I still treasure every affectionate moment we shared. Your heart might not have been in them, but mine was. If I can ever accomplish anything beyond seeing you hold on to the empire, it'll be finding out what it's like to kiss you when you really mean it."

An unwelcome heat flares under my skin. I can remember too well what his kisses feel like—all over my body, provoking more pleasure than I wanted them to.

Does he really think we could get to the point where I *do* want him that way?

Do *I*?

The second question sends an unsettling shiver prickling under my skin, but his passion is so earnest I can't simply dismiss it.

I grope for the right response. "Marc, there's been so much— I don't know—"

A shout reverberates from outside my window. I cut myself off, tensing instinctively, and a couple more hollers follow the first.

With a skip of my heart, I hustle to the door.

The natural part of Marc's face pales. He stays at his post on the threshold. "Aurelia…"

I motion him aside. "I need to know what's going on."

His jaw tightens, but he opens the door for me. The rest of my guards still stand tensed in the hall outside.

"Let's see what the commotion is," I say, and set off down the hall.

By the time I've made it to the central staircase that leads to the palace's main entrance, several nobles have emerged from the common rooms around me. I'm halfway down the stairs when a few imperial guards burst through the doorway.

At the sight of me, they stall in their tracks.

"Your Imperial Highness," one says, and seems to falter.

I draw myself up with all the fortitude I have. "What is it?"

Her stance stiffens, but she forces out the words. "A convoy's just arrived from Lavira. Tribune Valerisse is declaring war on you as a false empress, on the grounds of ineptitude and that… that you faked your confirmation rite for Sabrelle. They say they have evidence to prove it."

My guards' heads tick toward me, even Marc's, probably expecting me to deny the accusation as ridiculous. A queasy chill sweeps through me, pooling in my gut.

I can't deny it, not honestly. I *did* fake my completion of Sabrelle's confirmation rite.

How could Valerisse know that?

Chapter Six

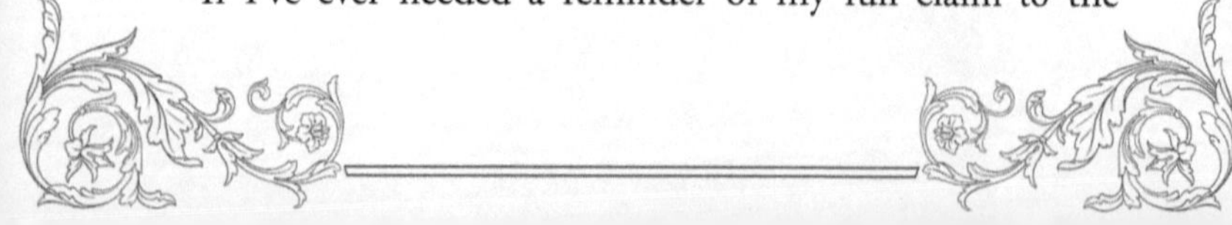

Aurelia

The warble of conversation filling the audience room only diminishes a little when I step onto the dais with its thrones. I hold my head high and adjust Coraya so she's nestled even more deeply in my embrace.

She peers up at me for a moment with her perfect blue eyes and nuzzles my breast, but the gesture is half-hearted. I fed her just before heading in here; she's sated enough that her eyelids drift shut a moment later.

An ache closes around my heart. I hate using my daughter as a political prop… but she was conceived as one. It was inevitable that there would be moments like this, wasn't it?

It was simply easier to accept that fact before she was a living, breathing, fragile human being I could hold in my arms.

If I've ever needed a reminder of my full claim to the

Darium throne, it's now. The discussions buzzing through the room center on Valerisse's declaration of war and her claims of my unworthiness.

"Silence!" Marc hollers from his place amid my personal guards. "Her Imperial Highness will speak."

His altered voice still carries the unshakable authority he cultivated as emperor. The nobles swarming the room hesitate, perhaps recognizing the familiar tone with a shiver down their backs.

If they had any idea that the emperor who often terrorized them still walks among them, if in his less sadistic form…

I gather myself and gaze out across the many dozens of tense faces, keeping my own tone as calm and steady as I can. "You've all heard the accusations and the threat one of the empire's tribunes has made toward me. I stand before you as both the chosen wife of the last emperor of the imperial line and the mother of his heir, prepared to act as regent empress until she is of age."

Before I can go any farther, a voice breaks out from somewhere in the midst of the swarm. "Is it true? Did you fail Sabrelle's confirmation rite?"

Another noble joins in. "The messenger said Valerisse has proof. The traitor you were supposed to execute still lives!"

Someone else makes a scoffing sound. "It could be all lies."

Pressure coils at the base of my throat. I'd like to believe that Valerisse has no real evidence of her claims, but I know they're true. The proof could exist.

Not even the imperial advisors gathered at the edge of the platform look confident. Axius keeps his usual foreboding stance, but Etta's expression is dour and Severo's hands twitch where he's clasping them in front of him.

In their own cluster near the platform, the foster princes

shift on their feet. Bastien's face is drawn. Raul glowers at the crowd, and Lorenzo meets my eyes with a subtle flick of his fingers: *Stay safe.*

I can't, though, can I? If I deny the claims now and Valerisse presents her evidence, I'll lose far more trust than if I face the accusation head on.

My only comfort is that the Lavirian rebel whose life I spared can have no idea that my lovers were involved in his escape. All he'll know is that he woke up still alive far beyond Vivencia's walls.

I've been preparing to give this statement since the moment I heard the messenger's proclamation a couple of hours ago. That doesn't lighten the words as they pass over my tongue.

"When Emperor Marclinus set out to perform the confirmation rites, I joined him as an additional show of my devotion to this country and my role in the empire. I'm the first imperial consort to carry out the rites at all. Nonetheless, I did complete all of them to the satisfaction of the presiding clerics."

I pause to fill my lungs, the ache between them expanding. "It is true that I did not fulfill Sabrelle's rite in the traditional way. The request that I commit murder conflicted with my dedication to Elox, who has always guided me well. So yes, I found a compromise that allowed me to fell the prisoner without ending his life. I believe I still proved that I *could* have ended his life if I'd wanted to, which is the most important aspect of the rite."

A renewed wave of murmurs passes through the crowd.

I clear my throat and speak louder to still be heard. "You all know I've gone above and beyond what's been expected of any past imperial spouse, including the few who've needed to act as regents. I fully completed the other three confirmation rites. I met every challenge my husband placed on me while we toured the rest of the empire over the past several months."

"That's right!" Bianca moves to the foot of the stage, pitching her voice to carry. "Our empress showed her strength and courage alongside His Imperial Majesty at every opportunity. To say she's unfit for the job because she made one small adjustment to a rite that wasn't even required of her is absurd. There wouldn't have been anything wrong with her declining to participate to begin with."

One of the marchions huffs. "Maybe she should have done that, then, instead of play-acting at it."

"There was no play-acting," I cut in. "The traitor did his very best to kill me. The injuries I took were real. The only difference is that what felled him was a potion lacing my blade rather than the force of the strike itself. I still had to cut him."

As more uneasy complaints rise up, Axius strides abruptly to the front of the platform near me. He holds up his hands for attention. "People of the court—you know me. I've fought for Dariu for decades; I fought well enough that Emperor Tarquin named me his military advisor. I can tell you from my experience that what Empress Aurelia did in the rite required *more* skill and perseverance than if she'd set out to merely stab the prisoner."

I hadn't expected the high commander to throw in his lot with me quite so blatantly.

I blink at Axius before jerking myself back to the problem at hand. "It certainly wasn't *easy*. And who is this woman who wishes to attack me? Tribune Valerisse has now proven to be a traitor herself, attempting to wrestle the empire from its legitimate leaders. What trials of rulership has she carried out? Why should we let her decide what's right for the entire country when she doesn't respect any of the traditions she's threatening? Do you want someone so underhanded and disloyal choosing who leads the empire?"

The tenor of the clashing voices seems to shift in my favor. My personal guards call out, "Long live Empress Aurelia!" and several guards along the fringes of the room echo the chant.

Baronissas Hivette and Damina, who've always set themselves a little apart from typical court politicking, join Bianca at the front of the room. I catch fragments of their praise for my accomplishments.

As the atmosphere in the room settles down, most faces are scowling at the injustice of Valerisse's betrayal and smiling encouragement my way.

I wave for their attention. I think I've spoken enough for now... but the court's opinion isn't my biggest challenge.

"I swear I will fight for the imperial line every way I can —to the death if it's required to protect the rightful heir. If I have offended anyone with my adjustment of that one rite, it will be Sabrelle. I'll go now to the palace temple to meditate with her and see what our godlen would ask of me."

The crowd of nobles murmurs in approval. My guards stiffen their postures as they prepare to escort me out of the room. I beckon to Cleric Pierus as well.

In this matter, I could use all the religious guidance I can get.

Near the ballroom doorway, I hand Coraya over to a nursemaid, who's surrounded by her own host of guards for my daughter's protection. The ache around my heart tears at the separation. How do so many of the noble parents stand sending their children off with the staff for the better part of every day?

None of them have to fear for their children's lives the way I do.

I swallow thickly and force myself to continue into the

hall. Whatever message Sabrelle might grant me, I'd rather not subject my infant daughter to her scrutiny.

If I want to keep looking after Coraya in any way at all, *I* have to be alive and in power to do it.

Cleric Pierus has fallen into step beside me. Once we've left the audience room well behind, I glance over at him, pitching my voice low. "As much as I'd like to believe I can find common ground with Sabrelle in one prayer session, it seems I've offended her greatly. Have any past rulers run into opposition from the gods? Any way I can better align myself with their divine will, I'll attempt it."

Pierus frowns, but an energized air comes over his stout body. "I can't think of any examples offhand, but I could certainly delve into the temple records and other accounts. Would you want to consider even examples that don't involve imperial figures?"

I smile at him. "Any information you think would be relevant, I'm most grateful for. I'm glad I have an expert so close at hand to turn to."

He bobs his head with an eager smile of his own at the praise. "I'll begin the research at once."

When we reach the temple, Pierus hustles off, I assume toward the records room. All of my guards except for Marc stop at the doorway.

With the extra familiarity he's been allowed through his position as my rescuer, the former emperor strides several paces farther into the domed room and stands in the middle beneath the bands of multi-colored light that streak through the stained-glass panels.

I turn toward the golden statue of Elox first. With a tap of my fingers to my forehead, heart, and gut and then a clench of my hand over my sternum, I acknowledge the godlen whose brand I bear on my skin. *Let me find some understanding with your fellow deity.*

Then I walk to the gleaming statue of Sabrelle poised in her own alcove almost directly across from the godlen of peace.

It's hard not to feel intimidated by this version of her, even if it's wrought in mortal materials. She's clothed in armor from helmed head to booted feet. Her heel pins a stag's carcass.

Her hard stare seems to follow me as I approach.

I kneel down on the scarlet pillow before her and repeat the gesture of the divinities. Inhaling slowly to center myself, I tip my face toward her and close my eyes.

Sabrelle, I swear that any insults you've perceived in my conduct were not intended. I have nothing but respect for the power you command and the might you inspire in your dedicats. I may disagree with some of those dedicats' actions, but I'm not out to completely destroy their legacy. I simply want to amplify the good that exists in the empire while discarding that which diminishes the people's lives. Please, what would you have me do?

At first, the light that wavers across my closed eyelids remains formless, ruddy blotches that match Sabrelle's totem color. Gradually, the vague shapes shift and solidify.

Movement ripples through my vision, like a marching army. Palace and temple spires gleam. Faint cheers reverberate at the edge of my hearing.

A hand—a hand that would have to be mine from the angle—reaches out and clasps the handle of a dagger. It turns the point of the blade toward my body.

Then it slams the weapon home, straight into my chest with a spurt of blood.

My eyes pop open, my lips clamping against a gasp I barely stifle. My stomach roils as the impressions echo through my mind.

When I glance back up at her, Sabrelle's cold expression looks like a sneer.

That's her answer, then. All she'd want from me is for me to kill myself and give the empire over to whoever would fight hardest for it.

My resolve hardens inside me. I push myself to my feet, tensing my legs against a wobble.

Fine. She'll just have to see that the person who'll fight hardest for it is me.

Whatever Valerisse thinks is at stake, it can't be as much as the hopes and pain of every conquered country on the continent.

I return to the doorway with my jaw firmly set. Axius stands in the hallway just outside.

"Your Imperial Highness," he starts. "I realize that Emperor Marclinus dismissed me from my position, but—"

I lift my hand to stop him. "I appreciate all the guidance you've already given me and the support you've shown today. As far as I'm concerned, you're still the imperial military advisor. And in that role, I'd like you to tell the tribune's messenger that Empress Aurelia will not be abandoning the throne."

Chapter Seven

Raul

When Aurelia steps into the military workout room for her fourth training session, none of the imperial soldiers who glance over look surprised. Sauntering in behind her, I catch several smiles before they yank their attention back to their own exercises with the expected strict discipline.

They like having an empress who'd stand a chance at whooping their asses in a fight—and who'd want that chance.

Captain Evando nods to me after his brisk bow to Aurelia. "Prince Raul—we haven't seen you in some time, Your Highness."

I pick up one of the training swords and test its weight in my hand. "I thought it was time to brush up on my skills, seeing as all of us may be called on to defend the rightful rulers of our empire as we're able."

His answering hum sounds approving. Better they all think I'm here out of devotion to their blasted empire than to the woman I love.

Conveniently, both versions of devotion look very similar at the moment.

As Aurelia stretches and goes through a few basic exercises to warm up her limbs, the gem on the pommel of her sword gleams by her hip. A few nearby soldiers peer at it with surreptitious curiosity.

This is the first time she's brought the Sabrelle-blessed blade anywhere outside her chambers. Before we left, she declared it was time she started getting some practice with her most powerful weapon.

It is an incredible sword. The way the steel sings as she pulls the blade from its sheath sends a shiver over my skin. I wouldn't mind a chance to stab and slash with that beauty.

But the honor is all Aurelia's. As it should be, if she's going to convince our godlen of war to stop being such a fucking idiot.

A hush falls over the room at the sight of the blessed sword. None of the soldiers know its history, but there's no mistaking the craftmanship or the sigil on the hilt.

Captain Evando pauses, studying it. "You've brought your own weapon this time."

Aurelia slices the blade through the air. "I've been informed that this sword is sacred to the family I married into, a treasure that will belong to my daughter when she's grown and one meant to defend the imperial line from all threats. It seemed appropriate that I make use of it for that purpose now. May Sabrelle look kindly on me."

She flicks her fingers down her front in the gesture of the divinities, but I catch a hint of dryness in her tone. The godlen hasn't shown any signs of relenting in her campaign of disapproval so far.

"A reasonable decision," Evando says, and raises his own sword. "I look forward to seeing it in action. It's a little larger than the blades you've practiced with before—we'll go through the forms more slowly to start."

I want to bristle on Aurelia's behalf, but in the glimpses I get of their tentative sparring while I engage in my own mock-battles, it appears he had a point. Aurelia's been working with the blessed sword in the privacy of her chambers, but I suppose I've gone too easy on her.

As Evando picks up his pace, a tremor runs through her arm. Her shoulder tenses with the strain.

A remark carries from the cluster of guards watching her performance. "A solid defense still needs to deal out a little pain on your opponent."

At the authoritative tone, my hand tightens around the hilt I'm clutching. My sparring partner nearly smacks my sword from my grasp before I recover from my annoyance.

Knocked down from his lofty position as emperor and still unable to keep his mouth shut. When I sneak a look at Marc, he's standing at proper attention, his expression somber.

Who asked for his opinion? And does he have to fucking stare at the woman who no longer belongs to him as if no one else exists in the room?

I'd like to go over and cut his eyes right out, but sadly he hasn't done anything that would justify the act to anyone watching. They all think he's the hero who saved her.

Never mind the shit they don't realize he inflicted on her before that point. She wouldn't have *needed* saving if he'd smartened up and dealt with his brother months ago.

Between bouts, I step back to gulp water and wipe the sweat from my face. Aurelia is jabbing and feinting with total determination, but it's obvious how much effort she's having to exert. Her jaw has tightened. She barely manages to raise the blade in time to deflect a blow from Evando that wasn't terribly fast.

I love watching her determination. So much strength radiates through every beautiful inch of her body even though she's struggling. Damn, she's a wonder.

Not everyone appreciates her the same way, though. The soldiers are watching her practice more openly now, but there are fewer smiles showing. Are they starting to worry that their empress isn't up to the task after all?

Maybe she brought her shiniest toy out too soon.

I cast my gaze over her current host of personal guards. Alongside Marc, I don't spot any of the soldiers we've determined have the ability to sense magic usage.

Aurelia's been sending the few who do possess that gift to guard Coraya rather than herself. I suppose her daughter is the more prominent target, and the rest of the court will probably approve of that consideration.

Most of the time I'd rather Aurelia had every bit of protection she can get. At this particular moment, I'm grateful for the lack of surveillance.

Casually, I circle around the imperial sparring match so I'm standing near a shadow cast by one of the room's pillars. The streak of darkness falls between Aurelia and Captain Evando.

As if stretching my fingers, I dip my hand into the shadow and send up an appeal to my patron godlen.

Kosmel, let my gift be as discreet as a breath. Let no one suspect any subterfuge.

Once I'm touching the darkness, it firms automatically against my grip. I will the streak of shadow to shift ever so slightly: lifting it a bit here, widening it a bit there. Keeping it filmy, not too forceful.

With Aurelia's next swings, I brace the weight of the blade so it glides through the motions that much more easily. With a nudge, I help her send Evando's blade swinging aside.

Aurelia's gaze flickers my way. She doesn't look directly at me, but she must have sensed the assistance and guessed that I'm behind it. It'd be a little much to expect her not to pick up on the intervention.

No one else has any clue, thank the godlen of trickery. I ease her way through a few more clashes, until admiring murmurs are spreading through the growing audience. I haven't pushed for anything flashy, just polished her technique a bit.

Evando stops and motions to the soldiers who've fallen out of their own practice. "You're here to train, not gape."

As the abashed soldiers turn back to their own concerns, Aurelia swipes her sleeve across her forehead. "That's enough of a session for me today. I'll see you again tomorrow."

"You did well, Your Imperial Highness," Evando says. "It won't help anyone if you push yourself too hard."

I fill another glass from the pitcher for my empress. "Water, Your Imperial Highness?"

Aurelia smiles at me obligingly if a tad crookedly. When she comes over to receive the drink, she drops her voice so no one but me will be able to hear. "I was managing all right."

"Hmm. But you manage a little better when we combine our skills. I want the army as impressed as you deserve."

"I'm not sure I can say I earned it if it's with help."

"And didn't you earn my help?" I tsk at her teasingly, but my own words have lit a glimmer of inspiration in my head. "Bastien and I did accomplish some interesting things by combining *our* skills. I wonder if that's an area of possibility we haven't delved into enough. The Coteans think collaborations between gifts are worthy of an entire school."

"Somewhat harder when you're avoiding showing you

have those gifts at all," Aurelia points out. "But let's think on that all the same."

As she drains the last of the water, Marc ambles over. This once, he's looking at me rather than her.

I'm not sure I like that better.

His cool gray gaze rakes over me, just as irritating as it was when a crown was sitting over it. At least he has enough sense to keep his own voice hushed. "Aurelia steadied a fair bit toward the end there. I don't suppose you had anything to do with that."

I gaze back at him blankly, but I can't stop an edge from creeping into my words. "Isn't that the point of practice—for her to get better as she goes?"

One of his eyebrows lifts at a skeptical angle. "The one time I had the chance to observe your full gift in action, I was distracted by other matters, like ensuring our empress didn't *die*. How exactly did Kosmel really bless you?"

I smile at him tightly. "I don't see how that's any of your concern. Hardly my fault if you couldn't be bothered to take note when you had the chance."

Marc's eyes narrowed. "As our foster brother from Rione noted the other day, we'll all have a much easier time supporting Aurelia if we know what resources we're working with. He volunteered to demonstrate his gift."

"Well, as fond as I am of Lorenzo, he and I don't always see eye-to-eye. And I'm not all that interested in your version of 'support.'"

Aurelia exhales with a note of exasperation. "Men—"

"It was a simple question," Marc breaks in, his voice hardening. "If your ego is that much bigger than your consideration for—"

A thumping of footsteps breaks through his growled retort and brings all our eyes jerking toward the doorway.

Neven is just skidding to a halt in the hallway beyond,

his face flushed. He gathers himself with a sharp breath and then appears to hesitate. His gaze darts uneasily over the gathered soldiers, many of whom have also glanced his way.

His attention settles on Aurelia with a twitch of his hand at his side that looks almost frantic. *Come.*

My stomach knots. What new catastrophe is about to crash down on us?

Aurelia knows better than to let any panic show herself. She glides over to the doorway as if she's in full imperial regalia instead of a relatively plain training dress and aims a gentle smile at my younger foster brother. "Prince Neven, have you decided to train today after all?"

The simple question seems to put him more at ease. He bobs his head respectfully. "Not right now. There was something I wanted to mention to you. If this isn't a good time…"

His beseeching eyes imply it had better be good.

Aurelia motions him back into the hall. "I was just finishing up. My late husband's foster brothers should have my ear as they need it. What's on your mind?"

As her guards trail after her, I decide no one will think it odd if I tag along to see what's bothering my fellow prince. I follow at Marc's heels, resisting the urge to wallop him in the back of the head. Not that he wouldn't deserve it.

As usual, Aurelia's guards give her space for her conversation while keeping a close eye on her surroundings. When I reach them, Neven is already partway through his hushed but urgent explanation.

"It's just a feeling… Like she's preparing me—and maybe any other dedicats she has around—for something important. Telling us to be ready to see… some kind of unveiling or reveal? I'm sorry I can't be more definite."

Aurelia pats his arm, a brief reassurance that's all she can offer as empress to subject. "It's all right. The godlen are rarely explicit in their messages. I appreciate the warning."

She steps back to the doorway. "Captain Evando, I may have need of additional guards this afternoon. If there's anyone you feel could leave off their training for more immediate matters, please have them join me."

The captain knows his place—he doesn't question her request. With a few efficient gestures, he points out several soldiers and calls them over. "Get on your full uniforms and stay with Her Imperial Highness until she dismisses you."

In a matter of minutes, Aurelia has set off with nearly three times her previous entourage of armed men and women. I watch her go, grappling with the tension coiling ever tighter in my gut, wishing I had an excuse to stay with her too.

"Signs from Sabrelle?" I ask Neven.

He nods. "I think so. I just didn't like the feel of it."

"Better safe than sorry."

The words have barely left my mouth when a trumpet blare reverberates through the palace walls. My spine goes rigid.

Whatever trouble Sabrelle has planned, it's here.

Chapter Eight

Aurelia

After Jinalle has finished adjusting the last bit of lacing on my gown, I stare down at the sheathed sword I hastily set on the vanity. The belt now circling my waist feels insubstantial in its lightness.

"Go on," I tell my maid. "I'll come out to meet the delegation in a few minutes."

She ducks her head and scurries out the door. Moments after it clicks shut behind her, the panel in the wall by my bed slides open.

Raul emerges on his own. I don't know if my other lovers have even heard the news that more delegates from Valerisse have arrived.

He strides straight to me and tugs me tight against his massive frame. "You can handle her, whatever she thinks she's going to throw at you. Both the tribune and the godlen."

My laugh comes out choked. "I wish I wasn't having to

face two formidable foes at the same time. Do you think—should I go out like this, like I normally would? Or should I bring the sword?"

I turn away from him, resting my fingers on the polished scabbard. Marching out to meet Valerisse's representatives with a weapon of war at my hip would be matching their aggressive tone. Presenting myself as a warrior rather than a peacemaker.

My body balks at the idea of even hinting at violence, but maybe that's what's needed at this point. Both those loyal to me and those faltering in their loyalties need to see I'm willing to fight with more than just words.

Sabrelle certainly won't be impressed by my typical hand-length knife.

Raul cocks his head, stroking his knuckles over my cheek as he does. "Are you ready to use it if it comes to that?"

Rather than answering automatically, I picture a scenario, prodding my will. My spine pulls straighter. "Yes. If that's what it takes."

"I wish *I* could take on the challenge for you." He turns my face toward him and claims a kiss so searing it stokes the flames of determination inside me.

I lean into Raul, soaking up his strength and the faith he has in me, and reach for the sword. He lets me fasten it to my belt myself.

Am I imagining things, or does it already feel easier in my hands than it did when I wielded it during my training session less than an hour ago?

Raul gives my arm one last squeeze. "I'll round up the others, and we'll be watching outside. You always have us at your back. Don't let anything shake you."

Once he's vanished back into the hidden passages, I gird myself and reach for my bedroom door.

Marc remained outside with my other personal guards

while I hastily changed clothes. When he takes in the sword I've re-donned, his mouth shifts with a slight curve of approval.

Nobles have gathered along the main staircase to wait for my arrival—one of the main reasons I took the time to swap my combat training gown for a properly formal one. I have no idea who Valerisse has sent today, but it won't do my cause any good if they look more imperial than I do.

As I walk past the members of the court, they stream along behind my guards. The additional soldiers Captain Evando assigned to me form a wider ring of protection, skirting the walls. When we pass through the doors into the palace's front courtyard, they pull in closer.

Apprehension taints the fresh mid-day air. More of the court has already swarmed out to peer at the delegation alongside the regular guards posted around the entrance and throughout the grounds. It isn't much of a spectacle, though.

A couple of soldiers who I'd say look a little uneasy flank a slim, middle-aged man in the red tunic and trousers of a Sabrellian devout. A pointed beard extends his equally pointed chin.

Next to him hunches a younger, burlier man with tangled hair drooping over his sullen face. The younger man's hands are shackled behind his back with the devout holding the short chain. Another chain runs between the prisoner's ankles.

The murmurs of the nobles dwindle as I descend the steps between them. Several paces from the delegation, I halt and fix the new arrivals with a firm stare. "What's this about?"

The devout clears his throat and offers me a thin smile that makes my gut squirm. "My godlen and all those who want to see Dariu under a true ruler would like to know whether you'll fulfill the rite you cheated her in before. I bring another traitor to the empire before you. Will you battle and slay him as he deserves and as Sabrelle would wish?"

How much was he guided by his patron godlen and how much by Tribune Valerisse? For him to have appeared here now, I'm not sure there was time for the message of my refusal to reach the tribune and her response to make it back to the capital—but she may have assumed my reaction and already prepared for it.

I open my mouth—but before I can say anything, a ruddy glow flares around jailer and prisoner. For the space of a couple of heartbeats, crimson light hazes their hair and skin.

As I blink, the supernatural glow fades, but the voices around me rise in volume again. There's no denying that public statement.

Sabrelle wants me to know she's watching my response as much as my court and the closest members of my army are.

I set my hand on the hilt of her blessed sword. My fingers curl around the leather binding of the grip as if it was made for my hand, but my stomach keeps roiling.

I could battle the supposed traitor, make an actual spectacle of this confrontation. Would murdering him be enough to appease the godlen or the tribune?

Would I be demonstrating my devotion… or my willingness to be bullied into following someone else's orders? How is it showing true strength to be coerced into an act that's against all my principles?

It feels as if Valerisse is managing to back me into a corner even though she's hundreds of miles away.

I stay where I am, weighing my options. "Do you have proof of this man's crimes? Dariu is a country of lawful justice, not unmitigated vengeance."

At least, its people would prefer to believe it is. And I'd like to make that statement true.

The devout scoffs. "Do you think Sabrelle would present a false challenge just because you treated the first one dishonestly? This man was brought straight from his prison cell. Will you accept the fight or not?"

"I'd like to know what exactly he was imprisoned for and why it's worthy of a death sentence."

"So little faith you have in our gods." He raises his voice, obviously wanting all our audience to hear. "I present you with a criminal who harmed our empire, and you want to debate the details? It sounds like a diversion to me. You're still unwilling to carry out the duties a real Darium empress should accept without hesitation."

He's trying to browbeat me into caving in. The realization stokes my instinctive defiance.

A real Darium empress wouldn't be badgered into committing a fatal act she didn't believe in, would she?

I lift my own voice as the devout has. "I believe Sabrelle values strength of mind and will as well as of body. I will seek guidance from all our gods."

I tap my fingers through the gesture of the divinities and tip my face toward the sun gleaming wanly in the overcast sky.

I only want what's best for the people of the empire—I want to see all of the continent thriving and happy. Elox, can you guide me? You've encouraged me to endure and accept so much… Do you really want me to accept this too?

My silent appeal wisps away from me. A renewed hush falls over the crowd, broken only by a few indistinct mutters from the devout to his military escort.

If even my own godlen feels I should give way here, carry out an execution of a man for unexplained crimes…

The dim beams of sunlight fragment. I get the impression

of a man and woman standing atop a sprawling palace, their hands clasped, serene white light emanating from them over lands that stretch far and wide around.

Scarlet flares between them, with a swing of a massive blade. The figures tumble to either side; the palace cracks apart. More scarlet flows like blood, swallowing up the peaceful glow that lit the countryside, swelling alongside a sense of hopelessness from deep in my core.

A lump fills my throat. Elox did want me to accept and endure alongside my husband—because he thought it would bring the empire peace in the end. But he didn't count on Sabrelle's meddling. I think I've just watched his dreams shattered, nothing left but ruin.

Even as that understanding forms in my head, the despair gives way to a rush of calm resolve. When I blink, the vision shifts. One figure clambers back onto the fractured palace and flings her hand toward the blood-drenched lands. A new glow burns away the horror.

A hitch of my pulse brings me back to the palace courtyard. Everyone is studying me, a few uncertain murmurs traveling through the crowd of nobles at my daze.

I swallow hard. Elox hasn't given me any definite answers. I still have to carve my own way. But my godlen has offered me a gift all the same.

He's telling me he trusts me. That he believes even if I can't hold together the empire as it was, I can transform it into something better.

And to do that, I need to act.

I draw the blessed sword. The hiss of the blade from the sheath startles the crowd back into silence. Even the devout presses his lips flat, his gaze turning wary.

I take a couple of steps toward him and his prisoner, holding the sword low so it's not an immediate threat. "You came here following your godlen's will—and I assume

Tribune Valerisse's as well. What were your intentions if I refused your request?"

The devout juts out his chin. "Your lack of commitment would speak for itself. We can't have someone unfit for the throne ruling our empire. And if you think your hesitation doesn't reflect badly on your capabilities already—"

I interrupt in a clear, steady voice. "So you're insulting me and inciting rebellion against your rightful empress by marriage and motherhood."

His eyes flash. "If rebellion is what's need to set—"

"Then I'll deal with the real traitor here, as Sabrelle should wish it."

I don't give him a chance to respond. I leap forward with a thrust of the sword and stab the devout right through the center of the chest as both Raul and Captain Evando have taught me.

In a proper fight, it wouldn't have been so easy. But it clearly never occurred to the devout that I might harm *him*. By the time he starts to react, the blade has already driven home.

Blood to match the pommel ruby spurts out over the shining steel. My stomach lurches, but I keep my expression placid as I jerk the sword free.

The devout staggers. He clutches at his chest, a cough sending blood dribbling across his lips. The crimson liquid is barely visible anywhere else, darkening the red fabric of his tunic.

The prisoner's chain slips from his fingers. As the devout slumps over, the chained man shuffles to the side. The soldiers who arrived with him close in, one catching his arm.

The devout tries to speak, but nothing comes out of his mouth but a broken groan. One of his soldiers reaches for his own sword, and several blades whisk from sheaths all around me.

I speak before my guards have to, holding my sword at the ready. "Sabrelle challenged me to kill a traitor. I've done as she asked. Will you have me execute more than one today?"

A tendril of cool wind licks around my calf beneath my gown—a reminder that my princes are standing with me too. I meet the soldiers' gazes without flinching.

The one who moved for his weapon drops his hand. His grimace suggests he isn't happy about backing down, but I'll take what victories I can get.

"We'll be reporting the outcome of our appeal to Tribune Valerisse," he rasps.

"Good. You can let her know that there's nothing meek or feeble about the ruler the empire already has. If she doesn't retract her call to war, we'll all be clear that *her* intentions have nothing to do with what's best for the empire after all." I motion to the prisoner. "And return this man to wherever he came from, to face the sentence he was originally given."

One of the other soldiers draws her lips back in a snarl, but when my guards press forward, she backs up a step. Dragging the prisoner with them, they hustle toward the gates where the horses they rode in on are waiting.

I exhale slowly, resisting the urge to sag with momentary relief. Behind me, Marc calls out in his rough new voice, "Now that's an empress!"

A ripple of cheers passes through the court. When I turn back toward the palace, a few of my guards and other soldiers stationed nearby salute me.

I smile at them all, pretending my gut isn't still churning at the sight of the blood drenching the sword in my hand.

I can be this kind of empress if I have to, but it's not who I ever wanted to be.

How much more blood will I have to spill before Sabrelle is satisfied?

Chapter Nine

Aurelia

Chatter and laughter carry through the imperial gardens in the glow of the evening lanterns.

I meander between the flowerbeds and hedge sculptures, wondering at how easily the court can shrug off this afternoon's events. The atmosphere might be slightly more subdued than usual, but you'd never suspect we're on the verge of civil war.

Or that I murdered someone a few hours ago.

A flicker of the memory passes behind my eyes, and my pulse hiccups with a heavy thud. The taste of bile seeps through my mouth, overpowering the delicate perfume of the first spring flowers.

Before my lingering horror can drag me too far under, Coraya squirms in my arms with a burble of sound. A smile tugs at my lips alongside the ache in my heart. I dip my head to press a kiss to her soft head.

Part of me wants to shut us away in my apartment so I can simply lie on my side and stare at her for hours on end, pretending the rest of the empire doesn't exist. I'd rather help change her soiled swaddling cloths a thousand times than face another scene like today's.

Unfortunately, I don't expect I'll get the option of making that trade.

I adjust her so she's positioned more upright, which she often seems to prefer. As she takes in our surroundings with her head leaned against my shoulder, Bianca ambles over to join me with a few of the other noblewomen trailing behind her. Coraya blinks her wide eyes and lets out a soft coo.

The vicerine has never shown any interest in having children of her own, but she smiles at my daughter warmly enough. "They really do grow fast, don't they? Look at her, taking the measure of us all already."

I chuckle. "It can't hurt for her to get started early. She'll have far more to learn than I did."

"We can all contribute there." Bianca pauses and glances over her shoulder at her companions: Baronissas Hivette and Damina, who've often stood by me when I've taken my minor stands; the elderly Marchionissa Lucrene, who's always seemed to hold herself above palace gossip; and a couple of middle-aged vicerines I'm not as familiar with, who duck their heads at my gaze.

Her smile turning wry, Bianca shifts her attention back to me. "The six of us were talking about joining in the combat training you've taken up. If you don't mind having the company, and if the soldiers will tolerate the occasional additional intrusion."

Of all the proposals she might have made, I'd never have expected that one. "You want to learn how to fight?"

Bianca lifts her shoulder with a careless air, but her eyes are sharp as ever. "The men of court generally learn some of those arts in their younger years. But not all of us have a husband around to defend us—and why shouldn't we pitch in to defend our empire if there's need? Plenty of commoners become full soldiers despite being women. There's no reason we can't pick up a few tricks. Our empress has inspired us."

She outright grins, and I can't help grinning back. She has a point there. And she must be feeling a little unsteady in her position with her husband banished to their estate, as welcome as his absence might be.

The two baronissas are married to each other, with no interest in entangling themselves with men. The marchionissa is a widow. I believe one of the other vicerines has never married, and the other… She's attached to that viceroy who tends to be lost in his cups before dinner's even over, isn't she?

Perhaps if they set the standard, more of the court's ladies will expand their horizons as well.

"I don't see why that should be a problem," I say. "I'll speak to Captain Evando, who's been overseeing my own training, during my next session."

"Perfect." Bianca gives me a sharper smirk. "We can't let any tribunes get ideas about this palace being easy pickings."

I bite back the comment that it's probably not the tribune we most need to worry about. From what Bianca has reported over the past several days, attitudes throughout the court have remained mainly in my favor, but today's events might have shifted them. It's impossible to know who the godlen of war could be working on through dreams and visions they don't dare speak of openly.

As that thought passes through my head, I catch sight of Neven's white-blond hair where he's strolling around a nearby fountain. I meant to speak with him when I had the chance.

"I look forward to seeing us all increase our might," I tell the noblewomen, and glide off toward the young prince.

Neven glances up at my approach, his shoulders momentarily tensing. Even when he relaxes, his stance remains a little awkward.

The prince of Goric has never looked as though he's sure how he fits in here.

I veer to fall into step beside him, and he gamely wanders on as if there's nothing unusual about my coming over.

"I'm glad you got through the challenge today without any harm done… to you or those of us at court, anyway," he says after a moment.

"Thank you again for your forewarning. You're obviously well in tune with your godlen's moods." I grapple with the phrasing of my request. "I don't suppose you've gotten any sense of how she feels about my handling of the challenge. I was hoping to impress rather than offend her, but I realize it was a tricky balance considering the circumstances."

Neven's mouth twists. "I haven't gotten any impression that she's celebrating the outcome. I suppose I'll see what dreams come tonight."

"If you can read any signs in them, good or bad, I'd like to hear about it. I do want to make peace with her… however exactly one does that with a godlen of war."

A strained guffaw tumbles out of the prince. "It might take some time with how riled up she seems to be. *I* think you showed plenty of strength."

With Neven having become one of my biggest critics until recently, I'll take that comment as a victory in itself.

The corner of my mouth quirks upward. "It's easier to show your true self when you're not cast in a much longer shadow."

Neven rubs the back of his neck. "Yes, I can see… why you had to make certain compromises."

Axius crosses our path. He takes in our odd pairing before dipping in a brief bow to me. "Your Imperial

Highness, you look rather serious. You know if you have any concerns about your security, you can come to me."

He's one to talk, when his grizzled face is as grim as always. Perhaps he's recalling that Neven and his princely foster brothers were there to help rescue me from the fire when he wasn't.

"No new concerns," I reassure him. "Neven has felt Sabrelle's divine influence in the past... After today's confrontation, I thought he might have useful information to share." I cock my head. "Are you dedicated to Sabrelle yourself, High Commander?" It's the most common godlen dedication among military folk, for obvious reasons.

Axius shakes his head. "I made my appeal to Creaden. It was always my goal to lead our might as well as I could and to build on the empire's strengths."

At least I don't have to worry about the godlen of war muddling *his* head with unnerving dreams, then. Assuming she's the only divinity who's taken an issue with my conduct.

"I don't suppose Creaden has blessed you with any dreams or visions about our immediate future," I ask in as casual a tone as I can summon.

"As far as I can tell from the prayers I've made, he wants me to continue to direct you along the best path I can."

"Well, I'm certainly grateful for your direction." I hesitate before asking, but if anyone should be able to pry, it's an empress. "You mentioned making an appeal—did your dedication ceremony include a gift?"

Axius doesn't look offended by the question. He taps his side. "Just a moderate one. I gave up a rib. When sending a squadron or group of squadrons into battle, I have a knack for arranging them in the most effective formation."

A very soldier-esque talent to fit the godlen of rulership and construction's areas of expertise. I let my tone turn dry.

"Let's hope we don't need to make use of that gift anytime soon."

Coraya shifts against my shoulder. I'd think she's just getting restless, except then she starts mouthing at my neck as if she thinks it might start producing milk.

I have to laugh even as my breasts twinge in anticipation of her need. "Please excuse me. My daughter is hungry."

I've tucked myself away on a secluded bench and brought Coraya's mouth to my chest when Marchionissa Lucrene drifts over to me. She beams down at the imperial heir. "We have to cherish these times while they're young. They grow up so quickly."

"I'll be happy if she simply gets the chance to grow up at all," I say without thinking, and then clamp my lips shut with an embarrassed flush of my cheeks.

The elderly marchionissa shows no sign of offense at my baldness. The fine lines at the corners of her eyes crinkle deeper. "You're facing an unusual challenge. It always seems harder for the empresses than the emperors, though even the one I knew long ago never had to deal with so much resistance."

The one she knew before—Emperor Tarquin's mother? Lucrene must have been a young woman when that lady reigned. I wonder what color her silver-white hair used to be.

I tip my head in politer acknowledgment. "I'm following the best course I can."

She nods. "From what I've seen, that's all you can do. Fighting and talking prettily are both important, of course, but her greatest strength—the way she led—was in her resolve. You reminded me of her today. Keep that conviction, and I think you'll find the way through."

The earlier ache spreads through my chest again. "I'll do my best."

"There are always going to be people with different

opinions in a country this big, let alone the whole empire." Lucrene tsks her tongue. "So many different needs. But I've seen how well you've managed to balance them so far. Just take your allies wherever you can find them. You never know when one person might make the difference."

The thought of relying on even more people than I've already drawn into danger around me sends a jitter through my nerves. But perhaps an ally's support doesn't need to be that perilous. Lucrene is making a difference right now, isn't she?

A lump rises in my throat. I adjust Coraya against me as I compose my response. "Thank you for your advice. I may want to speak with you again about how that past empress handled herself. Of course, it'd be my pleasure to reward you for your service to the empire—"

The marchionissa waves off my comment before I can finish. "Not at all. You've already given me a reward in letting me speak so freely."

She hesitates as if she's afraid I might punish her for her honesty after all, and it occurs to me that she's admitting to the lack of freedom she felt under her past rulers. My throat tightens even more.

"I'm glad I could offer that much," I say quietly.

A bright smile curves Lucrene's thin lips. She bows to me just as the night nursemaid bustles over.

The nursemaid clicks her tongue at me but lets me finish the feeding before holding out her arms for Coraya, who's now dozing. "You need your rest too, Your Imperial Highness. Especially today."

I can't argue with her. When I push back to my feet, my whole body feels leaden.

I slip away from the continuing revelry in the garden. At my chambers, Marc follows me inside while the other guards remain in the hall. He spreads his usual pallet without a word while I unravel my hair from its pins. I'd rather not bother with maids tonight.

"I think you did well today," Marc says softly. "My mighty empress."

His gaze catches mine and holds it with his usual intensity. The skip of my heart is unnerving but not totally unpleasant.

My hand flexes at my side. "I'd rather have avoided killing anyone."

"Sometimes we don't have a choice. What matters is that you act when you must."

Gods grant me as few "must" situations as possible.

That thought brings my attention to my trunk that holds my brewing equipment. Marchionissa Lucrene's remarks linger in my head.

I want to hold on to my convictions. I don't have to fight these battles the way Sabrelle and Valerisse envision.

I have my own methods.

When I open the trunk and take out the cauldron, Marc lets out a puzzled sound. "Aren't you going to bed?"

I shake my head. "I have something I want to start brewing first. It shouldn't take long."

My gift is already unfurling behind my eyes, adjusting the giddying hallucinogenic I concocted so many times before without its aphrodisiac aspect.

I turned the worst side of my husband into putty plenty of times with a prick of the hidden needle on my ring. Perhaps I can use a similar tactic to diffuse one or another future hostility so no swords need to be drawn to begin with.

CHAPTER TEN

Aurelia

By the time my potion is ready to cool, its herbal scent drifting through the room, Sprite has curled up on my lap and my head is drooping. I set the cauldron aside with a rub of my ring. I'll bring it into the bathing room to fill it so Marc won't see the trick.

I'd rather not give him any more information he could use against me than he already has, claims of full allegiance or no.

As I give my cat one last pet and displace her gently to stand up, the hidden panel whispers open. Bastien emerges, tentatively and then striding across the room with more confidence and only a flick of a glance toward Marc.

He wraps his arms around me and just holds me for a moment. "You were amazing this afternoon. I'd have been standing right there by your side if I could have been."

"She did have plenty of protection," Marc intones from where he's standing stiffly on his bedroll.

Bastien ignores him, peering into my eyes. "How are you holding up? I can't imagine the strain, after all the extra training you're doing on top of it…"

I give him a playful swat. "I'm fine."

But then a yawn stretches my jaw with a wobble that runs right down my body. The prince of Cotea notes it, and his gaze firms alongside his tone.

"Sit down on your stool. You need to stop worrying about being fine for a bit and let someone else look after you."

I'd argue, but that commanding voice he can bring out never fails to send a giddy shiver down my spine. And I don't actually object to sitting anyway.

I sink onto the cushioned stool in front of my vanity. Bastien leans over me, sweeping my hair back with a subtle caress of my neck. He rests his hands on my shoulders and meets my gaze in the mirror. "Lean into me. Let me take as much of the weight you're carrying as I can."

As I tip into his steady hold obligingly, there's a rustle of fabric by the door. Marc keeps his voice low, but the edge is still cutting. "That's not how you talk to your empress."

As if he and his twin didn't order me around hundreds of times in the past year?

Bastien's attention remains on me. He digs his thumbs into the crook of my shoulder with the start of a massage before answering. "It's how I talk to the woman I love." His voice softens without losing its possessive note. "The mother of my child."

He dips his head lower to press a kiss to the top of my head. Only then does he glance Marc's way. "*Someone* needs to care about how she's coping."

Even from the corner of my vision, I can tell Marc bristles. "I've been ready to defend her every second of—"

"What, for the last four weeks after months of torturing her?"

"I never—"

I pull away from Bastien, cutting my gaze toward Marc. "Stop squabbling. I don't need any defending right now, definitely not from Bastien." I tilt my head backward to look up at my prince directly. "And it'll be a lot easier to relax if you're not taking jabs at each other."

Bastien grimaces apologetically. "Message received. I meant to focus on you anyway."

In the silence that follows, he resumes his massage. As he works at the knots along my shoulders and upper back, I gradually sag into his touch. I hadn't realized just how much tension I was holding in my muscles until now, feeling the aches he's drawing out of them.

Bastien eases lower, running his thumbs down either side of my spine. When his hands come to rest on the sides of my waist, he leans in to brush a quick kiss to the side of my neck.

There's no demand in the gesture. He immediately continues kneading at the kinks strung through my back. But the warmth of his lips wakes up a quiver of sensation that travels straight to my core.

One of my princes has slept beside me every night since the fire, but their embraces have stayed relatively chaste. Between my body being in flux after giving birth and the stress caused by Valerisse's threats, there hasn't been much room for desire to bloom.

Until now. It unfurls with each stroke of Bastien's fingers. Warmth tingles through my sex and flushes the back of my neck.

Perhaps the quiver creeps into my breath as well. Perhaps

the warmth seeps through the silk of my dress. Either way, Bastien's massage turns into more of a caress.

He eases forward from where he's now kneeling behind me and kisses the corner of my jaw. "Would you like to be taken care of in other ways, Star? Just say the word."

Marc lets out a strangled sound. When I look his way again, his stance has gone taut, his eyes blazing.

His irritation sweeps away any doubts I might have harbored. Why should I spare him from the exposure to my real lovers? He knows Bastien fathered Coraya—it's not as if it's a secret how intimate we've already gotten.

He can't have any real place in my life if he'll never be willing to at least tolerate the men who've already earned theirs.

"If you don't like what you're seeing, you can look the other way," I inform him.

Marc just glowers at me, but Bastien recognizes the permission in my words. His commanding tone returns. "Turn around."

As I swivel on the stool to face him, a twinge that's not entirely pleasant runs through my belly. "I may still be a little tender inside."

From what I know of the healing arts, the medics' efforts should mean anything I might want to do now is *safe*. Whether it'll be fully enjoyable is a more subjective matter.

Bastien cups my face. "I'll take good care of you. Exactly what you need. But if anything does hurt, smack me."

At my snort, he smiles and then claims my mouth. The kiss sends a fresh rush of heat through my chest. As his tongue tangles with mine, my fingers dig into his shirt.

I have the vague impression of Marc's gaze still boring into us, but I can't say I care. There might even be a little thrill in the knowledge.

My true lovers have had to watch him—and mostly his

twin—grope me whenever they please for over a year. Let him find out how it feels to have to watch.

Let him witness what a touch offered out of love should look like.

Bastien kisses me again and again, gentle but intent. His hands travel along my sides and up to fondle my breasts through my gown.

My nipples spark with a sharper pleasure than I'm used to. Their other recent purpose has left them extra sensitized.

My breath catches. At the heightening flares of pleasure, I press into Bastien's touch.

"Oh, I've got more for you, Star," he murmurs against my lips with another swivel of his palms against my breasts. "Spread those lovely legs for me."

With a crackle of anticipation, I obey. Bastien sits back on his heels and gathers the layers of my skirt before shoving the heap of fabric nearly to my waist.

He kisses the inside of one knee and then the other. The brush of his mouth travels back and forth up my inner thighs.

By the time he reaches the edge of my drawers, I'm trembling. A pang has formed between my legs.

Bastien trails a delicate finger over the growing dampness at the crotch of my drawers. The jolt of sensation brings a gasp to my lips.

"Up," he says, soft but firm. At my brief bob off the stool, he yanks my drawers from my thighs.

The moment they've pooled on the floor, he lowers his head to my sex.

The first swipe of his tongue shocks a groan out of me. It's been so long—I'd almost forgotten just how good the men I love can make me feel.

My fingers curl into Bastien's rumpled hair. He delves

deeper, swirling his tongue over my clit, sucking that nub between his lips.

I sway with the waves of pleasure, clutching hold of him. He traces my folds and strums my clit before applying his mouth again, but not once does he press tongue or fingers into my channel.

Any lingering anxiety melts away. I rock into his attentions, riding his face. Every flick of his tongue sparks new tremors of bliss.

Bastien grasps my hips to pull me even tighter against him. He plunders me like I'm the only meal he'll ever want to eat, and the sensations swell all through my body.

I bite my lip against a cry. One more lap of his tongue and press of his thumb, and I'm careening over the edge.

My thighs clench around his face. A shudder runs through me from toes to head, as if I'm going to float right off the ground.

When I come back to myself, Bastien is grinning up at me, licking his lips. Not a trace of disappointment that he didn't get any physical gratification for himself shows in his expression.

Marc stands by the door so rigidly he might as well be made of marble, but he's still watching us. The stark heat of his gaze—how much lust and how much anger, I can't determine—sends another jolt through my nerves.

Bastien is just easing my skirt back over my legs when Raul and Lorenzo emerge through the hidden entrance. Raul takes one look at the two of us, at my cheeks flushing hotter under his scrutiny, and clucks his tongue playfully. "You've gone and hoarded her all for yourself, Bas. That's hardly sporting."

Bastien raises his eyebrows back at his foster brothers. "Maybe you should have figured out she headed back to her rooms sooner, then. I wasn't going to make her wait when she needed attending to."

I laugh and start to get to my feet. Lorenzo hustles to my side in time to grasp my elbow and steady me through one final tremor of aftershock.

He kisses my jaw with a teasing nip of his teeth. *"I'm just glad to see our empress looking so satisfied."*

Raul hums, giving me another onceover and a cocky smile. "It does appear that our brother did the job well."

Their companionable warmth wraps around me, lighting a glow inside that's much more than just bodily pleasure. When they're with me, every consideration—even the man who's technically still my husband poised across the room—can fade into the distance.

Watching them, inspiration flares like a lantern in my head.

I've been trying to appease Sabrelle, to court her favor… an awful lot like I once courted Marclinus's.

But I could never count on him to actually help me survive. It was the other men I turned to and won over who helped me achieve the heights I've gained.

Even Lucrene told me I should take my allies wherever I can find them. Strike a balance between all the empire's needs.

That advice could apply to more than just my subjects.

I wet my lips. "I think… I think I might have been looking at this rebellion all wrong."

CHAPTER ELEVEN

Marc

What exactly has this woman reduced me to? She's standing there amid three men she lets paw her with abandon, her skin still flushed from the way one of them pleasured her just moments ago. And I can't tear my gaze away, even as my hands clench at my sides and my jaw aches with the gritting of my teeth.

I want to rip their heads from their bodies and wallop them across the room in a bloody game of croquet. I want to stomp their fucking corpses to pulp.

But I won't, because *she* would hate me. Because I'd lose any chance of her warm, sparkling gaze ever being aimed at me with the same kind of affection, and that thought agonizes me even more than the sharp sear of my jealousy.

So I'm left here seething as ineffectually as a toddler who's had his favorite toy snatched, biting back the complaints even I know would sound pathetic.

She was mine first. She was mine more than yours.

Can I really say that's true? Aurelia's certainly not mine now. I'm only in the room because of the barest thread of fidelity I earned by stopping Linus's final madness.

I saved her life, and I get to sleep by her door while they share her bed.

As with every time my mind veers so far into resentment, an image rises up of her face bent close to mine in the dimness of that secret basement room. The eyes now sparkling then hard with pain and fury. The matching emotions rippling through her taut voice.

Who hurled knives at my head? Who burned my hands raw?

You played along with his games. Even when you finally 'let me into the family,' it was all another test designed to crush me.

I doubt you'd have done much different in my position, whether you believe it or not.

The rage that was swelling inside me deflates.

In her eyes, I deserved much worse. And in her position, I doubt I could have found even the shred of compassion that led her to keep me alive.

She beat me in both might and kindness. I've never encountered a force as formidable as this astonishing woman. How the fuck can I be angry with her?

My foster brothers are another matter.

They hover around her, all smug eagerness, relishing their proximity to her even more while I have to watch from afar. Prince Bastien and Prince Lorenzo don't bother to disguise their disdain when they glance at me. Prince Raul likes to outright smirk when Aurelia won't notice.

He isn't smirking at the moment, though. They're all completely fixated on her—on the urgent tone her voice has taken that yanks my attention back to her too.

"Sabrelle's been working against me for *months*," she's saying. "Almost the entire time I've been in Dariu. Neven started getting those dreams not long after I was crowned empress."

"She didn't like you offing the emperor she put on the throne," Raul suggests, speaking of my father's murder so casually I have to restrain myself from throwing him out the window.

If I even could. I've seen the prince of Lavira win enough arena battles to know he's no slouch in a fight.

Aurelia waves her hand as if dismissing the details. "Whatever the initial reasons, she's only continued to like me less. It wasn't until the coronation tour that she ramped up her efforts to encouraging assassination."

Yes. Through that wretch Valerisse, who deserves my wrath more than any of the traitors in front of me. If I have the chance to get my hands on *her*, there won't be any hesitating.

Lorenzo's illusionary baritone, a voice I'm not yet used to him wielding, carries through my skull. *"I'd have expected her to soften at least a little after seeing you display your might openly. What could she want from you?"*

Aurelia's mouth twists. "I don't know. It's possible… there isn't anything I could do. That's my point."

Bastien is studying her with a gaze more incisive than I remember recognizing before. Did he play a dope around me in the past, or did I never bother to consider him properly?

"Where are you going with this, Aurelia?" he asks.

Her gaze darts to me. My heart leaps at the momentary attention and then sinks at the tightening of her expression.

She aims a wry smile at the princes. "I'm thinking about the strategies that have served me best in the past. When I couldn't win over my husband even a little, instead of continuing to throw myself into a hopeless cause, I found other allies to turn to."

My teeth grit, but I manage to keep my mouth shut. What could I say that wouldn't add to her point?

Raul shoots me a cocky glance. "So if Marclinus is Sabrelle in this comparison, then we are…"

"The other godlen. They must have their own opinions about what happens in the empire's half of this world they watch over. There are *eight* of them—surely if they were all on my side, they could overcome whatever animosity Sabrelle is holding on to."

A wobble runs through my gut. Does she really think—

Before I can put my apprehension into words, Bastien is diving into the idea. "You can already count on Elox. I can't imagine any of the other gods would harbor ill-will against you."

She shrugs. "I don't know whether they'd have any feelings about me at all right now. I need to find ways of showing I'll honor each of them in the way I rule the empire. Give them a reason to stand up to Sabrelle and her dedicats on my behalf."

I can't keep quiet. "To focus on eight instead of one—"

Lorenzo's voice overwhelms mine. *"After those sick challenges Linus demanded while trying to put himself on their divine level, it shouldn't be hard for you to look pious in contrast."*

Aurelia gives a soft laugh. "I hope not. You may be able to help with that. If you can meditate with your own godlen on what they'd most want to see from the empire—or consider from your past experiences… I can use all the guidance I can get."

But not mine. I open my mouth again, and Raul glares at me before a sound can slip past my throat.

Fine. I'll just wait until they're not hovering around her. I still have the one advantage of being able to openly walk at her side, if in a much-diminished role.

After a brief negotiation, it's decided that Raul will be spending the night. While Aurelia vanishes behind her dressing screen to change into her night garments and he sprawls out on the bed, I force myself to lie down on the now-familiar sleeping roll.

The rustle of his caress and the murmur of their kiss lance through my awareness. It's a small blessing that I don't have to endure any more gasps or moans.

I've become accustomed enough to my new position to fall asleep once Aurelia's breaths have evened out. My instincts jerk me awake at the first purposeful stirrings on the bed come morning.

In the thin dawn light, Raul leans over to give Aurelia another kiss and pads over to the hidden panel in the wall. As he disappears behind it, Aurelia sits up on the bed with a swipe of her eyes.

I gather myself onto my feet. I have a short opening before her maids arrive to ready her for the day.

"I don't think dismissing Sabrelle is the wisest idea," I say.

Aurelia blinks at me. She slides out from beneath the covers and pushes her rumpled hair back from her face. The nightgown is chaste enough, but seeing it summons images from all the times I thought we came together in one bed or another.

Mostly hallucination, she said. And every bit of affection she actually offered me was feigned.

She folds her arms over her chest, which only emphasizes the curve of her breasts. "Is there any particular reason, or do you simply not like me ignoring your chosen godlen?"

I grimace. How long will it take before she knows I want to advise her properly, not based on petty concerns? "It's a simple matter of practicality. It should be far easier to sway one godlen than seven—with the assumption that Elox already favors you."

"If everything were equal, I'd agree. But Sabrelle has already proven particularly vengeful and resistant to my appeals. If she's ten times as unyielding as any of her fellow divinities, I'm better off focusing on them."

There's logic to that statement. The idea still twists me up inside in a way I can't quite pin down.

Perhaps it's this. "Don't you think it's possible that catering to all the other godlen ahead of her will only turn her more against you? You can't win a war against a god."

Aurelia turns her back on me to head to the bathing room. "I'm trying to avoid any war at all. She's the one turning this situation into a catastrophe."

"It's not that simple. Aurelia—"

When she keeps walking, a noise of frustration escapes me. I stride after her. "You don't know the sway Sabrelle can impose. She was a driving force in the creation of this entire empire. You have to listen to me."

As I catch up with her by the bathing room doorway, Aurelia whirls on me. "No, I don't. Not when you have a personal stake in appeasing her. I have plenty of other people to advise me."

My temper slips its reins. I snatch at her wrist where the gold band still gleams, my voice coming out harsher than I'd have intended. "I have a personal stake in *you*. I'm still your husband."

Aurelia wrenches her arm back. The wedding band flashes in the wan light.

Her gaze turns to steel. "You're no longer my emperor. I'll listen to you and consider what you have to say, which is more than you or your brother offered me most of the time you held the throne. But I don't have to agree."

My frustration curdles in my gut. "I didn't mean—"

"You did," she says, quiet but firm. "You still think you can order me around if it's important enough to you. I know I can benefit from your understanding of the empire, but you need to remember that I make the final decisions now. I earned that right. Or do you no longer believe that?"

Heat flares across my face, pricking hotter beneath the strange scarring that covers so much of it. Reminding me that I don't even look like the man she strove to marry, the emperor who reigned over half the continent.

Every part of this situation is a mess, down to the muddling of my features. How is she ever going to want me when I'm permanently stained for all to see?

When I keep making mistakes no matter how hard I try to prove myself.

My stubbornness prevents me from giving way completely. "I'm not ordering you. I just think the matter deserves more of a conversation—"

Aurelia cuts me off with a shake of her head. "No. I've been considering what Sabrelle might want for weeks, and it hasn't gotten me anywhere. I'm running out of time before Valerisse makes good on her threats. I have to try another way. *My* way, for once. Go back to your post."

The coolness of the command seeps through to my bones. I set my jaw and drag myself back to the apartment door.

I think it's over, a brief squabble like others we've had before. Maybe my words will sink in and she'll give them more weight once she's mulled them over.

The maids arrive to fuss over her, and we all proceed to the dining room for breakfast. As we step into the large space, Aurelia turns toward her host of guards, her gaze singling out me.

"I don't need all of you attending to me quite so closely

in here. Marc, why don't you make a circuit of the room and watch for signs of ill favor."

My spine jerks straighter even as I restrain a wince. She may as well have slapped me. It's a dismissal, a declaration that she wants me farther away from her.

Fine. I can show all due respect to my empress.

I tip my head. "As Your Imperial Highness wishes."

The weight of the other guards' gazes follows me as I set off along the edge of the room. They're not sure what to make of their empress's recent reliance on me. They may be glad to see her casting me off.

None of them has any idea that she's been keeping an eye on me at least as much as expecting me to watch over her.

I commit myself to the duty she's asked of me, keeping my ears pricked and my eyes keen as I tread along the outskirts of the rows of tables. The nobles take no note of me while they engage in their everyday chatter, other than an occasional twitch of disgust when someone's gaze passes over my discolored face.

No one appears to be talking about Valerisse or yesterday's challenge. I'll consider that a good sign.

As I continue my patrol along the back wall, a different name catches in my ears. "…if Marclinus were still here."

I pause, not looking toward the speakers. Are they comparing Aurelia to me—criticizing her while mourning their late emperor?

A different voice answers. "Thank the gods he isn't. Did you hear about all his grandstanding on his tour? Acting like he was a god himself… He's lucky Sabrelle didn't strike him down before he ever got home."

Someone else snorts. "He probably figured that if any of the godlen objected, he'd just order his soldiers to run them through like he would any of us." She pauses, the dry humor fading from her tone. "I can't help thinking about all those girls. If he'd gone ahead and married Aurelia in the first place…"

"He had to be sure it was the right choice," a fourth figure puts in, though he sounds awkwardly uncertain. "It's good that we know how hard she'll fight for the imperial family."

"Did the others really deserve to *die* because they couldn't fight quite as hard? They weren't even prepared… I'm not sure all of them even wanted to marry him in the first place."

Yet another table-mate makes a shushing sound. "I never heard you talk like that while His Imperial Majesty was still around."

"Who would have? We didn't want *our* throats cut."

From the corner of my eye, I see one of the noblewomen in the group glance toward the head table. "Our empress does seem as though she'll be less eager about bloodshed, even if she isn't afraid to deal it out as need be. It'll be nice getting used to speaking without panicking over any slight slip of the tongue."

Faint chuckles carry around the table with a chorus of agreement.

I propel myself onward, their words churning inside me in a noxious stew. Is that what my court really thought of me?

Well, me and my brother, but as Aurelia pointed out so incisively, I bear responsibility for his actions too. We were a duo, a partnership, the closest sort of collaboration any two people could take part in.

He fucked so much up… and I let him. Because it was easier than fighting with him about it and risking the whole house of cards tumbling down. Easier to hope I could eventually find a way to moderate his growing madness.

I can't place all the blame on his shoulders. I agreed to the trials. I helped carry them out.

I put Aurelia through the wringer even after, called for punishments on a whim. While I thought of those whims as forceful authority, how much thought did I really give to any of the pain I dealt out?

All this time, I assumed the court followed me because they believed in the power of the imperial line. Because they respected the choices my father and I made.

Were they actually cowering in fear every moment they were around me? Faking their admiration and loyalty just as Aurelia did and feeling nothing but relief with me gone?

By the time I reach the far corner, a lump has congealed in my throat too thick for me to swallow away.

Force is necessary, sometimes. A little fear can be a useful instrument. But I never intended it to be the only tool in my arsenal. That's pure carelessness. An authority as hollow as the devotion Aurelia feigned.

I didn't want to rule that way, just as I didn't want a marriage won through terror. I wanted to see my people— the whole empire—actually *thrive.* And all the while, they were holding their breaths whenever I was nearby, trembling at the thought that one mistake would cost them their lives…

I wondered last night what Aurelia has reduced me to, but it seems I reduced myself to a shadow of an emperor before she ever arrived in Dariu.

Even this morning—do I really think her strategy is wrong? Or am I more rankled that she's perpetuating the same ploy that worked against me, that I'll be able to contribute even less if she doesn't need my insights into my own godlen's attitudes?

I look toward the high table myself. I take in the warmth in the smiles aimed Aurelia's way, the way the nobles around her exchange conversation in harmony rather than a jockeying for dominance.

It's not an atmosphere I'm familiar with.

If I want to stay by this incredible woman's side, I need to do more than be useful to her. I need to show I can be part of the new version of court she's creating. Build something real rather than pressing on her fears.

I'm twenty-seven years out of practice. Maybe it's too late for me to find a new way.

But I'll be damned if I don't prove myself just as much a fighter as she is. And this time, I'll fight for the things that matter most.

Chapter Twelve

Aurelia

When the light from the overhead lanterns glances off my sword, an image flashes through my head: scarlet staining the steel, a dying gurgle.

A tremor runs through my pulse. I gather myself and manage to block Captain Evando's next strike, but a kernel of horror stays lodged in my stomach.

How much time will it take before the memories of my first violent kill fade? Or will they always linger, no matter how much time has passed, no matter how sure I am that I made the best choice I could?

I can't dwell on those uncertainties—not when I have so much more to accomplish.

I aim a smile toward the several noblewomen who showed up to train this afternoon. Bianca and the companions she gathered are moving through a few simple sparring moves the soldiers have shown them.

Please, don't let them regret throwing their lot in with me even this much.

From what I've seen, the palace military force hasn't resented the intrusion. Evando even suggested to his underlings that teaching skills to others can reinforce their own. But I'm keeping a close eye on the volunteer tutors all the same.

I need all of the palace's inhabitants, noble and staff, to be a united front behind me. If I don't have their support in whatever appeals I need to make to the other seven godlen, I won't get far.

And then I might be responsible for bringing down outright war on us all.

I don't want Sabrelle to assume I'm completely dismissing her, though. Improving my combat skill both increases my chances of surviving this coup and endears me to my main defenders, so I'm not giving up my practice sessions.

Evando tuts at my next block. After our multiple past sparring sessions, he's become more confident in correcting his empress. "You'll be better off angling your blade more on a diagonal when someone comes at you like that, Your Imperial Highness. Don't be afraid to keep the sword fairly close to your body so you're not straining your arm more than you need to."

As I nod, Neven gives a cough where he's paused in his own training to watch our mock skirmish. "Why are you sticking to just the sword work? If she's keeping her forms tight, she could knee an attacker in the balls while she's blocking. That'd knock him right over."

The captain stares at the prince as if he's suggested I dance a waltz with my enemy's entrails. "I hardly think— The empress needs to follow proper combat decorum."

Neven snorts. "Decorum is for performing. In a real fight, all that matters is not getting stabbed. She isn't going to feel good about being properly sportsman—er, woman—like if she's dead."

Evando narrows his eyes. "I'm not saying she shouldn't do whatever she can to defend herself if her life is on the line. But if you develop enough skill with your weapon, no one needs to resort to base tactics."

"I hardly think anyone who decides to murder an empress is going to be worrying about sticking to morally upright fighting strategies."

"That isn't the point. It's my duty—"

I hold up my free hand before their tones can get any more heated. "I appreciate both of your commitments to ensuring I remain unmurdered. If the empress gets a say in what she's taught, I do want to learn every possible move that could protect me. Captain, I promise I won't bring any of them out in respectable company unless it's absolutely necessary."

Evando's mouth tightens, but the dip of his head looks more abashed than annoyed. "Yes, of course, Your Imperial Highness." At the peal of the bell that signals the end of my session, he shakes himself, his shoulders relaxing more. "Next time, we can incorporate more, ah, street tactics into your practice."

The noblewomen head toward the door as I do. Baronissa Hivette glances at me while dabbing the sweat on her brow. "We'll see you in the hall of entertainments, Your Imperial Highness?"

"As soon as I'm presentable," I say. "Thank you all for your company today. The empire's strength comes from all of us!"

As I clean up and change in my chambers, my current host of personal guards switches off. I emerge to find Kassun among those on duty… and High Commander Axius standing in the hall where I'd have expected a fourth guard to be.

He speaks without preamble. "There's something we need to discuss, Your Imperial Highness."

Marc's gaze flicks over his new colleagues from where he's emerged behind me. "What's happened?"

Axius frowns. I step in before he feels the need to chide Marc for his presumption. "I'm sure we'll find that out in a moment."

The former emperor looks as if he's restrained a grimace, but he tamps down his impatience.

I motion from Axius to my door. "Do you want to step inside? It'll be as private in my apartment as any of the official military rooms and save us time."

The high commander hesitates—I suppose my suggestion isn't proper military decorum either—but he appears to think efficiency is more important. "All right."

The guards all file into my bedroom, presumably to protect my modesty. I come to a stop by my vanity. "Well, what's the matter?"

Axius's expression manages to turn even grimmer. There's something unusually deflated about the large man's posture. "One of your usual guards is missing."

I knit my brow. "Missing? What exactly does that mean?"

"It appears he's abandoned his post. He left quietly in the middle of the night, made an excuse about being on an errand to the guards at the gate, and never returned."

Dread starts to pool in my gut. "The errand could have taken him longer than he anticipated," I say, but I suspect if that was likely, we wouldn't be having this conversation.

Axius holds my gaze. "If he had reasonable intentions, he'd have reported them to his commanding officer—or to me. He was dedicated to Sabrelle."

Ah. "You think he's defected to Tribune Valerisse's forces."

The high commander inclines his head slightly. "All the evidence points to that conclusion."

I swallow thickly. "Well, I suppose that's better than him attempting to assassinate me while he was here." Whether that was out of some remaining shred of loyalty or more practical concerns, gods only know.

"He… He may not be the only one." Axius appears to gird himself. "No one's seen Severo since dinner yesterday."

I stare at him for a moment before my mind catches up. "My *counsel?*"

"Yes. *He* wouldn't necessarily have felt the need to report his reason for stepping away from court if it's only for a day or two, but at a time like this…"

Nausea pools in my stomach. "He was dedicated to Sabrelle too, wasn't he?"

"He was," Marc mutters from behind me, and shuts his mouth firmly at my sharp look.

Axius attempts to rally. "It's possible his absence is temporary and unrelated. And we've had defections in the other direction. A few soldiers who were stationed in Lavira or nearby have been arriving in Vivencia to offer their support."

My stomach churns harder. "Why would they feel they need to do that?"

If Axius's jaw clenched any harder, I think his face would snap in half. "From what they've said, Valerisse has been stirring up a lot of hostility toward you among her local forces. She's building her own personal army just outside Rodrige, and it's already grown to a concerning size."

None of the soldiers stationed that far away have had much of a chance to get to know me as a ruler. I only spent a few weeks in Lavira months ago, and then my presence was overshadowed by my husband's. The one challenge I carried out was solely for Linus's benefit and conducted with only my personal guards as witnesses.

A handful of those soldiers have returned to me, but all the others... How can I sway them in my favor when they're several days' riding beyond my reach?

I know the answer, but I can't help asking, "I don't suppose the local Lavirian forces can stand up to them?"

Axius shakes his head. "Even if we could coordinate with the local authorities, their military has been kept small and spread out—for obvious reasons. We may see some revolt from the Lavirian citizens... but I'd imagine most would prefer to stay out of the conflict."

A contingent of Raul's people revolted against Marclinus just a year ago. They might *enjoy* seeing the empire attack itself.

How much support do I have even here in Vivencia? "Have we lost many other soldiers—or anyone else—from the palace?"

"I know of a couple from the infantry, but that's all."

Kassun draws himself up straighter. "My colleagues are more than honored to serve you, Your Imperial Highness."

"That sentiment seems to be shared through much of Dariu," Axius goes on. "We've called in troops that could be spared to the surrounding towns so they're nearby if we need them. I have messengers standing by to summon more reinforcements and sentries posted farther abroad. She can't march on us without us knowing."

One of the other guards scowls. "We should march on *her*."

Marc inserts himself with an authoritative tone only I know he's earned. "If we go to meet her on what she's made her turf, she'll have the advantage. And the Lavirians are much more likely to fight with her if we bring the battle to their home soil."

"And she hasn't actually carried out any of her threats yet. Until she brings her forces onto Darium soil against imperial orders, there's still a chance of avoiding a real war." I drag in a breath. "We have to keep waiting to see what moves she'll make. In the meantime, we'll solidify our position as much as possible."

Including my individual position as empress.

Those thoughts are buzzing through my mind when a gentle knock sounds on the door. Kassun opens it to reveal one of the nursemaids with Coraya.

She takes in the guards surrounding me and draws back. "I didn't mean to interrupt. I heard you were going to join the court and thought you'd want to have Coraya."

"Yes, I was about to head to the hall of entertainments." I step into the hall and hold out my arms to accept my daughter. "Thank you. Just a little imperial business getting sorted out."

It'll have to be sorted out enough for now. There's nothing I can do to put down Valerisse myself at the moment.

Coraya coos and grabs at the neckline of my dress. I've had to stop wearing the necklaces my maids would like to drape me in to make sure she doesn't pinch her tiny hands on the elaborate finery. No great loss.

"Come now," I say to her. "Let's go see your court."

My daughter is becoming increasingly pleased with the attention of the nobles she'll someday rule over. As we circulate through the hall of entertainments, she offers more coos and even a couple of burbling laughs. The viceroy who earns the second of those beams back at her as if she's just granted him a chest of gold.

Our audience is less impressed by her spitting up on my

shoulder, only partly caught by a maid who dashes over, but that simply provokes some giggles.

"Babies will be babies, even when they're also the heir to the empire," Marchionissa Lucrene remarks with a fond smile.

I pass the cards tables but decline an invitation to join the game because I don't trust Coraya not to mouth the edges of the cards.

I'm just skirting the dart throwers when a plaintive voice reaches my ears. "Your Imperial Highness…"

One of the younger noblemen who's a newer arrival at court this season is hunched in a chair by the wall. With a pang of concern, I hustle over to him. "Are you quite all right, Baron—"

Before I can dredge up his name from my memory, he springs from the chair like an arrow unleashed. His arm whips out, and a globby shape flies at me.

Flies and splatters against the magic barrier one of my guards flings up a few inches from my face. The dark green substance hisses as it streaks across the gleaming shield and splatters to the floor instead. The pool of it sears a burnt mark in the rug.

"What the fuck are you doing?" Marc snarls. He's already on the baron, heaving him face first into the floor just inches from the sizzling acid.

As I catch my breath, clutching Coraya so tight against me she grunts in protest, the rest of my guards and hers pull close around me. Their eyes dart around the room for other threats, but no one stirs. The nobles around us have frozen, staring at the scene of the attempted attack.

I had no time to activate my drugged ring. None of my combat training did any good either when my assailant lashed out so suddenly. When I had nothing on me that could defend me against a chemical rather than a weapon.

When I was carrying my daughter in my arms.

The young baron yelps when Marc digs his knee into a soft spot on his back. "I honor Sabrelle. We need to pave the way for the empire's greatness. It'll never happen—"

Marc wallops his head against the rug hard enough for the other man's tongue to stumble. As the baron mumbles in a daze, Axius strides into our midst.

The high commander jerks his hand toward my guards. "Get this traitor out of here and lock him up for proper questioning. Empress, do I need to call for a medic?"

"No." My voice comes out fainter than I intended. I gird myself. "I was only startled."

Perhaps sensing my tension, Coraya starts to whimper.

Two soldiers from my doubled contingent of guards hustle over to haul the baron to his feet. Marc backs up, his teeth bared.

When he turns to me, his expression softens. His gaze drops to the baby I'm cradling. "Coraya—is she all right? He didn't hurt her at all?"

The thickening of his voice makes my throat constrict. He really is worried—not just for me but for her as well.

"Yes," I say. "Thank you—thank all of you—for leaping in so quickly."

Marc's gaze meets mine again, so fraught I can't look away. "I always will," he says, so quietly I'm not sure anyone else hears him.

All the regrets he's confessed to swim up from my memory. He failed to protect me so many times in the past... but he really has come through every time I've needed him since then.

I don't know what to make of the twinge that passes through my heart.

Marc isn't the only man who'll be worried about us. My attention flicks beyond my guards.

My eyes lock with Bastien's across the room. A glint of panic shines in his dark green irises.

I sweep my hand over my hair with a hasty gesture. *All well.*

His shoulders come down slightly.

The nobles closer by are murmuring to each other now. Several ease closer—as close as my now doubly-wary guards will allow.

"What a disgrace, Your Imperial Highness."

"To try to harm a *baby*..."

"Surely Sabrelle would never approve of that! He must have been insane."

They sound much more horrified that Coraya might have been harmed than their empress—which is fair enough, because so am I. But as my panic simmers down, watching them fuss and shudder around me sends a tingle of inspiration through my thoughts.

For all their snobbish and imperialist views, Dariu's nobles do care about children. I can't count how many times my appeals to Marc's fatherly instincts helped win his compassion when he was torn between me and his brother.

Perhaps I can expand our court's compassion to all the children of Dariu—and pay tribute to Inganne, the godlen who watches over those children, at the same time.

My attacker might have intended to knock me down, but instead he's nudged me one step closer to victory.

Chapter Thirteen

Lorenzo

As we step into the vast storeroom in the depths of the palace, one of Aurelia's guards makes a gesture that lights up the magic-blessed lanterns along the ceiling. Their enchanted glow sweeps over stacks of crates topped with glittering material and row upon row of decorative furniture and vehicles.

The empress blinks, her lips parting with awe. "I—I didn't realize we had such an extensive assortment of festival equipment."

One of the other guards—Kassun, who always seems particularly eager to impress her—grins as if he was directly responsible for building the collection. "The imperial family always loves putting on a good show for the people when it's time to celebrate. I guess you haven't gotten to see much of that here in Vivencia since we were on the tour most of the past year."

Aurelia nods as if in a daze and drifts through the stale air between the looming paraphernalia of past revels. She beckons me. "Let's see what we can find, Your Highness."

This once, the woman I love can consult with me openly. I'm the highest ranked member of court who's dedicated to Inganne, after all.

For show, I pull out the sheaf of papers and pencil I keep in my belt pouch. As far as the guards know, that's how I'll be communicating with her.

I might feel it's wisest to let our closest allies know my full gift, but spreading word widely isn't likely to work in our favor. The more secret powers we have up our sleeve when Valerisse makes a real move, the better.

Aurelia trails her fingers along the side of a vibrant gold-and-green sedan chair and gazes up at a massive wooden statue of Estera, which would be pulled behind a carriage on the wheeled platform it's poised on. She's taken a meandering path designed to draw us out of view of her guards—except Marc, who she's allowed to trail closer behind us so the others don't fret. As if an assassin would bother lurking down there.

"I suppose there's some level of organization—materials grouped by the festival they're meant to be used for?" she says just loud enough for the former emperor to hear. "Where would we find the Inganalia supplies?"

Marc's mouth twists apologetically. "I've never been down here myself. The staff has always brought everything out."

"Hmm. Well, it can't hurt to explore and see everything that's on offer. Inganne does value creativity."

Aurelia shifts her attention to me, with a smile that washes a warmer glow over me than that of the lanterns. "What do you think would win your godlen's respect the most—what would convince her that I'll uphold her ideals if I remain on the throne?"

I've been mulling that question over since Aurelia first mentioned her plans. *"You're focusing on her devotion to children and encouraging the same devotion throughout Vivencia, but you don't want to neglect her other domains. It's easy to bond through play—we should offer plenty of games where the citizens can mingle. And artistic activities—not just showing off spectacles of art but creating it together."*

Aurelia nods thoughtfully. "We want to put everyone on equal ground, the nobles seeing how little difference there is at heart between their children and the commoners'. I don't think it'll do to try to raise up the city folk, so perhaps we encourage the nobles to let down their airs. Have fun, make a mess for the sake of fun or art."

"That sounds perfect. Although you'll need to be careful how far and quickly you push them. Not many in the court like the idea of embarrassing themselves in public."

"We can ease them in… Oh, I see some orange over there! That must be Inganne's section."

As she picks up her pace, I can't help glancing back toward Marc. He's giving us plenty of distance even with his shadowing, hanging some ten paces behind, but his gaze remains fixed on Aurelia as if she's the only thing he can see.

As if she's the only thing he'd *want* to see.

The intensity in his eyes and the yearning I can practically taste emanating off him set my skin prickling. I have to suppress the urge to step closer to Aurelia and wrap my arms around her in a shield of affection, as if I need to ward off his. If what he feels for her could even be called affection.

We need to work with him. I believe he wants to protect her. But I can't shake the feeling that he'd claim her for only himself all over again if he could, whether she agreed or not.

He doesn't make any move to interfere or even interject himself into our conversation, which I've let him overhear my end of. Aurelia doesn't pay him any mind, so I force myself to dismiss his presence as well as I can.

It's my help our empress needs most right now anyway. The success of this festival could depend on how well I guide her.

As we move between the decorations and apparatus splashed with Inganne's favored color and many others besides, I dredge up as many memories as I can from the festivals I attended as a child, especially those back in Rione before I was dragged here as a hostage.

My home kingdom values the godlen of creativity's contributions more than Dariu ever has. They think life is all about might and dominance. We've always wanted to foster artistic inspiration.

I point out a couple of familiar items. *"Those discs make for a pretty elaborate game of collaboration that the kids usually find entertaining. There are opportunities for their parents to get involved too, to make it even more of a joint effort. And that long banner—I don't remember seeing it played here in Vivencia before, but in Rione there's an activity that's sort of a mix of obstacle course and follow the leader that's popular."*

"You'll have to explain the rules of that one. I never saw that in Accasy either." Aurelia stops to finger the edge of a swooping silk canopy embroidered with a complex pattern. "Usually there's some paint that gets thrown around."

More memories from back home swim up. *"We can do better than that. Maybe large murals on the walls of buildings that children and parents can add to together, or a swath of fabric they could paint and then you display it at the palace. There's a game you can play with the art, each person attaching one shape or symbol to the one before."*

"I like that." She taps her lips, studying a carriage that

holds a sculpted tree dotted with silk butterflies. "If we include a parade, we could get the children involved with that too. Show off minor talents, dance around, all in good fun. Although the nobles might balk at their children mingling with the commoners to begin with…"

"*We could save that for the end, once they've already gotten comfortable.*"

"Yes, perfect. It doesn't feel like quite enough, though. We want the festival to have a lasting impact that Inganne will approve of. The art might help with that. I'll need to think on what other elements could be more permanent."

"*Simply making the festival an official annual event might be enough,*" I point out. "*An additional honor to her alongside her usual yearly celebration. I'll keep mulling over other possibilities … I should stop by the library. There might be some references to older practices from the Inganalias of centuries past that we could incorporate. There's a whole section of books in Rionian I could check.*"

Aurelia smiles at me. "Go ahead, if you think that's where you're most likely to find more inspiration."

She takes a quick glance around to make sure no one but Marc is in view and then steps closer to give me a quick kiss. The brush of her lips leaves heat coursing through my veins.

I squeeze her hand before weaving back through the stacks of equipment toward the doorway.

The posted guards don't spare me a second glance. I hurry past them into the halls, not slowing until I've reached the vast imperial library.

The foreign volumes are kept in an out-of-the-way nook in a far corner. As I walk over to that section, the familiar stillness settles over me like a balm on my nerves.

Out of all the godlen, Aurelia shouldn't have any trouble winning Inganne to her side. There's no denying how much she loves her daughter, and she's sacrificed so much in the hopes of making a better life for all the empire's children.

Inganne should want the suffering of the conquered countries to be replaced with joy just as much as Aurelia does.

But we can't take anything for granted. The court will need to be convinced this new festival is worthwhile if she wants them to support any other schemes later on.

What will she have to do to impress Kosmel with his love of trickery? Or Creaden, for that matter, after all the efforts past emperors have dedicated to him?

When I reach the shelves of Rionian texts, I scan the spines for anything from times long past that might mention more playful activities. I've pulled out a couple of volumes to peruse when my gaze snags on a slim book squeezed so tightly between two thick ones it's barely visible.

I ease it out, my fingers smearing the dust that's gathered on it. No one's looked at most of these texts in quite a while.

The faded title on the front cover doesn't speak of festivals or the arts, but I can tell from the style of the script that it's from at least a few centuries past. *The Principles of Rionian Statecraft.*

It's possible it says something about the running of celebrations. And it might be the oldest book in this bunch. Anything that could have since fallen out of common knowledge will be useful.

Since it's the smallest, I crack it open first after I settle into my chair. I page through cramped print detailing the system of governance across the old duchies and the rules of inheritance, scanning for anything more relevant.

Then I turn another page and find myself looking at rows of whorled lines like orderly abstract art.

I peer closer. It's a code—laid out efficiently for the

officials the author obviously expected might need to use it. A method of conveying messages that no one outside the Rionian governing bodies should be able to recognize.

As my hand lingers on the page, my mother's voice drifts up through my mind. *This is still a war, even if they want to pretend we're at peace. And we have to make use of every resource at our disposal.*

My pulse kicks up a notch, but at the same time, queasiness grips my gut.

I can also remember, ever so clearly, the sadness and resignation on my mother's face and in her voice when I tried to tell her to have faith in Aurelia. Her melancholy dismissal of my comments as the result of my soft heart.

"Did you find something useful?"

My heart outright skips a beat at the sudden voice, even though I recognize it in the same moment.

I raise my head. Bastien has come up by the nearest bookcase, peering at the volume in my hand and the others stacked next to my chair. I was so lost in thought I didn't hear the prince of Cotea approaching.

Maybe, I convey with a twitch of my hand, and switch to speaking through illusions. *"I might have found a method to convey a message to my mother from a distance without any risk of the Darium forces in Rione stumbling on it. It occurred to me… maybe we should be reaching out to our home kingdoms. They have more to gain than anyone if Aurelia can hold on to the throne."*

Bastien lets out a soft huff of breath. "They do. But it'd be a tricky thing, letting them know that without the military and the governors catching on to her full intentions before she's in a position to carry them out."

"Yes. This could help solve that problem. But I don't know if I can solve the problem of getting my family to listen to my advice once I give it to them."

Bastien grimaces. "I suspect we'd all have a struggle there."

The doubt that shadows his face at my words sends a sharper spike of nausea through my abdomen. A surge of defiance carries me above the wobbles of my own self-doubt.

Why should we cringe at the thought of facing our families? We've done more to improve the empire than they ever have.

We've gotten an empress who'll free us all onto the throne, protected her, championed her. We're fighting to support her cause even now. At her side, we've overturned two emperors and convinced so much of the empire to admire a woman who isn't even of the imperial line.

We can't shy from a challenge now, no matter how personal or difficult it is.

"We have to try," I say, putting all the conviction I can into my words. *"Open the lines of communication, prepare them for what might come and encourage them to see what's possible. We owe it to Aurelia to win as many allies as we can from outside this country while she's working on Dariu."*

My foster brother's stance straightens to match my tone. "You're right. Of course you're right. I don't have any secret codes myself… Perhaps I should go digging in the Cotean shelves. But you can at least make a start of it."

"There's only the question of how to send the coded message. If I convey it by regular means, some Darium authority will check it before it gets into my mother's hands—and question why anyone from the palace is sending a letter so secretive."

Bastien's eyes go distant with thought. "When we were in Accasy, one of the baronissas—I think it was Hivette?— mentioned something about a gift for sending messages by magical means."

A smile crosses my lips for the first time since I discovered the code. I set out today to bring the city of

Vivencia together for a common celebration… but I may be on my way to uniting this entire half of the continent.

"Let's discuss it with Aurelia tonight and see what the baronissa can do for us."

Chapter Fourteen

Aurelia

"We're supposed to do what with all this fabric?" one of the marchions asks, grasping the edge of the vast swath of orange silk as if he's afraid it might smother him.

On my temporary platform in the midst of Vivencia's largest city square, I adjust Coraya against my bosom. Motioning to all the gathered figures with my free hand, I summon the explanation Lorenzo gave me.

"You can see the path marked with paint on the cobblestones. The parents' job is to guide all the children through the channels until they reach the end. Lift it or sway it or whatever else you need to do to direct them the right way and help them through the obstacles."

One of the girls poised at the start of the funnel game

claps her hands, her eyes sparkling as she watches the fabric already shifting ahead of her. "This is going to be fun!"

The adults lined all along the pathway that winds through the square look less certain. The nobles, despite the encouragement I've given in the few earlier activities, have mostly grouped together apart from the commoner parents. The commoners watch them with a mix of awe and wariness.

I suggested that everyone wear orange today in honor of Inganne and had shawls and tunics handed out for those who had no appropriate clothing in their wardrobes. But even garbed in the same hues, there's no mistaking the division between palace and city folk.

I want to break down that barrier as much as possible by the end of this festival. Remind all of them that the people they rarely mingle with *are* still people, with many of the same hopes and fears.

Just as all the people outside Dariu are.

If I can stir more understanding between the Darium nobles and the ordinary civilians of their home country, will they find more compassion for the plight of those in the conquered kingdoms as well?

Of course, the day is mainly about honoring Inganne's love of children and play. I gesture to the court musicians next, and they strike up the lively tune Lorenzo taught them.

"Move with the music!" I call out to the players. "With every laugh and dance we can stir in our city's children, we pay homage to Inganne."

The nobles have at least loosened up enough after the playful games they've already participated in to swing the fabric with the rhythm of the music. The noble and commoner children spring forward with no shortage of laughter as they spin and tumble between the shifting silk panels.

They accepted each other quickly enough. Some

evaluating glances were exchanged to start, but as soon as they were called to a challenge together, they threw themselves into the simple joy of it.

As they bound on through the sort-of maze, Cleric Pierus comes over to join me. He takes in the revelry with a pleased sparkle in his eyes. "A festival of children. We might never have had one of those before, but the people appear to be taking well to it. Of course the regular Inganalia includes some activities for the benefit of the youth."

"I hope our most whimsical godlen appreciates the gesture," I say. "No matter what conflicts the empire faces, we can't forget that our children are our future."

The cleric nods. "I believe you've captured the spirit of that belief and our godlen well. Our deities do like to see reverence through action rather than mere words."

Pierus helped me organize today's events, but I haven't touched on my larger purpose with him yet.

I pause before going on. "In the coming weeks, I'd like to show all our godlen how well my goals as regent align with theirs. Dariu should hold up every divine principle."

The cleric rubs his mouth, his eyes gleaming even brighter. "I'm not sure any previous imperial ruler has approached worship in quite that way. But perhaps it's what our empire needs after so much turmoil. Re-establishing ourselves amid all the divinities. Hmm." His gaze slides in the direction of the palace. "I may need to venture beyond our own library to advise you fully."

"I wouldn't want to take you from your other necessary duties."

He shakes his head with a smile. "Not at all. There couldn't be a higher duty than ensuring the empire has the favor of the gods. It's an honor to be tasked with such a quest. Thank you, Your Imperial Highness."

He hurries off as if to get started on his additional

reading right away. Buoyed by his enthusiasm, I step down from the platform and drift along the edges of the fabric funnel game.

My guards stick closer to me than usual, their gazes twitching over the mass of people all around us. So far no one's had anything but grins and cheers for their empress.

A day of celebration will do that. When was the last time any of these people felt they could really let loose in the presence of their ruler?

I'm not just encouraging them to collaborate with each other but to see how they can relax in my presence as well. How different an atmosphere it is when the leader of the country wants to share in their joy rather than hoarding it for himself.

Here and there where the parents and other adults who volunteered are clustered more tightly, I call away a figure or two and place them elsewhere along the path of silk. A couple of regular civilians find themselves amid a few baronissas. A viceroy and a baron end up among a group of commoners.

After an initial hesitation, they become absorbed back into their task. Voices holler encouragement to the children. Giggles and chuckles ring out alongside the music.

Coraya bobs her head against my shoulder, watching all the commotion avidly. When the activity shifts to painting the vast banner I'll be displaying by the palace gate, I sit on a hastily procured cushion and help her pat her hand into the paint and then onto the fine linen.

Our joint host of guards hover over us, as if fencing me off from the other revelers who are adding their decorations to the banner all along its length.

I glance up at the soldiers, keeping my tone light. "I don't need to be outright suffocated. Why don't— Marc, you could make a few circuits of the square, see if you pick up on any signs of trouble that might head my way. Hilara, you too. I think six will be plenty to protect Coraya and me when we're not even moving."

Marc's jaw tightens as if he's offended that I'm sending him away, although I only picked him because he's most likely to recognize a real threat to my security. He dips his head in acknowledgment all the same. "As you wish, Your Imperial Highness."

He and Hilara stride off through the crowd in opposite directions.

Coraya burbles through placing another handprint and waves her feet when I add those too. One of her nursemaids hustles over, looking as if she's restraining a disapproving tut and bringing a wet rag to wipe her off, but several of the other amateur artists nearby catch my gaze and grin.

It's good for everyone to see that the empress doesn't hold herself above her people, not when it comes to celebrating our children.

As the nursemaid fusses over her charge, I get to my feet. Bianca glides over to me, resplendent as always in a peach-orange gown. I'm not sure the vicerine ever met a color she couldn't turn into a fashion statement.

She looks at Coraya with an upward quirk of her lips. "Barely past a month and already an artist. Our empress-to-be is quite ambitious."

I laugh. "We'll see how she feels about it when she's old enough to give her opinion. She does seem to enjoy all the company."

Naturally, at that moment my daughter breaks out in a wail.

The nursemaid gathers her up. "She sounds hungry. I'll get her to the wetnurse." When I start to protest, she does let herself tut. "It's your festival, Your Imperial Highness. You shouldn't be diverted from it."

She does have a point. And Coraya doesn't go far, the wetnurse taking her to one of the little tents set up for shade from the sun. A few of our guards peel off to follow, but I hardly feel unprotected with three of them still around me.

Bianca's gaze follows the baby and her entourage. Something shifts in her expression, as if a shadow has crossed her face. "She's lovely, and I'm glad she delights you so much. And yet seeing motherhood firsthand hasn't made me any more inclined to have it for myself."

Her tone turns wry with that observation.

Another guffaw tumbles out of me. "It's certainly not a role without its challenges. I'm sure you could meet them if you did want to, though."

It doesn't surprise me that she wouldn't, considering how little interest she has even in the act that brings about a pregnancy.

The vicerine gives herself a little shake. "Well, I'm committed to being an excellent auntie. That seems an important contribution too. All the good parts, none of the work."

She shoots me a teasing smile, but I can't help thinking it looks a bit tight around the edges. Is she worried that I feel she hasn't contributed enough?

I smile back at her with all the friendly warmth I can summon. "You're welcome to that part. I'm sure she'll appreciate having all the devotees she can get."

I no longer question whether Bianca means her comments genuinely. She might like the prestige of being the empress's friend and doting honorary aunt to the empire's future ruler… but I know she actually cares for our own sake as well as hers. Any doubts about her loyalties have long since vanished.

I was just talking with my princes a few days ago about whether we could trust Baronissa Hivette to send a message to Lorenzo's family. She never knew what the paper I had her transport with her gift said on it, but that didn't appear to worry her at all.

She did worry about being able to transmit it correctly. *I have to be able to picture the place where it'll arrive*, she'd told me when I first asked her.

Then when Lorenzo conjured an illusion of his mother's office, her eyes widened. *Oh, yes. That will be enough. I could send a message almost anywhere with the help of a gift like that.*

Remembering that moment, Raul's comment about how he and Bastien combined their gifts to batter the fire—and Marc—tickles through my head. What other benefits could we discover in merging gifts, if such a thing is possible on a broader scale?

Would that be enough to give us an advantage against Valerisse and her growing rebellion if need be?

To experiment with that idea, I have to know what gifts are around me that could help secure the empire. I'm not even sure which godlen Bianca dedicated herself to.

Months ago, I might have suspected Ardone, the godlen of love and beauty. The vicerine's disinterest in bodily pleasure for its own sake makes that seem unlikely.

As we accept glasses of sparkling juice a servant is carrying around, I study her more thoughtfully. "Are you dedicated to Inganne? I don't think you've ever told me." That could fit the vicerine's appreciation of other sorts of delights.

"Oh." Bianca touches her bodice over the place where her godlen sigil will be branded. "No, I put my lot in with Prospira. Dreams of other sorts of bounty. Which I've happily achieved." She pats the gold necklace at her throat and strokes her hands over the ornate skirt of her gown.

I should have realized. She did tell me when I first spoke to her about her husband's abuse that she'd rather endure it than lose the wealth and prestige she's gained through her marriage.

"No gift," the vicerine goes on before I have to ask. "I couldn't decide on what I'd want to ask for, and anything that seemed worth asking required more of a sacrifice than I liked."

I shrug. "Fair enough. Perhaps you can give me a different sort of gift. I'd like to honor Prospira in the near future too. If any ideas for how to best appeal to her come to you, do pass them on."

Her expression goes distant for a moment, and the slight stiffness returns to her smile. "I'm not sure how much inspiration I can offer, but anything that occurs to me is all yours."

My brow knits. "Are you all right? If anything is troubling you—" Have other nobles been harassing her over her husband's banishment?

Bianca dismisses my concern with a flick of her hand before I can fully express it and bumps her elbow against mine with her usual companionable air. "Not at all. I just wish I could offer you more in the face of such adversity."

I give her hand a quick squeeze. "Your friendship is a gift in itself."

We drift over to admire the artworks several local painters and sculptors have displayed at one corner of the square. Bianca gets caught up in conversation with a couple of the other vicerines, and I meander onward, skirting the backs of the billowing tents and watching the celebration from the fringes rather than its center.

I'm about to make my way back to my platform when a familiar voice reaches me from the other side of one of the tents. "Come on now, you don't need to do that."

It's Marc's new gravelly baritone, mildly chiding. I ease partway around the fabric wall to see who he's talking to.

He's standing a few paces beyond the tent, his back to me, poised between two boys who look to be around seven years old. One is clearly a court child, his velvet jacket trimmed with gold embroidery and the leather of his shoes polished to a shine.

The other must be a commoner, and not the wealthiest of them either. Mended patches cover his baggy tunic, and the sole of one of his shoes gapes at the heel.

I can just imagine who the former emperor will look more kindly on. I tense in anticipation of needing to intervene.

The court boy swings a fist at the commoner, who smacks him in return while clutching his other hand close to his chest.

"Hey!" Marc's voice sharpens. He pushes the boys farther apart so they can't reach each other, gripping their shoulders to hold them in place.

"He took my glow-ball!" the court boy insists. "Thief!"

"It was mine. You tried to steal it from *me*."

I expect Marc to snap at the commoner boy for daring to harass and slander a member of his court. But instead my husband turns to the lavishly dressed boy, the profile of his face showing a scowl.

"I saw you go over to him and snatch it away. Why shouldn't he snatch it back? There are a hundred of those balls rolling around this courtyard for you all to play with. Go look for one of your own rather than taking one someone already found."

The court boy stomps his foot. "But I want *that* one. It has just the right colors."

Marc's tone turns dry. "We don't always get what we want. He's got just as much right to it as you do—more, since he had it first. Don't you have enough already without making yourself into a bully? Is that how you'd want your empress to see you behaving?"

The boy opens his mouth, closes it again, and ducks his head with a chagrinned expression. "No. Sorry, sir. You won't tell her?"

"If you stop making trouble, I see no reason to mention it."

As the court boy darts off, Marc shifts his attention to the commoner. The other boy stares up at him, still hugging his treasure close.

Marc's voice softens. "Are you all right? He shoved you pretty hard before I could step in."

The boy shrugs, but his shoulders relax with the motion. "No big deal. I'm fine." He hesitates. "Thank you."

Marc pats his head—a little awkwardly, but his voice is warm. "The security of the empire should be for everyone, not just the people from the palace."

"Yeah." The kid flashes a smile at him and lopes off in a different direction.

I hold myself still by the wall of the tent, observing Marc watch the kid he defended disappear into the crowd. A trace of a smile touches the corner of his lips in my view.

He looks actually… pleased. And I'll be damned if he isn't still stunningly handsome with that delighted satisfaction lighting his mottled face.

He couldn't have known I'd witness his intervention. He did it solely because enforcing fairness mattered to him.

A flutter of warmth spreads through my chest. I swallow thickly against the sensation, but it isn't totally new.

There've been other moments when I caught glimpses of goodness, kindness, and understanding in my husband, even before the fire. I haven't let myself think of them often, but I shouldn't act as if they never happened.

There was his recognition of how horrible Linus had

treated Lavira's children after we argued about it—and the steps he took to fix his brother's horrible scheme. The birthday feast and ball he put on in my honor, with all my favorite foods and symbols of my godlen. The softened punishment he gave Neven after the wretched trial in Goric.

That evening on the road when he promised to do whatever it took to see me safe… and told me so tenderly that he loved me.

Perhaps I'd have seen more of that side of him if his twin hadn't been ruining what little trust we were able to build in between our moments together.

But Linus isn't here anymore… and Marc is deciding who he's going to be from here on. He's accepted his new, much diminished role with barely a complaint. I think he's actually listened to the criticisms I've made.

That the man I married has become the man I'm seeing in front of me… It's rather incredible, isn't it?

I'm jerked out of my reverie by footsteps rapping against the cobblestones behind me. Marc is already marching off across the square again anyway. I swivel to where my guards are waiting.

One of the palace pages has just arrived, her hands clasped in front of her. She dips into a bow. "Your Imperial Highness, it's time for the presentation of artworks. If you'd still like to participate."

"Of course." It was my idea, after all.

The palace staff have set up a wooden throne on my platform, the back and the boards around it festooned with orange blooms the same hue as my dress. As I settle onto the cushioned seat, a line of children forms in front of me, each holding an artistic offering they made for me to admire.

They approach me one by one. I ooh and ahh over every image formed out of paint or clay, remarking on my favorite details, and thanking the child for sharing it with me. Each receives an orange ribbon marked with the imperial crest and Inganne's sigil. All that matters is that they created *something* and were willing to show it.

I've already applauded a couple dozen offerings when Lorenzo's illusionary voice slips into my head.

"Be careful. Raul saw one of the parents fiddling with her kid's craft, looking very intense about it, and now the mother's staring daggers at you. We think she might have added an effect that'll hurt you. It's the girl with the long reddish-brown hair in pigtails, about five back in the line."

My chest constricts. I spot the girl he described clutching a sculpture of colored paper and bits of wood, her brow knit as if she's more worried than excited about meeting her empress.

Does she know what her mother did to her artwork? Is this Sabrelle's influence working against me yet again?

The godlen inspired one of her dedicats to attack *my* child, so I suppose I can't be surprised that she'd rope other children into her cause, knowing or not.

Dread pools in my stomach. A trace of red seems to tinge the edges of my vision.

Is that Sabrelle's influence cast over us, or am I simply imagining it in my unsettled state?

As I summon as much enthusiasm as I can for the next kids I greet, my mind scrambles for the best response.

How will it look to my huge audience if I have guards haul off the child with no clear provocation, before she even reaches me? How will *she* feel about that treatment if she had no conscious part in her mother's plans?

This festival is meant to be for Inganne and the childish innocence she so treasures. Can I uphold her principles even here?

One more child remains before the pig-tailed girl. I pull together a few bits of inspiration and pick out Lorenzo in the crowd. Holding my hand where he'll be able to see it, I sign a quick command. *Bastien lift up.*

A moment later, a trickle of breeze across the back of my neck tells me the prince of Rione passed on my message, and my master of wind is at the ready. The girl steps up to the platform, and I brace myself behind my smile.

"Wait," I say brightly before she can reach me. "What you've made looks particularly special. I think Inganne herself might want it."

With those last words, I twitch my fingers upward.

Bastien's gust of wind sweeps across the platform and tosses the paper sculpture up toward the sky. Which is a good thing, because with the sudden jostling, it bursts apart in a shower of shards.

The wind whips those sharp fragments away across the rooftops. The audience gasps and claps, with no idea that what I've turned into a divine marvel was meant to be an assassination attempt.

The girl stares at the sky wide-eyed. "You did so well," I tell her, just as a swarthy, sour-faced woman shoves over to us.

"What are you doing with her offering?" she demands, using her outrage as an excuse to push right up to the platform. "No empress of Dariu should—"

"I hear you." My mind scrambling, I flick at my ring as I stand and reach to interrupt her. My fingers graze the bare skin at the crook of her neck before resting on her shoulder.

My guards step closer, with a tingle of magical protection thick enough that it quivers against my skin. I look only at the woman who meant to aim that blast at me.

"Hasn't it been a lovely day? Inganne thought your daughter's creativity was beautiful enough to make it even lovelier. Let's all celebrate the joy our godlen of play and art brings into our children's lives—and our own!"

Amid the cheers that ripple through the crowd, the woman glares at me. "You don't— I'm not going to—"

The new hallucinogen I concocted acts as quickly as I hoped. Her legs sway under her, and then a dreamy smile crosses her face. "It is beautiful, isn't it?"

Relief rushes through me. "Yes. Why don't you and your daughter come up and dance with me and mine?"

The woman takes her daughter's hand and spins the little girl around. Her giddy laughter mingles with the song the court musicians have just struck up.

As the wetnurse returns Coraya to me, I lean closer to my guards. "When we're done dancing, escort this woman off discreetly and find out why she'd want to harm me."

For now, it doesn't matter. For now, all my people see is the happiness I summoned in the place of her anger.

CHAPTER FIFTEEN

Aurelia

The memory of the music and mingling laughter buoys me through my walk back to my bedroom through the late-evening shadows. The moment I step through my doorway with Marc at my heels, my mood deflates.

I walk over to my bed and flop down on my back. The weight I'm carrying inside only eases a little.

Marc shifts on his feet at his post by the door. "Are you all right?"

Like he asked the little boy in the square this afternoon—except the ripple of concern is intense enough to roughen his voice more than its usual new gravelly timbre.

I close my eyes. "Naturally. Sabrelle wants me dead even in the middle of celebrating the most joyful and innocent aspects of humanity, she's got unknown numbers of people from all levels of society willing to do her bidding, and I don't really know if I can win the war Valerisse seems to be planning. But otherwise, everything's wonderful."

Venting my frustration barely takes the edge off it, and then I'm hit with a smack of shame. Who am I to be complaining when I'm in the most privileged position in the empire?

I'm not going to win any wars or impress any gods by lying around whining about my troubles. I need to get up and keep going.

In just a minute.

I breathe in and out, recovering my scattered nerves. Sprite leaps onto the bed and pads over to join me. As I rub her back, her purr reverberates through my heart.

All right. Here we go.

I force myself upright and onto my feet. My head still feels muddled. Perhaps a soothing cup of tea would help with that. I have plenty of options for clearing the mind and setting one's spirits in order.

My cat trots with me over to my trunk and twines around my ankles while I take out my brewing equipment. I sit on the rug with her nestled beside me and glance over at Marc. "I don't suppose you'd like a cup of tea while I'm making some anyway? If you want to help me think."

He blinks at me, and then one corner of his mouth ticks upward. "I'm honored that you'd include me after I so hastily dismissed your skills before."

That early day after I arrived at the palace, I brought him tea in his office. He chided me for acting like a servant and sent me away.

It was only a year ago, but it feels centuries distant.

As always, the process of picking out the blend and preparing the cups soothes me. I have enough water in my pitcher that I heat it in my little cauldron rather than calling for a kettle from the kitchen.

As the steaming liquid flows over the dried leaves and herbs, the crisply floral scent winds down into my lungs. I inhale deeper automatically.

"That woman during the presentation of the crafts," Marc says as I wait for the tea to steep. "A couple of the guards took her back to the palace after. The way you handled her daughter's offering—how it burst apart—she meant it to hurt you."

"It appears that way."

"How did you—" He halts. "The princes. Bastien can manipulate the wind, not just rain clouds, can't he? He helped you dispose of it in an unthreatening way. Did my foster brothers warn you beforehand?"

I tread into this delicate territory carefully. "They've helped me many times over the past year. I doubt I'd still be alive without them."

And many of the dangers they protected me from, Marc himself was a party to.

The former emperor is silent for a moment. "I didn't notice anything amiss. Obviously your regular guards didn't either. I'm grateful my foster brothers watch over you so well."

That might actually be true, even if he'd rather they didn't have to.

Before I can decide how to respond, he tilts his head toward me. "You touched her, by the neck and shoulder, right before her mood mellowed out. Did you do something —" His gaze sharpens. "Your ring. You've always worn it."

Even with everything that's already passed between us, my pulse stutters. I might have been willing to throw the ways I've manipulated him in his face, but I'm not sure I feel safe giving him the means to prove it.

"The ring has served me well too," I say noncommittally. "I'm not the sort to wait for anyone else to defend me if I can do it myself." I pick up the teacups and carry them over to him. "It should be ready now."

Marc's gaze stays speculative, but he doesn't push for a full explanation. Perhaps he can guess at my reasons for not wanting to give it.

My thoughts flit back to his peacemaking with the squabbling boys. He has been learning to take on perspectives different from the one he was raised with.

He takes the tea and sips at the same time I do. The hot liquid flows over my tongue and loosens some of the knots that've formed in my stomach.

With his next sip, Marc's stance relaxes enough that I can't help noticing again how striking he is even with the odd scar discoloring his face. My pulse skips for a different reason, and I pull back a step, grasping for an appropriate change of subject.

"I have gifts on my side, but I know Valerisse does too. She barged straight through a door after she tried to murder me. And then there are all the talents of the many soldiers she's pulled into her rebellion that we don't know for sure."

Marc nods, not showing any sign of offense at my retreat. "I gather she gave up a kidney or similar to Sabrelle. The soldiers… We do have records, but we can't be sure exactly who's defected to her side or simply fled the conflict. She may have drawn in people who weren't part of the military as well. Any way we engage with her forces, we'll need to be prepared for a variety of magic."

I grimace. "I was considering sending a few trusted soldiers to pretend to defect and spy on her so we have a better idea what we'll be up against. But it'll be so dangerous…"

"That's what they've trained for, Aurelia. They'll want to head into that danger if it means protecting their empress."

What he's saying is true, but it doesn't soothe my guilt all that much. I suppress a sigh. "There's still the matter of conveying messages back and forth at a distance. Baronissa Hivette can only send messages out, not retrieve them. Spies won't do us any good if they can't tell us what they've observed."

Marc perks up. "I think we have something that'll help with that. There are blessed communications boxes used sometimes for quick missives from forts and the like in the outer territories. Most are quite small, meant to be used while on the march. The spies wouldn't be able to communicate with anyone other than the palace, and they'd still have to be careful not to be discovered, but we could strategize around those considerations."

My own spirits lighten at the remark. "Axius never mentioned those."

Marc's smile turns crooked. "If you haven't specifically asked about secret communications, he wouldn't have. They're precious enough that they aren't used without just cause. Each one took decades to enchant well enough that it'd work properly. But for this purpose—if it gives us the information to make an effective defense against Valerisse's forces, that's more than worth it."

The other hesitation that stalled my planning before creeps through my mind. "For us. The soldiers I send—if she catches them…"

"That's their job," Marc points out, reasonably enough. "They went into service specifically to defend the empire, with their lives if need be."

That doesn't mean I like the idea of asking them to potentially give up those lives. If there was any other way…

But I can hardly infiltrate Valerisse's forces myself. And risking a few soldiers now might save thousands in the weeks to come.

I swallow more tea, willing aside my uneasiness and

sorting through my thoughts. "We'll still need to make that defense once we know what's needed. Before, you've been fighting citizens rising up, most of them without any military training. Now we're asking the soldiers to face off against their own colleagues… It's going to be a bloody battle no matter how you cut it."

A shudder runs through my abdomen at the thought of that blood drenching the city streets. Will this conflict really have to come to that?

Marc lets out a soft huff. "The soldiers loyal to you have just as much skill as those she's gathering."

"So it'll be a simple matter of numbers?" I shake my head. "We need an advantage, something to ensure we protect as many lives as possible, maybe even intimidate her before she launches outright war. Has… Has the Darium army ever experimented with combining gifts?"

"Using two or more talents in collaboration to produce new effects? I know they've attempted that in Cotea, but the results always seem somewhat unpredictable… Not ideal on a battlefield." Marc's expression tightens. "And we've never wanted to risk edging at all close to scourge sorcery."

The scourge sorcerers who brought the gods' wrath down on the continent centuries ago—setting the stage for the Darium empire to rise—didn't work quite like that. "They forced other people to give up their gifts, to sacrifice their whole lives to pass on magic so the scourge sorcerers could strive to be on the same level as the godlen. Two people working together as equals is nothing like that."

Marc's smile comes back, gentle around the edges. "No, I suppose it's not. Another area we can look into. There are certainly plenty of intimidating gifts among the palace soldiers and those stationed around Vivencia. I shouldn't have mentioned it—I can't imagine you ever encouraging anything remotely like that maniacal magic."

"If anything, I'm surprised the imperial family never toed the line," I mutter.

Marc's laugh surprises me. "I suppose after everything you've seen of us, I deserve that remark."

No hackles raised or prickly defensiveness. I study him more closely over the top of my teacup.

He really is becoming something more—something better—than he used to be, isn't he?

"Thank you," I say. "For listening. For hashing these strategies out with me."

"Without trying to shout you down, you mean?" Despite his wry tone, his gaze turns intense. "It was good, talking with you like this. I'm glad we can have this much."

The tenderness of the words sends a pang through my heart. "I always wanted this."

Marc's voice roughens more. "I know. And I made it a battle. I—"

He glances away from me, his gaze catching on his reflection in the nearby mirror. "I can accept that it was my fault, and that I ruined what we could have had." His next laugh holds no humor. "And how can I expect to ever recover what I threw away now that *I'm* ruined?"

I furrow my forehead. "What are you talking about?"

He waves toward the vanity. "Why would *anyone*, let alone an empress, want a man who looks like this? It's all right. I can moderate my expectations. I played unfairly and I lost, and this is what I'm left with. It's not as if I could have counted on earning your full forgiveness even if I wasn't a warped version of myself. I'll take whatever I can get."

Does he really think I look at him with revulsion because of that strange stain on his skin? The pang expands until a lump fills my throat.

He's been trying so hard to be everything I need—and

nothing that I don't. To leave behind all the parts of himself I did revile.

How can I not admire that—and how well he's succeeding?

"Marc…" I ease toward him, setting my teacup down on the vanity.

My hand rises of its own accord to rest against his discolored cheek. Marc stares at me as if transfixed, his stance rigid, his gaze unwavering.

I stroke my thumb over the smooth skin of his odd scar. "The way you looked before—that was the face of the man who tormented me. This is the face of the man who saved me. I'll always prefer this one."

A smolder lights in Marc's eyes, but he holds himself perfectly still, his hands at his sides. Absorbing my touch but afraid of sending me running.

I swallow hard, caught in a crash of conflicting emotions. One thread of desire pierces through them all.

Before I can second-guess the impulse, I bob up on my toes and brush my lips to his.

It's one of the chastest kisses we've ever shared. Our mouths merely graze each other, Marc tipping forward slightly to meet me but restraining himself from a more emphatic claiming.

All the same, heat blooms under my skin all the way down to my toes.

Part of me wants to lean right into him, to grasp his jacket and meld our mouths more firmly together. To find out what a full kiss might feel like.

Just picturing it sends a skitter of panic through my veins alongside the quiver of desire.

I pull back, my hand dropping, cutting off the contact between us. My gaze locks with his again. I don't back away.

The hunger in Marc's expression sets off a fresh tingling

straight to my core. Ever so carefully, he touches my cheek the way I did his. At the stroke of his fingers, my heart thumps harder.

His voice has gone hoarse. "And this will always be the face of the woman who conquered me: body, mind, and soul."

"Not heart?" I can't help asking.

His wry smile returns. "I don't know how much of a heart I can claim to have. But however much is there, it's yours too. However long it takes. Whatever you need from me. We were meant to do this together."

I draw back then, slowly so it doesn't seem like an outright rejection. My heart keeps thudding on.

How can those words feel so undeniably right?

Chapter Sixteen

Aurelia

In the small basement room, I light the enchanted lantern and perch on the settee. As I wait in the wavering light for the panel in the wall to open and admit my princes, my hands twist together on my lap.

The image of Marc's face when I told him I was going to meet them swims up from my memory. His jaw clenched, but he kept his voice even. *Why not here, where you're properly guarded? I should at least come with you.*

No one will know I'm there except them. I've got nothing to fear, I told him. *I'm allowed an occasional private conversation.*

The pointedness of that last sentence quieted him. Maybe because he can guess why I particularly need to talk to his foster brothers right now, and why I'd rather he wasn't around to listen in on the conversation.

I signaled them in the dining room not long ago. It only

takes another few tense minutes before the panel whispers open.

They emerge one after the other: Raul looking fierce, Bastien pensive, and Lorenzo concerned. As I stand to meet them, Lorenzo takes one look at my face and strides past the others to my side.

He tucks his arm around me and tips his head close. His warm, tangy scent envelopes me like a second embrace. *"What's wrong, Rell?"*

My mood is that obvious, then?

I let out a shaky laugh and hold up my hand as if I can ward off Raul's instinctive bristling. "It's not— I'm perfectly fine. There's no new catastrophe." At least not of the typical sort. "I just needed to talk to you about something."

Naturally, Bastien has already noted a key defining feature of this talk. "Without Marc around."

Raul manages to loom even taller. "Did *he* try to hurt you? After all his—"

"Raul." I touch his arm to stop him. "He didn't do anything wrong either. This is about me."

Lorenzo cocks his head to better study my expression and presses a gentle kiss to my temple. *"Go ahead. We can manage not to interrupt."*

He shoots a pointed glance at the prince of Lavira, who grunts his displeasure but settles for clasping my hand.

Now that I have the stage and their full attention, my throat closes up. I spent most of the night trying to decide how to broach this subject, knowing I had to, wishing every part of my life wasn't so tangled.

I drag in a breath. "I need you to know that nothing I say changes our relationship. I love all three of you as much as ever; I want you by my side as long as you're willing to stay."

"Then you have us forever," Raul says gruffly.

I twine my fingers with his. "I know this might sound

insane, but I'm recognizing that… there's a part of me that's starting to want Marc too."

Raul can't restrain a growl.

Bastien's stance stiffens, but he still manages to speak evenly. "As more than a guard."

"Yes. I— I'm not going to say he wasn't awful. But he was never *only* awful, not like Linus was. There were enough moments, and so much of what happened was influenced by his father and his brother…"

I pause and rub my forehead. "It still seems insane even to me. But the way he reacted when I told him the truth—the fact that he chose me over his brother, over keeping the throne… He's been cast down to one of the lowest stations in the palace, ordered around constantly, but he hasn't lashed out. I think he really does want to be someone better. And he *has* been."

Raul grimaces. "That doesn't mean— All the shit he put you through—"

I meet his pale gaze. "The three of you weren't exactly kind to me when I first arrived, and you didn't have a lifetime of being molded into a tyrannical dictator behind you. People can change. It isn't as if I never saw anything appealing about him even before—only that his behavior too often got in the way of any real affection developing."

Lorenzo strokes his hand up and down my back. *"And now it has developed?"*

"Something has. I don't know…" I shake my head. "I can't tell whether it'll go any farther or whether I want to act on it. But I can't deny that the feelings are there. We had a moment, last night—only a brief kiss, but I initiated it… I didn't want to hide anything from you. Marc has never pushed. You come first. If you can't stand him being anything more than my guard, then I don't even need to make any decisions, that's how it is."

I'm not sure how much sense I've made with that jumbled explanation, but Raul smiles thinly at my last words. "Then I don't see why you should even contemplate giving that prick the time of day. We can't trust him. He could be playing a long game."

Bastien's forehead furrows. "I don't *like* it. But I haven't seen any reason to think he doesn't regret his past actions. He's had plenty of chances to sabotage Aurelia in the past month without taking any of them. Hell, if he wanted to reclaim the throne, his best opportunity would probably be going over to Valerisse's side and giving her so much more ammunition against Aurelia. But he's still here."

Raul rounds on him. "So you want to see him—"

"No," Bastien cuts in. "I said I don't like it. But that's not what matters most, is it? I didn't like the idea of sharing our empress's affection at all to begin with, even with the two of you. And… strategically speaking, it would work to our benefit if Marc has even more tying him to Aurelia. Harder to shake devotion that's returned."

The other prince lets out a strangled sound and throws his hands in the air. But Lorenzo speaks up before Raul can keep arguing.

"What's most important is what feels right to Aurelia." He nuzzles my hair. *"I don't want to see you hurt. Only you can decide how much you can forgive Marc, what you're comfortable with, how strongly you feel about him now. If you decide he's worthy of being a husband in more than name, then I trust you and your judgment."*

"He's never going to shove us aside," Raul snarls.

I catch his gaze again. "I told you, that couldn't happen. If he tried, it'd shatter any affection I might have started to feel. And it could be years before I'm sure of whether that affection can overcome everything else. I won't— Nothing else will happen unless I've talked to all of you first. I shouldn't have let it go even that far last night."

My massive prince looks mildly mollified. He swoops in and claims a kiss so scorching I think he must be aiming to sear away any traces of Marc on my lips. As he pulls back, a flush tingles over my skin.

"You're ours—and we're yours," he declares. "Until he can say the same with his whole being, he doesn't deserve anything."

I don't think this is a good time to mention Marc's offering of body, mind, soul, and heart to my authority. Raul probably wouldn't believe it anyway.

Bastien steps in to caress my jaw, his dark green gaze steady. "Like Lore said, I trust *you*. He is your husband— we're lucky to have you at all, hard as that may be to accept."

My throat constricts all over again. "I think I'm the lucky one, having the three of you."

"Then it's luck all around." He leans in for a kiss that's more tender but no less passionate than Raul's and gives me a bittersweet smile. "I suppose you have to get back to the business of running—and not losing—an empire. We'll keep fighting right beside you."

"Yes," I say, thoughts of all the meetings and appearances and plans I need to make rushing over me. But as Bastien and then Raul head into the secret passage, something in me balks against following them.

Lorenzo glances back at me when he reaches the panel, taking in my stance. He hesitates. "Do *you need to go right back?*"

My mouth twists. "I probably should. There's so much— It's just a relief to be away from all the expectations for a few minutes."

Heat sparks in the prince of Rione's eyes. He closes the panel and returns to me.

As he sets his hands on either side of my waist, he dips his head for a lingering kiss of his own. *"Then let's make it a little more of an escape. You deserve all the love in the world, Aurelia. I don't want you ever to forget that."*

It's impossible not to melt into his embrace. I give myself over to this kiss I don't need to question or doubt from the man who devoted himself to me first, the man who's always wanted to see the best in me.

A hungry sound reverberates from Lorenzo's chest. As I loop my arms around his neck, he pulls me tighter against him. *"You always feel so good."* His hands skim up my sides so his thumbs can trace the curves of my breasts through my gown. *"Do you want— Are you recovered enough—"*

I can taste what he's asking in the desire that ripples through his illusionary voice. In that moment, there's nothing I want more. It's been too fucking long since I've been fully adored by any of the men I love.

"Yes," I murmur in answer to both questions, and dive into another kiss.

Lorenzo nudges me toward the settee as his deft fingers loosen the lacing on my gown. He eases me down on the cushioned seat, sliding the bodice down my body at the same time.

He kisses me at the same time as he kneels on the floor in front of me. His hands cup my breasts fully, palms swiveling over my sensitized nipples to provoke the sweetest jolts of pleasure.

I gasp against his mouth and kiss him harder. Heat floods every particle of my being around a knot of my own hunger.

I've missed this. I almost forgot how much.

Lorenzo bends to suck the tip of one breast into his searing mouth. At the nip of his teeth, I whimper and curl my fingers against his thick hair.

As he works over my chest with lips and teeth and one set

of clever fingers, he tucks his other hand beneath my skirt. It grazes teasing patterns over my skin all the way up my calf and thigh, until I can't restrain a moan.

My hips sway toward him impatiently. Lorenzo hums, the vibration tingling through my breast, and strokes me through my drawers.

Fuck, yes—but I need so much more. The intimacies I've had to set aside, the pleasure that might have brought too much pain before—I'm starving for it.

The flames of need flare higher as he eases aside the silky layer to caress me skin to skin. I yank his head up so our mouths can meld together once more and then mumble, "Please. I've been waiting too long for this already."

Lorenzo's chuckle tickles through my head. He kisses my cheek before yanking my drawers right off. *"Whatever you need, Rell. Always."*

I reach down to fumble with his trousers. It takes a few excruciating moments to free his cock. Once the rigid length rests in my hands, I can't resist pumping it in my hand, feeling it twitch with a desire to match my own.

Lorenzo muffles a groan on my shoulder. He tugs me to the edge of the seat where he can line himself up against me perfectly.

As he plunges into me, I lean toward him. Our mouths collide again. His shaft fills me with the blissful burn I was craving, not a shred of discomfort in the sensation.

A moan tumbles out of me. I clutch him tighter, rocking to meet his thrusts, urging him deeper. "I love you. So much. So good."

Lorenzo lets out a ragged breath. His lips skate along the edge of my jaw and down the side of my neck. *"I love you too. No matter what you decide you want, no matter who you consider letting into your heart—it should always feel like this, Aurelia. Never accept anything less than this good."*

That's a promise I think I can make.

He presses against the sweetest spot inside me, and I can't hold back a cry. We crash into each other again and again, mouths and hips, every collision sending me soaring higher.

I careen over the edge on a final surge of pleasure, clinging to Lorenzo as if he's my anchor in a storm. A few thrusts later, he follows me with a shuddered exhalation.

In the aftermath, we stay entangled, our breaths falling into a matching rhythm, his warmth wrapped all around me.

I don't know where else my heart will lead me, but what I feel for this man and his fellow princes has never been wrong. If I use that as my standard, I can't help but find the right path, can I?

Chapter Seventeen

Raul

As Aurelia and High Commander Axius address the five soldiers lined up in front of them, I hang farther back in the meeting room. Theoretically I'm here in case any of them have questions specific to Lavira, but really I'm reaching through my awareness of the shadows into every pocket and pouch on their uniforms.

Axius and Captain Evando might have vetted these five as closely as they're capable of, but after the recent attacks, I'm not leaving anything to chance. No hidden weapon, vial of acid, or exploding device is getting past me.

Thankfully, this bunch appears to be free of treasonous intentions. They hold themselves rigidly at attention as Axius gives their instructions.

"We can only give you two of the communication boxes. Guard them carefully, using whatever measures are available to you to avoid any of the opposing soldiers seeing them or noticing you using them."

All five soldiers give a jerk of a nod, impressively synchronized.

Aurelia picks up the thread in her gentler but equally firm voice. "If you have anything to report, write it down in the agreed-on code and place the note in the box. When you close the lid, it'll be transmitted to its coordinating box here in the palace. We'll only send messages back in case of extreme need to avoid the chance of anyone else discovering them. I want you all to stay as safe as possible amid the immense risk you're taking."

The soldier in the middle bobs his head again. "It's our honor to serve you as we're best able, Your Imperial Highness."

A sad smile curves her lips. She hides it well, but I can pick up on how much even this mission pains her.

She could be sending these soldiers off to their deaths. There isn't much our empress hates more than putting other people in the line of fire on her behalf.

It took a ridiculous amount of reassurance before she'd even rely on *me*.

"I appreciate it all the same," she says, "and I'm sorry you've been put at odds with so many of your colleagues. I hope that we'll be able to put an end to this sedition before many lives are lost."

Axius folds his arms over his chest. "If we can disrupt their plans before they can get very far with them, we'll have a better chance at that. Anything you can report on the enemy's intentions and expected movements will be invaluable to the imperial family."

Captain Evando steps in with an intensity to his bearing that looks a bit anxious to me. As the main officer in charge of the soldiers who guard the palace, he had a lot of input when choosing Aurelia's spies. I can't imagine he likes the idea that he might let her down.

"These five men and women are among the most capable and dedicated soldiers I've ever met," he says. "I'm sure they'll succeed in this mission and help restore peace to the empire."

Right. The kind of peace where the only people suffering are those who aren't from Dariu.

At least none of these five is dedicated to Sabrelle. Axius made that a defining condition of who we'd send out. It's not worth risking the godlen working her divine voodoo on our most precarious mission.

As the five soldiers salute their empress and file out of the room, I think of my mother and brother off in Lavira, watching this very different rebellion form under their noses.

Would they prefer to trade one dictator for another? Did they see enough of Aurelia's goodness during our visit months ago to trust that they're better off siding with her—as much as they can with Valerisse right there?

If they didn't, it'll have been my failing more than Aurelia's.

Aurelia glances at me, and I offer a brief smile to say I didn't catch any concerning signs. I can't risk any gesture warmer than that is wise with the other men and her personal guards looking on.

My gaze slides from her to the most distinct of those figures. Marc's attention is fixed on Aurelia with its usual intensity.

I stop my teeth from gritting only through immense force of will. I'd like to take a swing at him.

I'd like to punch his scar-blotched face right off.

How the fuck has he persuaded her to warm up to him enough that she'd set aside all the awfulness of their past? To consider actually getting close to him?

Gods only know how much intimacy she had to feign in

the past. They've shared plenty of kisses and more. But none of it *meant* anything. She avoided anything beyond what was absolutely necessary.

For all her sharp mind and ruthless determination, she's got a soft heart at her center. I can't let him exploit it.

This new façade of his has to crack sometime, doesn't it?

Before I can follow that train of thought any further, the guard who was posted outside the meeting room door nudges it open. "Prince Neven would like to speak with Her Imperial Highness."

Aurelia makes a beckoning gesture. "Of course. Let him in."

My youngest foster brother hustles into the room. Aurelia steps off to the side to consult with him, their voices hushed.

I'm guessing he's reporting some impression he's gotten from Sabrelle. Whatever it is, the slant of Aurelia's mouth suggests it doesn't involve sunshine and roses.

When is the godlen of war going to get her head out of her ass and recognize that our current empress is twice the fighter anyone in the imperial family was?

As Neven turns to go, Captain Evando clears his throat. "You haven't been by the training room lately, Your Highness. Did you decide you've elevated your skills enough already?"

There's a slight edge to the words I don't totally like. Neven bristles, so he must have picked up on it too.

"I have a more important duty to attend to," he says brusquely. "It's easier for me to focus on Sabrelle's influence when I'm on my own rather than surrounded by other people."

Evando raises an eyebrow. "Really? I'd have thought being around a lot of dedicated soldiers, especially when many of them are dedicated to *her*, would be the perfect setting to watch for her involvement."

Neven scowls. "What does it matter to you, anyway?"

"I'm just surprised, after how committed you were to seeing that your empress learns every possible strategy."

Aurelia steps closer, looking as if she's considering intervening, but Neven breaks the tension of the moment with a bark of a laugh. "If that's still bothering you, we can settle it pretty quickly. Sparring match, fifteen minutes, in the main training room? We'll see whether politeness beats determination."

Evando hesitates as if he didn't expect to end up quite so committed to Neven's training himself. Then a gleam lights in his eyes that I'm not sure what to make of. "Yes, we will."

Aurelia cuts a glance toward me with a bemused expression. I can almost hear her saying, with a dollop of exasperation, "Men!"

I doubt she'd appreciate my recent hostile thoughts, so I keep them to myself other than a quick gesture. *We'll come. Your room. Soon.*

She can piece together my meaning well enough. As she heads to her chambers with her guards, I set off to find Lorenzo.

Several minutes later, I confirm it's only Aurelia and Marc in her bedroom and step out past the sliding panel with the prince of Rione beside me. From the tic of his face, Marc wasn't expecting us.

Good. Let him remember that no matter how much he's wriggled into our woman's good graces, she doesn't tell him everything.

Aurelia is sitting at her desk, petting the cat that rarely leaves her side when she's in residence. "I'm guessing this isn't just a social call."

I flex my hands. "I've been thinking more about

combining gifts. How we can ward off talents like Valerisse's that rely on ferreting out other people's intentions rather than carrying out their own. Most shielding gifts only work with physical attacks. Marc's gift is along more analytical lines too, isn't it? We should see whether we can deflect it."

Marc's mouth tightens even more. "I suppose that's accurate. How do you imagine you'd 'ward it off'?"

He's game, then. Let's see how he reacts if this works—if we can strip him of even more power.

I let myself grin. "It won't be much of a gift for long, I suspect. *My* gift can obscure what's around us. Lorenzo's can warp perceptions. Between the two of us, I figure we could create a sort of smoke screen against other magic. A secret shield that both conceals and diverts."

Lorenzo signs, *I'll try*, and swipes his hands together. I filled him in on my idea while we made our way to the apartment.

Aurelia glances between the three of us and appears to resign herself to the impromptu competition. "It'll certainly be interesting to see the results."

As she leans back in her chair, Marc takes a few steps toward Lorenzo and me. "You know what I'll be attempting to do."

"Discerning my greatest physical weakness. I don't think I have any of those anyway."

If the former emperor is bothered that Aurelia shared the details of his gift with me, he doesn't show it. He studies us with an expression I can only call bored—his retaliation for my heckling. "Let me know when you're ready, and we'll find out."

I reach toward the shadows cast at my side, explaining for Aurelia's benefit. "When Bastien and I blasted this fool, we didn't consciously combine our powers. We were simply focused on the same goal, and I'm assuming they merged into something more based on that. So Lore and I will use the same tactic—concentrating our own gifts in tandem to deflect any magic that's aimed at us—and let the magic work as it will."

Marc narrows his eyes at me. "You still haven't mentioned what exactly your full gift is."

"She knows. Why should I mention it to you and give you that advantage?" I shoot him another grin and motion to Lorenzo.

He squares his shoulders, his face setting with concentration. I grasp hold of the nearby shadows. With all the mental effort I can summon, I disperse them into a filmy barrier between Marc and us.

Let it obscure any sense of our bodies and minds. Let any opposing gift get lost in the haze. Let us trick him even more thoroughly than either of us could alone, Kosmel.

I press my other hand to my sternum over the brand that connects me to my patron godlen. A tingle ripples through the air.

Something is happening, even if I can't say quite what.

"Go ahead," I tell Marc.

His jaw works. He fixes a piercing stare at me—rather than Lorenzo, naturally.

I focus on the shadows flowing between us, the faintest haze in the air, disguised by Lorenzo's powers winding through them. Marc's brow furrows.

He takes a small step closer, his expression tightening. "I can't quite— It's as if you're not exactly there. But I can *see* you still, right—"

His head twitches, and a smile flits across his face. "Ah. I'm sure all your training and your practice in the arena has benefitted you, but you still have a bit of a defensive gap when it comes to the left side of your neck. Best make sure no one rams a blade there, because you might not react quickly enough."

A chill washes over me, and I lose my grip on the shadows. Not that they were contributing enough anyway.

"It took you longer than usual to get a sense of it," I say, biting back the words I actually want to spit at him. I don't think telling him to fuck off would endear *me* more to Aurelia.

To my surprise, Marc inclines his head in acknowledgment. "It did. I needed a fair bit more concentration and finessing of my gift. You might be on to something."

My instinctive urge to argue with him collides with his obvious compliment and leaves me momentarily speechless. "Yes. Well. We will have to practice more."

Lorenzo makes a triumphant gesture, and Aurelia beams at us. "And no ill effects that I can see. We'll have to try more experiments—without straining your gifts, of course."

I allow myself to bask in the pride of her approval for a moment, only to be interrupted by a knock on the door.

With a hitch of my pulse, I hustle to the hidden passage, Lorenzo right behind me. As we shut the panel behind us, Aurelia's voice carries through. "What is it?"

Axius's voice replies from the other side of her door. "We've just gotten two letters by messenger, one from Rione and one from Cotea. I think you'd better have a look at them, Your Imperial Highness."

Chapter Eighteen

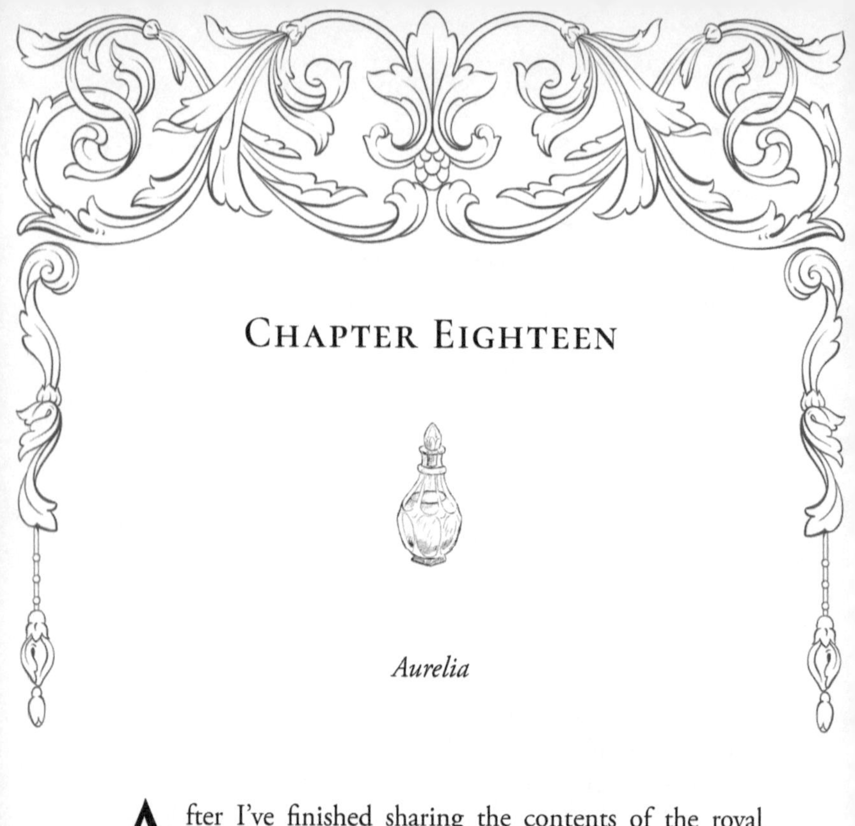

Aurelia

After I've finished sharing the contents of the royal letters with all four of the princes in the privacy of my chambers, a gloom settles over the entire room. Lorenzo's head droops.

He hoped so much that his overture would benefit me—that he could persuade real allegiance from his parents.

"It'd be a little much to expect them to declare themselves ready to send their people to war on my behalf when they barely know me," I say. "Cotea would have a hard enough time joining forces with us without getting cut down by Valerisse's army on the way."

Lorenzo grimaces. *"They could have offered some willingness to help. Or even real sympathy. But I suppose that isn't Mother's style."*

The brief letter from Queen Anahi is indeed light on sentiment. She barely even gives away that she knows about the brewing civil war I'm facing—which might be true in Rione's somewhat detached position from the rest of the continent, except I know Lorenzo informed her.

She framed the missive as a congratulations on Coraya's birth, with the most generic of well-wishes, followed by a remark that she looks forward to the next visit from her own younger child. Reading between the lines, she's saying I'm on my own and I'd better figure out some way to make sure Lorenzo survives the coming war.

I examine the second paper in my grasp. "It's not as if it's any less supportive than the message from Cotea."

Bastien steps closer to peer at the letter alongside me, a frown darkening his expression. "I don't know why Father bothered to send a letter so meaningless in the first place."

King Stanislas's letter congratulates me on the arrival of my daughter even more briefly than Queen Anahi did, before speaking about how the winter's chill is over and how all of the empire can look forward to spring's bounty. I'm not sure whether he realizes it never becomes all that chilly in Dariu or if he's trying to remind me of the hardships his people have faced.

Or maybe there's something more to it. I worry at my lip. "I feel as though he's trying to convey more than he's actually saying. To go on about the trees and the flowers... He didn't strike me as a particularly poetic type."

When I spoke with the Cotean king in person, he was most concerned about how well I used my gift—whether I stretched its limits and found new uses to adapt it to. The fact that he mentions lapinslay specifically...

What do I know about that flower? The name tickles at my memory.

Marc shifts on his feet by my door. "If you *want* them to fight for you, all you have to do is order them. They answer to you, no one else."

Bastien's jaw tightens, but I don't even need to think about my answer. "Valerisse has proven by example that soldiers who aren't dedicated to you can be as bad as enemies. And I'm aiming to better Dariu's relations with the rest of the continent, not make even more demands of the conquered countries."

Raul pauses where he's started pacing near my bed. "They might not come even if you ordered them. If they think Valerisse has a real chance of unseating you… Right now, some might figure they're better off waiting to see what leadership she puts in place than risking their lives supporting what they already know."

"Most of the continent is in a difficult position with Lavira right in the middle of everything and Valerisse building her army there," Bastien points out. "I'm sure she has people loyal to her watching the borders. She might be able to cut off any contingent that attempts to join you in Dariu, and none of the local armies could stand against even a portion of the Darium forces alone."

Raul huffs. "We certainly won't be getting any letters from the Queen of Lavira."

Despite his gruff tone, anguish shadows his face. The prince of Lavira has never been one to back down from a fight. I can only imagine how much he hates feeling his hands are tied.

I rub my forehead. "I can't hope for much assistance even from my former kingdom. Accasy is too cut off up north… I doubt the snow will have melted enough for people to make it through the passes for at least another week or two. There's no way to even talk to my family."

But thinking of my home country stirs up memories from the twenty-one years I spent there. The days I strolled through the gardens and the less tamed lands beyond with the Eloxian devout who was most well-versed in herbs and potion-making, taking in his raspy voice as he described the uses of each plant…

Lapinslay won't be much use in your healing arts, but it makes an interesting pigment when mixed with basil.

My heart hiccups. My head jerks toward Marc. "Go down to the kitchen and get a few sprigs of fresh basil. They must have some."

His brow knits, but he ducks out of the room without protest. I grab my mortar and pestle from my brewing supplies.

Neven prowls over to watch. "What are you going to do with basil?"

"I think King Stanislas is testing my ingenuity again."

Bastien barks a laugh. "That wouldn't surprise me. But how?"

I spread the letter on my desk, face down. "We'll see. It could be a coincidence… I've never seen lapinslay used exactly like this…"

But innovation is what the Coteans are best known for, isn't it?

Marc returns a few minutes later with a whole bundle of basil. He hands it to me and steps back to watch, his gaze avid.

I grind several of the sprigs into a thick paste, the pungent scent wafting into my nose. Then I smear the stuff on the back of the letter, rubbing it into the paper thoroughly.

As I wipe the mashed leaves aside, a faint scrawl emerges across the page, the ink almost luminescent.

Raul sucks in a startled breath. "Well, fuck."

Bastien's eyes gleam with renewed hope. "What does he say?"

I squint at the gleaming words, angling the paper to the light so they're more visible. "That if I can work out how to read this, it shows I've got much more to me than the tribune's brutal approach. The Coteans would rather see me on the throne than anyone she'd pick. But that preference doesn't matter if joining the conflict damages his people more than sitting it out and seeing her win would. Perhaps I can find some way of reassuring him."

A scoffing sound breaks from Marc's throat. "How are you supposed to guarantee his soldiers won't get hurt in a war?"

"I don't think he means that. Only that he needs to be sure whatever I'll do if I stay empress will balance out the sacrifices they'll have to make."

Bastien takes the paper from me and scans it. "Yes, that's how I'd interpret the message too."

"How do you do *that*?" Neven asks.

Another silence descends on the room.

I haven't the slightest idea. What can I promise Bastien's family that they'll believe? How can I prove my intentions?

Any of the conquered kingdoms might be able to turn the tide in this war... but I don't know how to invoke enough loyalty to make them want to.

It doesn't look as though any of my princes or the former emperor has an easy answer either. Lorenzo's eyebrows draw together. Raul opens his mouth and then closes it again with a scowl.

The silence is broken not by any of us but by shouts of alarm reverberating from outside my bedroom window.

My stomach lurches in anticipation of some new catastrophe. I rush to the window, but all I can see outside are several of the palace soldiers hustling across the front courtyard to the gates that lead to the city.

I motion the princes into the bathing room out of view and go to the door with Marc beside me. I poke my head into the hall just in time to see another soldier hurrying over to speak with my guards.

"What's going on outside?" I ask.

The soldier makes a pained expression. "We're looking after it—I didn't mean to bother you, Your Imperial Highness."

I shake my head. "It's not a bother. I need to know anything that concerns my people."

He draws his posture straighter. "We're still investigating. There are reports from the city of prominent divine omens around the Sabrellian temple near the arena… Unsettling ones."

A shiver travels over my skin. Omens intended to undermine my rule, no doubt.

I hesitate for only a second. "I'd like to see them for myself."

The soldier balks. "I'm not sure— Until we have a handle on the situation—"

"There's no actual danger being reported, is there? Omens have never harmed anyone." I turn to the rest of my host of guards. "You're all prepared to defend me as you always do if any new threats emerge, aren't you?"

They all nod briskly alongside a salute from Kassun. "Of course, Your Imperial Highness!"

"Then it's settled. Let's head out."

By the time my escort and I reach the palace's front steps, the staff have been alerted and sent a carriage around. As I clamber inside while my guards take their places on the outer benches, Axius jogs out of the palace with Cleric Pierus hustling behind him. "If we could join you, Your Imperial Highness? We'd both like to get a look at these phenomena."

I wave them inside. "It'll be useful to get your opinions on these omens too."

It's a short ride to Vivencia's main Sabrellian temple. The

driver stops the carriage at the edge of the growing crowd of civilians there.

I ease out with my guards forming a close ring around me. My gaze fixes on the temple.

At first, there's nothing to see but the formidable stone face of the building. Other soldiers have gathered all around its base, and a few devouts in formal red tunics and trousers are watching alongside the rest of us.

A ripple of ruddy light crosses the gray stone. An image like a crown forms, only to be slashed through by a sharper bolt of light.

Next to me, Pierus sucks in a breath. "My gods."

Murmurs pass through the crowd. Several civilians glance my way. The arrival of my carriage hasn't gone unnoticed.

I swallow thickly. Sabrelle isn't exactly being subtle. It's incredibly unusual for any of the godlen to create signs this blatant.

I'm trying to decide what I could say to the crowd that might diffuse the tension when a paler light gleams overhead. An impression of a dove, glinting as if it's made of sunlight, swoops toward my head.

A giddy wobble runs through my pulse. I press my hand to my godlen mark.

Elox is watching over me, just as openly right now as his fellow godlen is acting against me.

The murmurs rise, punctuated by a few gasps. I can't imagine any of these people has seen a divine spectacle quite like this before. I certainly haven't.

I glance at Pierus. "Is there any past precedent for a display like this?"

The imperial cleric's jaw has gone slack. "I… I don't believe so. You truly have caught the attention of the deities, it's clear."

Another carriage draws up behind ours, with more soldiers following behind it. All four of the princes spill out into the street, keeping a careful distance from me but obviously intent on witnessing this event for themselves. Several more soldiers from the palace fall in around us, including Captain Evando, who catches my gaze with a tip of his head.

Axius strides ahead of me and pitches his voice to carry over the growing crowd of city folk. "I know this is a tremendous event, but let's all keep our heads and simply contemplate what our godlen are showing us."

As if in response, more reddish light flares across the front of the temple. It traces a line like the rooftop of the palace... and then drains away in a bloody gush.

The crimson glow has barely faded when another flash of white draws everyone's gazes to one of the neighboring buildings. A shimmering crowned figure I have to assume represents me opens her arms to the crowd as if welcoming them all into an embrace.

It's a battle of omens, the only way our divine figures can express their disagreements to us directly. What will the city folk make of the holy chaos?

As I wait for another symbol to form, Neven pushes over to my ring of guards. "Aurelia!" He drops his voice to a lower but no less urgent tone. "I think you should get back to the palace."

Kassun grunts, looking displeased—possibly because of the familiarity with which the young prince addressed me, but that only shows how worried Neven is.

My body tenses. "Why? What's the matter?"

"I'm just getting the impression... She's pushing her influence harder. Trying to stir people up. I don't think you'll be safe."

Marc doesn't question the prince's statement. He waves

to the people who've gathered behind the carriage. "Clear a path through the street!"

Captain Evando joins us, with a sideways glance toward Neven. "I'm not sure there's any benefit in panicking when—"

A thump and a cry carry from the other end of the small square. A tussle has broken out between a few of the civilians and one of the palace soldiers.

"Might should rule!" someone yells. "We can't leave an imposter on the throne."

The current of aggression races through the crowd. Civilians and soldiers shove against each other. Someone throws a pot that shatters on a wall. Shouts collide, filling the air with a jumble of words.

Kassun all but heaves me back into the carriage. "We need to get you out of here, Your Imperial Highness."

Captain Evando is staring at Neven, wide-eyed. "I stand corrected," he says, and spins to brace himself against any rioters heading our way.

The other princes have pushed forward too. Axius is hollering for everyone to stand down and calm themselves, but I can't see that anyone is listening.

More light glimmers all around us: splashes of angry red and soothing white clashing. When I blink, a spiral of shimmering orange butterflies seems to be drifting down over the crowd as if trying to divert them to more joyful ends.

Despite the violence, a tingle of hope shoots up through my chest. Is that Inganne lending me her support too?

Some of the civilians stop and point, but more hostile figures keep pouring in from the streets. Perhaps Sabrelle has propelled them to this spot.

The road is too clogged with pedestrians for the carriage to retreat. As I watch from the window, Raul shoves aside a woman who lunges toward the vehicle. Even Lorenzo wades into the fray, holding up his hands as if appealing for peace but aiming a swift punch at the nose of a man who leaps at him.

Another man charges at the prince of Rione from behind, carrying a jagged hunk of wood like a club. A cry lurches out of me.

Lorenzo whirls, an instant too late. The club is already whipping toward his head—

And Marc hurtles into the attacker, sending him tumbling to the ground with his makeshift weapon only glancing off Lorenzo's shoulder.

The former emperor wallops the man's skull against the cobblestones hard enough to knock him unconscious and hefts himself back up. His posture stiffens slightly when he locks eyes with Lorenzo, but they share a brief nod of acknowledgment. The prince offers a flicker of a smile.

A glow lights up right inside me.

Marc might very well have saved Lorenzo's life just now. He didn't have to. He could have pretended not to see the threat.

If my husband can manage to set aside all the reasons he has to wish my lovers dead, surely some kind of peace can be made here in the city.

Ignoring Kassun's yelp of protest, I scramble out of the carriage and up onto its roof as I did once in a convoy nearly a year ago. Poised over the crowd, I lift my arms and call out with all the power of my voice.

"People of Vivencia! Your empress asks you to lower your weapons and your fists and listen. We're all on the same side here. We all want what's best for our country."

The voices of the many civilians who aren't under Sabrelle's influence echo my own. "Enough! Listen to the empress!"

A wash of white light sweeps over the crowd in the wake

of my words, and most of the figures go still. The few still struggling find themselves hemmed in by soldiers and their neighbors.

I speak into the quietened space. "I'm here with you. I want to see every one of you thriving. Let us be at peace and not harm each other, and I'll use all the might I have to ensure no one outside this city harms you either. I stand for peace, but I'm willing to fight for it."

More pale glow swirls around the square, laced through with gleams of yellow. Either it overwhelms the red, or Sabrelle has overextended her influence.

A whoop goes up, and then another. "Here's to Empress Aurelia! The gods stand with her!"

I ease down from the top of the carriage on wobbly legs, my heart heavy despite the cheers. Two of the gods stand with me, at least, but all these people have also seen how much the empire's patron godlen stands *against* me.

Valerisse might not have marched on us yet, but Sabrelle has brought war to my doorstep all the same.

Chapter Nineteen

Aurelia

Axius and Counsel Etta approach me just after breakfast, the high commander's grizzled face so solemn my heart is sinking before they've even drawn me aside into a private room.

"We've had messages back from two of the soldiers we sent north," he says without preamble. "They've arrived and integrated into Valerisse's forces without much questioning."

My apprehension starts to ease. "That's good news."

"Yes. What's less good is *why*. It seems she's had quite an outpouring of support. Soldiers who were stationed across Lavira, Cotea, Goric, and northern Dariu have all been flooding to join her growing encampment. There've even been significant numbers of Darium civilians from the cities nearest the border offering themselves as infantry."

Ah. My heart resumes its plummeting. "All people dedicated to Sabrelle, I assume?"

Etta grimaces. "It sounds that way."

"The civilians, almost certainly," Axius agrees. "The soldiers… I'm sure a large portion of them are, but others will have gotten caught up in the propaganda from those under Sabrelle's and Valerisse's influence. They haven't seen very much of you as a ruler. Many of them know the tribune far better than their empress. They *should* remember their loyalties—"

"But it's human nature to trust those you know better." I gird myself. "How do our actually loyal forces fare in comparison?"

"I believe we may be significantly outnumbered if it comes to a battle. If we're relying purely on human strength."

Who can say how the gods might factor in? Sabrelle has continued to flare up omens in the city at least a few times every day, often followed by contrasting symbols from Elox.

As I absorb that additional bad news, Etta jumps in. "There is a bright side to the current situation. The shifting of manpower means that there are fewer soldiers monitoring the local forces in Cotea and Goric. Obviously Lavira is essentially occupied, but if we could call on the other territories as I gather you were hoping, it'd be easier for them to act without Valerisse catching on or any local commanders objecting."

Because we can't count on even the commanders who've stayed at their posts being loyal to me, especially if I call on the conquered countries to attack Darium soldiers.

"That assumes I can convince them to stick their necks out." I restrain a sigh. "I was going to consult with Prince Bastien on possibilities for combining gifts, which could give us more of an edge in whatever battles might come. Maybe he'll also have new ideas on how to appeal to his family."

Axius nods. "Any strategies you suggest, I'll do my best to implement them. I just don't know how much time we'll have before Valerisse feels secure enough in her position to march."

I leave the meeting room with those ominous words hanging over me and almost immediately run into Captain Evando in the hallway.

"Your Imperial Highness." He draws himself to attention and then appears to hesitate. "There was actually something I wanted to speak to you about…"

Great God help me, has some other disaster occurred?

I stop to give him my full attention. "What's the matter, captain?"

"I'm not sure anything *is* exactly the matter…" He pauses as if to think through his words. "I'm concerned about Prince Neven. I understand you're relying on him to report on how Sabrelle has been reaching out to her dedicats, and clearly he's provided valuable insights. But I've noticed—he's seemed more withdrawn than usual—if Sabrelle realizes he's been helping you against her wishes, he might be experiencing some ill effects…"

I study Evando as he trails off. I don't see anything but genuine worry in his expression. "I hadn't realized you and Prince Neven had gotten close."

"I wouldn't say exactly close. He was coming for the regular training, and I see him around the palace, and—well —I suppose I've been thinking about the entire situation rather a lot given recent events."

A hint of a flush creeps up his neck with his stumbling words. It occurs to me that the captain isn't that much older than I am, perhaps in his mid-twenties—he must have risen quickly in the ranks. Which speaks well of his abilities, but also means he's not completely beyond youthful awkwardness.

For all their apparently clashing, perhaps Neven has caught his attention in matters beyond the military.

In any case, he isn't wrong to be concerned.

"I appreciate you looking out for a colleague," I say. "I've tried to make sure Prince Neven isn't pushing himself too hard, but I'll have a more thorough discussion with him the next time we speak. I'd never want him to neglect his own needs."

Evando bobs his head. "Exactly, Your Imperial Highness. Thank you for listening. I'm sorry if I overstepped."

He hurries off down the hall as if he's afraid of what else he might end up blurting out if he lingers.

I end up reaching the library later than I'd planned. Cleric Pierus is just bustling out, a couple of aged volumes clutched in his arms.

He pauses to give me a quick bow. "I continue my studies on your behalf, Empress. So many fascinating developments in these past weeks."

The eager gleam in his eyes has taken on a bit of a manic quality. With Evando's remarks about Neven lingering in my mind, I study the cleric carefully.

There's a sauce stain on his robe as if he dropped food on it and never bothered to change. As bright as his eyes are, dark smudges have started to form in the sallow skin beneath them.

My stomach tightens. "As important as your help has been, Cleric, I'd never ask you to set aside all other concerns. Make sure you're getting enough rest and looking after yourself, won't you?"

Pierus's posture sags slightly. His mouth twists. "My wife has been complaining I've barely been home these past several days—but there are so many more records to search through—"

I hold up my hand to stop him, the tension inside me thickening with the knowledge that I didn't even realize he *has* a wife. "The records will still be here after you take some time with your family. I'm not leading an empire by running all my supporters into the ground. You deserve a life outside your work. Go home for the rest of the day, enjoy it, and come back fresh tomorrow."

The cleric blinks at me as if I've spoken a language he doesn't understand. Then he bows lower, his expression softening. "Thank you, Your Imperial Highness. I'll do that." He chuckles. "And my wife will thank you for it too."

As I head into the vast room with its looming bookcases, most of my guards take up their usual position by the door. Marc trails behind me through the rows of shelves.

Bastien is already paging through a book in the section of Cotean language volumes. He glances up with a smile and a slight narrowing of his eyes when they slide to the former emperor.

He shifts his attention back to me as if Marc isn't there. "I think this text could be helpful. It details various experiments in combining gifts that were conducted at the School of Entwined Magics. Do you think your grasp of Cotean is solid enough that you'll be able to read it yourself?"

I take the book from him and contemplate the page it's open to. My Lavirian and Rionian may be a little shaky, but my tutors ensured I was decently fluent in the languages of Accasy's most frequent trading partners. And I've always been better at deciphering text than spoken words.

I nod. "There are a couple of terms here I'm not totally familiar with, but I think I can piece together the meaning from the context. These are relatively recent experiments?"

"Yes, I think that book is part of the small collection my parents sent along with me when I first arrived."

Bastien turns back to the shelves of books. "I hadn't really bothered with this section before since I assumed I'd already be familiar with the information from my home country. I didn't realize..." He touches a gold-gilded spine of aged leather.

"There are texts here that I've only heard spoken about back in Cotea. I think these are the only copies left." His tone darkens. "The empire wanted all the best for their personal library."

Marc folds his arms over his chest. "The empire rules all. Why should any of the outer territories hoard their most precious knowledge for themselves?"

Bastien cuts a glance toward him. "Whichever emperor or empress stole these books could have simply asked for a copy if they only wanted the knowledge. From the amount of dust on them, no one here has read them in decades if not centuries. This was about taking what we considered valuable from us, not spreading information."

"Perhaps there's nothing in them of any importance at this point anyway."

"This one is a record of the reigns of our most prominent rulers from before the Great Retribution. I think many in Cotea would like to be able to reflect back on that time."

But the empire wouldn't want them to remember there ever was a time when they ruled themselves.

Marc looks as if he's bitten his tongue. He shakes himself. "Well, that's fair enough, but I don't see how that helps our empress with her current problem. Do you?"

Gazing up at the shelves, inspiration lights in my head with a tickle of exhilaration. "Actually, it might. You said there's a few ancient volumes here, Bastien?"

He points out three more spines amid the shelves. "Those are all considered lost treasures by the Cotean royal archivists. I don't think they even realize the empire has them."

"Then why don't we restore those treasures to their rightful home? I'd imagine Estera would consider the returning of knowledge to those who'd appreciate it a worthy gesture of support."

Bastien brightens. "She should. To bring them home

after all this time, in defiance of imperial tradition—it ought to count for something."

His enthusiasm bolsters my own. "And perhaps that would help show your father I'm acting in good faith. Although I don't suppose getting a few books back will be enough for him to want to send his people into war, no matter how precious those texts are…"

I glance at Marc, but he makes no protest, though his mouth is tight.

My eagerness fades on its own as more practical considerations rise up. "And we'll have to think carefully on who could deliver them. Most Darium citizens would be uncomfortable at the thought of their empress being so generous with the outer territories. I don't want to stir up more uneasiness about my rule than already exists."

But we're running out of time for thinking. I can't be so careful that I ruin my chances to succeeding that way.

Bastien is tapping his fingers against the shelf. "I'm sure we can find a way. You—or I—can write a note using the same trick Father did to convey any other promises you're comfortable making."

How much good will a simple note do, though? What promises will the conquered royals believe after so long under the imperial family's thumb?

I never had the chance to start showing my full intentions before this revolt raised its head.

What I'm comfortable with isn't the most important consideration, is it? My comfort shouldn't come from someone else's misery—not Neven's, not Pierus's and his wife's. It certainly shouldn't come before the security of all the people under my rule.

Another idea slithers into my thoughts, so obvious and yet so unnerving a chill shivers through my veins.

Pierus isn't the only one with a family who cares about him.

My stomach bottoms out, but the larger I let the idea grow, the more correct it feels. Even if speaking it makes me want to vomit.

Bastien frowns, his gaze intent on my face. "Is something the matter?"

I steady myself. "No, not at all. An answer that might solve an awful lot of our problems just occurred to me. I think… I think I need to ponder it a little more before I lay it out."

Clutching the book on combining gifts to my chest, I hurry toward the door. If I ponder my new plan in my lover's presence for even a second more, I might completely lose my courage to pursue it.

CHAPTER TWENTY

Aurelia

Normally I cherish every moment I can get alone with my princes. This once, I'm glad for Axius's presence standing across the round table from me.

The high commander peers at the four hostage royals sitting around the table and then meets my gaze. "You specifically wanted the foster princes included in this discussion, Your Imperial Highness?"

I haven't explained my idea to him yet. I might want the shielding from their full reaction, but it felt unfair to discuss it with anyone else before they heard.

I draw myself up straighter, focusing on Axius and not my lovers' curious stares or that of Marc standing guard just inside the door. "Yes. It's occurred to me as perhaps it should have sooner that the princes may be the key to ensuring the royal families of the outer territories support my rule over Valerisse's claims."

Bastien's puzzled frown is visible at the edge of my vision. "Of course we'll help however we can. We've no interest in seeing traitors take over the empire."

Neven leans his elbows on the table, his eyes lit up. "I can write to my parents—make an appeal, include anything you think would make a difference."

He's so eager to accommodate me that the ache already gripping my heart squeezes harder. It takes me a moment to recover my voice.

I open my mouth, and the words catch in my throat. My hands ball where they're tucked into the folds of my billowing skirt.

"At this point, I think we need more than letters," I say as if only to Axius. "We should send the princes themselves home, so they can make their appeals for me in the most direct and impactful possible way."

Neven jerks even straighter. "If it would make a difference—"

At the same moment, Raul blurts out a strangled, "*What?*"

The prince of Lavira catches himself before he protests any further, but his younger foster brother's mouth snaps shut.

Neven glances around the table at the three now-rigid figures. At the mental calculation that must go on behind his eyes, his posture deflates.

He has no significant bonds tying him to Dariu. Heading home would only benefit him. But he knows the other princes have a much different level of investment.

To be fair, even Axius looks skeptical. "Send the fosters back? We would lose any—well, they're meant to more closely connect their home countries to imperial interests.

Without their presence here, their kingdoms might feel *less* inclined to support the current imperial powers rather than more."

That's a very polite way of saying they're our leverage—which I think he'd have spelled out more blatantly if the leverage in question wasn't here in the room with us.

The ache in my chest has grown teeth it's sinking into my flesh, but I propel myself onward, still focusing on the high commander. "That's exactly why it will be such an impactful gesture. We're showing our good faith while asking them to act with their own. I believe the princes will make a solid case for us, and one which their families will be more likely to believe when they can hear it without any mitigating factors."

Axius would have a difficult time arguing either of those points. He saw how all of the princes, even those with little military inclination, leapt in to help during the riot the other day.

Bastien clears his throat. His voice still comes out strained despite its usual evenness. "Are you sure this approach wouldn't harm your case with the court—if they assume that we've 'abandoned' Dariu?"

I force myself to meet his gaze for the first time. "If anyone asks, I'll tell them you're on a mission for me. That will make my position sound more secure rather than less."

Raul makes a rough sound that draws Axius's head around, but the prince keeps quiet otherwise. I hate to think what furiously defiant thoughts are passing through his head at my proposal.

Doubt winds through my chest again, compressing my lungs. What if I'm asking too much, extending myself too far? Risking more than the gamble is worth?

I was never meant to be in this position in the first place. In the plans I made with my family and my godlen, I'd have been the picture of an obedient wife, gently nudging my emperor husband toward more compassionate policies bit by bit.

But here I am. This is the place I've ended up in with the hand I was dealt.

If I don't claim my role with all the conviction I have in me, I'll lose the throne right out from under me. I have to trust that my vision for the future is right… and that the royals who've been at odds with imperial rule for so long will recognize that too.

Axius is rubbing his jaw. "I can see the value of the plan. We certainly can't afford to be all that cautious at this point. I'd rather we didn't need to call on anyone beyond the imperial forces to begin with, but desperate times…" He smiles crookedly at me. "You've always been willing to make sacrifices for the greater good."

He has no idea just how much of a sacrifice this plan is for me.

I dip my head in acknowledgment and catch Lorenzo's pained expression at the corner of my eye. My heart wrenches.

How is it fair for me to be putting them through this conversation with Axius as a buffer, merely to make it easier for myself? I can't let them leave without giving them a chance to speak openly.

I'm not a coward, no matter how appealing that route looks right now.

I square my shoulders. "I'd like to speak with the princes alone to discuss our exact strategy. If they have any objections or concerns, they should have the opportunity to express those with minimal possible judgment."

Axius only hesitates for a second. Presumably he thinks the likelihood of the princes attacking me, especially when I've just offered up their freedom, is nil. As he heads to the doorway, I seek out Marc's gaze. "Please wait in the hall with the rest of my guards."

My husband's posture tenses, but he only flexes his jaw and follows Axius out of the room.

The second the door has thumped shut behind them, Raul launches into speech, if at a lower volume than I can tell is his natural inclination. "This is ridiculous, Aurelia. We should be here with you. If there's ever a time when you needed support— You know we don't want to go 'home' for our own ends. There's got to be another way."

Bastien grimaces. "And who says our families will listen to us even if we're right in front of them? We couldn't make much progress on your behalf during the tour."

Lorenzo fixes his gaze on me, so intent I can't look away. *"You shouldn't have to be alone while you're facing this. We've worked together through every step toward seeing you on the throne. We can do more together."*

Neven just watches the four of us, his expression drawn, as if he's a kid watching his parents fight.

I swallow thickly. "I didn't make this proposal lightly or without thorough consideration. If it was only about my immediate happiness, of course I'd want you right here. But in this one case, I think you can do so much more for me— and your home countries—if we work together from afar."

Raul pushes back his chair to stand up, with a wave of his hand through the air. "Fuck that. You don't need our families to win this war. You made it this far without a speck of help from them. I won't be able to do anything at all with Valerisse staked out near Rodrige anyway."

"I wasn't up against a god before, and I'm not sure how much support I can count on from the other godlen no matter what I do." A tight smile crosses my lips. "And I think you'd manage to get to your mother. You have a powerful gift and a trickster god on your side. Her support might be the most important piece of this puzzle."

Bastien sucks a breath through his teeth. "I still don't see how you can be sure a message directly from us would be better than one written. Axius might be right—the local rulers *could* see it as a signal of weakness. That would undermine everything we'd say."

"Not if you say what I couldn't say in front of him."

Even Raul goes still. Lorenzo gazes up at me, his brow knitting. *"What are you thinking, Rell?"*

I look down at the table and then back at them. "The mess we're in isn't just about defeating Valerisse. I already needed to find a way to set your countries free without the Darium citizens thinking I'm dissolving the empire willy nilly. I don't want you to go home and simply talk up how wonderful I am. I'm going to send letters with you, signed and marked with the imperial seal, confirming that if they support my claim on the throne, it'll be proof enough of their loyalty that we can remove Darium oversight from their territories."

For a few moments, the princes only gape at me. Neven lets out a choked sort of laugh. "An answer to both problems tied together with a bow."

Bastien's expression has turned pensive. "Even with the seal, they'd worry that you might go back on your word…"

This is the hardest part. I place my hands on the table to steady myself.

"But you'll leave the letters with them," I say. "They'll have proof of the promise I made. And as an additional show of trust… I'll admit to a crime that would end my reign if they ever revealed it. If I fail to deliver on my end of the deal, they can unseat me."

For a few seconds, none of the princes manage to speak. A strained noise escapes Bastien before he forces words from his throat. "You mean—you'd actually confess—if they want to lash out at you—"

All of them can no doubt guess the most obvious crime I could acknowledge. I gather all my resolve.

"It's the only way I can give them a guarantee. As you said, they're not going to trust mere words. I'm handing them more than that, because I believe we can convince them of the better future we're envisioning for the empire." A tight smile crosses my lips. "Don't tell me you're losing faith now."

"Of course not," Raul says in a growl. "But to take that chance…"

I meet his gaze steadily, ignoring the wobble running through my nerves. "And if I don't? I came here as a pawn, and for so much of my time as empress I've still been controlled by what everyone else expects of me. If I want to make a real change, I have to put my own neck out there." I pause, and my voice catches. "If I could do it without putting you all at risk too—"

"Aurelia." Lorenzo springs to his feet and wraps his arms around me. *"We don't* want *you to face this challenge on your own. Whatever you need from us, we're here. Even if it means leaving you for a short while."*

A sudden burn forms behind my eyes.

Bastien squares his shoulders. "You know we're all in, whatever it takes. And it *will* only be a short while, because we'll be returning as soon as we've done all we can to ensure our families' support. That should be more proof in itself— that we want to come back even though we don't have to."

Raul still looks anguished. "You can't seriously be going along with this mad idea? If those letters get into Valerisse's hands—"

Blinking back the threatening tears, I set my gaze on him. "I'm trusting you all to make sure they don't."

Silence settles over us. With the immense sacrifices they

made to their godlen, they've got stronger magic at their disposal than almost anyone in the world. Even if I only wanted to send regular messages, they'd be the most likely to get those missives safely to their destinations.

Lorenzo's embrace tightens around me. *"We'll do whatever we have to do to convince our parents and come back to you with good news."*

I lean into him, too choked up to reply.

Raul strides over and tucks his head close to mine on the other side. "I don't want to make the decision even harder for you, Shepherdess. I know how carefully you think things through. I just hate the thought of leaving you undefended —for any amount of time."

I sputter a guffaw. "How worried do you think *I* am? I'm asking you to go riding across a country on the verge of war, probably by yourself. At least I'll still have my guards and a significant portion of the army around me. I wouldn't ask you to do this if I didn't think it's our best possible chance."

"We know that, Star," Bastien says raggedly.

Raul presses a kiss to the crook of my jaw and draws back, wary of the guards who could enter at any moment. Lorenzo brushes his lips against my temple and eases away with equal reluctance.

I inhale slowly, doing my best to steady my nerves and my voice. "It won't be right away. We'll want to discuss the most ideal phrasing for the letters to persuade each of the ruling families. You should consult with Axius and possibly other soldiers on the safest routes for crossing the border unnoticed. And we should come up with at least the start of a strategy for how the other countries can support me most effectively if they agree."

Bastien nods. "But we won't want to leave it too long. We might not have much time."

"Yes." That's true too, as much as I wish it wasn't.

Raul covers his frustration with typical bravado. "We'll talk it all through tonight, then. Better not leave your guards wondering if we're disrespecting our empress with protests."

I step out of the room first, with a gesture to Axius to indicate the matter is settled. He and I will need to talk further as well, but the current conversation has left me wrung out.

I set off for my chambers with my guards at my heels. In the imperial wing, the wetnurse is waiting near my door, rocking Coraya in her arms.

She smiles at me. "I thought you might like some time with the little empress-to-be before you turn in for the night."

The sight of my daughter's wide eyes loosens a portion of the tension inside me. I reach out to take her and tuck her head right under my chin.

"I'll pass on word when I'm ready for her to go back to her room," I say.

Inside my chambers, I walk straight to the vast bed and sit down in the middle of it, still cuddling Coraya close. I nuzzle her downy hair, absorbing the sweet infant scent that reminds me of just how much I have to fight for.

The panel in the wall whispers open. I glance over to see Bastien emerging.

The prince of Cotea takes in my pose and our daughter and climbs onto the bed without a word. He slips one arm around my waist. When he caresses Coraya's cheek, she offers him a flicker of a smile and a gentle coo.

"We'll get through this too," Bastien says quietly, as if to both of us. "There hasn't been one challenge yet that we couldn't overcome."

Yes. We will survive. I have to believe that.

But I'll be enduring a broken heart for weeks while we do the overcoming.

Chapter Twenty-One

Marc

I never thought I'd see my lowered position as a benefit. Yet it is convenient that I can gather with my foster brothers while I'm temporarily relieved of guard duty without anyone wondering where I've gone or why.

I tap on the map that's formed on the huge round table in the meeting room. Thankfully, its enchantment is keyed to respond to anyone's gestures, not only the royal family's. Blasted palace deciding I don't count anymore.

Although I don't count to anyone else either. If our current conflict has taught me anything, it's that imperial authority is determined much more by other people's opinions of whether you should wield it than divine right or anything else I once believed in.

I motion Prince Neven closer. "You'll want to avoid the main road into Goric. Valerisse will almost certainly have sentries posted keeping an eye on things there. I'd stick to one of these smaller throughways"—I sketch my fingers across a couple of the lines that've come into clearer focus—"and then once you pass this town, veer right into the forests here. The riding will be harder, but you're unlikely to bump into any hostile soldiers."

The Gorician prince nods, his mouth pressed in a tight line. He holds his body as if he's avoiding getting any closer to me than he needs to while following my guidance.

It's clear none of the princes are happy that I'm leading this meeting. To be fair, I can't say I'm all that happy about it either. I only volunteered because there are a few imperial secrets even Axius doesn't know.

I indicate a spot near the base of the mountains just east of Goric's capital city. "Approach Andov cautiously and get a sense of what Darium military activity is happening there. If you don't feel it's wise to head straight in, there's a shelter a couple of hours' ride away that's stockpiled with food and additional equipment. Be as patient as you need to be. We won't get anywhere if you're caught before you can even talk to your parents."

"I know that," Neven says brusquely. "I'm not going to do anything stupid."

At the other side of the table, Prince Raul swipes his hands together in a dismissive gesture. "Our imperial foster brother is just covering his ass pretending to be helpful. He's actually hoping we'll all get rounded up and gutted so there's no chance we'll come back."

I shoot a glower at him. "It shouldn't be hard for you to believe that I want this mission to succeed. I'm better off with Aurelia on the throne than whatever new emperor Valerisse thinks she's going to stick there."

Prince Bastien gives me one of his narrow looks, as if he's trying to evaluate how to most efficiently gut *me*. "And you aren't at all hoping she might be persuaded to stick *you* there?"

I can't stop myself from rolling my eyes. "The court that spent most of their days around me doesn't recognize me. I hardly think she'll believe who I actually am. And—"

I cut myself off at the lance of pain that slices through my gut.

And even if I won that extreme gamble, I'd lose Aurelia. I'd have to label her a traitor and see her executed.

No. The palace's magic has refused me. The entire country has already mourned 'my' death. I can't see any way that making a play for the throne in my current state would end in anything but an even worse tragedy.

Nonetheless, the memories of the blank gazes that travel over me as if I barely exist, perhaps only pausing with a wince of disgust at my marred face, send the sense of loss jabbing deeper. You'd think these pricks could appreciate how much I've already given up.

"I'm trying to help you survive," I reply flatly, and sweep my hand across the table to swing the visible part of the map over to Cotea. "You could use that assistance more than anyone, Your Highness. The open terrain along the Cotean border makes it particularly difficult for travelers to escape notice."

I have the impression Bastien has restrained a sigh. "And how do you recommend I avoid that notice?"

"The hills just south of the river." I rest my hand below them. "There are two guard posts that can keep watch over almost all of them, but we have a secluded route for any small convoys we don't want the regular soldiers seeing. There's a hidden door and a tunnel through one of the hills —I'll show you the pattern for unlocking the door once you've uncovered it."

Bastien's eyebrows rise. "The imperial family always keeps their options open, don't they?"

"You don't maintain control over an entire continent—or half of one—for centuries without making use of every possible advantage. You shouldn't complain. It benefits you now."

Prince Lorenzo twists his hand in the air in a gesture I can't understand but that makes Bastien grimace. I don't know if that means the mute prince was speaking in my favor or against it.

Raul saunters closer, folding his arms over his chest. "And how can you benefit me, *Marc*? Can you whisk me into Rodrige right under Valerisse's nose?"

Ignoring his tone, I pull the map over to Lavira. "I've gathered that your gift can help with that. You can do something with darkness, can't you? Make any precarious approaches by night, and I'm sure you'll be fine. But if you're worried…"

I point out a small town about halfway between the border and the capital. "There's another imperial shelter in the woods just north of Eldovon. You could hole up there during the day if you can't make the entire trek past Valerisse's forces in one night. I'll go over the trick to unlocking that one as well."

Bastien glances at Raul. "The most precarious part for you will be after you've arrived. It might be difficult to keep word from spreading that Queen Benvida's younger son has come calling unexpectedly."

Raul huffs. "My family might thrive on conversation, but they know when they need to keep their mouths shut."

"Then you have nothing to worry about," I say.

Bastien aims a thin smile at me. "Other than you arranging our departure in such a way that we never come back."

I grit my teeth against another instinctive protest.

Why should I be surprised that they feel that way? It isn't as if I haven't wished more than a thousand times in the past few weeks that...

That they'd disappear and leave Aurelia to me? That I'd never have to see her grace them with the adoring smile she's never granted me with quite the same warmth? Never have to watch them caress and pleasure her?

I expected to take a bitter satisfaction at the thought of her lovers disappearing. Instead, I find myself picturing the scene I witnessed in my wife's bedroom just two days ago. The way the man who's still glaring at me embraced her so tenderly, the softening of his face as he gazed down at the child who's really *his*, not mine... The way Aurelia relaxed into his body as if shedding all the weight she'd been carrying...

Bitterness does sear through me, but it's focused on my own deficiencies rather than theirs. What I haven't been able to give her. What I failed to recognize while I had the chance.

Do I really want to see how her heart would shatter if even one of these men failed to return? It isn't as if I could comfort her through the loss. She's offered me a shred of affection, yes—a shred I cherish every time I remember that brief kiss. But that's hardly enough to sustain her.

She needs them. And they... I can admit they've earned it.

I fix Bastien and then the others with my firmest stare. "You'd *better* make it back. For Aurelia's sake. You've made a point of proving you're leagues more capable than I gave you credit for. Don't fall down on the job now."

Bastien blinks at me. Raul lets out a scoffing sound that Neven echoes like a parrot.

Lorenzo... Do the corners of his lips curve upward for just an instant?

"Believe me," he says in that unnerving voice that doesn't shift his mouth, *"there's nothing shy of a second Great Retribution that could keep me from her side any longer than she requires it."*

Raul grunts. "That's right. So you'd better make sure *she's* perfectly safe while we're gone."

I exercise immense self-discipline and avoid pointing out to him that I saved Lorenzo's life just a week ago. Do they not realize I'd let myself be flayed to the bone if it protected her?

And so would they. I can't deny that fact either. Their devotion shines on their faces now, reverberates through their voices—even Neven's, in his less heartsick way. It's showed in every move they've made on her behalf that I've seen in the past weeks and those I've heard about from the months before.

And yet they still have to meet with just me in this meeting room while Aurelia attends to other concerns, because she's already nervous about how much attention she's focused on them since she came up with her plan.

For fuck's sake, *I* get to enjoy her presence more than they do, as distant as it often is, and I've spent most of my time in her life as a villain rather than her hero.

An unexpected knot forms low in my gut.

I yank my attention back to the map and talk Lorenzo through the far easier passage he'll have heading in the opposite direction from Valerisse's forces. I spell out the exact markers that will lead to the imperial caches I've mentioned and demonstrate the necessary patterns for unlocking the entrances.

All the while, the pressure of the knot climbs up from my stomach through my chest to my throat.

When I'm finished, my foster brothers gather together in a circle that doesn't include me. They knock fists and exchange encouraging words, all of them girding themselves for the journey that's supposed to start in the early hours of tomorrow morning.

For all their bravado, the strain of leaving Aurelia behind shows in their shadowed eyes and tensed jaws. They're throwing themselves into more danger than most of the soldiers under her rule are facing, not because they like the idea, only because she's asked it of them.

And it's going to wrench at her just as much. It already is. She hides it well, but I can see it in every shift of her face when she's around them, every careful lilt of her voice.

If they don't return, she won't even be allowed to mourn them. While she gave my brother a public spectacle of grief he sure as shit didn't deserve.

No matter how I feel about them, it isn't right.

Instead of heading straight back to resume my duty watching over our empress, I head down to the palace barracks. The men in my assigned dormitory are all sleeping, various snores mingling together. I walk past them to my bed in the corner and pop open my small trunk that holds my possessions.

Digging through the layers of the two changes of clothes I now own, my fingers close around a thin, smooth metal band.

Not totally smooth. Without even pulling it out into view, I'm aware of the rough edges where the strip of metal was cut through.

My hand tightens around the broken band. I close my eyes, and the image swims up of Father fastening it around my wrist and activating the enchantment so my bangle would match Linus's.

Aurelia might have offered me one small token of affection, might have put a little faith in me, but she isn't even really my wife. I'm not the one who married her, not in the official ceremony that was supposed to establish our bond, if you believe both parties need to be literally present.

But perhaps I still have enough of a divine blessing lingering on me to do one right thing before the woman I'd die for risks the men she actually loves for the good of *my* empire.

I tuck the band away, my mind already spinning through the practicalities. When I leave the barracks, I make my way to the dining room where I know Aurelia will be having lunch.

Her gaze ticks toward the doorway the moment I enter. She's always aware of me, just as I am of her.

Let me put that awareness to good use.

When she departs the head table, I fall into step alongside the other guards. She heads to her chambers, offering compliments and smiles to all the nobles who pass, as if she isn't in the process of tearing her heart out.

My resolve firms even more.

I follow her into her bedroom and take my post inside the door. She scoops up her cat and turns toward me before I can decide how to broach the subject.

"Everything went fine with your meeting?" she asks. Because it isn't a given.

"There were no casualties," I say with automatic derision, and catch myself. "But I think there's one more important thing we need to take care of before they leave."

Aurelia frowns. "What's that?"

"I'll have to get everything in order. Just—delay their departure another day? I'll explain tomorrow when it's all prepared."

Her brow stays knit, but she tips her head in acceptance, because somehow I've earned that much trust already.

May I prove worthy of it in every way she could want.

Chapter Twenty-Two

Aurelia

The gray-robed cleric of Kosmel motions to the creatures scampering around the temple's looming silver statue of the trickster godlen. "I'd imagine Kosmel will approve of your intent. Please don't overly disturb the rats if you can help it. They do have as much of a right to use this temple as the rest of us."

He steps back, giving me, Cleric Pierus, and the cluster of guards and soldiers around us a clear view of the base of the statue. There must be at least two dozen of the large rodents, sleek and glossy-furred thanks to their portion of the temple offerings. Their bodies rustle against each other with a faint skittering of claws against the stone floor.

I tamp down an instinctive shudder. Kosmel looks after his patron animal well, and it was their example that helped my oldest ancestors survive to found my home country. All the same, my studies in medicine have made me all too aware of how many diseases the creatures can carry and spread.

I admire their resilience and resourcefulness as a symbol of those virtues, but I can't say I want the actual animals getting particularly close to me.

Turning to the two soldiers Axius and Captain Evando recommended for our first major experiment in combining divine gifts, I push a smile to my lips against the weight of gloom hanging over me.

Tomorrow morning, my lovers will vanish from my life for days if not weeks. We've never really been apart, even if we haven't always been able to communicate in more than glances and signs. I can't be sure all of them—*any* of them—will make it back safely.

But I can't let my distress show in front of my subjects who expect me to still be mourning my murdered husband. So the best I can do is ensure we have as many advantages as possible in place so the conquered countries can actually come to our aid… if they choose to.

I focus on the ruddy-haired woman named Tobelle first. "You're dedicated to Kosmel yourself, I believe? Your gift has to do with distraction?"

"Yes, Your Imperial Highness." She bobs her head respectfully. "I can divert attention from a specific person, object, or place. Usually only the attention of a few opponents and only for a short time, but it can come in handy."

When she speaks, I glimpse a flash of iron in the back of her mouth—the back teeth she replaced. It's a common dedication sacrifice for soldiers, though most at twelve aren't willing to endure the pain of giving up more than a couple, as she did.

I can't even imagine what agony Neven went through to have every one of his molars extracted.

"I'm sure it can," I say. "Let's see how it works on its own. Perhaps you could attempt to distract the rats into not noticing you and then approach them?"

"Of course." Her gaze flicks to Axius and Evando, two superior officers she may hope to impress even more than she does me, before settling on the scuttling rodents. The little animals haven't paid us much of any mind so far, clearly secure in their position here in the temple.

The soldier's eyes narrow in concentration. She waits through a few breaths and then steps toward the statue.

I'd assume that a gift that could distract at least one human being should be more effective on much smaller creatures. None of the rats look Tobelle's way at first, continuing their sniffing and exploring as if they have no sense they might be imposed on. Even when she sets her feet a little harder on the tiled floor, not one furry head twitches her way.

But rats are probably more alert to threats than even the average military-trained human. Or perhaps it's simply that nearly thirty of them is too many for the soldier to distract all at once.

Tobelle takes another step, just a few paces from them now, and one of the nearby rats locks its beady eyes on her. With a squeak of warning, it darts behind the statue.

Alarm ripples through the swarm. Several rodents glance toward the soldier and bound away or brace themselves defensively. Others follow the first behind the statue without even bothering to check the source of danger.

Tobelle stops where she is, her mouth slanting at an uneven angle. "I'm sorry. That's the best I could do."

"Still impressive," Evando says in a reassuring tone. "You wouldn't normally need to be distracting enemy forces from so nearby."

I match his tone. "We just want a baseline so we can see

how effective our experiment is. We'd better give the animals a few minutes to settle down now."

I shift my attention to her companion, a skinny man named Farro who looks like he hasn't quite lost his teenage gawkiness. "And you're dedicated to Prospira?"

He dips his head in a brisk nod, clasping his hands in front of him. The motion draws my gaze to the spot where his little finger is missing from his left hand. "When I consulted with the clerics before my dedication, they suggested taking an atypical route so my gift might be less easily predicted and countered. I can create fear in the enemy by giving them the sense that our forces have much more abundant resources and strength."

My next smile comes more naturally. "Very creative."

The rats quickly resume their previous scampering. At my signal, Farro's stance tenses.

It only takes a matter of seconds before several of the rats shiver and run off behind the statue again. The others remain where they are but slow their explorations to look around warily. I can't tell whether they're affected by his gift as well or simply reacting to their companions' behavior.

"Very good." I gather myself. "While we're waiting for them to calm down again, let's get you in position for your joint effort. You remember the techniques we practiced yesterday?"

Tobelle steps over beside Farro. "Yes, Your Imperial Highness. I'm ready to give it a go."

"Absolutely!" her colleague puts in.

I've been poring over the book on combined magical studies since Bastien offered it to me. The most beneficial part so far has been the notes on ways to increase the likelihood that two—or more—gifts will enhance each other when used simultaneously on the same target.

From what the author of the reports claims, Raul and

Bastien combined their gifts almost effortlessly because of the brotherly bond they share. The better two people know each other and the more emotionally close they feel, the more easily their gifts will mingle.

For people who aren't anywhere as familiar or connected, there are various ways to attempt to establish a sort of harmony.

One is physical closeness. Tobelle and Farro link arms at the elbow.

Another is a coordinating rhythm. When I see the rats returned to their previous activity and prompt the soldiers, they start tapping one foot, matching the beats to each other.

Tobelle's shoulders tense as she gives Farro's arm a quick squeeze to indicate they should both begin using their gifts. Their faces tighten into similar masks of concentration.

Maybe it's only wishful thinking, but I'd swear a quiver of magical energy passes through the air and over my skin. The rats start to mill about in a much more frantic fashion.

The soldiers take a few steps toward them, tentative and then dropping their feet with more force while keeping up the thudding rhythm that's connecting them. The rodents don't appear to notice them at all, too busy colliding with each other and heaving themselves out of view, not just behind the statue but farther away.

They definitely look more panicked than Farro was able to accomplish on his own, without taking note of the only real potential threat that's approaching them.

Even as my spirits lift, the soldiers tramp closer—and the spell must break. The rats that were still scrambling around each other go still and then shake themselves. They peer at the nearby humans, one of them letting out an indignant squeak, and trot off around the base of the statue at a leisurely pace.

The soldiers' arms sag apart at their sides.

Tobelle spins around, rubbing her temple. "I'm sorry. Maybe it's because I was trying so hard to affect all of them —I'm already feeling close to my limit."

The records in the Cotean book did also suggest that combining gifts often takes more energy out of the casters than if they were working alone—especially when they're not all that naturally aligned.

"That's all right," I tell her. "It was a great start."

Pierus gazes around the temple with obvious awe. "It was amazing. So many wonders this world holds with the blessings of the gods."

Axius claps his hands together. "It does. Let's get back to the palace, and we'll find other ways to practice going forward."

When he's climbed into the imperial carriage alongside Pierus, Evando, and me, the high commander lowers his voice for our ears only. "I wasn't sure this experiment would be worth all the fuss… but I can't deny there could be advantages, if we can match up the right gifts and put them to work in an ideal place on the field. When you have a smaller force, you do sometimes need to turn to creativity to win the day, even if it complicates your strategy."

A light laugh escapes me. "I hope our creativity is enough."

Despite his approval, the flare of exhilaration that lit in me when I saw the soldiers working their gifts in tandem has guttered. It's progress, yes—but are we going to make enough of that to have an effective strategy in time?

As the carriage rattles over the cobblestones, Evando adjusts his position on the cushioned seat. "The princes are definitely setting out in the morn?"

The innocent question hits me like a jab to the gut.

I manage to keep my tone mild. "Yes, the plans are set

now. They'll leave in the early hours when they're the least likely to be observed."

"May the empire's luck go with them," the captain says, but his expression turns brooding as his gaze slides to the window.

Is he worried about the princes' loyalties—or about how one particular prince will fare on his journey? It doesn't feel like my place to pry.

It doesn't feel as if I've done enough to ensure any of the fostered royals will make it back to Dariu safely.

I peer out the window at the passing buildings, and my gaze snags on the elegant towers of the city's largest Esteran temple off to the east. Will my gift of the stolen books be enough to win Estera over to our side, for whatever help the godlen of wisdom can provide?

How much have *I* even done, just putting those books in the princes' hands to carry out the perilous part?

The comments Bastien's father made to me months ago rise up from my memory—the questions about how much I've stretched my gift. A lump fills my throat.

I want to heal the empire. I want to cure anything that's gone sour in my relations with the godlen whose support I need.

Could I make a different sort of appeal work? It isn't that different from how I reached out to Sabrelle in the temple weeks ago—although she simply shunned me.

I can hope that the godlen of wisdom will be more open to hearing me out.

I focus on the distant spires and reach toward my gift. If I wanted to mend any ill-feeling between myself and Estera, make my relationship with her as healthy as possible… what would it take?

Images waver and flit behind my eyes. I see arms reaching up and a greenish light streaming down to meet them. A sensation of propelling higher, of soaring upward, ripples through my body.

I blink, and the impression fades, but my heart keeps pounding faster. I think I know what would catch Estera's attention.

Is it a little mad? Perhaps even a lot. But if it means Estera's blessing goes with the princes on their journey, some madness is more than worth it.

I turn to Axius, who's watching me as if he noticed my distraction. "We have one more trip to make today. But I need to retrieve something from the palace first."

CHAPTER TWENTY-THREE

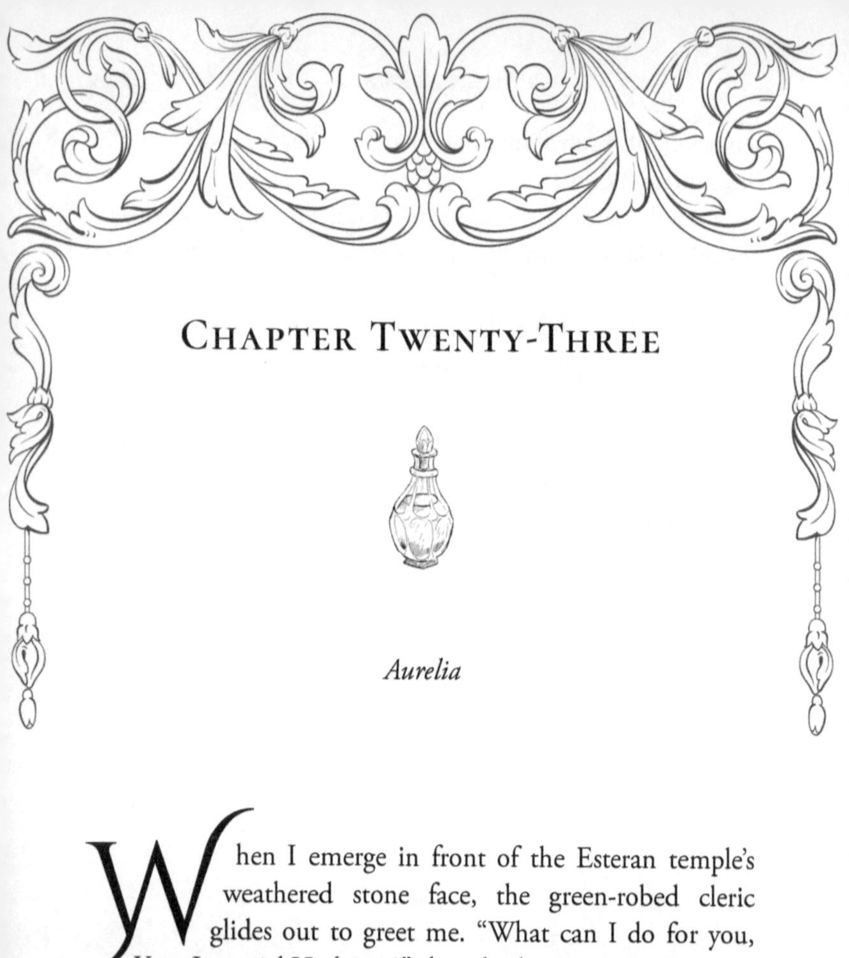

Aurelia

When I emerge in front of the Esteran temple's weathered stone face, the green-robed cleric glides out to greet me. "What can I do for you, Your Imperial Highness?" she asks, her gaze piercing.

I hug the ancient volume I've brought from my bedroom —one originally from Lavira that I intend to hand off to Raul before he leaves—against my chest. A whiff of the aged leather fills my lungs along with the cooling late-afternoon breeze. "I have a message to convey to your godlen. I believe my gift has shown me the way she'll be most receptive to it."

As my guards gather around me, the cleric knits her brow. "Of course you're more than welcome to present yourself in the worship room within."

I shake my head, my pulse kicking up another notch. "I want her to see how serious I am about honoring her principles and earning her favor. In her confirmation rite, I navigated a maze high above the ground. Now I'll ascend this building dedicated to her worship."

"Ascend…?"

I motion to the wall next to us. "I'm going to climb to the roof and make my appeal to her there, raising myself up as I would raise up wisdom and knowledge throughout the empire."

One of my guards makes a noise of protest. "Your Imperial Highness—"

I shoot a glance toward them. "No help from any of your gifts. If I slip, then it's my own failure of observation. I'll remember Estera's teachings and find the most secure way to scale the temple."

It sounds absurd when I say it. Rather than linger in the discomfort, I push forward to walk along the base of the structure.

My position affords me with enough respect that no one hauls me away, though from the tension etched in my guards' faces, it's a near thing. I ignore their and the cleric's stares as well as I can, focusing on the ridges of brick.

I know from my childhood studies that Estera likes her architecture to reflect her thoughtfulness—to allow necessary maintenance to be done even if no one with a useful gift is at hand and tools are lacking. There should be…

Here. Toward the back of the temple, one line of the stones juts out a few inches farther than the rest at the level of my knees.

Clamping the book securely in my armpit, I reach for the window ledge higher above and clamber onto the ridge.

Someone behind me sucks in a breath. For a second, my balance wavers, and a jitter runs through my nerves.

But I can do this. I navigated Estera's maze in the rain. I

led my court and my parents through twisting caves. I survived being buried alive and attacked by my husband.

For once, I'm carrying out my own trials for my chosen goals rather than being dragged into someone else's idea of a test.

I will make it to the top.

There's another ridge near my thigh. I set one foot on it and heave myself upward, grasping the side of the window to steady myself. My lungs hitch as the effort burns through my muscles, but gravity doesn't claim me.

All right. Two pieces of the ascent made, at least a dozen more to go.

It's a slow, careful process, especially when I also need to make sure I don't drop the book. By the time I've reached the level of the building's second story, sweat is dampening my forehead and the back of my dress. An ache is spreading through my shoulders like when I scrambled up the obelisk in Creaden's confirmation rite.

I completed that task too. I've never let any difficulty hold me back before.

The murmur of voices beneath me suggests I've gained a larger audience, but I don't risk glancing down. The sight of how far I've come might dizzy me.

I ease along another window ledge and step higher onto the next ridge. They're barely large enough to hold my toes, not proper footholds like in the climbing challenges I've faced before.

If maintenance workers could survive this route, then an empress should manage it too.

The wind whips past me, tossing my hair and ruffling my dress. Someone below lets out a brief shriek as if she thinks I'm about to be blown off the building with my garment. My fingers skitter in surprise, and I lurch before firming my hold.

I'm all right. I'm on my way. Maybe half the journey already over.

I cling and strain and heft myself by knees and elbows as well as hand and feet where necessary. When I reach the edge of the roof, a wave of relief washes through me that's almost as dangerous as my nerves. My legs relax slightly, and my feet wobble on their current ledge.

Just in time, I tense up to press myself rigidly in place.

The roof has a clever lip for diverting rain, stabilized by arches of stone beneath the protrusion. I set the book on the tiles just beyond the channel and wrench myself up after it in not at all graceful fashion.

Thank the gods Estera cares much more about intentions and insight than appearances.

On the roof, I stay low, crawling more than walking to the peak between two of the towers. There's no way I could ascend those delicate spires. But as the waning sun streams over me, the golden glow sinks into my skin with a comforting warmth that feels like a welcome.

I've arrived.

At the peak, I plant my feet on either side and straighten up. I tip my face toward the sun that can symbolize both Prospira's generous bounty and Estera's keen mind. Then I lift my arms, giving myself over to faith in my stance and the shifting wind, holding the book as high as I can.

I aim my thoughts after it, willing them to reach the godlen who's one of the three said to be most at home in the sky.

Oh great Estera, bestower of so much wisdom and spreader of knowledge, please recognize my offering. The imperial family has hidden away texts treasured by the other countries of the empire for too long. In your name, I will return these books to their rightful homes so that understanding can be regained and spread. I will raise the minds of the empire to new heights as I've ascended to this height myself to prove my resolve. Please bless my purpose and let all the royals of the continent trust in the plans I've crafted.

Let them not throw their lot in with Valerisse and toss me to the wolves, as they very easily could with the ammunition I'm offering them.

My heart thumps faster. No voice comes to me from on high. No divine touch whispers across my skin as I've sometimes felt from Elox.

Was it not enough? Or did I not understand what my gift seemed to be telling me?

I stretch my arms a little higher, restraining a wince at the pain in my shoulders—and a greenish glow flares around me. For an instant, the sprawl of the city buildings and the sliver of landscape I can make out beyond Vivencia's walls are tinted like sunlight passing through the leaves of a tree.

My heart leaps, and then it's over. As I blink, a smile lingers on my lips.

Estera wants to see the enlightenment I promised spread. Now I only have to make good on my promise.

And make it down from this temple without breaking my neck. That would be an excellent first step.

I retrace my climb in reverse as well as I can, with only a few wobbles. By the time I place my feet on the ground, my guards' expressions are so fraught that guilt squeezes my gut.

The words spill out of me. "I'm all right. And Estera— she showed her approval. It was worth it."

The cleric studies me with more curiosity than before. "You've shown yourself to be quite industrious in your pursuit of her favor, Your Imperial Highness. Estera values those who are willing to work toward their goals rather than taking the easy route."

I find myself smiling at her. "I've always preferred thoroughness over ease."

A few devouts and several civilians who ended up gathering to watch my climb move apart for my guards as they usher me back to the carriage. My audience gapes in silence.

I turn to them at the doorway and hold up the book. "Let us always remember the value of knowledge and see that it's shared freely, not hoarded."

With that, I sink onto the bench inside. I can hope my efforts today will bring favor not just to me but to the men I love on their hazardous quests.

Back at the palace, I descend from the carriage among my guards to discover that Marc is rejoining them. He took a leave for most of the afternoon to take care of some of that unspecified business that somehow involves the princes.

I bite back the questions I want to ask him, resisting the urge to return his dark gaze when it settles on me. I can't afford to look any more attached to a man who's supposedly just my guard than I already do either.

We're just in time for dinner. In the dining hall, I push my concerns as far to the back of my mind as I can so I can greet all the nobles around me. *They* still care more about how genial their empress is than how she's handling the war efforts beyond their view.

It's a relief when I can finally take my seat with Bianca at one side and Baronissa Hivette at the other. Neither of them are going to expect a performance.

But I have to give one anyway, because after a few exchanged pleasantries, Bianca glances toward the table where the princes are sitting with a sly curve of her lips. "So, you're sending off the foreign royals. I suppose that might solve certain problems."

My pulse wobbles. "What do you mean?"

She implied once that I might have an intimate interest in Lorenzo, but that was nearly a year ago and I dismissed the suggestion emphatically. She hasn't given any indication since then that she's noticed anything unusual about my interactions with my husband's foster brothers.

"Oh, well, with all the dissent being stirred up… I can't imagine they had the warmest feelings toward the imperial family that insisted they grow up here rather than with their birth families…" Bianca hesitates, studying my face, and seems to shrink in her gown. "Mostly I was making a joke."

I school my expression into total serenity and manage a chuckle. She's given me the perfect diversion. "I certainly hope you haven't observed any signs that they'd turn against me or my daughter."

"Oh, no, I'd have told you right away." The vicerine shakes her head, but her energy still feels deflated from the usual. "It's hard to get a good read on that bunch, though, isn't it? I wouldn't want to give you false confidence."

She has no idea how well my lovers have earned my confidence in them. Of course, she also has no idea that in a matter of days, my gamble could go wrong and she'll see me as the greatest enemy the empire has faced.

I swallow down my fears—for my princes, for myself. The course ahead may not be the safest one, but if I'm not brave enough for it, I don't deserve to be empress.

"Don't trouble yourself about that," I say. "I'm hardly one to throw caution to the wind."

"Of course." Bianca gives a brief laugh.

She stays oddly quiet through the rest of dinner, letting Hivette and Damina across from us lead the chatter. When the meal is finished, she slips away before I have a chance to speak to her privately. I watch her go, my smile stiffening.

Perhaps she's simply feeling under the weather. I'd like to believe it's only that.

I make a short appearance in the hall of entertainments but manage to duck out before too long with the excuse of tending to Coraya. With every passing minute taking me closer to the moment when my lovers will have to leave, my heart thuds heavier.

I do check in on my daughter, and then I make my way to my apartment. When I pause on my bedroom rug to gather myself, Marc touches my arm.

"Come with me," he says with a hint of his old imperial confidence, and moves to open the hidden panel in my wall.

Chapter Twenty-Four

Aurelia

Maintaining his mysterious silence, Marc takes me on only a short trek through the secret passages in the walls. I haven't traversed the narrow wooden halls enough beyond my few usual routes to decipher where we're going until we step out into a vast, shrouded sitting room.

"There you are," Raul mutters from where he's standing in the middle of the room with Bastien and Lorenzo, his massive form tensed. A lantern casts its amber glow over the three princes from where it's sitting on the floor near the wall. "Now are you going to explain what we're doing in this blasted spot?"

My gaze slides over the chairs and tables draped with protective sheets, the gilded wallpaper and dark wooden paneling, the thick rugs that've been rolled and leaned against the walls. A tang of tartly smoky cologne prickles my nose, thicker than it lingered in the temporary apartment I used while my own was restored.

Even with most of the furnishings packed away or concealed like ghostly silhouettes, even though I've only been in this apartment once, an uncomfortable twinge of recognition ripples through my gut.

I cross my arms over my chest instinctively, as if the room's contents might attack me as its occupants did more than once. "These are your old chambers."

This is the panel my princes and I stepped through that fateful night several weeks ago. Through the doorway across the room lies the bedroom with its different secret doorway behind the bookcase next to the hearth.

It's there that I called to Marc in a feigned panic to bring him out of the hidden room the twins shared, to drug him and carry him off to the basement where we interrogated him and meant to murder him.

Does he really want to stir up those memories now?

From Marc's faint wince when he takes in my expression, I have to guess not. "This isn't— I just assumed it was the safest setting for us to remain undisturbed, while still fitting my purpose."

Bastien tilts his head to one side. "Are we finally going to hear what that purpose is? We came as you requested— because you said it'd be for Aurelia."

Marc opens his mouth and closes it again. His expression stays mild, but when he takes a few steps away from me, more tension shows in his movements than even Raul's braced stance holds.

He stops between me and the princes and looks as if he makes a conscious effort to relax. His shoulders come down slightly.

He glances back at me. "You shouldn't think of these chambers as mine anymore. I don't. They'll be Coraya's when she's grown. I wouldn't be surprised if the people insist that you take them until that time, once you've crushed Valerisse's rebellion and proven yourself the rightful empress yet again."

I can't keep the tart note from my voice. "I'm perfectly happy with the apartment I have. What's going on, Marc?"

He shifts his attention to the princes. His hands twitch at his sides as if he's resisted the urge to clench them.

Despite that, his voice comes out even enough. I might even call it… warm.

"I'd be a fool not to see how good you've been to my wife," he says. "And I've already been a fool far longer and more often than I prefer. You've stood by her, comforted her, and protected her when she needed it, since before she even *was* my wife. You carried out the duties that should have been mine when I was too lost in my old attitudes to do it myself."

A trace of a smile touches Lorenzo's lips. He catches my gaze. *"I don't think any of us saw it as a 'duty' but as an honor."*

Marc lets out a choked sort of laugh. "As well you should. That only proves my point."

Raul swirls his hand in the air impatiently. "What *is* your point? We already know everything you just said. You're the one who's taken so long to catch up."

Marc grimaces at him but doesn't let a matching animosity seep into his tone. If anything, his voice softens. "You're about to head off on your own into highly dangerous territory on Aurelia's behalf. I know how much you're risking, and I know you're doing it for her. I know you'll put your allegiance to her over that to your families and do whatever you can to ensure their own loyalty and her safety."

His gaze returns to me. "And I know how hard it was for you to ask them to go and how worried you'll be while they're gone."

The sense of loss I've been trying to suppress all day

creeps up to wind around my throat. "So you wanted to arrange one last meeting? I'd have done that myself."

"No. I—I wanted to give you something better than that. I don't know how much of a difference it'll make, but I hope it'll mean something to have your devotion to each other validated beyond secret meetings."

He draws in a breath. "The palace might not fully recognize it, but technically I am still emperor. I was born of the imperial line with all the authority that should come with that fact. And by tradition the emperor has all the powers of a cleric should he choose to exercise them. I can sanctify a marriage under the gods' eyes."

My heart stutters. We all stare at him, speechless.

Raul attempts to recover first. "What— You really—"

Marc continues before the prince of Lavira needs to grope for words any farther. "I'm offering to oversee an official marriage ceremony between the three of you and her. You might not be able to celebrate it openly, but *you'd* know that your relationship is legitimatized, before imperial authority and the gods. If you'd all want that…"

As he trails off, he looks abruptly, startlingly awkward. I've never seen him quite so unsure of his footing.

The knowledge that he's made this offer despite his uncertainties, despite all the reasons he might have to want to hold on to the one exclusive claim he has on me, brings a swell of affection surging up inside me.

A smile stretches my lips. "Of course I'd want that."

I glance across at my lovers. Lorenzo is beaming now, the answer shining in his dark eyes before his illusionary voice passes into my mind. *"It would be the highest honor."*

Bastien's voice comes out rough. "I never dared to hope that would even be possible. Are you sure—would Ardone really give her blessing—when Aurelia's already technically married to you, and *three* of us—"

Marc smiles crookedly back at him. "I looked up historical precedent. It's unusual, but there have been occasional marriages of more than two people in the past. Even that blasted Signy who kicked us out of the western half of the continent… All Ardone seems to care about in those cases is whether the marriage is based on genuine love, and I doubt that'll be a problem here."

Raul still appears to be reeling. "Why would you— Are you serious? What's the catch?"

"No catch." Marc's face turns wistful. "I've had to do a lot of reflecting in recent weeks. The conclusion I've come to is that there's nothing I want more than to remain with Aurelia, acting as the partner I should have been to begin with, seeing her at peace and thriving alongside the empire. And I can see that binding you all together, confirming the support you'll keep offering each other, will get me closer to that goal."

I have the urge to kiss him again, more emphatically than the one time I allowed myself before. That gesture seems rather counter purpose to the one he's making, though.

He has come an incredibly long way from the imperial heir who once mocked my tea and hurled knives at my head.

Marc opens the pouch at his hip and retrieves a ball of pink silk… and three gold rings he displays on his palm. "I didn't think we could get away with each of you having a full band, and I didn't have enough gold from mine to make three of those anyway. But if I can still be her husband with it cut off my wrist, then I don't see why having a smaller band around your finger shouldn't be a more-than-sufficient symbol."

Raul's eyes flash. "You did grab the broken band from the servants' room! All this time…" His momentary consternation dwindles. "You held on to it all this time, and you're using it for this?"

"It's meant to be worn, and I couldn't wear it as is either." Marc pauses with a flick of his gaze toward me. "I had four rings made. I'll give you the other to set aside… until such time as you might decide you're happy seeing it on my finger as well."

The hope in his eyes makes my throat squeeze tighter. "I suppose we'll see about that part," I say quietly.

Lorenzo steps closer to me. *"You can conduct the ceremony here rather than in the temple? Right now?"*

"The temple seemed too risky, and I expect we're best off with me as close to my old imperial self as possible." Marc motions to the room around us. "It shouldn't take long, and then you can celebrate in private however you wish. I think I can pare down the typical ceremonial prayers."

Even Raul's face has lightened. I walk over, tugging Lorenzo with me, reaching to grasp Raul's hand and encompassing Bastien as well with my smile. "I couldn't have asked for better companions in everything that matters to me. We've been on this path together for so long, through so much. Let's make that commitment official in the eyes of the gods."

Raul dips his head to plant a kiss on my hair. "You know I'd make the commitment in front of the entire continent if we could."

We can't—we may never be able to announce our devotion publicly. Not while Coraya's path to the throne is still uncertain, at least. But this is still more legitimacy than I ever imagined our relationship might receive.

It won't eliminate the dangers my lovers will face or how much I'll miss their presence, but it'll make the bonds between us feel all the stronger, drawing them back home to me.

With a caress of my cheek, Bastien nods.

I turn to face Marc again. "How do we do this?"

"Much the same way you married 'Marclinus.' You can stay right there. You're ready?"

"We've *been* ready," Raul says gruffly.

Lorenzo links his arm with mine.

Marc taps his fingers down his front in the gesture of the divinities and tips his face toward the ceiling. His gravelly voice resonates through the room with the words I remember from that day in the palace temple over a year ago.

"Oh great Ardone, champion of love, beauty, and passion. We call on you today to witness and endorse the love shared by the four people in front of me."

As he continues through the wedding prayer, albeit with fewer of the extended flourishes the Ardonian cleric included, my princes ease even closer around me. My heart feels as if it's expanding, absorbing all the adoration they're radiating toward me and exuding my own back at them.

At them, and at the man who set this ceremony in motion.

Marc finishes the prayer with the final request. "May you watch over their love and honor them as they honor you with it."

A flutter of warmth passes over my skin, as if Ardone has literally touched me with her blessing. From the intake of breath behind me, I don't think I'm the only one who felt it.

We hold out our hands. Marc winds the cool strip of pink silk around each of the princes' palms, looping over mine in turn in between each. The words I've only said once before rise up in my throat automatically.

I meet Lorenzo's eyes first. "I swear before all the gods to love and honor you from now until my last breath leaves me."

When I said it to Linus, the promise fell heavy from my tongue. Now, it springs forth as giddy as a spring breeze.

I turn to Bastien at my other side. "I swear before all the

gods to love and honor you from now until my last breath leaves me." And then Raul, just next to him. "I swear before all the gods to love and honor you from now until my last breath leaves me."

I don't think Raul could grin any wider than he does before he repeats the oath back to me, his tone as tender as I've ever heard it. Bastien's penetrating gaze doesn't waver as he offers up his own promise. Lorenzo leans his head against mine and speaks the sacred words right into my head.

Marc holds out the rings again. He judges each of the princes' hands and slides the simple gold band onto the finger it'll best fit. They gleam against those digits—pale, tawny, and deep brown. Then he touches the band I still wear around my wrist as if to add it to the ceremony.

All those months ago, the fitted circle of gold felt like a manacle. Now it's an anchor, ensuring the men I love can never be flung too far astray.

Marc clears his throat before he speaks the last benediction. "Let it be seen that these four are married!"

Chapter Twenty-Five

Bastien

There's no audience to cheer on our newly confirmed union. No celebratory feast waits for us down the hall. But the memory of the first marriage ceremony Aurelia participated in is burned into my mind, even if the anger and pain I felt watching it has dwindled.

I raise my free hand, the one that now carries the light but noticeable weight of my new wedding ring. With a touch of her cheek, I draw Aurelia's mouth to mine.

We've kissed so many times, but this meeting of our lips comes with an exhilaration unlike anything I've ever felt before. There's something a little sweeter still, a little more satisfying, about kissing a woman I can call my wife.

In the heat that passes between us and the soft noise that works from her throat, I taste the certainty that no matter how far away I go, nothing can truly tear us apart.

That thought knots my gut all the same, because I do

have to go. In a matter of hours, I have to leave behind the woman I love and the daughter we brought into this world for gods only know how many days. I have to ensure my family treats her trust as a gift rather than a tool to unseat her.

And I will. I'll bring back the means to fend off this latest threat. We'll stand up to the traitor soldiers and the treacherous godlen and prove once and for all who's meant to rule the empire.

I deepen the kiss for a few beats of my heart before finally pulling away. Raul tugs Aurelia to him a moment later, with a mild huff that I got there first. As he claims her mouth in his demanding way, my gaze slides to the man who ruled the empire before her.

Marc is watching our intimate confirmation with a tightened jaw and an uneasy heat simmering in his dark gray eyes. It's never been easy to read my imperial foster brother's expression, and the unnaturally smooth discoloration of his face hasn't helped matters, but I don't think he's exactly *joyful*.

He offered us this validation despite his misgivings. I don't know how official anyone outside this room would consider the marriage given that Marc's current imperial status is questionable… but he clearly believes in it, and he's the one with by far the most to lose.

From the way he spoke, it sounds as if he genuinely doesn't see himself as losing anything. Nothing more than he'd already lost when his cruelty sent Aurelia into our arms to begin with.

He's acknowledged how important we are to her, how fiercely we've fought for her and defended her. Has he truly gotten to a place where he can appreciate our presence in her life?

It feels a little ridiculous to ask that question when he's

just turned his own wedding band into rings to honor our love.

All the observations I've made over the past few months whir like clockwork in my head. While Lorenzo steps in to claim a lingering kiss of his own from Aurelia, I keep watching the former emperor. A sense of resolve that's not entirely comfortable rises in my chest.

It's not until Marc speaks next, as Lorenzo eases away, that I'm sure.

He bobs his head to all of us, his gaze still intense but his tone relaxed enough. "I think you know where the bedroom is. Consummate your union for as long as you'd like."

Raul blinks at him, as if Marc's acceptance of our physical intimacies is somehow a step farther than making us Aurelia's husbands alongside him.

A trace of a flush touches Aurelia's cheeks—and the slight smile that crosses her face as she looks back at Marc is as sweet as the kiss we shared.

After what he's just done for us, I can't resent that smile or the fondness in her eyes. He's earned it.

No one's hurt her as much as he and his brother did… but not even the three of us can say we've sacrificed anywhere near as much either.

"Is her first husband going to deny his wife a kiss of approval?" I ask, calm and even.

Marc's expression twitches. His attention snaps from me back to Aurelia. "I…"

Raul shifts on his feet but doesn't protest. Lorenzo watches with a smile of his own curving his lips.

He might have suggested this himself if he hadn't been worried about how Raul and I would react.

Where our hands are still entwined with the silk sash, Aurelia squeezes my fingers. Then she holds out her other hand toward Marc.

I sidle over to make room for him to approach. His expression remains difficult to read, but there's no denying the elation that's lit there along with whatever else he's feeling.

He takes her hand in a gentle grasp and leans in.

I can't say no jab of jealousy runs through me watching them kiss. Aurelia sways slightly closer to him to accept the act, and part of me wants to punch him right off her. But that's a significant change from how I'd have felt even a couple of months ago, when *all* of me would have been completely for punching—and stabbing and gutting—if I'd thought I'd survive the attempt.

Marc has acknowledged everything we've done for Aurelia and how happy we make her. It'd be awfully hypocritical of me to deny that *he's* started to make her happy too.

It helps that the moment she pulls back from him, she turns to me and kisses me even more passionately than before.

By the time she's released me, my breath is coming short. Raul is already unwinding the strip of silk to allow us more room to move.

He dips his head to nip the corner of Aurelia's jaw. "Are you ready to take this to the bed?"

An airy laugh tumbles out of her. "Yes, please."

As our hands finally separate with the fall of the ceremonial sash to the floor, I turn to Marc again. "Do you think you can handle witnessing the consummation?"

His stare back at me verges on a glower. We both know my question is more a challenge than an invitation.

But Aurelia is watching for his answer too, with no objections. This marriage won't mean much if he can't tolerate all its implications.

"She's yours," he says, a little hoarsely. "I've ratified it before the gods."

"And we're hers," I reply. "Are you?"

His gaze slides to Aurelia, and that hopeful light comes back. As if there really isn't anything that could mean as much to him as her welcome. "Every part of me."

"Then come along."

I don't wait to see if he'll follow my order. Tucking my hand around Aurelia's arm, I join my other foster brothers in leading her into the imperial bedroom.

The furniture there has been draped with more protective sheets. With a nudge of my gift, I send the fabric covering the massive bed gusting off into a pile on the floor. I know Marc's still with us from the choked guffaw behind me.

Raul seems to have decided he'll just ignore the former emperor. He shoots me a glance with a teasing glint in his pale blue eyes. "Show-off."

I grin back at him. "Unlike your completely modest self."

"Hey, it takes one to know one."

He extends his hand into the darkness that cloaks the room nearly as thoroughly as the sheets, and a magic-blessed lantern on a side table flares on to bring the space into clearer focus.

"I won't be adding my gift to the atmosphere," Lorenzo says, slipping his arm around Aurelia's waist. *"No illusion could be as incredible as the reality we're celebrating."*

He ducks his head to kiss the side of her neck, and Aurelia leans into him with a pleased hum.

The giddiness that's been building in me since Marc started the ceremony sweeps every other concern from my mind.

This is my woman, *our* woman, and we're going to worship her as if we'll never get another chance.

I won't think about how true that possibility might be.

I stroke my fingers along her hip and up her side. As Aurelia clutches at my shirt, I tease them over the swell of her breasts through the thick fabric of her dress.

Raul tugs at the ties, pausing only to steal a kiss here, a squeeze of her ass there. The moment her bodice is loose enough, I dip my hand under to caress her skin to skin.

A gasp breaks from Aurelia's lips. She drags me in for another kiss, her grip on my shirt tightening as I strum her nipple to a stiffened peak.

My cock strains against the crotch of my slacks, painfully hard already. Great God help me, it's been too long since I was completely enveloped in the hottest, slickest part of her.

The gown slides from Aurelia's shoulders and collapses around her feet. We help her step free of it, pressing closer around her as we do.

I send the silk fabric drifting aside with a puff of breeze and graze the moving air over every inch of her bared skin our hands aren't caressing. Her moan is my reward.

I haven't forgotten her fourth husband, though. As Lorenzo turns Aurelia's head toward him for another kiss, I glance over at Marc.

He's stopped just inside the doorway, his arms loose at his sides but his posture stiff. Taking in our wife in her thin underclothes, his eyes smolder.

We're all with her now. All *for* her now—him included.

Why shouldn't he prove how well he can stand beside us as well as beside her?

I let my voice get a bit tart. "Don't hang back. You want to see her as pleased as she can be, don't you?"

Marc's gaze flicks to me. I can't tell how much he's surprised that I want him involved and how much offended that I'm daring to order him around.

Either way, he only hesitates for a second before striding to join our cluster.

When he's right in front of Aurelia, he pauses again. His hands flex at his sides.

"Tonight is supposed to be about the three of you," he says in a tone as stiff as his stance. "I don't want to overstep."

With us or with her, I'd imagine.

I don't know how far Aurelia is comfortable accepting his affections now either, but I trust she'll encourage him as she sees fit. I'm just giving him the first brief shove. "It is about us—and knowing we all serve her better in collaboration. You can let us take the lead and still… enhance the experience. So, let's see you contribute."

Aurelia tenses next to me, and my heart lurches. I open my mouth to take back my command—but then Marc lifts his hand, and she relaxes again, as if she was only concerned about *his* reaction.

He grazes his fingers along her nearly bare shoulder and down her side, making her silk chemise ripple. My fellow princes go still around her, waiting to judge his approach and her response.

I can't help egging him on now that we're all in. "You can do better than that."

Marc wets his lips and draws his hand back up to cup her other breast, ever so carefully. Aurelia's eyelids dip. She leans into our combined caress.

Sucking in a breath as if he can't believe this is real, Marc flicks his thumb over her nipple. I decide it's time to get back to pleasing our woman myself.

I tug the strap of her chemise down and lap the tip of her breast into my mouth.

Aurelia whimpers, clutching at my collar now. I drink in the sound and the sweet scent of her delicate skin, swiveling my tongue around the pebbled nipple and adding the friction of my teeth.

When I lift my head, she tugs at my shirt. I strip it off

without a thought to my thin frame. Marc's judgment of that doesn't matter when he's already judged me worthy in so many other ways, and no one else in this room gives a shit about my physical heft.

Aurelia kisses me hard. As Raul tucks his hand right between her legs, she moans against my mouth.

While she rocks into his touch, Lorenzo dapples kisses down the back of her neck and strokes her ass. Marc keeps tending to that one breast. After she's released me, he dares to lean in for another kiss.

Watching him, my sense of a threat diminishes even more. He's one of us, helping us take her to the heights we all agree she deserves.

Aurelia takes charge next, grasping the waist of my trousers and yanking me with her as she backs up. "Let's bring this encounter to the actual bed, hmm?"

I chuckle at her impatience and follow her. When we reach the bed, she glances around at all four of us trailing after her and appears to ponder the logistics.

With a determined expression, she nudges me down on the mattress on my back. "You've been a very good husband."

I had no idea those words would turn me on so much. My cock jerks to even sharper attention, springing free as she loosens my trousers.

She bends over to envelop my shaft in the heat of her mouth, and all I can do is sag into the bed with a strangled noise of approval.

Few pleasures could compare to the bliss of having this woman's lips stroking up and down my cock, her slick tongue tracing torturous patterns in their wake.

I'm vaguely aware of the other men around me—Raul tugging down Aurelia's drawers, Lorenzo massaging her breasts with her chemise completely discarded. My fingers tangle in her hair. I can't help bucking into her mouth, but even through the pleasure hazing my mind, I know I want more than this.

I tug her head so she looks up at me. So much desire shines in those bright blue eyes that I want to fall right into them.

"Ride me, Star."

Aurelia's smile is nearly as delectable as her mouth around my cock was. She shimmies farther forward and finds just the right angle to lower herself onto me.

Tipping my head back into the covers, I groan as she encompasses me. My hands drop to her hips, urging her to roll them over me, thrusting up to propel myself even deeper.

Her body doesn't look exactly the same as it did when we first enjoyed an interlude like this. Her torso curves with more ample slopes. Marks so pale they're almost silver ripple across her thighs and belly, the lingering reminders of the stretching of her skin to accommodate our growing daughter.

As I rock to meet her, I trace my fingers over those lines, delighting in the knowledge of what they represent. They prove her determination and strength just as much as the purple scars that dapple her forearms from her earliest potion-making experiments.

As far as I'm concerned, the new patterns on her skin are nothing short of magic. This life we've built together, the passion we create together—it's all magic, every part of it.

Raul sets his hands on Aurelia's waist just above my own and kisses her shoulder blade. His voice comes out even deeper than usual. "Do you think you can handle me here now, Shepherdess?"

He teases his fingers down the center of her ass.

Aurelia gasps and nods. "Yes. That sounds amazing. Just go slow."

"Whatever my empress needs." He plants another kiss on

the crook of her jaw and starts working her over with his hand and molded shadow to warm her up.

Aurelia bends down to kiss me and then sways back upright to meet Lorenzo's lips. As she melts into him, she trails her fingers down his chest to his slacks.

"Let our empress have a look at you," I demand, and he sheds his shirt and then his pants with a rough laugh.

As Aurelia closes her hand around Lorenzo's straining cock, Raul lines himself up behind her. He does ease in slowly, but her channel clenches around me at the increase in pressure. A headier pulse of bliss radiates through my body.

"Fuck," Raul mutters. "You always take me so well. We're going to make you feel fantastic. Just stay right here with us."

He keeps one hand on her waist and slips the other lower to rub her clit right above where she and I are joined. Aurelia's moan and the quiver that runs through her body give proof to his skills.

I don't know how much longer I'm going to last. I press up into her, angling for the sweet spot I know will provoke the most pleasure, straining against my release.

Lorenzo bestows kisses across Aurelia's face and shoulder, his chest hitching. Raul gradually speeds up his thrusts from behind her.

And Marc… Marc has hung back by the side of the bed, watching all of us with his face flushed and his posture tensed again.

I manage to speak if not at my steadiest. "Get over here, ex-emperor. Tend to your wife."

He stirs into motion. Climbing onto the bed, he finds a space next to us where he can trail his fingers across her breast again. Lorenzo matches his gesture on the other side, stoking the flames of Aurelia's pleasure all through her body.

Aurelia lets out another moan and shudders. Her orgasm ripples into me in the most ecstatic of floods. I can barely take a breath before I'm erupting alongside her, a brilliant haze sweeping over my vision, every nerve tingling.

Lorenzo comes with a spurt across her arm and my chest that I can't feel too bothered about. Raul nips her shoulder and comes with a groan that reverberates through the room.

Aurelia slumps partway over me, panting, and claims one more kiss. Then she eases farther upright to offer one to Marc as well.

Watching him embrace her even when she's entangled with the three of us, a warmth I never expected to feel expands through my chest.

We might have to leave her, but she won't be alone. I can trust that there'll be one man watching over her for whatever she might need until we return.

Chapter Twenty-Six

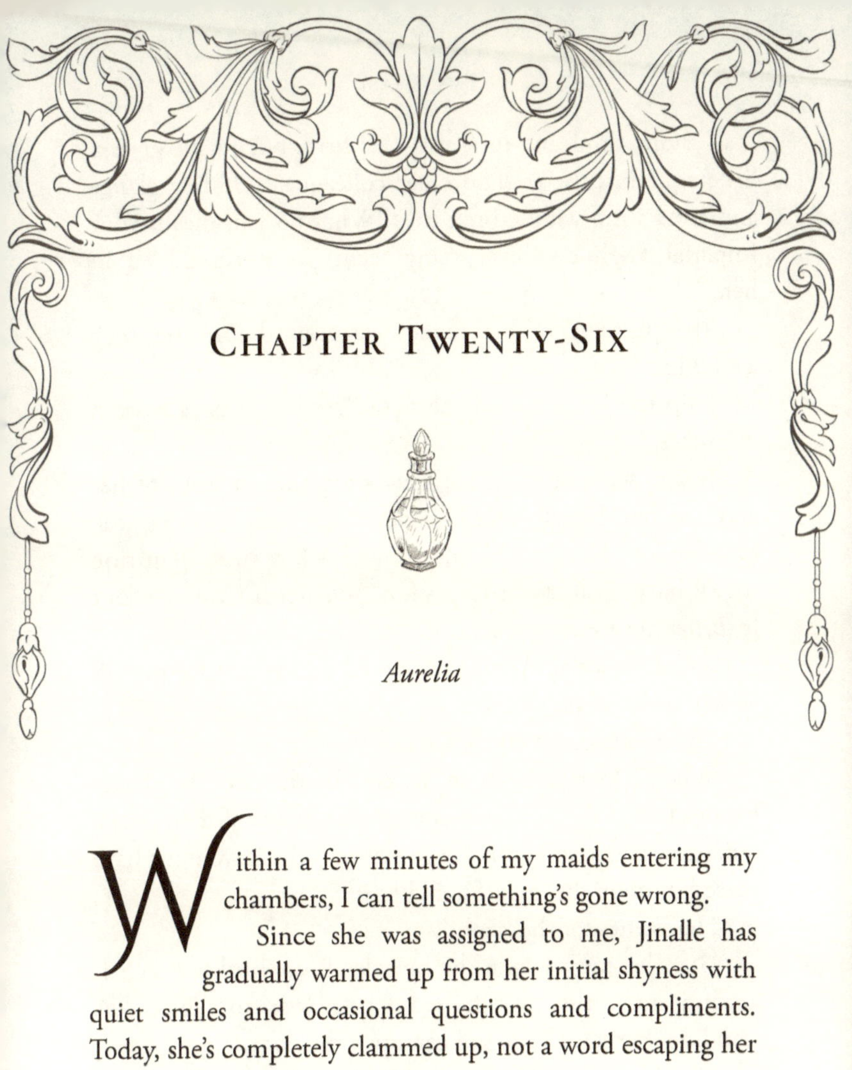

Aurelia

Within a few minutes of my maids entering my chambers, I can tell something's gone wrong.

Since she was assigned to me, Jinalle has gradually warmed up from her initial shyness with quiet smiles and occasional questions and compliments. Today, she's completely clammed up, not a word escaping her mouth other than her initial hasty greeting.

Eusette fills the gap with her usual chatter—except it *isn't* like usual. There's a frantic quality to her torrent of prattle, jumping from one subject to another with barely a breath in between.

I manage to hold my tongue until they've finished pinning my hair in its upswept style. As Jinalle scurries over with a bracelet to match my gown, I fix my gaze on both of them. "All right. What's happened?"

I didn't think my tone was *that* firm, but Jinalle gives a little squeak. Eusette shoots her colleague a chiding glance and aims a too-wide grin at me. "What do you mean, Your Imperial Highness? Everything seems as it should be in here."

The phrasing of her remark suggests the answer she's avoiding.

I tip my head toward the door. "And how does it seem out there?"

Jinalle starts to twist her hands together in front of her and catches herself when she realizes she's twisting the bracelet too. Her voice comes out in a low rush. "I'm sure they'll have it all cleaned up soon. You needn't worry about it. *Better* not to worry about it."

I swallow a sigh. "I think I should decide that for myself. Worry about what, exactly?"

The women exchange a wary glance.

When I look at Marc in his post by the door, he shakes his head. "I didn't hear any commotion… but if there was a quieter conversation with the guards outside, it wouldn't have passed through the door. Should I—?"

He reaches for the knob.

"No, let me." I take the bracelet from Jinalle, fasten it around my wrist myself, and stride over to where he's standing. He eases aside so I can open the door.

Despite my apprehension, my skin tingles at his closeness. Memories stir of his hands moving over my body alongside my princes'—my new husbands'—a few nights ago.

I tamp down those heated thoughts and peer out at the guards clustered outside. The fact that I find myself looking at five rather than the usual three sends any other consideration right out of my head with a jangle of my nerves.

"What's going on? Has there been—" Panic spikes through my veins. "Is Coraya all right?"

Kassun's eyes widen at my tone. He holds up his hands. "No one's been hurt. We just—there was an incident overnight—the high commander ordered extra precautions until we're sure it's dealt with."

"That *what* is dealt with?" I demand, not quite able to smooth my temper from my voice. Apparently I'm the supreme ruler of the empire until I want the answer to a simple question that directly affects me.

Do they really think I'm so fragile?

Kassun, at least, doesn't. He bobs his head, gives his fellow guards a stern frown as if daring them to object, and motions for me to follow. "It's just… a bit of a mess. In the audience room. Like I said, no one was hurt. The cleaning staff should have it back to normal by the end of the day."

I march along behind him with Marc at my heels and my other guards surrounding me on either side. As I reach into the well of calm at my center to settle my mood, a trace of absurd amusement passes through me.

We rarely use the audience room except for formal proclamations and assemblies. If this 'mess' is something that can be fixed in a day, I might never have found out about it if my staff hadn't been so nervous *about* me finding out.

Or maybe I'd have noticed something was off regardless. More soldiers than usual are patrolling the halls. Even the nobles I pass turn tight-lipped and tense at the sight of me, though they offer their usual bows and respectful greetings.

Outside the audience room, Captain Evando is pacing. Another soldier reaches him just before I do and murmurs her report.

Evando sighs. "Well, I suppose that's to be expected."

He turns to me, his posture drawing stiffly rigid. "Your Imperial Highness. We hadn't wanted to trouble you with—"

"So I gathered," I say, more dry than snippy now, and crane my neck toward the doorway. "Is it safe for me to go in and see this mess, or must I insist that you describe it to me?"

Evando grimaces. "It appears to be an entirely superficial defacing. Unfortunately, the likely culprits have fled in the night, so we can't get confirmation of their intentions. But neither had significant gifts we're aware of. You should be safe, but keep your guards close."

My gaze flicks over the men and women in their stubborn ring around me. "I don't think that'll be a problem."

I step into the vast room, and my heart sinks.

I have no love for the imperial audience room. It's been the site of some of my most traumatic memories from my time in the palace.

This is where I first stood before Emperor Tarquin and his heir and found out my betrothal was a sham. Where I watched as the first of my unwilling competitors had her throat slit. Where one of the twins—possibly the one flanking me right now—had me brand my three lovers with the imperial crest.

None of that makes the wanton defacement any less horrifying.

All across the walls that stretch the sprawling length of the space, thick red paint has been smeared. It gives off a tangy, chemical scent that turns my stomach. Some of it is just random blotches, but in many spots it forms Sabrelle's sigil or crude images of her totem symbols: stallions, hounds, swords and shields.

The two thrones on the dais at the far end of the room have been completely drenched in red, as if someone was slaughtered across them and left to bleed out. More red splatters the indigo rugs around them, where several servants are scrubbing furiously while a couple of others hold out their hands, perhaps working gifts.

I wrinkle my nose. "What—how did this happen without being noticed? *Can* it be cleaned?"

"No one uses the audience room at night, so there weren't any guards posted inside," Evando says. "With no access to the space from outside the palace, there's never seemed to be any reason to focus attention on it during the patrols. We're assuming the perpetrators slipped in when no one was watching this particular hall and did their work quietly. And the paint... They used a particular formula that's resistant even to gifted measures to clean it. But we have made some progress."

Great God help me, the room used to look *worse*? More nausea bubbles up.

I glance around, noticing the nobles starting to gather in the hall outside to observe my reaction—instinctively seeking out a particular icy blue gaze and head of auburn hair. Opening my mind as if a resonant voice might travel into it to reassure me.

But of course all I see and hear are regular members of the Darium court. All of the foster princes left before dawn three days ago.

My spirits waver like a candle flame in a draft. I catch a sideways look exchanged between two marchionissas and a baron's eyebrows arching at a judgmental angle.

Jerking my gaze away, I square my shoulders.

I can't let my court see me shaken. If I lose any more support here in the palace, gods know I'll face more troubles than paint on the walls.

I turn back to Evando, firming my voice. "And those perpetrators, the soldiers responsible—they've vanished like the earlier ones?"

Evando opens his mouth, closes it again, and appears to

gird himself before answering. "High Commander Axius is investigating now. The people we believe are responsible have abandoned their rooms here. But… it doesn't appear to have been soldiers." He lowers his voice so only I can hear. "Vicerine Saldette, Marchion Syrus, and all of their respective households departed rather hastily at a very early hour of the morning."

Ah. Understanding curdles with gloom in my belly.

Saldette and Syrus have both resented me, however much they've attempted to suppress the indications. They both had daughters who died in the trials that allowed me to become empress.

Syrus had an additional reason for animosity, considering Linus sent him off to tend to his estate rather than enjoying court several months ago. He only returned in the past couple of weeks, and I wanted to take that as a promising sign that he'd recognized siding with me was at least a better option than war.

It's difficult to imagine the stately vicerine or the pompous marchion slathering paint across the walls themselves. Although who can say what they'd be moved to do, given how long their resentment has been simmering? No doubt their personal staff at least helped to carry out so much vandalism in so short a time.

And soon if not already, the rest of the court will know that two of their own have rallied against me.

I have to do *something*.

I dip my head to Evando. "I appreciate all the work going into cleaning the room as quickly as possible. Let's not waste much manpower trying to track the culprits down when we can be reasonably sure they've gone to Valerisse." I shift my attention to my guards. "I believe it should be time for breakfast?"

As they escort me to the dining room, the clot of curious

nobles follows behind us. I walk straight in and take my place at the head table.

Counsel Etta catches my gaze from farther down the table and tips her head with a somber expression. No doubt I have a long meeting with my advisors to look forward to this morning.

There may be no princes I can turn to for comfort today, but at least Bianca is nearby, a few seats down from mine. The tightness of her smile tells me she's aware of the latest attack on my rule.

No one's taken the seat right next to me yet. I'm allowed some control over the table arrangements, aren't I?

I beckon her closer. She blinks at me with a hesitation I didn't expect, but then gets to her feet and glides over.

As she takes her new seat, I stay standing by my high chair, watching the tables fill up with my court. When the last few stragglers have entered, I clear my throat. The guards poised behind me stomp their feet to emphasize my call for attention.

The entire room goes silent.

I lift my voice, keeping it calm and steady. "I want to say a few words before we enjoy our breakfast. How sad is it that someone among us took out their grievances on this treasured palace that's held the imperial family and its court for many generations, rather than expressing their concerns to me directly? I hope if any of you have matters you'd like to discuss, you'll do so and let me address the issue rather than acting out."

With that, I sit down and accept the plate a server sets in front of me.

I'll need to be even more careful what tone I set over the next few days, but I think that was a good start. Framing their peers' actions as a childish temper tantrum rather than a legitimate act of protest should diffuse some of the power of the display.

A buzz of conversation rises around me. It's hard to concentrate on any strand of it when my thoughts are still whirling in my head.

Bianca lets out a quiet huff. "Idiots, the both of them. Sabrelle isn't the only godlen who watches over the imperial family anyway. I'd say Creaden would be proud of how much you've built here, as much as I know of him."

My lips twitch with half a smile. Something in her words niggles at me, like a spark gusted out before I can see what it's lighting. If I looked at it in the right way…

I can't quite put my finger on it when my mind is already so cluttered.

I speak wryly instead. "At least I've never known you to have much interest in painting."

I mean the remark as a joke, but Bianca's expression twitches.

"Indeed not," she says hastily. "And certainly not anything so garish as well."

She pauses, looking down at her plate with her forehead so furrowed I start to worry she thinks I was actually accusing her of plotting treason. When she speaks again, it's in a softer tone. "I'm glad we know each other so well. To be honest, you're the only person in court I've ever felt I could trust. I can't imagine wanting to give up something so priceless. You can always count on my support, however I can best offer it."

"I know that," I assure her, with a pang through my chest.

How much have I done to support *her*? Surely there's more Bianca would want out of the rest of her life than tagging at my heels? I believe the words she just said to me, but she's also seemed out of sorts these past few weeks.

Perhaps there's more I should do for my friend, as she's

done for me. When I have a break from godlen-driven traitors to focus on that problem too.

After breakfast, the court heads out to the gardens, but I veer up the stairs toward the imperial quarters instead. "I'm going to meditate briefly with my godlen and clear my head," I tell my guards, and ask a page we pass to have the nursemaid bring Coraya to me.

Once I'm in my apartment with my daughter in my arms, though, I don't kneel in supplication. I sink down on my bed as I did the day I told my princes they'd have to leave me, cuddling Coraya close.

Sprite leaps up and tucks her furry body against my thigh. I stroke her back too.

I just need to gather myself so I'm ready to face the coming conversations and jostling of the court. Clear all this chaos from my head, brace my spirits, set the fears and the grief aside.

My breaths glide in and out of my lungs at a slow, even pace, but the ache inside me only expands. How can I say for sure I'm doing any of this right?

What if I never see any of my lovers again? What if my confession doesn't earn the trust of the royal families but brings down doom not just on me but my daughter too?

A cautious voice carries from by the door. "Aurelia?"

I look up to meet Marc's gaze. He takes a couple of steps toward the bed and then halts. Concern shimmers in his eyes.

What do I say to him—this man whose place in my life has changed so much, who honored the men he should have hated, who proved he could accept every part of my relationship with them... and despite all of that, who can't ensure they return any more than I can?

A sob hitches up my throat before I can contain it.

Marc's expression stutters, and then he's striding the rest of the way to me without waiting for further invitation.

As he sits next to me and wraps his arm around my shoulders not so differently from how Bastien hugged me a week ago, I close my eyes against the burn of tears.

When I don't pull away, Marc tightens his embrace. "They'll make it back. I've seen how determined they are to be here for you. I can't believe there's anything they'd let stand in their way."

They could face obstacles they won't have a choice about, but it doesn't do any of us good to dwell on that possibility. And Marc still doesn't know about the greater risk I took that affects not just my lovers but my own security.

It doesn't matter. It was the right decision, the only way I could be sure of convincing the conquered royals of my intentions while it can still matter.

Valerisse stole my chance to gradually ease our world into the future I dreamed of.

I drag in another breath. "I know. I can do this on my own. I just... would rather not. And it's harder to stay focused here when part of me can't help wondering what's happening to them."

Marc brushes a gentle kiss to my temple. "You still handled this morning's incident well. I know you'll win the rest of court over even more when you step back out there today. Those two idiots were never going to be satisfied with you."

He pauses, and his voice gets rougher. "And that's mostly my fault."

"And also your father's and Linus's," I have to say. "But I suppose Saldette and Syrus might have hated me for taking away the chance that their daughters could become empress even without the violent trials."

Marc lets out a strained laugh. "We did drag you into a

lion's den, didn't we? But you keep rising above it. And you're *not* alone. I'm not going anywhere, not as long as I can serve you."

He goes quiet again, his head tipping against mine. I hear him swallow.

Then he says, even lower, "I didn't get to be the one to say it when the moment was official, but I don't mean it any less. I swear before all the gods to love and honor you from now until my last breath leaves me."

My throat constricts. Fresh tears well up, but they're bittersweet now instead of all grief.

I turn my head instinctively, seeking out his lips.

Marc cups my cheek through the kiss, steady but not demanding. When we draw apart, the gleam in his eyes reminds me of the way he looked at me naked while he added just a tiny portion to the pleasure my lovers were stirring in me.

No, not just lovers. By then, they were my husbands too.

Because of him.

A flicker of heat ripples through my limbs alongside my pulse, but I'm not in a state to pursue it. I can't offer him the gold ring he gave me to hold on to that night or repeat back the words that clearly mean so much to him either.

We've come a long way… but I don't know how much farther we'd have to go before I can completely give my heart over.

With his next comment, Marc reminds me of just how far apart we still are in certain ways. "And whatever you said in those letters, I doubt there was anything more you could have done to persuade the outer territories to fulfill their duty to defend the empire."

I have to bite back an ironic laugh. I've kept the details of those plans secret even from him because it's hard to imagine he'd approve of me offering those kingdoms their freedom from the empire—and confirmation of my past crimes to hang me with if I fail to deliver.

"We'll have to wait and see," I say.

Coraya has been dozing, but now she blinks and squirms in my arms with a disgruntled murmur. Marc studies her and reaches out, his hand hesitating for a second before he grazes his fingertips over her hair. "You be good to your mother, future empress."

Hearing the affection in his voice despite the fatherhood he lost provokes a renewed ache around my heart. "She's always good. She just doesn't have many ways of expressing herself." I click my tongue at her and earn a smile.

Marc chuckles. "Look at that face. You can tell she'll be just as clever as you."

I glance up at him and take in his expression as he beams down at her. The ache swells into a more tender sensation.

Maybe I can't return his full devotion, but I can offer him something.

I tilt my head to give him a peck on the cheek. "I consider Raul and Lorenzo her fathers, you know, in every way except the one only Bastien can claim. And you're her father too. You looked after her as well as you could from the moment you found out she was on the way."

Marc's hand stills, his gaze jerking to me. When he manages to speak, his voice has gone raw. "Not every way. I still think about—if I'd stood up to Linus sooner—"

"We don't know where we'd be then. All we have is where we are now. And you've been making something impressive out of that."

Marc gazes at me a moment longer as if awestruck. With a rough sound, he leans in and claims my lips with a more thorough kiss than before.

He only pulls back when Coraya makes a squawk of protest.

Her face starts to scrunch up on the verge of a wail. I laugh and yank at the lacing of my dress. "She's hungry. Just a moment's patience, little one."

Marc keeps his arm around me as I bring Coraya's mouth to my breast. Resolve ripples through his voice. "We'll make sure all her fathers come back, for her sake too. No matter what it takes. Anything I have to do to open up the way, I will."

His last sentence quivers through my mind like that remark of Bianca's did earlier. Perhaps because I've let out some of the anxieties that were gnawing at me, this idea takes deeper root.

My spirits leap. I put my gift to use to find more ways to open myself to the gods' support once. Why shouldn't I do it again—with the godlen who cares most about seeing all families thrive?

Chapter Twenty-Seven

Raul

I sit at the back of the darkened meeting room, reflecting on all the places I'd rather be right now: Tucked close against Aurelia on her bed while she sleeps. More than balls-deep inside her up against the wall. Dancing with her in the ballroom with my hands placed chastely for our audience.

Fuck, even sitting at a table across the dining room from her would be better. Anywhere I could see her, know she's all right, and be ready to leap in if the situation changes.

But this is the best thing I can do for her: sitting here in this stuffy room that smells faintly of the rosemary my mother uses to keep her mind sharp. The letter I have tucked in the inner pocket of my jacket could get my empress much farther than any other assistance I could offer.

How far the conversation I add to that letter will get her remains to be seen.

I take a slow breath the way I can imagine Aurelia would suggest to steady myself. I won't lose my temper. I won't be the idiotic kid my family has seen me as for so long.

I'm here on business that could change the entire shape of the empire and set my kingdom free. That's more than any of them have ever accomplished.

The darkness makes the room feel smaller, but it means I'll be able to hide myself if a random member of staff pokes their head in for whatever reason. I shift on the chair, rubbing my thumb over my new gold ring.

I will return to her—to my *wife*.

The giddiness of that new title sweeps through me, just as the door clicks open.

I brace myself, but within the first second, I can tell the arrivals are exactly who I expected. As my mother slips inside with my brother at her heels and flicks her fingers toward the magic-blessed lantern, I push to my feet.

Mother and Fernam stall in their tracks, the thud of the door shutting behind them emphasizing their silence. My lips twist into a crooked grin as I raise my hand in a jaunty wave of greeting.

I'd like to think they're only surprised because I'm supposed to be nearly half the continent away. I suspect it's also partly that it never occurred to them I'd have listened or remembered well enough to know the covert signal they share with key staff to indicate when a particularly urgent and discreet message needs to be conveyed.

But the signal I left—a tassel tied around the knob of Mother's door—brought them to this room, so it all worked out regardless.

Of course, Her Highness Queen Benvida is not one to allow herself to show she's rattled for long, even among her nearest relatives.

Mother lifts her chin and manages to peer down her nose

at me even though I've got half a foot on her. "My goodness. Raul, what are you doing here without any announcement of your visit? No one told me you'd arrived."

Fernam folds his arms over his chest and shakes his head with a fondly exasperated air I'm much too familiar with. "You didn't offend the empress so badly she sent you on your way, did you?"

My first urge is to glower at the both of them. That's also my second and third urge. Thankfully, I manage to find my way to a fourth option, which is to flatten both my smile and my voice just slightly.

"You didn't hear about my visit because I didn't want anyone knowing. I'm here to convey a message from Her Imperial Highness, for your ears only. Considering the precarious situation you're currently in with an army of traitors on your doorstep, I assume you can understand the need for subterfuge."

Mother blinks at me, a more subtle sign that she's startled. I've managed to surprise her twice in the space of a minute. Wonders upon wonders.

"She sent *you?*" she begins in a tone so puzzled it's definitely insulting, and then recovers herself again with a pat of her pale hair. "Well, I suppose there's a certain sense to that. She might not have wanted to risk any of her most skilled soldiers, and she'd know you'd be more familiar than any with the palace."

Naturally her first assumption would be that I was sent because I'm more expendable.

Before I can respond, she motions to the table. Her voice turns cloyingly gentle—affectionate, but the kind of affection you'd extend to a wobbly toddler. "Why don't you sit back down, and we'll discuss this message of yours? I'm sure you've had a stressful time getting here."

Yes, dodging the soldiers patrolling the highways at the border wasn't a laugh riot. I haven't had a proper bath in days, and my clothes probably smell of the poor horse I pushed to its limits getting up here that fast.

And I'd do it all over again in an instant if it means they'll listen to me.

I do sit, because it's a reasonable suggestion despite her delivery of the suggestion, and retrieve the letter from my jacket. "You'd better read Aurelia's message first. She lays out exactly what she's hoping for, and I can answer any questions you have. I assure you, she means every word of it."

As I set the letter on the table between us, my mother's eyelid tics. It occurs to me after the fact that I was a little too familiar in how I spoke about our empress.

Oh, well. Maybe that'll work toward convincing her that I know Aurelia's mind.

Stay focused, Raul.

Mother slides the letter closer, taking in the imperial crest pressed into the wax seal. She sits down in a chair at the other side of the table and works the envelope open. Fernam sinks into the seat beside her to read as well.

I clasp my hands on the table to stop them from fidgeting. It's almost amusing watching both the queen and the crown prince fight to control their expressions as they absorb Aurelia's promise—and the confession she's offering them as leverage.

Mother opens her mouth and closes it again. I can tell she reads the letter at least twice, as if she thinks it might say something different on the second go. Fernam lets out a bark of a laugh and then schools his face impassive again at Mother's chiding glance.

Mother aims her evaluating stare at me. "She can't be serious."

I splay my hands. "I don't see how she could make herself sound more so. She thought long and hard about how to convince you just how serious she is."

"There must be a trick to it. You're out of your depth here, Raul. There's no circumstances where the empress would agree to divest herself of her own empire. And she's making this supposed offer to the other conquered countries too?"

My teeth grit, but I manage to let the insult slide off my back. "All except Accasy, because she could hardly travel there herself to deliver the message, but she'll do the same for them too. Why is it so hard for you to believe? She started out as one of us, a royal under the empire's thumb. She lived that life for twenty-one times longer than she's been empress."

Fernam speaks slowly as if he thinks I won't understand otherwise. "But she did become empress. By all accounts, she worked very hard to obtain that position. That certainly speaks to a great ambition."

An edge creeps into my voice. "Yes, it does." I catch myself and drag in another lungful of air before continuing in a milder tone. "Her ambition is as it always was to free the rest of us, including her own suffering country, from the empire's claws. She obviously couldn't say so to you explicitly when she was here before, since she didn't have the power to make good on the ambition at the time and her husband would have executed her if he'd caught wind."

Mother clicks her tongue. "That's all easy to say, much harder to prove. If she expects us to throw our citizens into this civil war on her behalf, we'll need more than pretty words."

"She has given you more than words. She's offered up knowledge you could use to turn all of Dariu against her if you revealed it. What more guarantee *could* she give that she'll follow through on her promise?"

Mother's expression softens, and I realize my voice has risen. I'm playing into her impression of me as a hotheaded cretin again.

I tuck my hands under the table so she can't see them if they ball into fists. But instead of clenching them, I trace the line of my wedding band again.

Marc placed this ring on my finger. I can still see him with that small but warm smile as he declared us all Aurelia's husbands alongside her. The prick actually complimented us, welcomed us farther into her life.

He's back there right now, looking after her while the rest of us can't. And… I actually believe he *is* looking after her.

Somehow he's become something other than a prick.

If even the imperial asshole can reform himself in my eyes, surely I can get my family to see me as more than a fuck-up?

When I speak again, the steady tone comes more naturally to me. "I apologize. The urgency of the situation is weighing on me, but of course you need to take your time considering her terms. It is a gamble—neither of us would deny that. But I feel it'd be an even greater gamble to stand back and see what becomes of us if the empire falls into Valerisse's hands. You saw how she handled the rebels last year."

Mother doesn't let any discomfort show on her face, but her grip on the letter tightens just enough to crease the paper. "Obviously I'd prefer not to witness such a slaughter again. I'm simply unconvinced that sending our people to a different slaughter is the answer."

"That's understandable." I hold her gaze, keeping mine as firm as I can. "I realize I sprang this idea on you out of nowhere, and it's a decision that must be considered with all due gravity. But please do take time to consider it. I risked my life coming here because I believe this is the best thing for our kingdom. If you need more reassurance, think on what that would look like so I can tell Aurelia when I return. Is that fair?"

My mother considers *me* for a longer moment than is really comfortable, but I manage not to squirm. "I suppose it is. Although I assume the empress would prefer an answer as soon as possible."

"She wouldn't want to rush you. It isn't her way to force capitulation."

"What will you do in the meantime?"

My lips curve wryly. "I have a few old texts I think the palace librarians will be overjoyed for you to return to them on my behalf. Otherwise… it's best if no one other than you two catches wind that I'm actually here. I could hide in my old bedroom if one of you can contrive to get food to me there. Or I have a safe house I can go back to with arrangements to return in another day or two to discuss the matter further."

Mother hums. "I think we can see that you remain in the palace unstarved. I may very well have further questions once I've given the matter more thought. Let me retire to my chambers to do just that now."

Fernam and I stand as she does. I can't tell whether she's softened at all to the proposal. She sweeps out of the room without another word.

Was this whole journey pointless? Or worse, did we put ammunition in my family's hands that they'll use against Aurelia rather than taking her up on her offer?

Fernam's smile slants. "Well, you've certainly caught her attention." He casts a provoking glance my way. "I'd heard you'd made quite a ladies' man of yourself in the Darium court, but it never occurred to me you'd have weaseled your way into the empress's drawers."

I don't think he actually believes I'm fucking the empress —even though I *am*—but the heckling comment brings my temper surging back. Whatever he thinks of me, he shouldn't talk about Aurelia as if she's a whore.

A sharp retort springs to my tongue. I'm sure my anger shows on my face. But at the same time, the sensation of the silk cloth binding Aurelia's hand to mine whispers over my fingers.

I swallow my rancor.

What are older brothers for if not to heckle? He probably feels off-balance when I've arrived with such a major proposition, and he's trying to reassert himself as the more important prince in the room.

I don't have to let him.

I cock my head to one side and match his tone. "I hope you never let Mother hear that you think women who rule make their decisions based on who they've taken to their beds."

Fernam blinks at me. Then he lets out a fuller laugh. "You know, maybe Her Imperial Highness has had a good influence on *you*. I've never seen you like this before… but it's good. It was about time you grew up."

It's easier to stifle my annoyance when I can't say he's entirely wrong on that point. And when he steps around the table to cuff me fondly on the shoulder.

"Thank you for coming all this way to give us this opportunity," he says. "I know Mother is being cautious about it, but she has to see it could be the best way forward for all of us. And if Empress Aurelia truly offed Tarquin, we owe her a heap of thanks already. I'll do what I can to sway Mother."

It's my turn to stare. Fernam doesn't seem to notice my shock, simply giving me another pat and heading out with a promise to secret some extras from the kitchen to my room. I watch the door swing shut behind him, my throat closing up with an ache that's more sweet than bitter.

I brought him around. If I could accomplish that... then Mother shouldn't be impossible after all.

Chapter Twenty-Eight

Aurelia

By the time the carriage draws to a halt near the Prospirian temple, impatience is gnawing at my gut. This was the closest site dedicated to Prospira I could find that fit the impressions my gift gave me, three hours' trek from the capital.

The farmlands that surround the temple seem the perfect setting for a place of worship dedicated to growth and abundance. Even this early in the season, a few crops are poking up in tidy rows, while other fields have been recently plowed to churn the soil. A rich, loamy scent drifts in the breeze.

The temple sprawls rather than looms, its wooden walls still sprouting leaves. As I approach the entrance, a warbling sound reaches my ears from the river coursing past the back of the building. Thick strands of grass wave along its banks as if beckoning me over.

I head into the temple instead. The cleric hustles over to greet me before I've made it halfway down the entry hall.

He dips his head low. "Your Imperial Highness, we're honored to host you today. Is there anything I or my devouts can help you with?"

I smile at him, suppressing the anxious quiver in my nerves. I've tapped into my gift for this purpose before. Surely Prospira won't turn me away?

"I'm hoping that with some meditation I can determine exactly what would help most," I say.

The cleric motions to a nearby devout dressed in a similar yellow hue. "We can clear out the worship room for you. There are a few petitioners here today, but—"

I hold up my hand to stop him. "I don't want to displace any of my citizens. I hardly need the whole space. But thank you."

My guards follow me into the room at the end of the hall that's somehow both grand and homey. A hearth crackles with a lively fire at one end while beams of sunlight stream with a honeyed glow from the glazed windows above.

The statue of Prospira poised across from the hearth is sculpted from a living tree, the twigs of her hair dappled with budding leaves, her feet merging with the roots before they sink into the floor. As I've often seen, she's depicted pregnant, one hand resting on the swell of her belly with a sheaf of wheat tucked under her arm.

Her other hand is extended as if in offering, balancing a few coins that glint bronze and silver. It's common practice for those hoping to improve their financial situation to leave a small offering and pray to see the wealth come back to them many times over.

A carved rabbit nestles next to one of her legs. Flowers both etched and left as offerings decorate the space on the other side.

A couple and two solo petitioners are kneeling on the yellow cushions spread throughout the room, facing the statue. At my entrance, their gazes flicked toward me. They've frozen with widening eyes.

I don't want to disturb their prayers any more than I can help. Silently, I take a cushion near the wall. My guards form a semi-circle around me, shielding me from view but leaving my line of sight toward the statue of the godlen unobstructed.

Marc's curious gaze lingers on me, but I don't have answers for him yet even if I wanted to share them.

I inhale slowly, tap my fingers down my front, and open myself to both the divine energies of the temple and my gift.

Oh great Prospira, so many people of the empire are struggling to make ends meet rather than enjoying the abundance you would offer. How can I best champion that cause for you? How can I heal this rift that's cut through the realms?

I focus my gift on that last question. As with Estera, I need to convince Prospira of my commitment to following her principles and imbuing my rule with them. The opulence of my current living situation hardly matters if I can't share some of that lavishness with the people who need it most.

An image wavers through my mind: rippling waters coursing in a steady current. I have the impression of coolness lapping at my limbs, of my body buoyed on subtle waves.

My pulse skips a beat. Perhaps the river really *was* beckoning me, or this temple's patron godlen was calling to me through it.

I can only imagine what my guards will make of this development, but if they could tolerate me climbing onto rooftops, they'll have to accept this endeavor too.

Without a word, I slip out of the temple and go to the

carriage. As quickly as I can, I remove my jewelry, my belt with its pouch and knife, and my slippers.

"Your Imperial Highness?" Kassun asks.

I suppose my behavior is bizarre enough that he doesn't feel he needs to put more of the question into words.

"Prospira has shown me how I must make my full appeal to her," I tell him. "You needn't worry. I learned how to swim when I was a little thing splashing around in Accasy's lakes."

"Swim?" he repeats with a note of consternation, but I'm already striding toward the riverbank.

The tall grass hisses against my skirt. If I were being completely practical about this task, I'd strip my gown off too, but I can only imagine how horrified my guards would be by that immodesty.

No, I'm meeting Prospira as empress, so I must maintain some imperial decorum. I'm not afraid that she'll drown me.

Stepping into the water, I have to restrain a wince. Its chill nips at my skin, first up to my knees, then up my thighs to my waist.

By the time I've reached the center of the channel, the river flows around my chest. The cold water steals my breath, but I drag more air into my lungs, turn so my back is to the current, and tip over.

The river catches me, nudging me to the surface so I float as I pictured in my vision. The breeze dancing across my front amplifies the cold, but it's as much exhilarating as uncomfortable now.

I give myself over to the loss of control even as my heart thumps harder. *Lead me where you want me to go, Prospira. Let me witness what you want me to see.*

The current tugs me faster, and water sloshes across my chin. I press my lips tight against it, blinking the moisture away.

A shout I can't make out carries from the bank, where I

think my guards are jogging alongside me. I smile in an attempt to show I'm perfectly all right.

This supplication isn't going to get me anywhere if my protectors jump in to "save" me before I've reached whatever revelation the godlen would lead me to.

With another spurt of water across my face, I close my eyes. The floating sensation consumes me even more fully when my surroundings have given over to darkness.

I drift to one side and then the other. My foot grazes the bank before I whirl away again. The cold seeps right through to my bones.

Sunlight wavers across my eyelids. I open them again to stare up at the vast blue of the sky.

As I gaze toward the heavens, the imagery shifts before my eyes. The smattering of white clouds seem tinged with green. The endless blue streams around and between the tufts, like rivulets between patches of grass…

My breath catches. At the rush of understanding, my body tenses, and I go partly under.

The water sweeps over my head, tossing my hair free from its pins and across my face. Letting it wander wherever it most naturally goes.

Like it should always be.

The recognition of that fact grips me. I tilt my legs down and plant them on the ground. The current gushes around my shoulders, but everything inside me has gone perfectly still.

Yes. I should have seen it without her even showing me. It was just—I encountered the problem so many months ago and haven't returned since—the logistics of making the change…

No matter how complex it is, I have to make it happen. I knew even when I first saw the way Prospira's generosity had been warped that the situation was wrong, and now I have the power to set it right.

I push to the bank, absorbed in the resolve that's come over me. My guards cluster along the edge, Marc and Kassun bending down with arms extended to help me up.

As I reach for them, the wind whips faster across my face, flicking up a few stray hairs along my forehead despite their dampness. An inexplicable tug forms in my throat.

"Wait," I murmur, and turn back toward the center of the river.

The water flows around me—on and on, all across the realms. The wind buffets my skin again, forcing my eyes closed. Streaks of light stream across my eyelids.

A river mouth splitting into five. Separate currents racing away… and rippling back again?

I shake my head, blinking, but the second vision doesn't become any clearer in my head. Was that overture from Prospira at all? The hint of a divine presence that brought it didn't feel like her expansive warmth but something brisker.

Nothing further comes to me. I take Marc's and Kassun's hands and scramble out of the water with a heft of their arms.

As soon as I'm out in the open air, the chill hits me sharper than before. At my shiver, Marc lets out a sound of distress and wrenches off his jacket.

By the time he's wrapped the garment around my shoulders, one of my other guards has hustled over with a blanket she must have grabbed from the carriage. I tuck the folds of fabric close around me and run my fingers over my wild hair.

So much for imperial decorum.

"Did you see anything?" Marc asks, to chiding looks from his fellow guards who must feel he's overstepping with the question.

I answer anyway. "A lot. I'm certain of one thing… I need to speak to the cleric."

The other woman among today's guards tsks her tongue. "Let me…"

She retrieves a few pins from one pocket and hastily arranges my hair away from my face in the simplest of styles. At the lift of my eyebrows, she offers a wry smile. "It never hurts to have a few extras around. They can serve all sorts of purposes."

I can only imagine what sorts of uses a soldier would normally put them to.

A laugh tumbles out of me. "I'm glad for that."

We tramp back to the temple. The cleric and a few of his devouts have come out to watch my progress—and perhaps to wonder at my apparent madness.

As we reach them, I lift my head high and gather myself. So much of this plan might depend on how many allies I can prepare in advance.

I clasp my hands in front of me. "I believe Prospira has called on me to do a great work in her name. Cleric Drusus, how easily can you pass on word to other temples of Prospira —even across the Darium border?"

The cleric betrays only a twitch of surprise before he answers as if nothing all that odd has occurred. "We have temple messengers who can travel quickly enough, and subtle methods of magic that can convey broader signals between our temples, all across the continent. Any task you'd wish to put my fellow clerics to, I'm sure they'd be more than happy to support you and our godlen."

The threads of my conviction ground me like the roots of Prospira's statue. "Good. Then I expect you'll be getting word from me shortly."

CHAPTER TWENTY-NINE

Aurelia

As I approach the imperial strategy room, an unexpected sight meets my eyes. Kassun went off duty about an hour ago—and there he is down the hall, smiling avidly enough to dimple his cheek while the maid he's talking to peers at him through her eyelashes.

Why shouldn't my guards have their flirtations while they're on their own time? The sight hits me with a pang that's both warm and sharp, like an ember glowing a little too hot for comfort.

I'm glad Kassun has someone he'd like to flirt with. I can't help thinking of the men *I'd* usually look at that way, whom I haven't heard from in nearly a week.

All I can do is keep going, laying the groundwork so we're all in a better place when they return.

I motion for Counsel Etta to follow me into the strategy room. She peers at the vast, enchanted table with a nervous purse of her lips. "I'm not sure how much I can weigh in on any military matters, Your Imperial Highness. I believe High Commander Axius has advised you very well there on his own."

"He has." I shoot a smile across the table at the grizzled man who was waiting for us, my frequent companion in this room. "But this task involves more than just military might. I thought I should get your opinion too."

Marc watches avidly from the post he's taken just inside the door. I haven't mentioned the proposal I'm going to make in any detail to him either, though he's watched me digging through the library for records to inform my approach.

If he's going to disapprove, I'd rather find out after we've both heard two of the top imperial advisors' opinions on the subject as well.

I tap the table to bring up the conjured map and draw the area to the northwest closer. "When the coronation tour passed through Cotea, I heard about a longstanding problem afflicting the northern areas of that country. It seems the lowlands there have always tended toward dryness, and the empire has exacerbated that situation."

I sketch my forefinger over the routes I remember from the maps I studied. "Since the defection of the western half of the empire and the establishing of many additional forts along the Seafell Channel, several canals have been constructed. They divert water from the natural rivers and streams and funnel it to pass by the forts."

Axius clears his throat. "By necessity. The soldiers at those forts ensure that the dissention of the western countries never crosses farther into the empire."

I lift my eyebrows. "I was under the impression the forts were mainly there for the launching of new incursions *into* the western territories. The most recent emperors and empresses have spent most of the past century attempting to regain the ground they lost, haven't they?"

Etta pipes up. "They have—but it is partly a defensive function, I'm sure. If we didn't stay on the alert and show our power, there's no telling what they might do."

I shift my skeptical gaze to her. "Have Icar, Silana, or Bryfeen *ever* launched an attack on our side of the channel?" I can't remember hearing of any overt hostilities from the western countries closest to our border.

"There was that strange business several years ago near the Silanian city of Rexoran," Axius says gruffly. "The nearest fort got word that the king wished to treat with Emperor Tarquin in exchange for military support, but when our soldiers crossed the channel, they were ambushed."

Another incident I came across in my research. "The Silanians made no attempts to cross the channel to our side then either, from what I understand. And didn't it become clear that the note had been forged? The Silanian king was assassinated shortly afterward."

Etta's voice lowers. "We were never able to work out exactly what the circumstances of the request were. There's been all that unnerving business over there with the resurgence of scourge sorcerers and riven magic…"

"Nonetheless, there've been no aggressive actions taken against the empire's existing territory. That's true, isn't it?"

I fix Etta and then Axius with a firm look until the latter inclines his head in agreement. He grimaces. "It's generally been thought—to regain the rest of the continent, for the benefit of the empire—it's not a legacy easily abandoned."

I soften my tone in turn. "Of course not. But after more than a hundred years, I fear our efforts there have not served the empire *well*. How many soldiers have died without any ground regained?"

Axius opens his mouth to protest, but I hold up my hand

to stop him. "In any case, I'm not suggesting that we evacuate the border. Only that perhaps, at least until we see the outcome of this potential war, we greatly reduce the number of forts still active and the number of soldiers stationed in each. And that would allow us to stop up the canals, letting the waters resume their natural course as much as possible."

Etta knits her brow. "Are Cotea's problems really what we should best concern ourselves with now? With all due respect, Your Imperial Highness."

The corner of my mouth twitches upward at her belated caveat. "I'd like to return the natural waters to the plains of Cotea as a gift in honor of Prospira. Inganne has lent me her support after I honored her. I'd like all the godlen to recognize my position as empress. Perhaps if Tribune Valerisse realizes she has only one out of the nine on her side and the others approve of me, she'll give up this madness before it turns to war."

"Ah," Etta says, a glimmer lighting in her eyes. "That would be the best possible scenario."

Axius's expression turns thoughtful. He rubs his jaw. "I can see how the godlen of abundance would approve of sharing the resources more widely. And I suppose now would be the easiest time to call in a large portion of those soldiers. Those who've remained at their assigned posts, following their imperial orders, will be those most inclined to follow new orders you give them. If we should need to resupply those forts…"

Marc gives a quiet cough. "I believe a technique was investigated, before the canals—"

The high commander cuts off the supposed guard with a sharp glance. "You've never been stationed outside the palace. I hardly think you should be weighing in."

He returns his attention to me. "By the end of the day,

I'll put together a plan for seeing your intentions through. Unless Counsel Etta has additional objections."

She shakes her head. "I can see our priorities must be maintaining the territory we still have—and the peace and order we've built here. I only—old habits die hard."

"They do. Now, in case appealing to the gods *doesn't* dissuade Valerisse, I'd better go over the latest reports from our spies within her ranks and how we might make use of the information."

Etta's face tightens. I don't think she has much stomach for war.

I aim a wry smile at her. "Thank you for your input on the situation in Cotea. You can take your leave now if you'd like, unless you have thoughts on the military strategy after all."

She laughs with obvious relief. "No, I can certainly leave that subject to the high commander."

Marc opens the door for her to duck out of the room. His eyes meet mine briefly, dark and intense—but I can't say any more so than usual.

I suppose I'll find out how he feels about my plan when we're alone.

Axius pays the supposed guard no mind. He tugs at the illusion on the table to focus the map on Lavira. "I think the reports we got yesterday and today are promising. The influx of new supporters has slowed."

My smile twists. "That could mean Valerisse will decide it's time to move on us soon."

"Yes—but those who haven't gone over to her are on your side. We need regular men and women as well as the gods." He tilts his head. "The spies have observed that not all the conversation they've heard has been completely supportive of Valerisse. I've been thinking about the tactics we've seen used against you here—attempts to stir up ill-feeling about your rule. The attacks with the insults spoken against you, the imposing divine omens…"

"You want me to ask Elox to project threatening signs over Valerisse's army?"

Axius chuckles. "That isn't really his typical approach, is it? No, I wondered if there's a way we might spread more doubt and dissent within her own ranks. Other than the contingent who served directly under her, the loyalty of those soldiers will be shaky. They *are* going against their imperial oaths."

I mull the idea over. "How would we accomplish that? Surely anyone who spoke out against her openly would be cut down. I'm not sending our people up there to die just to shout a few accusations."

"True. But if we could come up with a subtle means… It's something I thought we should discuss."

Marc stirs at his post. "I'd imagine, if there were soldiers with ideal—"

Axius scowls at him, clearly annoyed by the second interruption. "Know your place, man. You've done a lot of good for Her Imperial Highness, but that doesn't give you the station to impose on her conversations. I've been running this army for decades longer than you've even been in it."

Marc's jaw clenches, but this time he doesn't back down. "I simply wanted to suggest—I thought I heard it mentioned that there might—"

"Enough," Axius snaps. "We're going to discuss the possibilities based on facts, not second- or third-hand information you overheard."

My hackles have risen on Marc's behalf. Can't Axius just let him speak?

Maybe I wouldn't feel this way if it were any other soldier. I suppose it is overstepping rather a lot for a new guard to be inserting himself into a discussion between the empress and her highest military advisor. But I know that this particular "guard" has far more experience and understanding than Axius realizes.

I grope for a diplomatic approach. "Your authority is undeniable, high commander. But I'd like to hear what my guard has to say, in case it sparks some new idea. Outside perspectives are often useful that way."

Axius's expression stays grim, but he isn't going to deny the request from me. He waves brusquely at Marc. "Go on, then."

Marc starts again in an unusually cautious tone. "I thought perhaps there might have been soldiers with gifts that would be useful for subtle methods of undermining… It might be something considered in the past, even if not implemented yet."

Axius's scowl deepens. "I don't see any inspiration in that, only a lot of vague imaginings. Of course we'll consider the gifts of the soldiers. If that's all you have to say, we'll get back to our discussion."

Marc looks as if he's bit his tongue. His gaze darts to me for just a second, and abruptly I understand.

He isn't just speculating. He *knows* something that either Axius doesn't or has forgotten—but it's something no ordinary guard could possibly be aware of. He can't say more without raising an awful lot of questions he knows I wouldn't want asked.

It mustn't be something he feels he could simply tell me and let me appear to discover it on my own, or he wouldn't have spoken up in front of Axius at all.

The huge secret he's carried on his shoulders for weeks is holding him back… from *helping* me. From serving me and his empire as well as he's able.

That doesn't seem right.

Axius is watching me, waiting for my agreement to

continue the conversation. How much farther could we get with it—with all our strategy sessions—if the man who once led the army alongside Axius could speak freely?

My heart thuds faster, but all at once my fears seem absurd. Axius wants to save the empire just as much as I do. He wouldn't use the basic fact of it to destabilize my rule. As long as the information isn't presented in an incriminating way…

And does any part of me believe now that Marc would act to hurt me?

The answer comes without hesitation, without thinking.

No, I don't. I might not be completely sure how I feel about *him*, now or at some future point, but I'm absolutely certain of his loyalty to *me*.

And perhaps that's exactly why there's only one sensible thing to do.

I look at Marc again, my voice steady despite the racing of my pulse. "Just tell him. He can handle it."

Marc's eyes widen. "Aur—Your Imperial Highness?"

"It'll make everything easier."

He just stares at me, his stance gone rigid.

I restrain a huff of frustration and turn to Axius. "Doesn't anything about him feel familiar to you?"

Axius is staring at me too, a furrow digging deeper into his forehead with every passing second. Gods, at this rate he's going to think I've gone insane. Does Marc really believe that's—

"Your Imperial Highness," Axius begins slowly.

Marc pushes forward, striding to the edge of the table a few feet away from me. He speaks swiftly but firmly. "Fourteen years ago, you and Emperor Tarquin discussed the possibilities of undermining rule across the border using illusionists. The project ended up abandoned, but only after you'd pulled together a team of soldiers with appropriate gifts and given them some additional training in subterfuge."

Axius's stare jerks to my husband. At first, he can only gape. "You—how would *you* know that? No one knew. You couldn't have been more than a child."

"I was thirteen years old," Marc says quietly, "and my father felt that was old enough to be a part of most of his strategy discussions for when I took over the throne. I was the *only* other person ever in the room when the two of you discussed it. Even the soldiers involved were never told what they were being assembled and trained for."

Axius's throat works. Most of the color has drained from his face beneath the graying beard.

His voice comes out in a croak. "Marclinus? But I—You —I saw—"

One side of Marc's mouth kicks upward at a wry angle. "You saw my corpse. That was… a rather complicated situation. Suffice to say I *did* die, and I'm now only Marc. I'm not sure it does anyone any good getting into the specifics. All that matters is Aurelia has earned her place leading this country, and I'm no longer in a position to do so, so I intend to support her every way I can. I hope you can accept that and do the same."

"Well, I—" Axius's eyes twitch to me and then back to Marc. "Of course. I shouldn't have forgotten that squadron we worked with… It was so brief a time, and with them never going into action for that purpose—it would serve us well for this. I'd imagine most of them are still around. I marked it discreetly in their records as Emperor Tarquin requested. We could train in more, but I'm not sure there's the time. It'll be faster to refresh their memory."

It seems like a reasonable time for me to rejoin the conversation. "Yes, that sounds wise. Perhaps along with reflecting on our approach to the Cotean canals, you could take today to identify where those soldiers have ended up and how many you can get orders to quickly?"

He dips his head even lower than usual, perhaps to acknowledge both our authority. "Absolutely, Your Imperial Highness. Er, and Your—"

"I don't have a title anymore, Axius," Marc interjects. "It's all right. You'll get used to it. My wife has adapted admirably."

The high commander still looks stunned, but he takes this latest bit of information in stride. "I'll get right on both of those tasks, then."

As he comes around the table, I turn to follow his progress. "High Commander—we feel it's best for the security of the empire that Marc keeps his full identity secret. I'm sure you can imagine the difficulty of believing it for those who knew him less well and how much chaos it would cause…"

Axius nods. His gaze slides to the former emperor with undisguised awe. "As you both see fit."

"She remains your ruler and the highest authority of the empire," Marc says evenly.

"Yes." The high commander swipes his hand across his face. Then he lowers himself into a full bow—directed at me, not my husband. "You can count on me as ever, Your Imperial Highness."

He hurries out.

As the door thumps shut behind him, Marc sags forward. He plants his hands on the edge of the table, his head drooping, his back curved.

My heart lurches. I dart to his side, but as I set my hand on his shoulder, I catch the brightness of his smile.

"You have no idea," he says hoarsely. "Having to pretend for so long—being looked at like a stranger— I swear, I won't let this undermine *your* position the slightest bit. But I feel as if I can fully breathe for the first time in…"

Marc straightens and spins toward me to frame my face with his hands, ever so tenderly. "Thank you. I never would have asked—but I didn't have to. Thank you."

He kisses me so soundly my head spins with the rush of desire. I clutch the front of his shirt as if I can ride out the wave, but even when he eases back, the sense of need keeps thrumming through my pulse.

I gaze up at the man who's been reborn out of the embers of his old self, and I can't come up with one reason not to welcome this hunger.

The words come out unexpectedly husky. "Do you know what I want most right now?"

A matching desire flares in Marc's eyes. "What's that, wife?"

"Why don't you take your turn and conquer me?"

Chapter Thirty

Aurelia

In the wake of my suggestion, the smolder in Marc's gaze sears hotter. His hands linger by the sides of my face.

His voice drops even lower than mine did. "What sort of a conquering did you have in mind?"

I wet my lips instinctively, feeling him track the movement like a touch across the sensitive skin. "I don't believe we've ever fully consummated this marriage, husband."

Marc sounds as if he's tried to stifle a groan. His mouth descends on mine again, the heat of the kiss washing away every other concern.

His hands drop to my hips. In one smooth motion that proves just how much strength his well-built body holds, he lifts me onto the edge of the map table.

As he presses closer against me, my head spins with

desire. I wrap one arm behind his neck and kiss him even harder. An embarrassing whine of need is building in the base of my throat, driven by the first traces of friction at my core.

I manage not to cry out in protest when Marc pulls back, but it's a near thing. He gazes at me, his face flushed and his eyes glittering, like I'm an astonishing treasure he's just uncovered.

His voice comes out with even more of a rasp than usual. "Gods know I'd like to take you right here on this table, but I don't trust that no one will come through the door. And I'd like our first proper time together to be more than a hasty rutting."

The promise in that statement sends a tingle all the way to my toes.

I manage to gather my composure. "Then I'd better retire to my chambers."

Even though he was the one to pause our encounter, Marc releases me with obvious reluctance. I take a few steadying breaths, willing the flush from my own cheeks, and stride to the door with him stalking a careful distance behind me.

In the hall, my full host of guards shifts into a semi-circle around me. They've been following me even more closely since the missing vicerine and marchion proved that even the nobles of my court might become my enemies.

I say nothing until I've reached my apartment. At the door, I give the assembled soldiers a grateful smile. "I need to contemplate our next steps. Please see that no one disturbs me until I tell you otherwise."

The guards offer brisk nods of agreement. After Marc has stepped in to take his usual post inside the room, the door shuts with a heavier click as I slide the lock over.

No one should be able to enter these chambers without my permission.

Marc is already reaching for me. He traces his fingers down my sides to my waist and walks me backward to the bed. "I want to see all of you. I'm going to admire every inch of this terrain I'm conquering."

A giddy laugh tumbles out of me, but a pang of tension squeezes my heart at the same time. He's admired me before, but never for long—not with a totally clear head.

As he reaches for the ties on my gown, I stop him. "We should start by removing this."

I slide off the gold-and-sapphire ring that's aided me in so many of my plans and set it apart from us on the bedside table.

Marc watches, his gray eyes darkening. He might not know exactly how I've used my ring, but he already guessed that I've been able to affect people with it somehow. I'd imagine he can deduce that it factored into my manipulations of our past intimacies as well.

But it'll have no part in our interlude this afternoon. Everything we both experience will be completely real.

I return to him, and he works at my dress with small caresses of my back and sides. As the bodice loosens and gapes, he can't seem to resist leaning in to brand the crook of my neck with his mouth. But then he eases back, nudging the fabric down to pool at my feet.

I lift my arms so he can strip my chemise off me too. He tugs my drawers down to join my dress.

His gaze rakes over my naked form, drinking in every inch of me as he promised. My skin may not be as smooth as it was before my pregnancy and my belly may not have lost all of its extra curve, but if anything, my husband looks more awed by my body than he did when he first saw me this way a year ago.

I let him get his fill before grasping the collar of his uniform. "Do I get to share in the admiring?"

The corner of Marc's mouth quirks upward. "I would never deny you, wife."

Together, we unbutton the shirt. Marc tosses it aside, the muscles across his shoulders and chest rippling.

The smooth gray discoloration that covers so much of his face seeps down his neck but peters out by his collarbone. It seems anyplace his skin was covered by his clothing, the combination of Bastien's and Raul's magic didn't imprint on it.

I trace my fingertips along the edge of the scar and up across his cheek. With a rough sound, Marc bends to kiss me again. Then he hefts me up as he did by the table and carries me onto the bed.

He lays me out on top of the covers, my head nestled on a pillow, and kneels between my knees. For all I'm spread out before him, his gaze doesn't leave mine.

"That one time," he says. "In Lavira. I didn't imagine any of *that*, did I? I never fell asleep."

The memory of how much pleasure he managed to stoke in my body even when I didn't want to feel it floods me with heat.

"That was all real," I confirm.

A full smile lights his face. "Then I'll start with what I already know you'll enjoy."

He doesn't torment me with the lead-up this time, perhaps as impatient to revel in the pleasure of this act as I am. After a few strokes of his hands up and down my thighs, he crouches down and laps his tongue over my sex.

That's all it takes for bliss to jolt through my torso. I bite my lip against a whimper. My bedroom door is solid enough to prevent most sound from traveling through, but I don't want to take the chance of getting too loud.

Marc hums approvingly and leans closer. He braces his arms on either side of my hips in the most intimate of embraces and buries his face between my thighs.

His tongue strums over my clit and delves between my folds. His lips work over every place I'm neediest with pulse after pulse of rising pleasure.

I can't hold back a moan, as much as I try to muffle it. My hips rock of their own accord, urging him on.

Marc doesn't bother to come up for air. He devours me as if I'm a meal he'll never get enough of, sucking and licking and pumping his tongue inside me.

I clutch his hair, the rising waves of bliss shocking gasp after gasp from my mouth. He swirls his tongue across my clit, and I come apart in a crash of ecstasy.

Marc replaces his tongue with his thumb, continuing to stroke that sensitive nub until I've sagged into the bed with my release. He grins. "I can't imagine a sight I enjoy more than watching you unravel with pleasure. I think I need to enjoy it at least a couple more times today."

I let out a breathless laugh. "I don't see any reason to argue."

He chuckles in return and kisses my inner thighs on both sides before making his way up my torso. His lips chart a path across my hips and belly before lingering on my breasts.

"I've never given these the worshipping they deserve, have I?" he murmurs, and laps one tip into his mouth. As he teases that nipple with his tongue, he trails a thumb over the other.

Heavy quivers shoot through my flesh. I whimper and squirm beneath my husband, a knot of need returning to my core despite my recent release. My hands trace over the muscles of his shoulders and down his back until he lets out a groan.

He lifts his head and surges up so our mouths can collide

again. As he kisses me, he fondles one breast and then the other as if he means to provoke every spark of pleasure he can from their slopes.

His groin brushes my sex through his slacks, and a desperate mewling escapes me. Our lips break apart; I grasp at his pants between us. "I've been waiting more than a year to be able to welcome you properly. Let's not delay it any longer."

Marc's next laugh comes with a brief hitch. "And I've been waiting more than a year to properly understand what it should mean to be your husband. I'll satisfy you every way you need, wife. And not just in this bed."

The promise brings a lump to my throat. He's already made good on it in so many ways.

The last lingering doubts I've held on to crumble away.

As he fumbles with the fastenings on his slacks, I touch the scarred side of his face. Marc pauses to glance up at me.

The words catch for a second before they spill out, propelled by the swell of emotion inside me. "I love you."

They come out so quietly that at first I'm afraid he didn't hear me. He stares at me, his expression blank.

Then the most brilliant smile I've ever seen from him stretches across his face. He draws my face to his and claims my mouth, long and lingering, until every part of me is trembling with anticipation.

When our lips part, his head stays bowed over mine, our foreheads brushing. "Then I've done one thing right with my life, no matter where else it leads me."

He kicks his slacks the rest of the way off. I open myself wider with a gasp as he slides his cock over my folds.

As Marc lines himself up, he holds my gaze, one elbow propping him over me, the other resting on my thigh. I raise my knees instinctively.

He presses in with a catch of his breath and a dip of his

eyelids, but his eyes stay locked with mine. He slides into me torturously slow, drawing out the sensation until all my nerves are tingling.

When I'm full of him, Marc stops as if he's absorbing every sensation of the moment. Gazing up at him, I'm hit by a smack of emotion—the knowledge that I resisted this act for so long, that I never believed I could possibly want it, and yet here I am.

Somehow the husband I reviled has become an irreplaceable part of my life. To go forward without him feels as wrong as losing any of my princes.

Something must change in my expression. The haze of pleasure on Marc's face fades with a frown. "Are you all right? If you don't—"

I grasp his arm before he can retreat and beam up at him. "No. I want this. So much. I was only thinking about how far we've come."

He catches my lips again with the tenderest of kisses. Just when I think I might die from waiting, he starts to move.

He eases back and plunges deeper, again and again, bringing a fresh surge of bliss each time. Delight radiates across my skin and breaks my breath into panting.

My thighs press around his hips. My arms loop around his shoulders, locking him with me. Our lips part and collide, more kisses smattering across cheeks and jaw and neck, wilder with every passing minute.

I'm already primed after my first orgasm. It only takes a few more slams of his cock against the giddying spot inside me before another wave of ecstasy wracks my body.

I muffle my cry against Marc's shoulder. He keeps pumping into me, urging the wave onward.

Then, as I start to come down, he flips us over so I'm lying atop him.

When I blink down at him, his grin returns. "I've found I

have a taste for being conquered too. Why don't you ride me like you did Bastien so well last week, my empress?"

I don't know what sends more of a thrill through me—his request or the fact that he can refer to my intimacy with one of my other husbands so fondly.

I shift my weight over him, adjusting his angle inside me, and the groan that tumbles out of him inflames me even more. I'm so sated, but I have even more capacity for pleasure I haven't unearthed.

Bracing my knees on either side of him and my hands on his sculpted chest, I rock up and down. It takes a minute to find the right pace, to hit all the spots that set off the hottest sparks inside me.

Marc reaches up to fondle my breasts again, adding more spikes of delight to the mix. When I start to buck faster over him, his eyes roll back.

"Fuck. I don't know how I ever thought I had you before. This is everything."

All I can manage in response is a wordless murmur of agreement.

Marc's breath turns ragged, but he trails his hand down my body. "You need to come with me."

He strokes his fingers over my clit, and I bite my lip against a sob of pleasure. The jolt sets me bobbing even faster, taking him as deep as I can bring him.

My fingernails dig into his chest. My head falls back. And just as Marc's control breaks with another groan, I hit a new peak.

A spurt of heat fills me as my whole body sings with the heights of bliss. Quaking with the sensation, I sag into Marc's arms.

He clutches me tight against him, the two of us still entwined as closely as any people can be. Alongside the heady rush and the affection filling me, a thread of relief ripples through my chest.

We have come an awfully long way, much farther than I could have imagined a year ago. I couldn't be more grateful for that.

But how much farther do we need to go before this fragile peace we've founded is truly safe?

CHAPTER THIRTY-ONE

Lorenzo

Mother reads the letter again, a small smile playing with her lips. I'd be happier that *she* seems happy if her mood hadn't shifted the moment I made my presence known to her at the palace, before she even knew why I'd come.

I expected concern and questions about whether I'd really thought this quest through. Insinuations that Aurelia has manipulated my emotions. Instead, the queen simply seems pleased to have me here.

When has she *ever* been really pleased with me since the sacrifice I made that took my voice with it?

"Well," she says now, setting the letter on the small table. "That's certainly something worth keeping in our back pocket."

She doesn't think it's worth acting on right away? Did she understand what Aurelia's asking? I'd have thought she'd have been the most prepared out of all the royal families after the vague but emphatic message I sent earlier.

I scratch my pencil across one of the papers from the stack next to me. The brazier that fills the high tower room with its thin heat crackles, waiting to consume my words once my mother has read them.

If Rione is going to offer our aid, it needs to be soon. It's unlikely to be long before war breaks out.

Mother considers the note and flicks her fingers to consign it to the flames. "We needn't worry ourselves with that. There are much more straightforward ways of gaining our freedom that don't rely on an empress's promise."

My stomach twists as if it's been snagged in seaweed. I scrawl out more hasty words on a fresh paper. *What are you talking about? She'll follow through—she's given you the means to guarantee it. Tribune Valerisse isn't going to offer any promises at all.*

"Oh, I'm not interested in hearing from the tribune either." Mother sits back in her chair, her gaze sliding away from me across the white-washed walls, and I wonder abruptly why it's just her and me in this meeting.

When she first ushered me up the tower stairs, I assumed she wanted to hear the message I'd come to deliver right away, that there wasn't time to gather my father or sister from whatever was occupying them. But I'm getting the impression that Aurelia's letter hasn't made all that much difference after all.

Mother's had something in mind since before I arrived. My appearance may have propelled her onward faster, but on a route she was already following.

Is it a route she doesn't think her husband or her heir would fully approve of?

I press my pencil more firmly against the next paper. *What are you planning?*

What could possibly be a better option for our people than the freedom Aurelia is offering? We're in a far better position than the other conquered countries—we might send a host of soldiers only to find the battle is won before they reach it and risk their lives. Our distance, across the sea strait from the rest of the continent, has always afforded us a little extra security from trouble on the mainland.

Mother sets her elbows on the table and rests her chin on her folded hands. A trace of the sadness I'm more familiar with crosses her dark face. "You don't need to worry about that. I'm just glad she sent you back to us, whatever her reasons. Now I have no reason to hesitate—the empire can't use you to punish us."

The strands of tension squeeze tighter around my gut. Is this what actual drowning feels like?

She's always trying to protect me, as if I'm not caught in the middle of this whirlwind of politics whether either of us likes it or not. As if I haven't been handling myself through it for the sixteen years since I was wrenched from my home— years that recently included the overturning of not one but two emperors.

I know the situation in Dariu far better than anyone here, I write. *If you're going to take action against them, you should let me weigh in.*

The queen's gaze softens even more. "Oh, Lorenzo. I think you've given enough for our family already. We'll set you up in your old rooms, make sure you have every comfort I'd imagine they denied you in that wretched palace."

She tosses my last paper into the brazier for me and stands. It's a dismissal—she thinks the important part of this conversation is over.

She thinks I'm never going back to Dariu.

I stare up at her, my hands balling, and a jolt of certainty crackles right through the center of me.

I already knew how far I might have to go to convince her of Aurelia's message. I just didn't realize it'd be because she had pre-existing plans that could lead to an even greater catastrophe.

In my own cunning ways, I've stood up to soldiers and emperors. I helped put the woman I love on the throne. I'm a gods-damned force to be reckoned with.

Hiding that from my family now looks to be much more dangerous than revealing myself.

I push to my feet too, drawing myself up so I'm slightly taller than her, my stance steady. And I project the illusion of my voice straight into her head.

"We're not finished here. You need to tell me exactly what you mean to do."

Mother freezes other than the drop of her jaw. She stares at me in silence for several thuds of my suddenly racing pulse. "Lorenzo. You…"

I keep my mouth firmly shut so there's no doubt about my voice being gift-driven. *"I have a lot more of a gift than I've let on. There are plenty of things about me that you don't know. Because I've been playing this game of politics for years right in the thick of it, and I couldn't risk jeopardizing everything I was working toward by letting my secret get out. But it sounds like you might be about to jeopardize it all right now anyway."*

"I— You—" Understanding dawns in her eyes, and her posture relaxes slightly. "You *are* dedicated to Inganne. It's all illusion. Just more than music."

I nod. *"It's anything I need to conjure. I did sacrifice an awful lot. It was a little too easy to convince everyone I was enough of an idiot to swap my voice for nothing more than extra artistic talent."*

Her mouth tenses against a wince, but then her expression brightens more. "Then it's even more wonderful that you've come back to us. There'll be so many ways you can help—"

And there it is. She's already jumping straight to how she can use me for her own ends.

I cut her off, letting my illusionary voice flatten. *"Help you with* what? *What are you planning?"*

A fierce smile curves my mother's lips, one I don't like at all.

Determination rings through her voice. "We have the perfect opportunity, Lorenzo. You haven't been here to see it. First, a handful of the imperial soldiers vanished after word of the tribune's declaration reached us. Then so many more were summoned to bolster the reserves around Vivencia. The governor and his ranking officers have tried to cover up the loss, but we estimate there are no more than a quarter of their usual numbers left."

My stomach bottoms out. I can already see where she's going with this line of thinking.

Aurelia—and Marc and Axius, advising her—must have assumed that as long as they kept some military presence in Rione, my people were too down-beaten after the last uprising less than a decade ago to attempt another. No doubt the high commander hoped to end the threat of civil war quickly and return regular forces to our island country.

None of them, not even Aurelia, could fully understand just how much fury our queen has been hiding behind her royal composure. Not even Aurelia knows what it's like to see hundreds of your citizens strung up around the city like hogs in a butcher shop.

Mother knows she may never get another chance like this again. Of course she'd jump on her first opportunity.

Except she didn't quite. She hesitated until my arrival… it sounds like, because she was worried what would happen to me if she rebelled while I was in Darium custody.

A lump rises in my throat, but her consideration of my safety doesn't make a difference now. She thinks that with me here, she can rush ahead without any dire consequences.

"You're going to order our soldiers to turn on the remaining forces and slaughter them," I guess. *"And hope that Dariu is too busy fighting with itself to intervene until it's too late."*

A sharp laugh leaves my mother's mouth. "They will be. We've been marshalling forces, and they haven't had enough presence here to notice a thing. I have men ready with a message that'll send the governor hustling off to the other side of the country, and the moment he's gone, we can sweep them all out of Santia and the rest of the island. Once we've cleared our territory, we can defend the strait so they never get another foothold."

It's a clever plan. It would probably work.

And it might ruin the chances of us ever being at peace with Dariu rather than in a constant state of potential war. It would *definitely* ruin Aurelia's chances of handing back true sovereignty to my foster brothers' kingdoms.

The people of Dariu will never accept the ceding of other territories right after they've been violently thrown out of one. Aurelia would look weak rather than wise.

My mouth twists. *"Don't you see that the empress is offering us something better than that? We could rule Rione again as allies with Dariu, without needing to defend the strait or see more of our people die in attempts to reconquer us."*

Mother waves her hand dismissively. "One is a sure thing. The other—Empress Aurelia has her own goals. I'm not going to let my people down by giving up this one opportunity for another that may never materialize."

I resist the urge to smack my hand against the table for emphasis. *"You're letting them down by turning against the only imperial ruler who's actually cared about us."*

That sad look crosses Mother's face again. "You really

believe that, don't you? If you'd been through as much as I have—do you have any idea what she'd have done with you if she'd discovered your true gift?"

A stunted laugh hitches out of me. I meet my mother's gaze with a smile nearly as sharp as hers. *"Mother, I told Aurelia a year ago. I helped remove Marclinus and put her on that throne. She's had a thousand chances to exploit me, but she's only ever worked toward getting to where she is now—where she can set the empire free."*

The queen goes still with her lips parted. "You told her before *me?*"

I motion at her much as she waved my concerns off moments ago. *"Because as soon as you found out, you bowled over anything I have to say to use me for your own ends. No, I haven't lived as long as you have—but I've lived in the Darium court for sixteen years longer than you've spent there. I know those people. I know Aurelia. For once, can you believe that I might be seeing more than you can, not less?"*

Through the space of one breath and another, we simply stare at each other. Mother's jaw tightens. Is she going to dismiss me all the same, stalk out of here and set her violent plans in motion no matter what I say?

I have to keep trying. *"Aurelia hates the empire just as much as you do. She's who you were when you were my age, seeing the injustices dealt against her country and aching that she couldn't do anything to stop them—except she found a way. And she's taken that way, no matter how much it's cost her."*

"I don't see that it's cost her all that much," Mother says tartly. "She's sitting on the highest throne in the continent."

My teeth set on edge. *"If you could just talk to her, properly…"*

A glimmer of inspiration lights in my head.

Maybe she can. Not by trekking across the strait and half

of Dariu to meet Aurelia in Vivencia, but there is another option, isn't there, if what Mother said is correct?

"You can," I go on. *"Put that first part of your plan in motion. Get the governor out of his house. He has a messaging mirror linked back to the imperial palace there, doesn't he? We reach out to her, and you see what she says… And if you still don't like it, you can send us to war against her rather than for her."*

Mother hesitates only a moment longer. "I would have started this way regardless. And there are… clearly some things I didn't know. I can admit that. Let us see. Although you realize that breaking into the governor's castle is a declaration of war right there?"

A warmer smile touches my lips at the growing acceptance in her voice. Maybe I can set this mess right after all.

"My gift can get us in without anyone being the wiser. Send him off, and I'll take care of the rest."

Chapter Thirty-Two

Aurelia

Governor Bodum shifts on his feet, looking as if he's restraining a frown. "Your Imperial Highness, you want me to… order the soldiers to take up shovels and fill in the canals?"

It's unsettling facing the man through a pane of glass. The full-length mirror hung on the wall is enchanted to project my image across the continent to the mirror hanging in the Cotean governor's residence and his to me, but we're still hundreds of miles apart in reality.

Still, I'm grateful that I can take in his body language and tone rather than relying on written messages.

"The soldiers can simply oversee the process," I say. "Unless they wish to join in. I believe you should have enough imperial funds in your coffers to hire Cotean workers who can handle the majority of the effort. I simply need you to ensure it's done with care, as Prospira would wish for the good of the land. We've let it suffer for too long—all imperial territories should thrive in her honor."

Appealing to the godlen and the authority of the empire seems to ease Bodum's initial hesitation. "Yes, of course. The forts may struggle with water supply once they return to their usual staffing, though."

I'm ready to address that concern. "I don't want any of my loyal subjects to go without. I've gathered that there's equipment for filtering the water from the Seafell Channel in place at the older forts. I'm already sending out skilled devouts to see that it can still work properly and to equip the newer forts. Then everyone will have the water they need."

Including the Coteans who've suffered from Dariu's selfishness for so long. Gods forbid our soldiers needed to drink water that wasn't quite as pleasant to allow the locals' farms to grow crops.

"Our great empire faces a great threat from within," I add in my best imperious tone. "I don't wish to see anyone under my rule feeling their interests will be served better by one who intends to destroy proper imperial order. It's best for Dariu if all our subjects and all our godlen know the empress has not forgotten them."

Governor Bodum certainly doesn't want to suggest we should encourage Coteans to side with the traitors. He dips his head. "Absolutely, Your Imperial Highness."

Off at the side of my vision, Marc raises his eyebrow. I recall the advice he gave me before this meeting and restrain a sigh. If it works, then it works.

I aim a benevolent smile at the governor. "Your own work managing Cotea shouldn't go unrewarded. Once this project is finished, I hope you'll visit the palace for a special commendation."

Bodum brightens, just as Marc thought he would. "I'd be most grateful. Thank you. I'll see that your directive is carried out as quickly and effectively as possible."

He will now that he knows he's getting something more out of it too. Well, it isn't as if I wasn't aware of Darium greed.

And bringing the governor back to the palace will make it easier to remove him from Cotea entirely when the time comes, not that I'm going to mention that part of my mission yet.

I make the gesture to deactivate the mirror's enchantment, and the gleaming surface wavers to show only my reflection. Stepping back from it, I rub my forehead and glance over at Axius. "I'll be alerted if we get new communications via any of the governors' mirrors?"

Until yesterday, I had no idea this small, windowless room even existed, branching off from the emperor's office. Axius retrieved me from a brief interlude playing with my daughter to let me know I needed to speak with Queen Anahi of Rione right away.

However Lorenzo contrived to get her to the connecting mirror in the Rionian governor's residence and willing to negotiate with me, I couldn't have asked for a better opportunity. After I'd shooed Axius and my guards out of the room, I confirmed my commitment to seeing her regain proper rule over her country, and I think… she might have believed me.

In any case, she tentatively agreed to an alliance. She'll prepare the local army to cross the strait and join my forces by the palace, and she'll know it's time to send them when I call to the governor to let them pass.

I don't want to play that hand too quickly—as soon as they move, Valerisse will know I'm making deeper alliances and crack down on the conquered countries closer to her that much harder.

In answer to my question, Axius nods. "I have a token I carry on me that's influenced by the mirror's magic. If I have to leave the palace without you, I'll pass it to one of your other advisors who'll remain here. Although I don't foresee abandoning you in the middle of this crisis."

"If you did, it wouldn't be abandoning—it'd be carrying out some plan to my benefit." I study the mirror. "So, each of the governors of the conquered countries has a mirror connected to this one. Are there any other portals of communication I haven't been informed of yet?"

Axius's mouth twists. "I apologize. None of our previous plans required your communication with the governors. I have the authority to use the mirror to convey military orders you've agreed to, and it didn't occur to me you'd need to know the means."

"It's typically reserved only for members of the imperial family," Marc puts in, his tone slightly wry. "Our high commander doesn't quite consider you of that line, even though he's farther from it himself."

Axius looks chagrinned, shooting his former emperor a wary look. I think he's still processing the idea that my guard with the mottled face was once his ruler.

"And fair enough, since I'm *not* of that line." I smile reassuringly at Axius. "And it's true that I haven't had any need to speak to the governors before now."

"My oversight is corrected." His brow furrows. "Other than the governors… I believe there have been smaller mirrors placed in key forts during long campaigns in the past, but that hasn't been necessary for some time."

Marc shakes his head. "They're probably collecting dust in the basement of the most recent forts now. There'll be records somewhere to determine where they are."

They won't be of much use to me if they're that far out of my hands anyway.

I gaze at the mirror a little longer, fighting the longing to reach out to the governor of Accasy. What message could I ask him to pass on to my parents, even if he wouldn't think it highly odd for me to use him as a messenger?

Accasy has less of an army than any other conquered country, with mountain passes to tramp through to get anywhere near Valerisse's forces. Would Father even agree to send our people if I asked? He was hesitant to get involved in imperial politics even when they were playing out right on his doorstep during my coronation visit.

I'll decide what other uses I can make of these blessed devices later.

I smooth my hands over the skirt of my gown and turn away from the mirror. "All right. We're honoring Prospira as she deserves, and I hope that Inganne and Estera continue to look favorably on me. May they shine on our efforts with all the abundance, creativity, and wisdom they can offer."

There are still four more godlen I haven't determined a way to appeal to. The knowledge itches at my skin.

I need to move faster. Sabrelle's omens keep haunting the city, and Valerisse has gathered all the might she can.

Our time is running out.

Axius clears his throat. "There's another matter—the estates of the two noble households who defaced the palace. We've turned up no sign of either of them, but their conduct makes their property forfeit. Vicerine Saldette's should pass to her nephew, who's remained in court and shown no sign of sedition, but Marchion Syrus has no line of succession."

Because his one heir died while competing against me for my husband's hand. I swallow thickly. "What would typically happen in such a case?"

Marc answers for the high commander. "Either the

imperial family would take over the estate and hire staff to oversee its business and taxation, or you'd grant it to another party, perhaps a worthy member of court with little inheritance of their own."

Little inheritance. A quiver of exhilaration passes through my chest. I might have the perfect use for that.

"I'll think on it," I say.

Axius tips his head and then motions to the door. "Then we're finished here. I believe many of the nobles were expecting you to join them for a combat training session shortly?"

Yes. The physical exertion might help clear my head— and it's always good for my court to see how determined I am to fight in every necessary way.

I swipe my hands together. "Let me change into my training gown." My gaze flicks over the lantern with its magical glow. "And let's get some fresh air. It's warm enough to train on the lawn, isn't it?"

"I'll have everyone gather there."

By the peal of the next bell, I'm standing on the lawn where I once played mindless games under Emperor Tarquin's watchful eyes, now armed with a practice sword and surrounded by other noble ladies similarly equipped, as well as our military instructors. It is heartening to see I now have a dozen noblewomen interested in improving their fighting ability alongside me, as well as the few noblemen refreshing their skills.

The glances and murmurs cast our way from the rest of the court cavorting in the nearby gardens don't feel entirely relaxed. Everyone is watching their empress even more anxiously than before two of their number smeared defiance across the audience room.

I can't appear weak or frantic. I'm leading the continent to a better future and refusing to bow to any more tyranny.

It's only unfortunate that some among us might prefer a tyrannical ruler.

As usual, Captain Evando leads the exercises, with his chosen soldiers walking among us to advise on our positioning and provide sparring partners as need be. The movements of my body and the effort rippling through my muscles grounds me. When I pause to get a drink from the table the palace staff have set up, my head does feel clearer.

Bianca laughs with Baronissa Hivette and lowers her sword. A memory tickles at the back of my mind—something she said not long ago brought me to the verge of inspiration.

I move to beckon her over, but before I can raise my hand, her gaze lands on me—and darts away, as if she'd rather not meet my eyes.

I lower my arm with a matching sinking sensation in my gut. I won't force her company if she wants her distance right now. Perhaps between the gossip of the court about her husband and my precarious status, she's starting to question whether her closeness with me actually works in her favor.

I'd hate for the friendship she's offered me to end up harming her.

Thankfully, there's another party I can nudge for some kind of answer.

Kassun has joined the training before it's time for him to return to guard duty. I carry my glass of the watery juice usually presented on hot summer days over to where he's standing farther down the refreshment table.

The soldier snaps to stricter attention at my approach. "Is everything all right, Your Imperial Highness?"

"We have no additional troubles to face, as far as I know. But I was thinking—you're dedicated to Creaden, aren't you?"

I've become rather thoroughly informed of the

dedications and gifts of most of the palace military staff. The godlen of leadership is the most popular choice after Sabrelle.

Kassun nods. "I'm sorry I didn't earn a gift so I could help you with that too."

I wave off his apology. "It isn't gifts I'm looking for right now but insight. Creaden deserves to be honored just as much as the other godlen I've appealed to. But…"

What Bianca said the other day, about Creaden appreciating what I've built—her words still niggle at me, not feeling quite right.

Kassun waits patiently until I go on.

I look around at the sprawling lawns and gardens, the vast palace grounds that could hold the imperial buildings ten times over. All of which existed before I arrived. "I haven't constructed anything for him to approve of so far. Whatever contributions I've made to the empire, they haven't been all that concrete."

And in some cases, as with the canals, I'm *un*-making what other emperors have built.

What if it's impossible to please even most of the godlen at the same time?

Kassun's warm smile soothes my nerves. "I wouldn't worry yourself about that, Your Imperial Highness. Creaden appreciates all kinds of construction and leadership. It isn't as if most of us dedicated to him can go around erecting monuments or whatever."

"No, I suppose not." I cock my head. "So what do you do to feel as though you're meeting his expectations?"

"I, well…" The guard appears to fumble a bit at my interest, but recovers quickly enough. "I figure as long as we're helping see the world run well and on solid foundations, we're supporting his goals. I mean, he's not just the patron god of emperors and empresses but all kinds of other rulers, right? Mayors and captains and the lot of them."

I have to smile back at him. "I suppose you're hoping for tribune someday. Or perhaps even high commander?"

Kassun ducks his head with a trace of shyness. "If I can earn it."

"I have no doubt you will."

His words have stretched out the uncertainty that was itching at me, spreading my misgivings into a clearer picture.

The imperial family claimed Creaden as one of the empire's primary godlen alongside Sabrelle… but he's just as much the godlen of the royals of the conquered countries, isn't he? Does he really approve of seeing those leaders' authority squashed so the empire can have more?

Past emperors have gone as far as to erect their own sorts of monuments right on the grounds of the various royal palaces, traveling residences so they can pretend they're still in Dariu no matter where they go. If we ever bothered to invite the kings and queens to enjoy our hospitality here—

The spark flickers to life so abruptly I have to catch my breath.

The imperial grounds *do* have room to accommodate several more palaces… Why shouldn't they? There's one very concrete way I could pledge my commitment to increased collaboration between Dariu and the other countries. To have the flow of culture and ideas move both ways instead of it always being Dariu imposing on the others. To meet with their rulers as equals rather than underlings.

And perhaps I should be thinking beyond physical travel. The royal families are more important in their kingdoms than the governors are—or at least they should be. Why couldn't they—

Across the lawn, Bianca lifts her arm to wave to another noblewoman—and her stance wobbles. A deep flush washes over her face, ruddying her smooth brown skin.

I set down my glass and start toward her. "Bianca?"

She stumbles with a sway of her legs. I leap forward, too late to catch her before her body hits the ground.

Her head lolls against the grass. When I touch her cheek, I flinch.

She's burning up. And a strange mottling of tiny red blotches is forming across her face.

Chapter Thirty-Three

Aurelia

The medic holds out her arm to stop me from passing through the doorway. "You'd better not come any closer, Your Imperial Highness."

What I can see from the threshold is already disturbing enough. It's the middle of the day, but the beds in this staff dormitory are nearly all occupied with maids, cleaners, and cooks twisting and turning under their sheets. Red dots stand out against their skin like a flood of ruddy freckles.

A lump clogs my throat. "It's spreading quickly."

The medic nods, her lips pursing before she speaks again. "Based on the symptoms, it's a variation of camp pox—usually only seen among soldiers on the march or in siege. It hits hard and fast, but we've developed methods of eliminating the contagion once it strikes. Unfortunately, whatever's hit the palace is resistant to our usual remedy.

Some of us have been able to use our gifts to soothe the symptoms, but there are only so many of us…"

They've been running themselves ragged. And reducing symptoms doesn't matter if the person is still just as sick when the medics have exhausted their magic.

"Will they recover on their own?" I have to ask.

"We're not sure yet. No one has, but the first cases were only yesterday afternoon. Traditional camp pox can last over a week if untreated… and used to leave many of those who recovered with permanent ill effects."

My throat constricts harder. "Is it ever fatal?"

The medic grimaces. "Only occasionally, usually among those already weakened for other reasons. But we can't be sure of that either with this stronger strain. Some of the more elderly palace residents have been hit particularly hard: Baron Daveno, Marchionissa Lucrene, Meritta who supervises the kitchen staff…"

Lucrene. She was training alongside Bianca and the rest of us yesterday when the illness first struck.

But if she's still alive, there's a chance to save her from what must be Sabrelle's latest offense.

"How is Vicerine Bianca?" I have to ask. I haven't been allowed to venture into my friend's rooms since the medics recognized the illness.

"The fever's addled her mind, but she's faring better than some." The medic's head droops. "I'm sorry I can't offer more solutions yet, Your Imperial Highness. We're applying all our skills to the outbreak."

I drag in a breath, willing away the impression that I'm feeling a tad dizzy myself. It's only the stress—it has to be. "I'll apply my own too and see what I can come up with."

The medic's expression softens with a trace of a smile. "I almost forgot your gift. But don't tire yourself too much, Your Imperial Highness. We need you well."

I need my court well. More than half of the palace staff has already fallen ill, and an equal proportion of the nobles on top of that.

When I head back down the hall, a soldier I vaguely recognize comes trotting to join me and my guards. I brace myself for more bad news.

"Another seven soldiers are down with the pox," he reports, dipping his head to both me and Captain Evando, who's assigned himself as one of my personal protectors now that some of my usual host of guards are sick. "That's almost a third of us stationed around the palace."

I grasp onto the one glimmer of hope I can find. "Your ranks haven't been hit quite as hard."

Evando exhales roughly. "From what I've seen, any of us who've caught camp pox in the past hasn't been affected by this strain so far. Most of us who've spent time at the borders or farther abroad have faced it before."

He glances over at Marc, who's poised even closer than usual by my shoulder. "I don't see where you'd have encountered it. Are you sure you should remain on the empress's guard duty? If you catch it and pass it on—"

Marc interrupts in a firm tone. "I assure you, I've recovered from the pox before. I'm no more a threat to Her Imperial Highness's well-being than you are."

Evando still looks skeptical, which I can't blame him for. As far as he knows, Marc only joined the imperial military forces very recently.

He has no idea that the man he's questioning led the march against the Rionian rebellion several years ago.

It seems best to divert attention from any questions of Marc's history. I stride on to the stairs that'll take us to the main floor of the palace. "Do we have any idea where this outbreak originated? How the first to catch it were infected?"

I don't think Sabrelle could have sent the contagion

straight into her victims' bodies, no matter how sure I am that she's the ultimate source of this plague.

At the same time as Bianca was fainting at my side, the first few pages collapsed in the palace halls. I can't imagine who all four of them would have encountered at approximately the same time.

Evando shakes his head with a defeated air. "We've had the typical messengers, deliveries, and changing of the guards, but nothing unusual. I don't believe any of them had interacted with Vicerine Bianca, although perhaps she caught it from one of the staff. There haven't been any reports of illness from the rest of the city so far… It doesn't make sense."

Or maybe it does. As we reach the top of the stairs near the broad windows overlooking the front courtyard, someone down the hall gasps. A crimson light filters through the glass.

With a lurch of my heart, I spin toward the windows.

A glowing image of a vibrantly red stallion gallops past the palace, hovering in mid-air, like some kind of demon horse. As it passes us, it tosses its mane defiantly.

The soldiers on the grounds below stare up at it, several of them flicking their hands through the gesture of the divinities.

I tap my fingers down my front myself, a chill gathering in my chest. "Sabrelle is responsible somehow. She influenced someone, encouraged the disease in whatever ways godlen can…"

I whirl on my feet again, this time toward my own quarters. A hot flush washes away the chill. "I need to make use of my gift now, before—"

Evando is staring at me, his face paling.

Marc's expression has gone taut. "Empress…"

The flush flares hotter—more than just determination. It's the searing of a fever.

A prickling sensation creeps under my skin. Have I already broken out in the ruddy blotches of the pox?

My legs wobble under me with a wave of lightheadedness. Marc catches my elbow, and Evando takes my other arm.

"We'd better get you to your chambers, Your Imperial Highness," the captain says, and calls to one of the remaining footmen nearby. "Get any medics who can be spared to the empress's apartment!"

He keeps muttering as they usher me up the stairs to the third floor. "We shouldn't have let you look in on the patients."

I keep my head enough to speak dryly. "I hardly think you 'let' the empress do anything, captain. And I won't have caught it from looking through a doorway ten minutes ago. It's a wonder I hadn't fallen ill sooner."

My sacrificed spleen rarely causes problems in my daily life, but it does make me more sensitive to sickness.

Is this Sabrelle's plan? She wanted to get rid of me, so she had my entire palace infected?

The feverish fog unfurls through my head. As we approach my chambers, all I want to do is lie down and escape the aches starting to wind up my calves.

Then one of the nursemaids bursts past the door to my daughter's rooms, her eyes wide with panic. A baby's wail splits the air from behind her.

"Medics!" she cries. "Someone bring the medics!"

I lose my breath as sharply as if I've been punched in the chest.

"Coraya?" I manage to croak. "Is she sick too?"

The nursemaid takes in my no-doubt blotchy face and backs up a step. "We'll do whatever we can for her. The medics have to be able to help her."

Evando tugs me toward my own rooms. "Come,

Empress. There's nothing you can do for your daughter right now. You both need to rest and listen to the medics."

Except the medics don't know how to cure us yet. And there is something I can do—what I was planning to do before the sickness swept over me.

When I've opened the door to my chambers, I veer not toward my bed but to my trunks.

"Your Imperial Highness?" Evando asks, wavering uncertainly on his feet as I shove open the lid.

"I can reduce my symptoms myself," I tell him, grabbing my tea box and brewing apparatus. "And then I need to see what kind of cure *I* can make. I'm not letting Coraya suffer if I can help her."

It might be more than suffering. The medic said even the usual camp pox can kill those with a weakened constitution. How hard will it hit an infant?

A hot rush of tears blurs my vision. Godlen or no, I'm not letting Sabrelle take my daughter from me. How dare she even *try?*

My arm wobbles, and Marc leaps in to steady my small cauldron before I drop it.

"All right," he says in a tight but even tone. "Let's see you use that gift of yours. Just tell us what you need."

He shoots a look much too imperious for his current station at Evando, but the captain is too out of sorts to react.

Yes. My gift. But first I need to be able to concentrate.

I detach the upper portion of the tea box to get at the medicinal supplies underneath. Dried waneberry leaves for fever. Vitch bark for the aches. I suppose I should be glad my stomach isn't churning as well. I might actually be better off than when Bastien inadvertently left me deathly ill.

Gods, if only he and the others were here now—

No, it's better that they're not. The princes would never have encountered this pox before. They'd fall ill too.

I can do this on my own.

I'm not entirely on my own, besides. As I chew the herbs, Marc studies my apparatus and does an impressive job of figuring out how to assemble the various parts. He crouches beside me, his gaze avid.

Behind him, Evando paces on my rug. "You shouldn't push yourself too hard. The medics will be here any moment."

"The medics don't know what to do." The fever is retreating, letting my thoughts sort themselves into better order. I inhale deeply and press my hand against my godlen brand in an appeal to Elox. "Let me see."

How would I cure this sickness afflicting me? What ingredients do I need, and what should I do with them?

To my relief, images start swirling behind my closed eyes almost instantly. There's *something* my gift can tell me rather than the blankness of impossibility.

Iffling root. Garlic. Oduna powder. A little wervid tincture. And…

In my mind's eye, delicate blue petals unfurl and drift in bubbling water. I can almost taste their tartly sour scent.

My stomach sinks. Opening my eyes, I paw through the lowest layer of my tea box.

I come up with one small vial of whole persinam petals, preserved in a clear gel, and a packet of dried ones. Even though I know the properties change with drying, I prod my gift again.

All I can see are the softly pliant petals amid the boiling bubbles. My gift wants them fresh, or as close to that as I can offer.

I only have maybe one flower's worth.

I sit back on my heels, rocked by a rush of despair. Fresh prickles break out over my skin. The curatives I took can only hold off some of the discomfort.

I'm going to get sicker, and I don't know what to do.

Marc takes in my expression and frowns. "What's the matter?"

I wet my lips against the growing dryness of my mouth. "The remedy I can see… It needs persinam blossoms. Fresh ones. It's not a very common ingredient—I only have a little. Not enough to help more than a few of the people who are sick."

Captain Evando makes a disgruntled sound. "You don't need to heal everyone. That isn't your job. If you can ensure your own and your daughter's safety—"

It takes all my will not to give in to the returning urge to lie down. "Curing the two of us won't ensure our safety. We need every soldier who's still on my side. A third of them are already laid low… If the new pox turns out to be fatal…"

Marc studies the vial in my hand. "We'll send out people who are still well to find more of the flowers. *I'll* go if you need me to."

"No. We can't. They only bloom when it's quite warm. We get them for just a few weeks in Accasy. Even down here, the blossoms won't be showing for at least another month or two."

Evando stands up. "I'm sure there's someone on staff who has a gift for encouraging plant growth." He pauses. "Hopefully as yet unaffected by this illness."

We can't count on that. And then there's the matter of *finding* the persinam plants to begin with—I haven't seen any on the palace grounds.

I rub my head against the renewed ache, and a few of his words strike against my mind like a flint. In the spark of inspiration, I see rats scurrying around a statue.

The words tumble out of their own accord. "Maybe there's a faster way we could expand the cure. If I combine my talent… Is Farro still well?"

Evando's eyebrows jump up, but he strides to the door. "He was the last time I saw him. What do you think he can do for us?"

A crooked smile crosses my lips. "He can give the sense of abundance, of his allies having *more*. Maybe in combination with my gift, Elox and Prospira will see that we can actually *make* more out of the ingredients we have."

As Evando sends someone off to find Farro, Marc focuses on me. "Do you want to start the brewing? Is there anything else you'll need?"

"I have most of the ingredients here… A bigger cauldron would be better. I'll need to boil water. And garlic—they'll have plenty in the kitchen…"

I sway, and he grasps my shoulder.

His thumb strokes across the peak. "Hey. If you tell me what needs to be done and then rest—"

A choked sort of laugh breaks from my throat. It hurts when I swallow. "I have to be doing the brewing. Both so I can combine gifts with Farro and to make sure I pick up on any subtle steps I might not have seen when trying to picture the whole process. I can make it through."

My husband's jaw clenches, but the squeeze of his hand is only reassuring. "It's incredible watching you work, even if I wish it was under better circumstances. There are larger cauldrons in the kitchens. Grab the ingredients here that you need and let's get you down there so you have more room."

I don't want to lean on anyone. Once I leave my chambers, I still have to project all the strength an empress should possess.

I manage to walk steadily if slowly, chewing another scrap of waneberry leaf and focusing on my intentions. My guards know better than to push for me to speak.

Marc keeps one hand ever-so-lightly on the small of my

back, pretending he's simply protecting me from attacks from behind rather than braced to support my weight.

One of the staff has cleared out the kitchen before I get there, which is a good thing. I step through the doorway and stagger. It takes several seconds, clutching the nearest cabinet, before I can convince my legs to hold me again.

Captain Evando runs to grab me a chair. I sit at the table and start crushing the garlic cloves Marc finds on one of the countertops.

The fever creeps back through my mind, growing ever hotter. I'm only vaguely aware when Farro arrives, looking both puzzled and nervous.

Marc explains what I want from him before I need to. Farro tilts his skinny frame to peer at the little flower. "I—I don't know if that will work."

"We try," I tell him, the most words I can pull together coherently, and motion to the cauldron.

Evando nods. "The water's boiling."

I beckon to Farro and trudge the few steps over to the large pot, carrying the vial. From deep inside me, I summon the sort-of prayer I need, hoping it'll make sense. "These petals will heal. These petals will be more than they are. They'll be everything we need."

Farro's eyes twitch, but he repeats my words and clasps my hand when I offer it. We tap our feet together the way he did with his fellow soldier in the temple of Kosmel.

A faint light, white and green swirling together, glints at the edge of my vision. With a hitch of my pulse, I toss the petals into the boiling water.

As they ripple across the bubbling surface, Farro and I keep tapping our feet in unison. I squeeze his hand in rhythmic pulses that he returns.

My guards bring me one ingredient and another. I toss them in and stir the mixture with the long ladle.

The tartly sour scent I imagined rises up as if we'd thrown a handful of petals in instead of just a pinch. A giddy trickle of relief washes through me.

"Done," I mumble. "Just needs cooling…"

My words stumble away from me, and the last thing I'm aware of is my body teetering over as my bones turn to jelly.

CHAPTER THIRTY-FOUR

Bastien

My father eyes the books we've just set on the royal archivist's desk as if he thinks they might leap up and assault us. "A few returned tomes are hardly cause to start celebrating our liberation."

With just one sentence, he can set my teeth on edge.

Through immense will, I force my jaw to relax. "That's only a fraction of what she's offered."

"It's the only concrete manifestation of her commitment." He turns on his heel and stalks back toward his office where we were talking earlier.

I follow at a brisk pace, checking the hall to make sure no servants are around to notice my presence. I made it into Cotea safely enough, albeit with a couple of diversions to avoid soldiers on patrol near the border, but the capital is crawling with nearly as many figures in imperial uniforms as when the coronation tour stopped here.

Tribune Valerisse is clearly wary of the country closest to her current base of operations. I don't want to stay here any longer than I need to, and not just because every day apart from Aurelia jabs at me like a thorn in my chest.

I don't want to leave without knowing the Cotean king is at least seriously considering Aurelia's proposal, though.

I keep quiet until the office door has shut behind us and then fold my arms over my chest. "Aren't you always badgering me about taking risks and seeing what's possible beyond what's right in front of us? I'm giving you the greatest opportunity any ruler of Cotea has gotten since Dariu swept in centuries ago. Don't tell me you're all about sticking to the straight and narrow now."

A muscle in Father's jaw ticks. Apparently I'm getting on his nerves too. Even the last time I visited, I wasn't bold enough to challenge him quite so openly.

That was before I watched Aurelia speak up to him on my behalf. Before I helped bring down Marclinus and saw my own child brought into the world.

Everything I've wanted to fight for since *I* was a child is within my reach. I'm not letting the chance slip me by.

Father's eyes narrow as he considers me. "I don't believe in reckless action either."

"What's reckless about this? It's a clear trade. She's proven her generosity before. She's given you a way of striking back if she reneges on the promise."

"Or lies that could make us look like imbeciles if we bring them up."

I restrain a huff of frustration. "Have you been paying any attention at all? She's exactly the sort of authority you should want to support. She's doing something *new*, going against the main god of the empire, daring to set out on a new path. And conveniently, it's a new path that would grant freedom to our country."

"It's easy to dream," Father retorts. "It's not so easy to follow through when it means going against what everyone around you expects."

"She already is going against them." I wave my hand vaguely in the air. "Do you see any innovation coming from the tribune and her brutish forces?"

Father's mouth twists. "We don't know where that path will lead yet."

All at once, I'm exhausted. So tired of clashing with my father every step of the way, of being a disappointment no matter what I say or do.

We've been having variations on this argument for two days straight, and we keep going in circles, ending up back where we started.

I have one more card to play, don't I? One that'll prove I know more about the inner workings of the empire than the man in front of me could ever hope to.

I don't think the sentimentality will sway him, but maybe the shock will.

"If you can't give me any better reason than that," he's starting.

I fix him with my steeliest gaze. "I can give you one more reason that should matter to you. If you let the empress and her reign be crushed, you're consigning your granddaughter to execution too."

Father gapes at me for a few seconds before his eyes widen. "You can't mean…"

I smile grimly. "I can. The 'imperial' line continues thanks to me. So you can be sure that I, at least, am going to do what I can to secure the futures of all the people I care about."

Before the king can formulate a response, footsteps rap against the floor in the hall outside. A frantic knocking sounds on the door.

I duck down behind Father's desk as he goes to answer the summons. "Yes?"

A servant's hasty voice travels into the room. "I thought you'd want to know, Your Imperial Highness—an imperial patrol has insisted on entering the palace. They want to look through all the rooms."

Including those supposed to be private to the Cotean royals, no doubt. My hands clench where they're braced against the floor.

There's no way this squad is acting on Aurelia's orders. They'll be minions of Valerisse's.

Do they have any idea that *I'm* here, or is it simply my bad luck that they've decided to conduct a more thorough survey of the palace right now?

Either way, I can't let them find out I'm in residence. If word gets back to Valerisse that Aurelia's been sending out her supposedly hostage princes to speak to their families, gods only know what she'll do to ensure we can't cooperate.

Father has thanked the page and closed the door. He turns toward the desk. "I don't think you can hide down there through this search."

"Obviously." I straighten up, navigating my mental map of the palace. After all this time, my memory isn't perfect, but it should serve me well enough.

Thankfully a building this big comes with plenty of exits.

"I'll go down the northeast staircase and head through the stables," I say. "I can find something to occupy myself with out of the way until nightfall. That'll give you some time to think this through properly."

Something shifts in my father's expression. "Bastien…"

I was already striding toward the door. When I pause to glance at him, he appears to waver.

"Be careful," he comes out with.

I nod and jerk the hood of my cloak up over my head.

Hardly anyone other than staff uses the northeast staircase. I'm able to slip out into the second-floor hall in time to dodge a couple of gossiping maids and then make it to the ground floor without any further encounters.

I'm no more than ten paces from the doorway that leads to the stables when I catch a glimpse of black fabric painted with skeletal bones on the other side of that arched entrance.

My heart lurches. I dart sideways into one of the storerooms.

The soldiers' boots—two pairs of them, as far as I can discern—thump across the stone floor. From the mutters passing between them, they're checking every room they pass.

Shit. Valerisse must have told them to be particularly thorough, covering every entrance to the palace. I can hardly hope that they'll ignore a hooded figure hustling past them.

Should I take my chances that they won't recognize me and pretend to be a servant? I'm dressed plainly enough to stay as anonymous as possible.

Either of the soldiers could have seen me recently during the coronation tour, though. And if they realize the Cotean prince is visiting in disguise, that'll raise even more questions.

The soldiers tramp closer. I gird myself—and reach out my gift to one of the rooms I passed, with a silent apology to the staff who'll be called to clean up.

A gust of wind drifts through the hall and picks up speed as it rushes into the large pantry. With a punch of force, I fling it toward the shelves I remember seeing.

Jars and bottles clatter to the floor with the sound of smashing pottery. One of the soldiers gives a shout, and they both charge over to investigate the commotion.

The moment they've stepped into the pantry, I slip out of my hiding place and bolt for the stables as quickly as I can while setting my feet softly.

My pulse doesn't stop hammering until I'm out the other

side of the stables and through the hidden door in the palace walls that only the royal family knows how to open. My remaining lung has tightened in my chest with a rasp of breath.

Pausing to gather myself, I smear a little soil on my face to further conceal my appearance. Then I set off through the streets as if I have no business with the palace at all.

Despite the panicked adrenaline still fading from my veins, I welcome the sun beaming down over the city. Winter crispness hangs in the air, but I can taste the spring growth on the horizon.

I did want to visit one particular place in the city before I left. One small bit of bright side: The intrusion has given me the perfect opportunity.

I wind through the streets in a round-about route until I'm absolutely sure no one has followed me from the vicinity of the palace. Then I veer down one of Delphine's main roads, one I sent Aurelia's carriage down months ago when we visited Cotea's capital.

Will I be able to walk these streets side-by-side with her someday, without fear or reprisal?

The answer to that question could depend on the information I dig up now.

Up ahead, the columns of pinkish marble twined with veins of silver come into view. My spirits lift at the sight as they have so often in the past.

I might not have had any direct experience with combining gifts before Raul and I accidentally collaborated to attack Marc, but I've always found the idea fascinating. It had never occurred to me it could be used for anything as extreme as what we accomplished—but then, I had no idea that being close with your collaborator allowed for more intense effects.

What other factors might I be unaware of? If there are

additional strategies that could work in Aurelia's favor, I need to uncover them at the School of Entwined Magics.

It's chilly enough today that no students are practicing their skills out in the tiled courtyard. I approach along one side, close to the wall, with the building of matching marble and silver looming over me.

Thankfully, the headmistress's office lies only a short distance down the main hallway. I rap on the door without hesitation.

Cleric Irma has been one of my family's closest associates for decades. She won't do anything to jeopardize my plans.

Not that I intend to tell her exactly what those plans are.

When her assistant opens the door, I keep my head ducked low so my hood obscures my face. "I need to speak with the headmistress. Privately. Important news from the palace."

As the assistant hesitates, Irma's warm voice carries from farther into the room. "Let him in, Nestor, and give us the room."

The assistant steps back to admit me and then scurries out with a respectful bob of his head.

Cleric Irma looks up at me from where she's sitting behind a broad desk of pale wood. She runs her fingers over her blond-and-gray hair, which is pulled back in its usual loose braid. "What can I do for the royal family today, good man?"

I tug back my hood with a swift swipe at the dirt on my cheeks. "I was hoping you could answer a few of my questions, cleric."

Irma's eyes brighten at the sight of me, but she's canny enough to drop her voice lower. "Prince Bastien. I had no idea you were visiting."

"And I'd like to keep it that way." As she can no doubt

already guess. "I'm on a mission for the empress. Part of that mission involves the techniques you teach here."

The cleric sits up straighter. "I'm happy to serve you and Her Imperial Highness however I'm able. What in particular did you need to know? Here, sit down, you look rather harried."

I can't say she's wrong about my emotional state.

I take the chair at the opposite side of the desk and clasp my hands on my lap. "There isn't really a 'particular.' You know Empress Aurelia is facing a rather immense challenge. We're hoping that if this war comes to be, combining the gifts of those on her side might help shift the chances of victory in her favor—to protect her and her daughter and preserve the imperial line."

One of Irma's eyebrows lifts slightly. "And preserving that line matters a lot to you?"

I gaze back at her evenly. "Preserving it from being overthrown by bullies who I doubt will have Cotea's better interests in mind does, yes."

Irma hums, her attention sliding away from me. Her expression goes distant with thought.

"I'm not sure entwined magics could be the advantage the empress is hoping for. They can provide fantastic solutions to small-scale problems, and sometimes small-scale problems can tip the scales for larger issues… but I suspect not quite as large as an entire civil war."

I frown. "Why couldn't the same techniques be used on a larger scale? If the dedicats involved were well synchronized and aligned in purpose, and their individual gifts were powerful…?"

I trail off at the shake of the cleric's head.

"It's not that simple," she says. "Or rather, there's a simple reason why it wouldn't work, not for long."

My heart sinks, but I'm not going to give up just like that. "And that reason is?"

Perhaps we can find a way around it as we have so much else.

Irma offers me a gentle smile. "You're familiar with the principles of how our gifts are granted in the first place, aren't you?"

"Of course. The bodily sacrifice shows emotional dedication and physical fortitude, and the gods grant their blessing proportionately to what's offered."

"Yes." She splays her hands on the desktop. "Are you aware that by combining gifts, they generally produce a greater effect than if the two effects happened separately?"

One side of my mouth quirks upward. "That's what we're counting on."

"Well, that's where the problem lies. For a minute here or there, it doesn't become a problem. But if you try to sustain a combined effort for longer, expand it further—you can easily lose your handle on it. And if you don't rein it in quickly enough, you can do damage to yourself before you even realize you've crossed that line."

"Damage?" I repeat, my stomach flipping over.

Irma's smile turns sad. "Your gift may start demanding more sacrifices of your body—permanent ones. And for those, you won't even get to choose what you give up."

Chapter Thirty-Five

Aurelia

I wake with an uncomfortable heat still coursing through my limbs and a more pleasant warmth against my back.

As I stir on the bed, my lungs fill with the tart yet smoky scent of my first husband. Marc's arm slides down to my waist, hugging me a little closer against him before his embrace relaxes.

Sprite leaps up to join me with a trill of a mew that sounds like a protest. Does she object to sharing the space?

I rub her head between her ears before rolling over to meet Marc's gaze. Aches sharp enough to make me wince reverberate through my joints.

Marc takes in my reaction with a knitting of his brow. He strokes his other hand over my hair, his gaze intent. "How are you feeling?"

I test my mouth and find it dry but my throat only a little tender. "A little feverish and achy, but not as bad as before. Did I faint in the kitchen? How long have I been out? What's happened?"

The corner of Marc's mouth quirks upward at my flurry of questions. He leans in to kiss my forehead. A contentment I never expected to feel with this man unfurls over me like the softest of blankets, soothing the edges of my anxiety.

"The medics kept you asleep so you could heal better," he says. "It's the next morning. They've been distributing the concoction you made all around the palace. The last report I heard, it isn't curing the pox completely, but it's easing the effects enough to allow a smooth recovery."

My heart leaps to the base of my throat. "Coraya?"

"She's had two medics with her since yesterday, ensuring her fever never gets too high and that she stays hydrated. The potion helped her too."

I sag into the mattress, a sharper thread of tension winding through my initial relief. "My cure wasn't totally effective."

"Maybe that's the best effort anyone could have made. Your gift doesn't always provide you with a recipe for instant healing, does it?"

"No, but I asked it for something that would make me totally well, and it felt as if I had the answer." I pause. "Combining my gift with Farro's might have weakened the composition of the potion. I've never tried anything like that before, and we were stretching the persinam awfully thin."

"That possibility occurred to me too. But it's better that everyone is partly well than only a few recovered and most still on death's doorstep. You were amazing."

The awe in his gaze brings a giddy flutter into my chest. "I serve my people every way I know how."

"And that's why there could be no better empress." Marc brushes another kiss to my temple. Then his expression tightens. "The cure didn't get to everyone in time. Baron Daveno and Marchionissa Lucrene... They were already too sick. A few of the staff as well."

Grief hits me in a wallop, drowning my initial relief. I blink at the tears that've sprung to my eyes.

Lucrene did her best to guide me, even trained alongside me despite her age. The others—I might not have known them well, but for any of them to have died because I failed...

My thoughts race to all the other people under my care. I push myself upright. "There'll be more cases—the pox will keep spreading. To make more of the concoction—"

"A few of the medics are already handling that. I watched everything you did carefully and gave them full instructions. They sent out a few of the unaffected staff yesterday in search of persinam bushes to bring into the greenhouse and encourage into bloom. It's sounded like they expect to have a decent crop within another day or two, and then we may have a potion that's a full cure after all."

I swallow thickly. "Then let's hope there aren't many more cases in the meantime. We'll have to arrange funerals. I should look in on the members of court still recovering..."

My body sways, fatigue still weighing heavy on it, but a knock on the door stiffens my posture.

Marc is already moving, pushing off the bed and stealthily striding to his expected post by the threshold.

"What is it?" he calls through, swiping his fingers through his mussed curls to set them in better order and tugging his uniform straight.

Axius's voice travels through. "Is the empress awake? There's a... development I think she'd like to know about."

My pulse thuds harder. I ease to the edge of the bed,

girding myself against the aches that cling to my bones, and comb my fingers through my own hair. Sprite prowls over beside me and leans against my waist as if to help support me.

Marc glances over, taking in the gown I'm still wearing, and turns back to the door. "She is, but she needs more rest. Better you come in to talk to her than her getting up."

I can't argue with that approach for now.

The high commander enters with an air of caution, but his expression softens when he sees me. "You look much better today, Your Imperial Highness."

I manage a smile. "I won't worry about how badly I must have looked yesterday for that to be true. What's the matter? Have more people taken ill?"

Bianca must be recovering by now, mustn't she? It didn't sound as if she had a particularly bad case.

Axius's jaw twitches. I think he'd rather not tell me, but he isn't one to lie to his empress. "The pox has started to spread in the city. But the medics are prepared to brew more of your cure as soon as all the ingredients are ready. They have the matter in hand—and that isn't what I came to talk to you about. Your sister has arrived."

The last sentence is so unexpected that it takes several thumps of my heart before I can quite understand it. "Crown Princess Soreena? Here at the imperial palace?"

A slight smile curves Axius's lips at my bewilderment. "It seems she felt it important to see you as soon as she could. She arrived just a couple of hours ago—I've kept her to an isolated room away from any possibility of illness. But she'd very much like to speak to you."

My older sister has come all the way from Accasy—it never occurred to me that might happen. I open my mouth and close it again, grappling with my conflicting impulses.

"Have her come to my chambers," I say finally. "But

warn her that she'll need to keep her distance as I could still be contagious. We can have a private meeting in here."

I stress the word 'private' with a flick of my gaze toward Marc. As much as I've come to trust him, Soreena will think it incredibly odd for me to let a guard overhear our conversation. Whatever she's traveled all this way to speak to me about, I doubt it's casual chitchat.

Marc inclines his head slightly and steps out when Axius does.

While my mind whirls about why Soreena might have come, I pad carefully to the bathing room to quickly freshen up and wind my hair in a simple bun. I don't think my sister will care how I look, but anyone who catches sight of me before or after our meeting will expect me to meet certain standards of propriety.

I'm weak enough from my bout of camp pox that my legs start wobbling halfway through my trek back through my bedroom. I decide sitting at my vanity will be a little more dignified than perching on my bed, with the benefit of requiring fewer steps to reach.

I've only just settled onto my stool when another knock sounds. I keep my voice as steady as I can manage. "Come in."

"Her Highness Princess Soreena," one of my guards intones, and my sister slips into the room.

She stops just inside the doorway, turning toward me. It's clear *she* hasn't had much time to freshen up after her journey. Her pale hair is rumpled, her pretty face drawn with hints of her own fatigue. She's wearing a riding dress, plain by royal standards and smudged with dirt on the sleeves.

Every instinct in my body clamors to throw myself at her and grab her in a hug. I hold back only with the thought of how awful it'd be if she made this journey only to fall ill.

"It's good to see you," I say, hoping she can tell how much I mean that. "I wasn't expecting a visit."

Soreena's lips curve in a slanted smile, but her eyes stay shadowed with worry. "It didn't seem wise to wait on official messages back and forth. I heard when I arrived that you've been ill. They said the worst is over—are you truly all right?"

I find a smile of my own in me. "Not perfectly, but I'm on the mend. It's safest to keep some distance. And I'll feel even better no longer having to speculate about what might have troubled you enough for you to come all this way."

My sister lets out a very unladylike snort that puts me more at ease. "What do you think? Word trickled out from the Darium forces stationed near Costel that your rule has been threatened. This tribune is still gathering her army intending to unseat you, isn't she? As soon as the snow cleared from one of the passes, I rode."

I blink at her. "Father approved?"

She shrugs. "I told Father I was going whether he approved or not. We needed to find out what we can do for you, and I can travel nearly as fast as any messenger if I take a mind to. I wasn't sure how much you'd trust a regular messenger to convey a request for help."

No wonder she looks weary. She'll have been on the road on horseback for more than a week with barely a rest.

The urge to embrace her grips me again, alongside an ache that steals my breath for a moment. "I don't know how much help you can give. We don't know what moves Tribune Valerisse will make next, and with Accasy so distant—I didn't want to put our people in danger for no real gain."

Soreena's smile grows. "We're not so distant at the moment. Several of our military squadrons followed me through the pass and should be assembling right by the border with Goric. The hardest part of the march will be behind them by the time I return with your orders, Empress."

As wonderful as it was just to see her, I'm not prepared for the rush of affection that sweeps through me with a sharper pang mixed in. "Soreena, that's— You know I wouldn't have asked you to attack Valerisse's forces on your own. *I'm* outnumbered. It might be suicide."

"You won't be outnumbered if you have support from the rest of the empire. We're just doing our part."

At the thought of all the frustrated thoughts I had when I was last in Accasy, I could laugh and sob at the same time. I hated the way our family and our nobles kowtowed to Marclinus and shied away from any trace of defiance.

But we are a people who know how to survive, how to bide our time and strike when the moment is right. Kosmel must be as proud of my sister as he was of those first Accasians who won the freedom to form their own country.

"I've been trying to arrange such a strategy with the other royal families nearer at hand," I admit. "It'll benefit us all in the end, if we succeed. I can point to your loyal support as justification for handing rulership over the kingdom back to you and Father."

I would have found some way to include my home country in that decree anyway, but having our soldiers fighting on their empress's behalf will make it that much easier.

A hint of sorrow crosses Soreena's face. "You've had to endure an awful lot on your own, Aurelia. I've hated every hour I had to spend up there not knowing what you were dealing with next, especially after we saw… Well, you're free of that madman now. I had to offer whatever help we could."

A lump fills my throat. "Still, to ride all the way here— you put yourself in so much danger—"

"I have plenty of reasons to want to keep you on the

throne for my own sake." She touches her belly. "We found out just a couple of months ago—you're going to have a niece or a nephew by the end of the summer. And hopefully others to follow, none of whom will ever have to be sent off to this palace to give the imperial family new leverage."

Which might very well happen if Valerisse or whoever she intends to set on the throne takes my place.

So many lives ride on my decisions in the coming days. There are so many more hopes I'm gambling with.

But it's either gamble or give up. Valerisse and Sabrelle have left me no good choices.

I summon enough genuine joy to beam at Soreena. "Congratulations. I won't let it come to that, no matter what I have to do." I'm not sure how convincing either statement is, but it's the best I can offer right now.

"I think you should stay here," I go on. "Away from anyone sick, until we have a definite cure for this pox that's afflicted the palace. It should only take a day or two, from what I'm told. We don't want you riding off only to fall ill and have no way of taking care of yourself. That'll give us time to work out a signal so you know when your soldiers need to press onward… Maybe I'll have news from the other outer territories so we can devise a cohesive strategy—"

"Your Imperial Highness?" Axius's voice carries from beyond my door.

My stance goes rigid. What's so urgent that he's interrupting my meeting with my sister?

"Yes? Come in."

He enters with a deferential bow and a cautious glance toward Soreena. I wave my hand to dismiss any concerns he might have. "Whatever you need to say, she can hear it too."

His mouth tightens. "We've just gotten a new message from our people among Valerisse's forces. A significant portion of them, including Valerisse herself, have remained near Rodrige for the time being. The tribune appears intent on some goal our spies haven't been able to decipher."

A chill washes over my skin. "A significant portion of her forces have remained—what about the rest?"

Axius rests his hand on his sword hilt, his eyes flashing. "About half of her illegitimate army has set off in a march toward the Darium border."

Chapter Thirty-Six

Aurelia

When friction of the chisel's handle against my palm breaks the skin, I suppress my wince. Gritting my teeth, I keep digging the tool into the surface of the stone block.

With each chip I dislodge, the shape of Creaden's sigil unfurls.

Purple light spills down over me from the stained glass windows in the temple's roof. Devouts in matching tunics and trousers watch me from a careful distance.

I doubt any of them expected to see their empress hunched over a row of five stones in the middle of their temple's worship room. But this is what my gift showed me when I prodded it for an idea of how to heal any rift there might be between me and the godlen of leadership.

Ordering my staff to build traveling palaces for the

continent's other rulers isn't enough. I have to show how committed I am personally to constructing a stronger foundation than the venomous ties of tyranny.

I finish the sigil in the first block without pausing. My palm has only reddened, no blood seeping through the raw spot.

Not enough. My vision was clear about that aspect of my act of dedication too.

I nick the skin deeper with the corner of the chisel. A few scarlet beads well up in the hollow of my hand.

A rough sound from behind me tells me that Marc has noticed the harm I've done to myself. I can imagine him stiffening against his urge to rush in and bandage my palm.

But the former emperor trusts me enough to leave me be, even if he doesn't approve of my current methods.

I let the blood drip onto the sigil and meld it into the stone with the tip of the chisel. The gray surface turns faintly pink.

How appropriate. The color of love, when I'm enduring this discomfort out of a love for all the downtrodden people of the empire.

I do wrap my hand after I'm satisfied with my first effort, to better get to work on the second of the five blocks. Now that I've found my rhythm, the process goes faster. I fall into a meditative state, imagining the conferences that could be held at the imperial palace with all the countries' royals speaking as equals. A pinnacle of leadership.

If we can reach that future. Please, Creaden, help me see the way through to it.

Why wouldn't he want to share my dream?

Perhaps the godlen Dariu has claimed as one of their two patrons celebrated the empire's victories when its forces first swept across the continent, bringing order and authority in the wake of the devastating Great Retribution. But now, after centuries of that authority devolving into bullying and torment? How many recent emperors and empresses have been admirable leaders to anyone except the people of Dariu itself?

They haven't served even the Darium citizens all that well, considering the animosities they've provoked against their home country.

By the time I finish the fifth block, both of my hands are aching, as is my back. Crimson droplets splatter the tiled floor.

Gritting my teeth, I straighten up and carry the blocks out to our carriage despite the guards hovering around me eager to help.

These stones will be the first laid in the foundations workers are already preparing on the grounds around Vivencia's palace.

Marc can't keep totally quiet. "We can see about calling a healer—"

I cut him off with a shake of my head. "The bandage will serve well enough. I'm not making this gesture for it to be easy."

I turn toward the temple, nodding to the cleric watching us go before tapping my fingers down my front in acknowledgment of the higher power whose attention I hope I've caught.

Cleric Pierus insisted on joining me for this venture as well. He makes his own gesture to the divinities and follows me into the carriage.

As he sits down on the bench across from me, he dips his head. "Your commitment to the gods does you immense credit, Your Imperial Highness. It's been fascinating to watch, but I don't know how much farther I can advise you."

I smile in return. "I'm grateful for your support all the same."

The carriage rattles down the road back to Vivencia. I didn't have time to venture all the way out to the country's most massive temple of Creaden, where I participated in the dedication ceremony a year ago, but this one a couple of hours from the city is nearly as prominent.

We aren't heading straight back to the palace, though. I've already instructed the driver on our next stop.

Partway through the city, we stop outside a different temple, this one tall and narrow and built of the palest limestone. Devouts of my patron godlen slip in and out of the doors, carrying satchels slung over their shoulders.

The Eloxian cleric emerges to meet me by the carriage. She hands me a satchel of my own, the lines at the corners of her eyes crinkling. "You don't need to exert yourself any more than you already have, Your Imperial Highness. I understand you were quite ill just a few days ago."

"I'm fully recovered now," I assure her, though the truth is my skin still pinches a little at the brush of the cool breeze. "It's my job more than anyone else's to look after this city."

I want the people who've suffered because of Sabrelle's wrath against me to see how much I'm on their side.

Two of the devouts join me and my guards, directing us through the streets to one they haven't traversed yet. We knock on each house's door and ask whether anyone within is ill and needs the cure I concocted—at its full vitality now that fresh persinam blossoms have been coaxed into blooming.

Many of the civilians gape at me in open awe, recognizing me even though I've left my crown in the palace and dressed for traveling rather than a formal event. I hand over vials of the potion with murmurs of encouraging words.

"We'll see the whole city well again, as soon as possible. I would never leave you to suffer alone."

In the past couple of days, the new strain of camp pox

has spread throughout Vivencia and started to trickle into the surrounding countryside. It swept through the literal camps of the Darium soldiers who've been recalled to defend the capital if need be. I visited some of the ill men and women at arms yesterday in an attempt to raise their spirits as well as cure them.

More than half Valerisse's army now squats just south of the Lavirian border. I don't know what she's waiting for. Perhaps she thought the disease would hit us harder, and now she's re-evaluating her approach.

She has more help than I'd like even here. We've just turned the corner when a few urgent voices peal down the street.

"Tribune Valerisse is following Sabrelle's will! Her army is coming to set the empire to rights."

"We must all show our proper dedication rather than supporting the false empress!"

"Those who turn against the godlen of war will fall to her blade! Don't you know where your loyalties should lie? She's already punishing us!"

My teeth set on edge. A few of my guards push toward the civilians, who I suppose are Sabrellian dedicats, but I call for them to halt.

I clamber onto a stack of crates so more of the passersby can see me. "Sabrelle wishes for bloodshed and violence. I don't claim to be an empress by birth, but I'm here to protect all of you as well as my daughter, the imperial heir, until she's of age. I stand for peace, and so does my godlen. Let us support each other and strive toward a future that's bountiful for us all!"

Several of the nearby civilians clap. Many others avert their gazes and hustle away.

My stomach sinks with my scramble downward. The illness might not have gotten too deep a hold on my people's bodies, but it's given Sabrelle another in-road into their minds and loyalties.

How much longer can this treacherously subtle war continue before I've lost without swords ever clashing?

By the time I make it back to the palace, the smells of the coming dinner are wafting through the halls. I mean to head straight to Coraya's apartment before anything else, but as I pass the parlor, I spot a familiar head of sleek black hair ahead of me.

Bianca catches sight of me at the same moment. Her posture goes briefly rigid, as if she's not pleased to have been noticed.

She's kept to her rooms the past few days, supposedly still recovering. I didn't want to impose. But if she's well enough to be on her feet now…

I don't think I can leave this uncertainty simmering between us any longer.

I stride toward her. "Vicerine, it's good to see you so well. I've been asking after you."

Bianca inclines her head and takes a small step back. "I appreciate your concern more than I can say. I didn't want to add to your responsibilities with so much else going on—I was never overly unwell."

"Checking in on a friend is a pleasure, not a responsibility." I hesitate and motion her to a nearby sitting room where we can speak more privately. "Would you give me a moment?"

"Of course, Aurelia."

Among the armchairs, neither of us seems to feel comfortable sitting. Memories of the aggressive shouts among the city folk ring through my head.

Surely Bianca hasn't changed her views of me completely?

Would she admit it even if she had?

It seems simplest to cut to the heart of the matter. "You've been awkward around me in the past couple of weeks. Sometimes even avoiding me? If I've offended you in some way—"

Bianca's eyes widen. She lets out a sputter of a laugh. "Offended *me*? You should never—if I gave that impression—"

She halts as if she can't find the right words. Her astonishment sounded genuine enough that my worst worries subside.

"Will you tell me what's the matter, then?" I ask gently.

"I only..." She sighs and rubs her temple. "After it became so clear that Sabrelle is acting against you, I started thinking— You've been doing your best to gain the favor of the gods, and here I am dedicated to Prospira but with no interest in having children or really any kind of family, so often focused only on myself."

Her gaze lifts to meet mine. "If I've let down my godlen, I don't want any ill favor to rub off on you through association."

"Bianca." My lungs constrict so tightly it takes a moment before I can breathe again. All this time, she was fretting about my security.

I rest my hand on her arm. "If I've learned anything from my communing with the gods, it's that there are so many ways to show our devotion. Prospira doesn't only cultivate families and that sort of fertility but the other sorts of abundance you talked about. I can't see why she wouldn't approve of you making the most of the rewards you've gained, the wealth you've come into."

The vicerine shakes her head, but her posture has relaxed. "You may be right. I didn't want to take the chance.

There's so much at stake. I'd hate to be an obstacle in your way."

She's been taking that responsibility on herself just as I've considered myself responsible for the lives of everyone in the empire. With a swell of compassion, I step closer to her and give her a quick hug.

"You're not an obstacle," I tell her when I step back. "I need different attitudes and ideas around me if I'm going to find every tactic that could get us through this mess. Please don't shun yourself on my behalf."

A wry smile tugs at her lips. "Fair enough."

The mention of shunning brings back another idea I toyed with earlier. I'm only more sure of my decision now.

"Soon you'll be able to shed even more of your family if you'd like." I motion vaguely to the world beyond the palace walls. "I need to choose a new guardian for the estate that once belonged to Marchion Syrus. If it was yours, you wouldn't be reliant on Ennius's lands to support your position. I don't see why you shouldn't be a marchionissa rather than a vicerine."

For the second time in this conversation, Bianca stares at me. "I—I wouldn't ask that—"

I grin, feeling as if I've gotten one thing utterly right. "Which is why you deserve it more than most."

We only have to get through the coming war with our heads still attached to our bodies, and then it can actually matter.

Chapter Thirty-Seven

Aurelia

When I finally reach Coraya's apartment, I sit in one of the armchairs with my daughter, offering her a meal from my breast before I see to my own dinner.

She's growing so fast, but after her own illness, her infant body feels even more fragile in my arms. Sabrelle tried to steal her from me—to destroy this innocent life who's never done a thing against her, solely to warp the empire to her own ends.

My arms tighten around Coraya.

Is the godlen of war always so heartless? Or has she gotten so caught up in her anger over my altering of the empire that she's let reason slip away from her?

Who can know how the minds of our deities work? All I

can do is protect my daughter with every ounce of strength I have.

I rock Coraya in my arms, debating just how vital it is for me to make an appearance at dinner in front of the court when they saw me at breakfast, and a knock sounds on the door.

"Your Imperial Highness? A messenger is here to speak with you. High Commander Axius says it's urgent."

My pulse hiccups. I press a quick kiss to Coraya's forehead, return her to the nursemaid's arms, and hurry into the hall.

Axius ushers me to the main meeting room. We're almost there when Captain Evando catches up with us.

The captain's gaze darts between the two of us. "Is there — I heard—"

Axius motions for him to come along. My heart thumps faster, not sure of what Evando could have been referring to.

Then we step into the meeting room to find two figures waiting by the map table—neither of them actually messengers. At least, that's not their main role.

Raul straightens up from where he was leaning against the table, his familiar cocky grin stretching his lips and his eyes smoldering with all the affection he can't openly offer in front of our audience. I swallow the lump that's surged into my throat, balling my hands at my sides to hold them back from reaching for him.

My gaze searches his massive body in its travel-worn clothes, confirming there's no sign of injury before shifting to his companion.

Neven has returned to us tonight as well.

The youngest prince tugs back the hood of his cloak to reveal his shaggy white-blond hair, which he has to swipe away from his eyes in its rumpled state. The dark circles under his eyes suggest he hasn't gotten enough sleep while traveling back to us, but that's hardly a surprise.

Captain Evando's mouth twitches as if he's suppressed a smile. "You made it back."

In theory, he's speaking to both of the princes, but I don't think his eyes have left Neven for more than a brief glance toward Raul. The prince of Lavira arches one eyebrow as he takes this in.

Is this why Evando was in such a hurry to join our meeting?

Neven shrugs and offers an awkward smile of his own, his gaze darting from the captain to me. "I thought the empress would want my report as soon as I could give it. The roads between Goric and here weren't too bad."

"I'm glad," Evando says, and draws in his breath as if he's going to continue, but then clamps his mouth shut.

Neven looks his way again. A trace of a flush colors his pale cheeks.

Hmm. I might not be the only one hoping for a more private reunion.

Raul drums his fingers on the table, still looking amused. "I can't say the trek from Lavira was much fun, but I dodged all of Valerisse's people easily enough. It took a bit of a detour getting around that swarm of them squatting across the border." His expression darkens. "She's getting restless."

I jerk my mind back to matters that should be more important than the ache in my heart. "I heard Valerisse stayed behind in Rodrige. Do you have any idea what she's working on there?"

He shakes his head. "My mother's people hadn't been able to determine, other than possibly she was hunting down citizens she thought would rebel against her rebellion. She and a pack of her pet soldiers were roaming the streets in the couple of days before I left."

Axius folds his arms over his broad chest. "What other news can you bring? Will the Lavirian royals support Aurelia against Valerisse as well as they're able?"

Raul's mouth twists into a grimace, and I know it isn't going to be that simple. "She isn't completely convinced… but I did make progress. She *wants* to believe joining forces with Dariu under Aurelia will solve her own problems in the long run. And the crown prince is completely on board."

He catches my gaze. "The queen just doesn't quite trust you yet. I'm not sure what it would take. If I could have pushed her farther by staying, I would have."

Regret roughens his tone. I resist the urge to squeeze his hand. "I know you would. Thank you for conveying my message and encouraging her as much as you did."

I shift my attention to Neven. "And your parents?"

"They want to help," he says quickly. "But they're concerned—to throw the limited military they still have into a full-out war… My family did get a good impression of you when you visited during the tour. Mother said if they see the right opening, they'll act."

The right opening. How can I know what that means or whether the Gorician royals will follow through on their word even if I can orchestrate it?

They need to trust me more too. To trust that I can bring the future I promised them into fruition.

How did I find myself in a position where my fate rested on so many people other than myself?

As that question knots me up from throat to gut, Raul lifts his chin. "What about Lorenzo and Bastien? No sign of them yet?"

He speaks casually, but his jaw flexes after he's spoken as if he's reining in a deeper tension. He'll be as concerned about his foster brothers as I am.

I inhale slowly to steady myself. "Lorenzo was able to

communicate with us briefly. He wanted to stay a little longer to continue planning with his family, but from what he said then, I expect him to be back within a day or two."

Assuming he isn't caught up in enemy action, which thankfully seems unlikely coming from the south.

"Bastien…" I go on. "We haven't had any word from him so far. But I didn't expect to. I'm sure he'll make his way back as soon as he feels the time is right."

Gods help us, let that not be too long from now.

I turn to Neven again, partly out of necessity but also to distract myself. "Have you been getting more impressions of Sabrelle's mood or intentions over the past weeks?"

The prince of Goric grimaces. "More dreams. More bits of visions. Lots of aggression and attempts at terrorizing. She's… definitely not happy. I think she assumed you'd give up by now, and it's frustrating her that you haven't."

I don't think I want to see how the godlen of war behaves when she's frustrated if she wasn't before.

"I'll attempt to meditate to her again," I say. Maybe now that I may have gained some favor with many of her fellow godlen, she'll be willing to listen to me. However distant that possibility feels. "And we'll keep shoring up—"

Knuckles rap hastily against the door. Axius opens it to find a breathless page outside. "I think Her Imperial Highness should see this—in the garden—we don't know what to make of it."

A chill floods around my chest. I stride forward in the midst of my guards, bracing myself for the worst.

The princes, the high commander, and the captain all hustle behind me. We reach the broad windows overlooking the garden—

And there, over the orchard, a narrow shower is dappling the newly budding spring leaves. It streams down in such a condensed streak of rain it only hits a few of the treetops.

I peer up at the sky and spot the single gray cloud floating like a bit of lint against the blue. After a moment, it drifts toward us, leaving a streak of rain across the grass and the garden planters.

The page wrings her hands. "It's been doing that since we noticed it. Stopping and then moving closer. One of the footmen got wet—he said it seems like normal water. But I don't know…"

Understanding lights in me like dawn peeking over the horizon. I can't hold back my smile. "It's all right. It's a friendly omen for once."

Bastien sent that cloud, blown by his gift. Giving us a message in the most subtle way he can.

He's on his way back to me.

With the afterimage of the rain, a vision wavers behind my eyes of a handful of streams streaking across the realms all the way from the other capitals to me. My princes coursing home as if there's no other path they could follow, as if they've always been connected to me.

A deeper spark of understanding flares to life, and my posture pulls straighter.

The second vision that came to me by the river near Prospira's temple—I think I know which godlen sent it and the means to gain his backing too.

If only I can convince the lower authorities of the empire to follow my commands, no matter how extreme they find them.

Chapter Thirty-Eight

Aurelia

As soft as it is, the whisper of the hidden panel in my bedroom wall opening tugs me from the fathoms of my unsettled sleep. I open my eyes in time to see a familiar lean frame emerging from the wall, shaggy auburn hair falling across his eyes.

My heart leaps. I heave myself right over Lorenzo, who arrived yesterday afternoon and has barely left my side since, and wake him in the process. When he sees the source of my urgency, he only lets out a grunt that sounds amused.

I scramble off the bed and wrap my arms around Bastien. He hugs me back so tightly I can barely breathe.

All the things I wanted to tell him, all the new plans I've been making and the hopes I've been building, fall away. All that matters is having him safely here against me.

Bastien tips his head to seek out my lips. As we kiss, a

snort reverberates from the other side of the bed, where Raul has apparently woken too. I didn't want to lose any minute I could get with all of my newest husbands.

"You're all right?" I murmur to Bastien when our lips ease apart. "I got your rainy 'message'—very clever."

He smiles crookedly and clasps my hand where I've rested it on his chest. It's hard not to think of him as more breakable than the other princes, even though he's proven himself hardier than the Darium court has ever seemed to give him credit for.

"I'm perfectly well," he says, his eyes shining as he holds my gaze. "Just overjoyed to be back here with you. And tired. But there's so much I need to report on—"

The urge that stopped me from blurting out everything that's been on my mind rises up again. I tease my thumb over his mouth. "Not yet. When we're all properly rested and clearheaded. There's a lot all of us need to discuss. Right now, I just want to enjoy having you with me again."

Bastien's expression softens even more. He kisses me harder, his hands tracing the sides of my body, and glances toward the bed. His tone turns dry. "Is there even room for me?"

Raul scoffs. "We've managed three before. Get your ass over here so our wife can have her rest too."

Lorenzo grins to show his approval. I lead Bastien to the bed, and Raul scoots over so the prince of Cotea can align his body with mine. Raul has nothing to complain about when he had me all to himself the previous night.

My attention slides to the form lying on the sleeping mat in front of the door. If Marc is awake and watching our reunion, he gives no sign.

He's allowing me this brief span of peace with my other husbands before we go back to preparing for war.

I aim a smile his way, in case he can see it, and pull my princes close around me.

I'm jolted right out of both sleep and peace hours later by a taut voice. "She did *what?*"

I flinch, my eyes popping open. When I peer blearily at the figures now sitting tensed on the bed around me, Bastien presses his mouth shut with a guilty expression. His hair is so adorably rumpled I want to run my fingers through it, but his green eyes look even darker than usual as his gaze sears into mine.

"Have you felt any unfamiliar physical sensations since you were ill?" he asks in an urgent tone. "Even something you might have dismissed as an aftereffect of the sickness or another passing discomfort?"

I knit my brow, sorting through my thoughts with sleep still blurring them.

Whatever my husbands have been talking about while I kept slumbering, it's clearly riled them up. Lorenzo is watching me, his face as somber as Bastien's. Raul has pushed right to his feet, clutching one bed post as if he thinks he's going to wrench it off and wield it at an enemy. Even Marc has approached from the door, his jaw tight.

"I did have some lingering symptoms," I say carefully, dredging up the memories. "Aches in my joints, sensitivity of my skin. But they passed within a few days."

Raul's fingers flex around the bedpost. "You haven't noticed anything since then?"

I shake my head. "Nothing out of the ordinary. Why? What's upset you all?"

Bastien tips his head toward the other men. "Marc was

just telling us about the camp-pox epidemic and how you concocted the first cure for the new strain. You merged your gift with one of the soldiers?"

Why would he be bothered by that?

I study him as if I'll find an answer in the set of his features. "Yes. One of the two who carried out the experiment with the rats. It didn't work perfectly, but it meant we got a lot of people back on their feet faster than otherwise. It might have saved Coraya's life."

Bastien's mouth twists. "And that's a worthy cause. But—you shouldn't extend yourself again. None of us should. I think we need to take any strategies focused on the combining of gifts off the table."

His statement kicks me into sharper alertness. "What? Why? It's the one definite advantage—"

"It might not only be an advantage," Bastien interrupts in a lower voice. "Aurelia… I spoke with the cleric who leads the School of Entwined Magics in Delphine. Most of their work, including the accounts in that book I found for you, focus on minor effects. I didn't know there's a reason for that."

Raul breaks in, sinking back onto the bed so he can grip my shoulder. "It could have hurt you. Sacrificed some part of your body at random. The magic you worked with the soldier might have done that already in some way you haven't noticed yet."

A chill ripples through my veins. I glance down at myself as if I might notice that I've lost a foot or a hipbone that somehow escaped my attention before now.

My sense of practicality steadies me. "If it did, it can't be anything very important, or I'd have felt the loss by now."

"You got lucky, then," Marc says, cool and even, but his gaze sears into mine almost as intensely as Raul's. "I agree with Bastien—it isn't a risk you should take again."

Lorenzo reaches over to give my ankle a gentle caress. *"Having you here and well is more important than anything your magic could offer."*

Their concern wraps around me, but it feels more suffocating than comforting.

Annoyance prickles through my belly. "I just told you that for all I know, Coraya might have died if I hadn't attempted it. Would you have preferred that outcome? What if there's another situation in the future where I might not continue to *be* here if I don't act?"

"Aurelia…" Bastien lets out a strangled sound and moves to slide his arm around my waist. He tips his head against my shoulder.

I can't suppress the ache of longing that wakes up at the touch of my lover who's been apart from me for so long, the last of my husbands to return. My throat chokes up.

He strokes his hand up and down the side of my arm and kisses my cheek. "We'll do whatever we can to make sure it doesn't come to that. Unless you're absolutely sure… What the magic sacrifices in you could be a death sentence in itself. It does you no good if you trade one awful fate for another."

"We have no reason to think it's even likely to be that bad," I have to point out, though my voice has softened. "You and Raul combined your powers in an enormous blast, and you're both still perfectly fine."

"It seems the length of the effect as well as its potency play a role. We weren't working together for more than a minute, if that. And it was only enough to sweep through one room. Once we start talking about tackling entire armies…"

I fold my arms over my chest. "And are you all going to avoid any further experimenting? Do you really think you'd be willing to stand back and not make an attempt if *my* life was in danger?"

Marc grimaces. "That's different. The empire depends on you, not the rest of us."

"*I* depend on you," I can't help saying.

Heat flickers in his gaze at the recognition that my statement includes him. Lorenzo runs his thumb over my calf again. *"We'll all go forward with caution. But it sounds as though it wouldn't be wise to experiment unnecessarily, at least."*

A sudden, horrible thought hits me. "Not just for me. We were talking about the soldiers combining their gifts more—even civilians, if it came to that. I can't ask them to take risks I wouldn't take myself."

Raul gives a dismissive grunt. "Of course you can. That's what being the empress means. If *someone* has to act and it could be anyone other than you, they're the better choice. That's how it works, Shepherdess."

He might be right, but my stomach has balled tight all the same. This mission was supposed to only be mine. It was hard enough even involving the three princes around me. It's gotten harder with every new request I need to make of the empire's people to reach the future I want to give them.

"We'll see what we face and how great the risks appear in the moment," I say eventually.

Bastien frowns. "Aurelia, you shouldn't—"

I rest my hand on his lean chest to stop him. "I know you don't want me to consider it at all. Your opinions on the matter will be taken into consideration. I just... don't think it's wise to make promises at this point."

A growl escapes Raul. Marc's jaw works, but he mostly looks resigned.

In some ways, my first husband is more familiar with my capacity for stubbornness than my princes are.

I shove myself toward the edge of the bed, doing my best to leave the weight dragging at my gut behind. "If we can't rely too heavily on that strategy, then we'd better move quickly on our other possible tactics. I have a bunch of governors to order around today."

The logistics I worked out in bits and pieces come back to me, and my innards knot up all over again.

I glance at Raul with a wrench in my heart. "And I'm going to need to ask something else of you."

Chapter Thirty-Nine

Aurelia

By the end of the next afternoon, my reserves of peace have dwindled to zilch.

The Darium governor of Goric peers at me through the mirror with a furrow digging deep between his bushy eyebrows. "You want me to bring this mirror to the Gorician royal family for *their* use?"

I keep my voice prim and steady. "Yes. Given the current atmosphere, I'd like to be able to communicate directly with Queen Dafina—and judge her responses directly—as needed. We can't be too careful when the empire's security is being threatened. If you have any urgent messages for me, they'll be obliged to give you and your representatives access, of course."

"Of course," he says, looking somewhat mollified. Framing the exchange as something I'm doing because I *don't* trust the local royals rather than because I do has made the request go down easier with all of the governors I've spoken to. "And once the present… uncertainty has been resolved, it can easily be returned."

"Indeed." Not if everything goes as I've planned, but I won't be mentioning that part to him. "I'm sure you can understand, the matter feels rather urgent…"

He jumps in before I need to finish that sentence. "Yes, Your Imperial Highness. I'll have the mirror transported to the royal palace right away and confirm with you once it's in place."

When the glass surface wavers back to my reflection, I step back, a breath rushing out of me. That's four of the conquered countries handled. I've already gotten confirmation of the move from Rione and Cotea, and the Accasian governor promised to carry out the task by the end of the day.

Now all that's left is the part that requires the least from me… yet is also the hardest.

I flick my hand through the gesture of the divinities. "This is only the start, Jurnus. I'll see these lines of communication permanently open between the kingdoms of the empire in your honor. Please watch over my allies who'll help make it so."

Particularly the one I'm about to send back into hostile territory.

When I reach my apartment, all four of the foster princes are waiting for me. They emerge from the hidden passage as soon as the door has shut with only Marc in the room with me.

I speak before they have to ask. "Goric and Accasy are done as well. All that's left…"

Raul moves to my side before I can find the heart to keep speaking. He hugs me to his massive frame even tighter than he did in my bed last night.

"I know what I need to do, Shepherdess. I made it into Rodrige and back once already with all my limbs intact. It'll be a piece of cake."

I press my face against his solid chest, inhaling his musky amber scent. "When you went in before, there wasn't half an army camped out near the Lavirian border. Before, you didn't have to steal a blessed imperial tool."

He manages to shrug. "Who better than a man who can work with the shadows? I won't let the pricks catch me."

Despite the breeziness of his tone, his stance tenses slightly. He kisses the top of my hair, his embrace firming again as if he's considering never letting me go.

I wish *I* didn't have to let him go another time. But there's no way I can openly ask the governor overseeing Lavira to give up her mirror without Valerisse finding out about the request. I've gathered the tribune has at least a few loyal soldiers stationed at the governor's estate.

Soldiers Raul will have to get past along with the governor's own guards to retrieve that mirror.

But he's right—no one has a gift better suited to carrying out this mission. There's no one else his family would trust to bring them what's really a gift from me.

I haven't fulfilled my gesture honoring the godlen of communication until every conquered country has a direct line of access to the imperial palace. I can't hope to sway the Lavirian royals into trusting me if I can't speak to them face to face.

It has to be done. I just can't make myself like it.

"Stay for as little time as possible," I tell him. "I'll need you back here. We don't know how much longer Valerisse will hold off on attacking."

Raul's chin grazes my hair with his nod. "Nothing could keep me away for long."

He cups my face and kisses me so hard my knees wobble.

Then, with a squeeze of my hand, he's slipping back into the hidden passage behind the wall.

Lorenzo moves to my side and tucks his arm around my back. His illusionary voice has never sounded more emphatic. *"He'll be fine. He's the toughest of all of us."*

Neven grunts as if protesting the evaluation, but not enough to outright argue.

The corner of Bastien's mouth quirks upward, though his eyes remain somber. "The rest of us are here for whatever new threats you might face. If I'd had any idea what Sabrelle would inflict on you—"

I reach out to touch his face. "It's all right. If you'd been in Vivencia during the worst of the pox, you'd probably have caught it too. I'm glad you were safely away."

He leans into my touch. "And I'm glad you still had people on your side while we were gone."

His gaze slides to Marc, who's stayed by the door. My first husband offers a crooked smile, though his gaze is only warm as he watches us. So much of that old hostility and jealousy has melted away in the past few weeks.

Whatever else we're facing, that one victory feels like a miracle.

He isn't the only support Bastien was thinking of, though. The prince of Cotea cocks his head. "How long will your sister be staying?"

I square my shoulders. "I was actually going to talk to her next. I think she'd better head home now that the threat of the pox has diminished and she can take some of the cure with her. The Accasian troops are waiting for her orders."

I find Soreena in the guest bedroom she's been assigned, not far from the one where I slept when I first came to the palace as a princess adrift. Thank the gods I was able to offer her better hospitality than I received.

My sister takes one look at my expression and appears to gird herself. "It's time?"

"I don't think we can afford to wait any longer." I clasp her hands in mine, grateful to be able to come this close to her now. "Is there anything I can give you to make the journey or the task at the end of it easier? I could send a few Darium soldiers with you for the road—"

She's already shaking her head. "That would only draw more attention to me when I want to go unnoticed. The best you can offer is a fast horse, a discreet note to ensure I can swap for another at the waystations, and a stock of travel rations so I have to stop as little as possible."

"I can have that prepared before the next bell." My grip on her hands tightens. It hurts nearly as much to let her leave as it did Raul. "Thank you again. For everything. Knowing you'll have my back, that we're fighting this uprising together —it won't be easy, but it won't be quite as hard."

"That's the best I could hope for. Stay well, little sister. Your Imperial Highness." Her eyes twinkle with mischief before she pulls me into a hug.

"Father will be able to get word from me through the governor's mirror," I say as I hug her back. "But I know it could take a long time for a message to reach you and the Accasian troops from the capital. So watch for my sign, and then march as quickly as you can."

Soreena dips her head briskly. "We may not arrive for the start of the battle, but we'll help you end it."

Before I can get any more caught up in farewells, one of my guards calls through the door. "Your Imperial Highness, you have a message to answer."

Gods, can I not get a moment to breathe?

But I don't want to delay my response. His phrasing means one of the royals of the outer territories is reaching out through the mirror. I expected as much soon but didn't know exactly when it would happen.

With my pulse thudding at a faster rhythm, I give Soreena one more quick squeeze and hurry out into the hall.

Marc leans his head close to mine. "The king of Cotea."

That'll be a good start. I square my shoulders, girding myself for more negotiations. "I'll need Prince Bastien with me for this conversation. Someone summon him to the office. And have one of the pages prepare everything my sister will require for her departure."

I give the page my instructions on my way back to the mirror room. Bastien catches up with us when we're just a few paces away.

Axius opens the door to the imperial office. "He's ready to speak when you are."

I lift my chin, thoughts of all the assurances I need to make to King Stanislas flitting through my head and rattling my pulse. "I'd like it to be just the prince and me for this discussion, to give every appearance of discretion. We should be perfectly secure with all of you stationed outside in the hall."

Axius only makes a slight grimace as he strides out of the room. I leave Marc and the rest of the guards behind as well, venturing through the long office and past the sliding panel concealed by a bookcase into the smaller, windowless mirror room.

The mirror is positioned so the viewer on the other side of the enchantment can't see the doorway. I gather myself a little more, shut the inner door firmly, and position myself in front of the mirror with enough room for Bastien to stand beside me.

His father peers back at us from surroundings I can only see hazily around him, presumably a space somewhere in the

Cotean palace. His crown gleams atop his brown-and-gray hair, and a frown turns his sallow face grim.

I don't think we're getting off on the right foot.

I strive to make my tone sound both measured and welcoming. "I'm so glad I can speak to you this way, Your Highness. Truly, communication between the imperial family and the royals of the outer territories should always have been this simple."

He motions to the mirror. "These blessed tools are certainly an innovation worthy of royalty. Thank you for granting me one for as long as that generosity may last."

There's the skepticism I knew to expect.

I offer a mild smile. "You know that if things go as I hope, my generosity won't have to come to an end. Gods willing, this is only the beginning of a long collaboration between our countries—one you can enter as freely as I do."

"Yes, I recall the promises of your letter." He shifts his lean frame. "It seems rather a lot has developed since you penned that missive, though."

I can guess what he means, but I'd rather he told me what he's most worried about. "You're referring to…?"

King Stanislas's next gesture seems to indicate the entire world beyond our respective rooms. "Your treasonous tribune's army has marched closer to Vivencia. She's instructed her soldiers here to intrude even more on my family. It was a near thing preventing them from discovering the arrival of this mirror. And I hear a more dangerous strain of camp pox has been spreading through the imperial capital."

Ah. So essentially, he's worried about everything.

I hold my smile in place. "All of those things are true, but we're conquering the challenges presented. It would be easier to do so—for both of us—if we could fully work together instead of relying on only our own resources."

Bastien speaks up before his father can. "I told Aurelia about your concerns, and it took her barely a day to find a way to address them. You have to see how important it is for her to make this joint effort work. If…"

He trails off at a twitch of the king's face. Stanislas's gaze has jerked away from us to stare deeper into the room.

I register that fact just an instant before a reddish glow flares at the edge of my vision.

My own head jerks around. A flicker of light in the shape of a hawk streaks across the white-washed wall behind me. Prickling heat pierces my chest.

Sabrelle. She's brought her omens right into my palace, right into one of its most private rooms.

Trying to ward off a man I hope to make one of my strongest allies in the coming war.

When my eyes snap back to King Stanislas, even more color has leached from his face. His lips part with shock. "You— She—"

Even though the impression of the warrior goddess staring down at me has my skin crawling, I can't let her ruin this meeting.

I grasp hold of all the calm I can summon inside me. "Sabrelle can't do anything except send omens to try to frighten people and push them into going her way. She wants to bully the empire into accepting a leader who plans more war and violence. Is that what you'd truly prefer, Your Highness?"

His jaw tightens. "I'm not sure I'll have a choice."

"You will. I stood up to two emperors, and I'll stand up to a godlen as long as it takes to bring about the peace I've imagined. Peace for *all* the countries of the empire."

I draw my posture as straight as it will go. "I swear before you on my life and my daughter's that Cotea and all the other conquered countries will get your freedom of rule if you help me push back this threat. That's all I wanted since before I ever stepped into this palace. Help me make my dream real."

More light glimmers around me, but even as my pulse hitches, I realize it's a pale glow like sunlight. White and pure, shining over me.

As it washes across my body, my heart swells with gratitude to my own godlen. Elox is watching over me, standing up for me, in his own way.

King Stanislas blinks, stunned into total silence now.

Bastien looks as if he's restraining a grin. "We have gods on our side too, Father. It's up to you whether you fight for more war or for true peace and freedom."

The Cotean king takes a few rough breaths and firms his expression. "Well, I— That certainly is something to think about."

The words sound noncommittal, but when he considers me again, there's a sharper spark of interest in his eyes than I've ever seen before. "I do like the future you speak of, Your Imperial Highness. It's a dream I can support. Let me see exactly what *sort* of support I'll be able to muster."

I hold back the full giddiness of my smile. "I appreciate that, Your Highness."

After I've dismissed the image in the mirror, Bastien pulls me close. "You were amazing."

I let myself get lost in his kiss before I turn toward the door. "We still have so much more to prepare."

Outside the office, I find Axius waiting alongside four of my guards. Kassun immediately waves toward the length of the hall. "You wouldn't believe— Your Imperial Highness, there were Sabrellian omens flashing across the walls."

"I saw one in the meeting room as well," I say, my heart sinking. Were they all through the palace? What will the court be thinking?

And— "Where has Marc gone?"

Axius answers first. "I believe he went to investigate after the omens appeared. He said he'd return quickly."

He's barely finished speaking when Marc does indeed emerge from around a nearby bend in the hall.

The former emperor strides over to us, his posture rigid and his mouth unusually flat.

I brace for bad news, but at Axius's raised eyebrow, he only says, "I found no source, but Sabrelle stopped her display quickly."

Marc doesn't sound relieved, though. And when his eyes meet mine, a darkness smolders in them that sets a peal of alarm coursing through my veins.

Chapter Forty

Marc

I keep my mouth shut and my expression impassive through Aurelia's reassuring speech to the court, through her overseeing of the construction efforts on the palace grounds outside and her mingling with the nobles in the parlor, through dinner and other entertainments. All the while, memories of glowing red omens float in the back of my mind, alongside her soft but steady voice.

"I swear before you on my life and my daughter's that Cotea and all the other conquered countries will get your freedom of rule if you help me push back this threat."

Every time the words come back to me, I have to restrain my jaw from clenching. Part of me wants to grab her in front of everyone and shake more answers out of her.

Part of me wants to shrivel up like a shrub wilting in the winter chill.

I do neither, but my wife is nothing if not perceptive.

The moment her maids have left her chambers at night, she turns to me with her arms folded over the bodice of her nightgown. "What is it?"

I meant to confront her. I should have expected that she'd initiate the confrontation first. It gets us to the same place anyway, doesn't it?

I don't see any point in beating around the bush. "You aren't planning on preserving the empire. You're going to break it apart."

Her deep blue eyes only show the slightest flicker of emotion. I can't tell if she's even surprised that I know.

"You overheard my conversation with King Stanislas. How?"

Calm as ever. So little rattles this woman. This time, my stomach twists through my automatic pang of admiration.

I gaze back at her, equally unyielding. "There's a hidden area behind the mirror room where people can be stationed to make a sudden appearance or simply follow discussions unseen. Axius would normally have been back there, but he took you at your word that you wanted the conversation to stay private. I assumed there was nothing you'd say that you wouldn't mind *me* being privy to. After Sabrelle started conjuring her omens…"

I worried about Aurelia's safety. I lied to my supposed colleagues and slipped away so I could protect her.

And got to hear her offering up the territories my ancestors conquered centuries ago in simple barter.

Aurelia's mouth tightens. "I suppose you needed to find out eventually, but that isn't how I'd have wanted it to happen. I probably should have told you sooner. I'm sorry I didn't."

No apology for the scheme itself, no explanation. Just acknowledging her plan as an unshakeable fact.

My hands do clench then, despite my best efforts. "You

kept it from me because you knew I'd disagree. My foster brothers—they all know, don't they? They made the offer for you in person with their visits. And all the while you acted as if you were only doing what was best for Dariu."

All the while she acted as if she'd come to trust me.

She gave me her body and perhaps her heart, but not everything. Some part of her still lies out of reach, and I didn't even realize.

The shriveling impulse comes back. I stifle it.

I may not be emperor to the people of this palace any longer, but I know who I was. I know what responsibilities I shouldered. I haven't tossed them aside.

"Marc." Her voice is so gentle it spears right through the center of my chest. "I *am* doing what I think is best for Dariu. For all of us. This isn't what I pictured to begin with. I thought I could transform the empire into something that allowed all the kingdoms within it to flourish. But in our tour across the continent, I saw so much… It became clear that the systems that stifle the outer territories are too deeply entrenched. And they harm the people of Dariu too. We'll be stronger as an ally rather than as the tyrannical force we are now."

"The people of Dariu are never going to accept this!"

"They will. If the other kingdoms come to our aid in our time of greatest need and I frame the drawing back of our authority as a reward, they will. I'll ensure it comes with benefits for everyone that are more concrete than the impression of superiority."

Too many thoughts clash in my head. My father's lectures on just how superior we *are*. The dissidents who've slaughtered our soldiers and spat in our faces. The false smiles the other royals offer me.

Aurelia moving among them, turning those expressions

into something warmer. Earning cheers from the crowds both here in Dariu and abroad.

What if she's wrong? How will we ever recover?

What if she's *right*?

That last question brings a tinge of bitter bile into the back of my mouth. "This is the way it's been for centuries. We won the right to rule fairly. My ancestors proved we were the strongest, that we could rally in the face of the Great Retribution."

"Yes." Her agreement somehow stings as much as her arguments. "But that *was* centuries ago. Everyone has rebuilt. Half of the continent proved they could shrug off your family's control a hundred years ago, and they seem no worse off for it. What did you, or your father, or your grandparents, or your great-grandparents do other than maintain a system put in place ages ago?"

"If there isn't any need for change—"

"How can you say there isn't?" she asks. "Look how easily Linus terrorized every other kingdom around us. My whole life, I've watched Darium soldiers do the same on a lesser scale throughout Accasy. Most of the people of this empire live in fear, not prosperity. They aren't giving Dariu their best, only what it takes to most easily survive."

The conversation I overheard between the nobles weeks ago comes back to me. I have to restrain a flinch.

It isn't just the outer territories where people live in fear. I hated the thought of ruling that way.

Still, to throw everything we've built away…

My lips part, but I don't know what I can say that won't make this situation worse.

I don't even know what outcome I want.

Just looking at Aurelia, at her lovely face with its kind eyes and the slight furrow of concern that's formed in her brow, twists me up even more.

The words tumble out. "I need—I need space to think this through."

I need to get away from the woman who's consumed so much of my being that I can't pick apart what's really me anymore.

I brace for her to insist that I stay under her watch, for the tables to turn so she's more guard than I am. But apparently she trusts me more than I've assumed.

Or else she believes there's no real damage I could do to her cause regardless.

She nods, with a smile I can only call sad. "Of course. You've devoted an awful lot of your time to me these past few months. Take what you need for yourself."

The compassion in her response only sets me more on edge. I dip my head in return and stride out of the room.

The guards stationed outside blink at me.

"I'm feeling a little under the weather," I say hastily. "It's better for the empress if I sleep in the dormitory rather than nearby."

They accept my explanation without question. It was more odd that I spent so many nights watching over her from within her room than that she go without.

And she won't be without. No doubt Bastien or Lorenzo —or both of them—will be joining her soon enough.

I can't even be mad about that. I gave them the highest permission there is to stay by her side.

On the lowest level of the palace, I march into the guards' dorm where I've only spent a fraction of my time since my immense demotion. I lie down on my cot, yank the blanket to my shoulder, and close my eyes.

I thought I'd stew in my thoughts for a while, navigating through them until I determined the route that feels right. I must have been more exhausted than I realized. Sleep rolls over me in a heavy wave and drags me down.

Fatigue might not be the only force acting on me. In the depths of my doze, familiar images that I thought I'd left behind flood my mind.

Aurelia flees down the palace steps, her dress billowing behind her, shrieks and wails rising from an unseen crowd all around us. I fling a knife, and the blade buries itself in her back.

As blood spurts from the wound, she crumples at the base of the steps. Cheers erupt. A warm rush of approval wraps around me.

Civilians careen toward my wife's fallen body. They tear apart her limbs and raise the bloody chunks to their mouths. As they feast, the city grows taller and brighter around us.

Then I'm standing on a battlefield, armies in uniforms of half a dozen colors arrayed before us. Aurelia, back on her feet, sweeps her arm toward them—welcoming them. They charge into our midst, severing throats, stabbing guts, until my vision is hazed with red.

A lightning bolt spikes down from the sky and rips the empress in two. The enemies disintegrate around me. Sobs of relief rise up from my people.

On and on the dreams come, blood-soaked and vicious, presenting Aurelia as a monster to be slaughtered. I must toss and turn with them, because when I finally wake up, my sleepshirt is damp with sweat and my blanket is tangled around my legs.

I slump back on the bed for several minutes as the frenetic thudding of my pulse evens out. Nausea pools in my gut.

When the nightmares first came during the coronation tour, I blamed them on Linus's mad schemes. Aurelia and my foster brothers suggested they might have had a divine source.

Does Sabrelle sense that my faith has been shaken, and this is her way of prodding a potential opening?

I close my eyes. The dreams were never quite this emphatic or insistent before.

I spent my whole life swearing to bring glory to the empire. To defend it to my last breath. Am I abandoning that promise if I stand by Aurelia now?

What would Father have made of her claims? It's easy to picture him sneering at the idea of cooperating rather than dominating.

We have a legacy to uphold. The gods themselves deemed us worthy of shepherding the empire.

How ironic that Aurelia herself is devoted to the godlen who takes sheep as his symbol. Is that why Raul calls her "Shepherdess"?

The empire *is* a legacy. A legacy no one I've met had all that much to do with. The entire continent was conquered generations upon generations before I was even born.

How many legacies did we break when we stormed into all those capitals and claimed them as our own?

I rub my forehead, but my path isn't becoming any clearer to me.

Daylight is starting to creep through the small windows near the ceiling. I need to go back on duty soon or Aurelia's other guards might become suspicious. Especially when there's been an epidemic not just of camp-pox but of people around her turning traitor.

I gulp down a quick breakfast and make it to her apartment just as she's emerging for her own morning meal. Her nod of acknowledgment is nothing but professional. It shouldn't be anything else when we're in public.

In the dining room, I stand at attention behind her. She laughs with Vicerine Bianca and discusses the architecture of the new visitor palaces with Baron Nisto. Every word, every movement exudes serene certainty.

She conquered me so thoroughly I was ready to give myself completely over to her. Did I miss something I should have seen sooner?

How could every principle I've been raised on since birth be *that* wrong?

After breakfast, the court moves out to the gardens. Aurelia glides among the nobles with her usual encouraging remarks and friendly conversation.

How can Sabrelle see her as such a threat? My wife may exert different kinds of power, but there's no denying her might.

Or is that exactly why the godlen of war despises Aurelia —because she's showing that brute force was never the only option?

As my thoughts keep running in circles, one of the nursemaids hands Coraya over to the empress. Aurelia gathers her daughter in her arms with a kiss of the infant's forehead that's all delighted affection. Coraya leans against her shoulder, peering at her subjects-to-be and shaking a wooden rattle toy in her tiny hand.

Lorenzo ambles by. He only glances at Aurelia with a subdued smile, but his hand moves by his side.

Aurelia brushes her fingers over her hair, curving them in a way I'm suddenly sure is a message.

I've seen gestures passed between my foster brothers before, haven't I? It just hadn't occurred to me that the mute prince might have a more complicated vocabulary beyond my understanding.

There *are* things I haven't seen, but an awful lot of them happened before Aurelia ever walked among us.

Lorenzo walks off with more energy to his strides. A few minutes later, he positions himself near one of the planters and starts playing his vielle with all his usual skill for the entertainment of the court.

He never volunteered his talent under my father. But then, Father called on him often enough that I can't imagine the prince would have felt inclined to offer more.

How much has my foster brother strained that actual gift of his? He fainted at least once…

I never let myself worry about how any of the princes were faring in the past.

Through the haze in the back of my head, a prickle of apprehension wriggles forward. Something… Something in the garden doesn't seem quite right.

Tension winds through my limbs. I shove my internal debate aside and scan our surroundings with sharper eyes.

What's niggling at me?

One of the maintenance staff is perched on a ledge by the roof of a shed we're walking toward. She looks as if she's simply checking the tiles—there's nothing so strange about that, is there?

A man in staff uniform ducks off between the trees in an unnervingly furtive way.

Is that a gleam of metal amid the flowers in the planter just up ahead?

The breeze ruffles through the leaves on the nearby trees, and my ears catch an odd creak.

A page steps out from behind the shed and beckons to Aurelia. "Your Imperial Highness, you should see the roses just starting to bloom over here."

Does her tone sound a tad too urgent?

I make a swift gesture to my fellow guards to be even more on the alert, just as Aurelia steps forward to follow the page.

"I think you'll like the roses too," she's murmuring to Coraya when the tile beneath her foot gives way.

A small pit must have been dug beneath the tile. Aurelia pitches forward, her leg plunging into the path nearly to her knee. At the same moment, a gardener snatches up a knife that lay among the flowers and hurls it toward her.

A chunk of the shed's roof snaps off and plummets straight at Aurelia's head. A branch whips off a tree just a few feet beyond. Three of the palace hounds bay and hurtle along the path.

It's not one attack but several all at once—to try to overwhelm us guards? My colleagues are shouting and flinging out their various gifts.

I throw myself forward, toward the baby slipping from Aurelia's jostled grasp.

I catch Coraya a second before her head would hit the ground and press her close to my chest, positioning myself so I'm between Aurelia and most of the danger. The hounds have already been diverted, the knife smacked aside. The branch thumps to the ground inches away from us.

Kassun slumps with a grunt where he deflected the broken piece of roof, so close his sleeve brushes mine.

Aurelia scrambles up, blood streaking down her shin from a scrape, the elbow she threw out in an awkward attempt to break her fall bent at an unnatural angle. Even though pain tightens her face, all her attention focuses on me. "Is she all right?"

I look down at the baby I'm clutching. Coraya blinks at me and lets out a brief babble that sounds more startled than frightened.

Then she sticks the rattle she's still clutching in her mouth to gum its ridged surface.

My mouth twitches with unexpected amusement. It's hard to look away. This small life could have so much power in the future… or none at all.

Either way, she's every bit her mother's daughter. Cool and composed despite the chaos around her.

She might not actually be *my* daughter, but I can't see her as anything but incredible.

As I straighten up and show Coraya's unharmed form to Aurelia, one of my fellow guards calls for a medic. The others grab the worker who was poised by the roof and the one who hurled the knife.

"There were others!" I call out. "The page who beckoned Her Imperial Highness this way—and there was a man who ran off, I think to loose the hounds."

A whole conspiracy of staff against our empress. Would any of them have been dedicated to Sabrelle?

How does this latest attack make sense?

"Thank you," Aurelia says quietly. She takes Coraya from me with her unwounded arm and murmurs to her daughter while the medic sets the broken bone she's impressively ignoring.

Her gaze falls on Kassun, whom another medic has just bent down beside, and her stance tenses. "Is he badly injured? What happened?"

"I'm fine," Kassun mutters, but the blood caking his hair where the chunk of roof banged his skull says otherwise. He sways where he's kneeling.

The medic sets a steadying hand on his shoulder and hovers her hand over his head. "We got to him quickly enough. The damage can be mended."

Aurelia's face stays pale. "Go with them to the infirmary, Kassun. You'll need rest to properly recover."

More concerned about her guard than her own injuries. Just like our empress.

Axius comes up beside me with a clap of my shoulder, more familiar than he'd ever have allowed himself when I wore imperial purple. "There'll be more challenges ahead, but if you keep acting that swiftly, the empire has nothing to worry about."

I hold back a rough chuckle. As his words sink in, they don't feel quite as absurd after all.

I've seen what my wife is capable of. Out of the options I have, it is possible that seeing her remain on the throne is the best thing I could do for the empire.

Over Aurelia's protests, the medic insists that she should retire to her apartment for some rest herself. "The first few hours after the healing are the most important. Your arm will give you a little pain for a week or two, but more if you don't take plenty of time to recuperate from the start."

And so, less than a day after our last argument here, I find myself back in Aurelia's bedroom.

She frowns at the fabric sling the medic gave her to remind her not to strain the healing limb. I can't help remembering the morning she came to me with her shoulder dislocated, trusting me to mend what my twin had broken.

"That's your sword arm," I find myself saying. "You won't be able to train with the soldiers for a few days at least."

Her frown deepens. "It is what it is. Better my arm broken than my head. Or Coraya." Her gaze returns to me. "I know you're still upset. But you helped us—you helped her—without hesitation."

There's only one way I know how to answer that statement. "She's my daughter too."

She is, and she will be, in the ways that matter most.

A trace of a smile softens Aurelia's expression. She motions me over to her, farther from the door, and takes my hand in hers. "I *am* sorry I kept something so important from you. It's been a long journey to determining where I stand with you, how much we can rely on each other. I haven't always been certain of my way."

My throat tightens. "It has." Mainly because of my and my family's behavior, not hers. "I can understand that."

I wish she'd trusted me more… but I can't say I have a right to be insulted that she didn't.

Her thumb strokes over my knuckles, sending shivers over my skin. She looks down at our hands and then meets my eyes again. "I'm sorry about your father too, you know."

The statement knocks the words from my mouth for a few beats of my heart, it's so unexpected.

"You don't regret killing him," I say, with no doubt about that fact.

"No. But I regret that it was necessary to reach my goals. And I regret that losing him hurt you. It was hard for you—I could see that. You've had to navigate a lot of things alone that you expected to have more guidance for."

That sentiment is just like her, isn't it? She notices every impact her actions make, even when I'd done nothing to deserve her concern back then. Nothing she does is without compassion or consideration.

Even Sabrelle couldn't honestly claim otherwise, as many bloody visions as the godlen might send into people's heads.

My voice turns even rougher. "You haven't had any guidance at all."

She lifts her shoulder in a slight shrug. "I've had my godlen. The princes, once we found our way to each other. And sometimes your advice has been welcome as well."

"I've been grateful for every time you've listened." I grope for the right phrasing. "I suppose you aren't sorry for giving away my empire."

A wry glint comes into her eyes. "I believe it's my and Coraya's empire at the moment. But no, I'm not sorry about it. It'll be for the best. We don't deserve so much of what we're still demanding from those kingdoms."

She squeezes my hand. "I'll promise you this. If after ten

years the separation has gone badly instead, I'll lead the charge to take them all back."

The promise is equally wry, but I know she means it all the same. The firmness of her grasp travels up my arm in a pulse of warmth to squeeze around my heart.

I don't know whether this is right. I don't know just how wrong or not I've been. But I've never been more sure of how much I love this woman.

May that love prove my salvation and not my undoing.

Chapter Forty-One

Aurelia

The gardener sits sullen-faced in a corner of his dim cell. He looks at the stone floor, but it's obvious he's speaking to Axius rather than me. "I didn't plan anything against her. I just saw the knife there and thought I should use it. For Dariu's own good."

Where I'm standing outside the bars next to the high commander, I resist the urge to hug myself, as much as the defensive stance would comfort me. "Why do you think throwing a knife at me would be for Dariu's own good?"

The man's lips stay sealed.

Axius clears his throat. "Answer your empress. You owe her that much."

"I owe her nothing. She's only empress because she married Marclinus. That doesn't mean much."

I completed all the same trials—and more, I want to shout

at him. *I've helped the people of the empire while he tormented them. Doesn't* that *mean something?*

But I know getting angry isn't likely to encourage more answers.

I drag the dank air into my lungs and keep my voice carefully calm. "I'm not sure why it'd mean I deserve to die. I'm doing my best to look after Dariu while my daughter—Marclinus's heir—grows up."

Again, the gardener ignores me. His theoretical co-conspirators have behaved the same way. Even the page who called for me to see the roses—who denies that she had any idea of the trap set in the path—and the man we believe let the hounds loose—who claims they were already out when he saw them—haven't been able to meet my eyes. The best answers they've given me have been shrugs and shakes of their heads.

Axius steps closer, right up to the bars. "If you were pushed into this course of action by another party, your punishment will be much more lenient. We don't wish to see you take the fall for someone else's evil intent."

The gardener turns toward the wall. "It was all me. We just happened to do something at the same time. We saw a chance and took it."

As if there's *any* chance that the hollow under the cracked tile appeared of its own accord, that there happened to be a knife in a nearby flowerbed and a slab of roof breaking free and a tree branch on the verge of snapping all in the same small area at the same time.

It doesn't matter if we believe his story, though. If we can't convince him to elaborate on who else might be part of the conspiracy, we get nowhere.

Axius looks as if he's squashed a sigh. He motions for me and the guards clustered behind us to head to the stairs out of the palace's small prison area.

I don't speak to him until we're out of hearing range from the cells. "What do you make of it? Could it have been Sabrelle's influence, more coordinated than before, even though none of them are dedicated to her?"

Axius frowns. "That seems unlikely. From what Prince Neven has reported of the dreams she sends and the reports and behavior we've had from other dissidents, her calls to action have never been anywhere near that detailed in their planning. She's stirred up a general sense of dissention, nudged people toward violence. But to lay out so many specifics, especially when their minds shouldn't be particularly open to her…"

That's how I saw the situation myself, but my stomach knots at his matching assessment. "Then there's a *person* in the palace who did the coordinating. I suppose if we could determine who they've all talked to recently, that might lead us to the culprit."

"I already have guards making inquiries. Unfortunately, I'm not sure how easy that thread will be to follow. As staff, they regularly talk to other staff, supervisors, and even members of the court in the course of their duties. And they often carry out their work in areas of the palace where no one is keeping close watch. It'd be fairly easy to arrange a small conspiracy of servants unnoticed."

I swallow thickly. "Then we also need to speak with anyone on staff who'd have at least a little authority over those five who *is* dedicated to Sabrelle. Even without proof, their guilt might give them away."

Although I don't have a tremendous amount of hope for that possibility. Sabrelle has given no indication that she's conflicted about her campaign against me, so why would her supporters be?

As if to confirm my thought, a flicker of red courses along the wall up the stairs next to us. I get a glimpse of a filmy glowing stag charging forward before it fades into the late-afternoon daylight streaming from a window above.

Axius tracks the movement of the omen too, his jaw setting. Sabrelle has penetrated the imperial palace in more ways than one, and she's shown no inclination to draw back.

As we come out into the hall, the high commander glances over his shoulder at my contingent of guards. I gathered he's personally interrogated every man and woman assigned to my protection over again since this morning's incident, although those who were with me in the garden all responded impressively to the attack.

"Stay even closer and be even more on the alert than usual," he orders them before turning back to me. "You have your meeting with the princes?"

"Yes. Perhaps if we can rouse their family's armies for certain, we can put an end to this threat once and for all. I'm expecting communication from Goric around the eighth bell."

And Lavira too sometime today, if luck has been on Raul's side. It's been long enough that he could have made it back to his home country, but I can't fault him if it took more than a day to pilfer the governor's mirror out from under her.

Once I can speak to all the royals… will *I* be the one declaring war, on Valerisse? Sending all the troops loyal to me to the northern end of Dariu to tackle her there?

The idea makes my stomach churn harder, but even Counsel Etta and Cleric Pierus are starting to advise me in that direction. The waiting amid Sabrelle's growing influence is fraying my chances. I may be safer fighting Valerisse on territory more comfortable to her if that means we can get the battle over with sooner.

I just hate the thought of all the innocent Lavirians who'd no doubt be swept up in the conflict so close to their border.

Axius parts ways with us at a branch in the hallway. I pass a couple of barons and a few members of staff on my way, with brief nods of acknowledgment and a creeping of my skin. My hand rises to rub over the sore patch on my forearm where the bone was broken.

Any of these people could be scheming to bring about my downfall. I have enemies lurking within my home, spurred on by divine approval, and I have no idea how to tackle them.

A more welcome figure jogs over to join us. Kassun's face still looks sallower than usual, but no sign of his actual wound remains on his head.

He comes to a stop in front of me and bobs in a quick bow. "I'd like to return to duty, Your Imperial Highness."

When I blink, I can still see the scarlet staining his tawny curls. Every particle of my body balks.

The man who's defended me valiantly on so many occasions nearly died in the gardens today. How can that be right?

How can I ask more of him? He never expected to find himself in the midst of the most twisted sort of civil war.

I clear my throat. "Actually, Kassun, I'm putting you on leave for at least a couple of weeks. You've more than fulfilled your duties as it is."

The guard blinks at me with a stutter of his gaze. "Your Imperial Highness? If I let you down today—"

I hold up my hand. "No, not at all. You went above and beyond. You should be rewarded with a little peace."

His forehead furrows. Then he draws himself up straighter. "I wouldn't consider peace a reward while you're still in danger. I want to keep defending you from whatever threats are coming."

"Kassun… You were badly hurt today."

"And I'd take the same wound or worse again if it means

you don't." He hesitates before clenching his jaw defiantly. "I'll follow what orders you give me. But won't you give me the reward of getting to decide what matters to me?"

The question pierces my heart. I swallow hard.

Can I not protect even one man from the troubles that are dogging me?

But he's right. I'm fighting the war we're already emmeshed in to give every citizen of the empire more freedom to decide their own fate. How can I deny Kassun the same freedom—just to make *myself* feel better?

Standing aside clearly wouldn't make him happier.

More guilt winds around my gut, but I manage to summon a smile. "All right. If that's how you see it. I hope you know how grateful I am for your dedication. But I do think you should take the rest of today off for a full recovery, so you can serve me as well as possible."

I didn't realize Kassun could draw himself to even stiffer attention. "Yes, Your Imperial Highness. It will be my honor to return in the morning."

So much for imperial authority. At least I enforced a few more hours of leisure.

As we head toward the sitting room where I planned my informal meeting with the princes, my gaze slides toward Marc. The former emperor catches my gaze and offers me a crooked smile, as if nothing is all that different from usual.

I think we reached some kind of agreement over my ultimate intentions for the empire. By the end of our last conversation, his stance had relaxed and the tension smoothed from his voice. But I can't blame him for being upset.

I wouldn't blame him if he's *still* upset, only mastering the emotion better now. This is why I hesitated to tell him my full plans in the first place.

If he decides he's not satisfied with my explanation after all… what is he going to do about it?

The memory comes back to me of his awed expression when he confirmed Coraya was all right after he shielded her in the garden, of all the affection that's shone in his eyes when he's gazed at me so many times before.

He gave me his throne, gave up his entire identity, to stand by me. I'm not giving up all sense of caution, but I won't let doubts cloud my mind either.

Neven is already waiting by the sitting room, talking with Captain Evando next to the doorway. The captain bobs his head to me, his brow furrowing as he looks me over. "Your Imperial Highness, are you faring all right since this morning's incident?"

I hold up my arm. "Just a scrape and a minor fracture that were healed quickly enough by the medics. But I'll have to hold off on sparring sessions for a short while."

"Healing well is more important than a bit of training."

His gaze slides to Neven, and the softer expression I've noticed before crosses his face. His tone lightens. "That doesn't mean *you* should shirk your own training, Your Highness."

Neven's eyes light up in turn. He cocks his head. "If you're so keen to lose your sword, I'll spar with you as soon as this meeting is over."

Evando looks nothing but delighted at the prospect. "We'll see who loses their grip first."

As they toss more banter between them, a pang forms around my heart. Will there ever be a time *I* can be so openly friendly, even flirtatious, with the princes I've fallen for?

It isn't any of those princes who appears next, but Axius, hustling toward us all stormy grimness.

My pulse stutters. "What's wrong?"

He jerks to a halt close enough that only my guards and I

can hear his low, strained voice. "You need to come to the mirror now."

"Have the Gorician royals called on us early?"

"No." His face somehow turns even solemner. "It's Tribune Valerisse."

My heart outright lurches. "*What?*"

"Come. We have to see what she's got to say, and she won't speak to me."

Chapter Forty-Two

Aurelia

My thudding pulse chases my footsteps through the halls. I gesture for Marc to follow me all the way into the mirror room along with Axius.

I'm not facing the woman who's determined to crush me alone.

The air in the hidden room off the imperial office tastes even staler than usual. It fills my lungs with a weight I can't shake off.

I step in front of the mirror slowly, with my head held high. Tribune Valerisse's image shows on the gleaming surface. Her dark eyes narrow at the sight of me.

She stands with a strict military posture, her lean frame emanating the athletic strength I've seen from her in motion. The tightness of her thrice-braided hair looks equally strict, securing every chestnut-brown strand away from her coppery face. She's still wearing a high officer's uniform, her gray-

and-black jacket and trousers perfectly smooth and unblemished.

There are no ambitions of imperial purple on her… yet.

"Aurelia," she says in her brusque voice, as if we're equals —or as if I'm below her, from her disdainful tone. "Good. I wanted to give you one final chance to step down with a little grace before I knock you off that throne."

I stare right back at her, summoning all the calm I can. "That won't be happening—either part of it."

"I wouldn't be so sure about that." She flicks her fingers toward the mirror. "Did you really think I wouldn't hear about your plotting with the minor royals? I've confiscated all of these blessed relics. The only one who'll be communicating with you through them is me."

My gut hollows out. My one clear connection to the royal families is lost. My offering to Jurnus has been ruined.

How much does she suspect? What are my chances of persuading them to help if she's scrutinizing their movements even more warily than before?

Valerisse isn't finished. Her lips curl with a trace of a sneer. "The discovery inspired me to conduct a more thorough assessment of my forces. You won't be hearing from any of your spies again either. The people of Rodrige will be admiring their strung-up corpses until the birds pick clean their bones."

The well of cool serenity inside me turns to ice. The chill spreads through my veins.

I only keep my horror from my voice through sheer force of effort. "All of this is treason, tribune. I'm acting in protection of the empire by the rights granted to me—"

"Sabrelle has removed her favor," Valerisse interrupts. "The empire wouldn't exist without her support, and she wants you gone. I'm pleased to be her champion. And she's given me such a gift to bolster my divine mission."

She shoves up the sleeve of her jacket in a jerk. Her arm beneath is bare nearly to her shoulder—where, just below the short sleeve of her shirt, a steel armband grips her bicep.

A hound and a stallion bound across the metal ring. Their eyes flash with tiny rubies.

Beside me, Axius sucks in a hitch of breath. I can't breathe at all.

This must be why Valerisse lingered in Rodrige despite sending some of her army onward. She was searching for the same relic Linus sent me on a hunt for months ago, the one I purposefully refused to find while giving him a replica instead.

The Sabrelle-blessed armband Elox felt was too dangerous to remain in mortal hands. The ornament designed to give the wearer all possible boldness in battle.

Now it encircles Valerisse's arm like a divine mandate.

I open my mouth, but no sound comes out.

Valerisse scoffs and lets her sleeve drop. "We march on Vivencia with no further delays. Your days are numbered, false empress, and that number is dwindling faster than you can imagine."

Before I can say a word, the image in the mirror wavers and snaps away.

I sway on my feet for a moment before my legs stiffen enough to catch my balance. My voice comes out hoarse. "Summon my other advisors. We need to meet at once."

Less than an hour later, I rest my hands on the tabletop in the strategy room, needing all the steadiness I can gain from its cool, solid surface. "And how long will it take before Valerisse's forces are at Vivencia's walls?"

The scowl that's marked Axius's face since the tribune

delivered her announcement deepens. He motions to the map of Dariu expanded on the table's surface. "Most of her followers are infantry, traveling on foot. Even if she sets a hard pace, we have about a week. And I doubt she wants them exhausted when they reach us."

Counsel Etta speaks up. "But she's using even that timeline against you. We've already gotten a report from one of the border towns her army passed by—they pillaged the place for supplies and declared it your fault for refusing to back down."

Cleric Pierus winces. "She wants all the common people to blame the war and its hardships on you even though she initiated it."

"If she can convince them that I'm holding on to the throne illegitimately, they'll believe her." I pinch the bridge of my nose as if that sensation will bring my frantic thoughts into better focus. The uncomfortable weight in my chest has only grown with the passing minutes, as if I'm carrying a boulder.

A boulder Valerisse and her patron godlen heaved at me. And I have no one I can hand it off to.

"We have no real choice, do we?" I say. "We need to face her and put all our power into shutting down this incursion."

The high commander shifts uneasily on his feet. "By every report, her army far outnumbers the forces we've been able to gather—and some of our people are still recovering from the pox. We may be a little better off by the time she reaches Vivencia, but to order them to take up a strenuous march right now…"

I might be sending them to certain death, with plenty of discomfort along the way.

I swallow a sigh. "If the other kingdoms will contribute—"

Etta frowns. "We can't count on them. Gods only know how she's threatened them after discovering the mirrors."

Which could work in my favor, making the thought of her victory even less palatable… or very well work against it, making the risk of supporting me feel too great. And we have no way of knowing which it'll be when I can't get a message to them and a response back in the time it'll take for Valerisse's army to arrive at my doorstep.

"I've signaled my sister," I say. "What support Accasy can supply will be on their way."

But marching little faster than Valerisse's people are capable of… We might already have fallen by the time Soreena reaches us if we're otherwise left to our own devices.

Axius looks as if he's carrying a boulder on his shoulders as well. "I've been scouring the last missives we received from our spies for any details that could indicate a weakness… Perhaps she missed one or two of them and we'll hear more still."

"You haven't gotten anything in the past couple of days, have you?"

He shakes his head. "No, but there was often a day or two between notes even before. They'd need to be even more cautious now. There's a chance."

A chance. How flimsy must it be?

Neither of us mention the prince we sent off into Valerisse's domain. I have no idea if Raul even reached Lavira.

Was his attempt to steal the mirror there what alerted Valerisse to my gambit?

If her soldiers caught him in the act, I can't imagine there's any chance at all she's allowed him to live.

An ache squeezes tight around my heart, bringing the burn I've been struggling to suppress back into my eyes. I blink hard and drag in a breath.

None of the advisors around me has any idea just how much Raul meant to me. They wouldn't understand how shaken I am.

I can't appear weak even before them, not when I'm barely holding on to this empire as it is.

"We have time to gather more information and devise additional strategies," I say finally. The statement doesn't feel definitive enough, but I'm not going to give orders I can't say for sure won't screw us over rather than bring us closer to victory.

How did I ever believe I was going to win against a woman so bolstered by the godlen of war?

Axius nods sharply. "I'll have more possibilities to present to you in the morning."

The cleric clasps his hands in front of him. "You should speak to the court tonight. Murmurs are passing through the halls—they need clear information and reassurance."

I'm not sure I have much of either to offer, but I'll have to conjure some no matter how I feel.

I dip my head in acknowledgment. "Have them gather in the audience hall at the ninth bell. I need a short while to think through what I'll say." My gaze slides over the tabletop. "Perhaps this image of our great country will inspire me."

It's more that I don't want to have to step out into those halls and face the murmurs myself just yet, but my advisors take my request at face value. With a few respectful parting words, they file out of the strategy room.

When it's only me and Marc at his post by the door, I slump over the table, my head on my arms. The weight pressing down on me might as well be an entire mountain.

Careful footsteps cross the floor. Marc sets his hand on my back. "We aren't going to let her win."

I force myself to raise my head with a hasty swipe of my

eyes. "So many people have suffered—so many people *are* suffering—because I've refused to back down."

"And how many more do you think will suffer in the future if you let her steer the empire to her ends?" He grips my shoulder with a firm squeeze. "I know that's not the empire I want to be living in."

"It's closer to your family's legacy than anything I planned," I mutter.

The moment the words have tumbled from my mouth, a jolt of regret hits me. But Marc only chuckles roughly and gives me a gentle tug to my feet.

Face to face, he holds my gaze, his hands wrapping around mine. "We're going to make our own legacy. I don't know exactly how it's going to look or if I'll approve of every part of it, but I want to see what this world can be when you get to stretch your wings."

My throat constricts. Apparently he's forgiven me for wanting to destroy the dominance the imperial family established so long ago.

The knowledge doesn't touch the deepest pain inside me. The thought of the other man who might never stand with me like this again, who I might have sent to his death, digs into my chest like a shard of glass.

Something must show in my expression, because Marc touches my cheek. He doesn't have to ask what else I'd be anguished about.

"Raul will make it back," he says, like a promise. "I've never met a man more devoted or more stubborn."

"I don't think devotion or stubbornness are all that good at deflecting swords."

"She'd have to catch him first. He's got plenty of talent to ensure that doesn't happen."

Which is why I sent him. Why he might have insisted on

going even if I hadn't. But what does any placing of responsibility or blame matter if he's gone?

I inhale with a hitch of my lungs. "I've tried so hard to be fair to everyone, to minimize any harm… but maybe I reached too far, too fast."

Marc makes a dismissive sound. "Do you think he'd have encouraged you to do anything other than try for everything you can? I know I wouldn't."

As I meet his eyes again, he leans in to brush his lips to mine.

It's the first time he's kissed me since he discovered the full extent of my plans. The offering is tentative at first, as if he thinks I might not welcome *him*.

I loop my arms behind his neck and kiss him back with all the affection I have in me.

Does Marc have any idea how much it means that the man who once looked at me with such skepticism now throws himself whole-heartedly behind my schemes—even to his own detriment? What I feel for him could never threaten my love for my princes, but our bond is just as special no matter how different.

They stood by me through the worst I faced, schemed alongside me every step of the way.

He gave himself over, choosing to lose his brother, his throne, and his empire rather than lose me.

When our lips part, Marc tips his forehead so it rests against mine. He traces the line of my jaw in a caress that only softens the ache inside a little. "If I could do anything to bring him back faster, to stop Valerisse before her soldiers get anywhere near you…"

"I know. You've already done a lot. Maybe we all simply need to sleep on this problem, and answers will come to us."

I don't really believe it'll be that easy, and I doubt Marc does either. But he doesn't argue, only teases his fingertips over my hair with a soft smile. "I have every faith that you'll prevail."

I can't stop myself from bobbing up on my toes to claim one more kiss. Marc hums encouragingly and nudges me up against the table—and the door hinges squeak alongside a gasp.

The two of us jerk apart, far too late. As a flush burns across my cheeks, I find myself staring into the shocked face of the footman who pushed open the door, his lips parted as if frozen before he could speak a greeting.

Beyond him, several more faces set in equally startled expressions stare in at us: my other guards and a baron and baronissa whose eyes have gone totally round.

"Your Imperial Highness," the footman fumbles. "The—er—Baron Nonum and his wife wished to speak—"

"It's all right," the baron interrupts. "We can see the empress is… otherwise occupied."

He and the baronissa scurry off, no doubt to share the gossip with the first members of court they can find.

My stomach flips over. I've certainly given them something to talk about.

Have I just shaken the court's faith in me even more?

Chapter Forty-Three

Aurelia

When the ninth bell peals outside, the jitters in my gut haven't resolved. I step onto the dais at the front of the audience room and come to a stop before the imperial thrones, deciding it's better to be on my feet before the assembled court so they can see me standing tall.

As the clusters of nobles turn toward me, they fall silent. No one has commented to me directly on my dalliance with Marc, but I notice several gazes slipping past me to study my current array of guards. He stands among the others with the implacable air that served him well as emperor, not a hint of concern showing.

Other nobles study me more intently. Lips curl with derision; chins lift haughtily. Their judgment wafts over me like the fumes from a refuse heap.

The last thing I need right now is them questioning my own judgment. Wondering whether I'll be distracted from the crisis we're facing by the attentions of a man they consider far below me, without the slightest clue he's my husband—and was once their emperor.

As much as I'd like to keep my intimate activities private, they've been wrenched into the public sphere. I'm going to have to address them.

As a ruler should, I start with the most pressing matter. "Some of you may already have heard that the treasonous tribune who's rallied soldiers against me and our imperial heir has begun marching her army through Dariu. We've always known the conflict could come to this point and have been preparing our own forces for weeks. If I have my way, it'll be resolved as swiftly and bloodlessly as possible."

"Not much chance of that now," someone farther off in the room mutters, just loud enough for me to hear. The rest of the court stirs restlessly.

"We always have options," I say. "I've made no secret how important it is to me to see our realms at peace, both for the sake of all the people within it and to honor the godlen who's guided me so well."

Another voice rises from the other side of the room. "And what about what Sabrelle wants?"

I firm my stance. "Sabrelle is not the only godlen the empire looks to for approval. My own confirmation trials and my husband's appealed to Estera, Prospira, and Creaden as well. We cannot let one godlen with a taste for violence dictate the future of the continent any more than I'd expect you to lay down and surrender to our enemies for Elox's sake. Although even Elox wouldn't ask that of you."

The crowd before me doesn't look convinced. If even the nobles' resolve is shaken here in the lavish protection of the palace, how will the soldiers and the common people be feeling as the news spreads?

Will I find myself even more outnumbered by enemies when Valerisse's army makes it here?

"I have extended my gift in directions I never before considered," I go on. "I've given myself over to the hands of the gods to discover what messages they would give me. I've bowed and bled to find the best way through this conflict. You know me—you know I've served you as well as I'm able to. Tribune Valerisse wants the rest of Dariu to serve *her*. That selfishness doesn't befit a ruler. The gods will not remain on her side."

A scoffing sound carries from a figure hidden in the crowd. "But maybe you're too occupied with entangling yourself with your guards to care how the rest of us fare."

One of those guards strides forward with a fierce expression, but I hold out my arm to stop him from leaving the dais.

Despite the thudding of my heart, my voice remains steady with the words I've thought through so many times in the short while before this announcement. "Many of you have heard that news too—that I've taken some comfort in the arms of one of the soldiers who's watched over me. A soldier who's fought more than once with incredible courage and honor to save my and Coraya's lives. Whatever his station, he's earned immense respect."

"And more," someone else says in a mocking tone.

"Just months after Marclinus was laid to rest..." another mutters.

I manage to stop my teeth from setting on edge. Yes, let's talk about Marclinus.

I let my head droop in a show of mourning. "No one misses my husband as I do." That is, with all the relief and lingering trauma from the horrors he inflicted of me. "But even when he was alive, there was no expectation of restricting our attentions. I'm sure everyone in this room saw that he bestowed his freely on many other parties, as was his right. I hope you won't shame me for sharing mine on some small scale after the loss of him."

The words came out calmly enough, but several mouths snap shut around the room. Eyes lower and lips twist as people must remember all the indiscretions they witnessed their emperor carrying out during our marriage, often right in front of me.

They can hardly hold him up as a model to be emulated and honored, and then chide me for following in his footsteps to a much-moderated degree.

In the sudden awkward silence, a voice I didn't expect to hear pipes up.

"What's so wrong about the empress being interested in a soldier?" Neven pushes forward so he's standing in front of the dais, his brown eyes flashing as if daring anyone to argue. "Those men and women put their lives on the line to protect all of you and the empire, don't they? I don't see how that makes them somehow *less* than us. I—I'd be proud to have any member of the imperial military as a partner."

A trace of a blush creeps up his neck. For all the tension in me, I have to suppress a smile.

Somehow I suspect there's one particular military figure he's picturing at his side.

I pick up the thread he handed me. "Indeed. How lucky we are to have such fine fighting men and women working for us. They're the ones who'll see us through the conflict ahead. I hope you'll continue to offer them all due respect. And if any of you have the means and inclination to contribute more to the protection of the imperial line, please approach me or any of my advisors. Now let us retire to the hall of entertainments."

I sweep off the stage as if I'm nothing but confident in my declaration. My pulse is still skittering at a sickly pace, but I don't let my stride falter.

Bianca falls in next to me in the hallway. After our talk the other day, she's resumed her usual friendliness with no more anxious hesitation.

Her lips curve in a sly smile. "So you do have it in you after all. He's a little odd to look at, but he obviously can't be faulted for integrity."

If only she knew. But her approving words bring my gaze sliding to my friend with more consideration than before.

She teased me once about my possible interest in Lorenzo, without showing any sign of disapproval even though my husband *was* still entirely alive at that time. Does she really enjoy seeing me pursue my own freedoms and pleasures?

It's been more than a year since she last looked at me as a rival. She's risked her own life to protect me, as dedicated as any of those soldiers. She nearly gave up the benefits of our friendship when she feared the association might harm me.

Maybe I shouldn't even need to ask that question.

Looking at her smooth brown face, the tangle inside me loosens.

Marc and I have our strange, twisted relationship that often feels as much like obsession as love on his part. My princes wanted to tear down the empire before I ever came here. Bianca is a part of Dariu and the imperial court. She profits from the empire's continued power more than just about anyone.

If I want confirmation of whether my plans are leading us toward a better future or total disaster, who better to ask?

The vicerine knits her brow. "Is something wrong? I mean, more than the obvious."

"I'm not sure. Could we talk for a moment, just the two

of us, before we join the rest of court for tonight's entertainments?"

If I were nervous, the pleased expression that softens Bianca's features melts most of that anxiety away. "It's far from a hardship to spend more time with you rather than the lot of them. Whatever's on your mind, I'll do my best to oblige."

Does she think I'm going to ask her for a favor? I suppose in a way I am, but not at all the sort she could imagine.

We duck into one of the palace's many sitting rooms. I leave all of my guards outside, with a pointed look at Marc to hold him at bay.

He shoots me a brief glower, but he trusts Bianca enough not to raise a fuss no matter what I say to her.

Let's hope our instincts are right.

The vicerine settles into one of the chairs, but now that I've decided to make this confession, I can't bring myself to stay in one place. I pace across the rug, pulling together the right words.

"I want to know what you think about something," I say finally. "I'd like you to be honest with me. I'm hoping this step will make all of us better off in the end, but it may be a little difficult, in the transition…"

The furrow in Bianca's forehead deepens. "I'm not sure how much help I can be when it comes to addressing an uprising. It is a little outside my experience."

I have to laugh at the dryness in her tone, even as a lump chases the sound up my throat. "No. Not like that. I—"

I force my feet to stop and look her in the eyes. "If I hold on to the throne against Valerisse as I mean to, then once she's dealt with… I intend to focus solely on Dariu's security and prosperity. To form alliances with the other kingdoms but remove our authority over them, so we can collaborate as equals rather than tyrant and conquered territories."

Bianca blinks at me. I brace myself for her reaction, but the first thing that spills out of her is a guffaw of her own. "*That's* why the new palaces. It isn't just for Creaden's sake— or it is, but you really mean the recognition of the other royals as more than a show."

"Well, I didn't think it could *hurt*. And I doubt Creaden would be swayed if he thought the gesture was only superficial."

Bianca swipes her hand back over her dark hair and shakes her head. "You had me worried, Aurelia. I thought you were so frightened by this errant tribune that you were desperate enough to think I could help win a war. Instead, you're already planning on restructuring the entire empire in our presumed victory."

"And that doesn't bother you?" I press.

She pauses, her gaze going distant as she considers. "Will it mean we lose out on anything we currently get from those other countries?"

"We'll need to offer them fairer payment for the goods and services we require," I say. "But I think that balance has been tipped in Dariu's favor so long we can hardly complain. And we get to lose out on the continued hostilities and rebellions, the underhanded trading and conflicts of interest."

"I could do without all of those. Sounds like a reasonable exchange."

Her easy-going words send relief rushing through me. Of course, Bianca doesn't have direct business interests that will be affected. Many of the other nobles aren't likely to be quite as accepting.

Her total lack of horror makes the ground beneath my feet feel that much more solid, though.

I can do this. I can defeat Valerisse and Sabrelle and whoever else tries to wrench the empire I've fought so hard for from my grasp, and leave even the nobles of Dariu happier once the dust settles.

As long as this palace and the city around us are still standing when that time comes.

Bianca leans back in her chair, watching me eagerly. "How *are* you going to put that treacherous viper in her place, Empress? I've never had to see you at war before."

The answer rises up as if it was already there, just beyond my reach. "We're not going to let them even reach Vivencia's walls. We'll meet them where the fewest possible innocents will be harmed and bring every skill and trick we have to bear."

Which means I too will venture beyond the safety of these walls.

Marc once rode into battle against the Rionian rebels. How could I refuse to do the same for the people who are now mine?

Chapter Forty-Four

Raul

The stomp of my horse's hoof yanks me out of sleep. I roll onto my feet in a crouch before I've registered more than the noise and the answering hitch of my pulse.

As my blanket tumbles off me, I peer through the darkness. The night is thickened further by the grove of trees I crashed in for shelter. Its chill prickles into my lungs.

How long have I been out? My thoughts slosh and collide in my head in woozy fashion, but it's hard for me to tell how much that's from exhaustion and how much the lingering aftereffects of my straining my gift.

An ache still throbs dully at the back of my skull, the pain winding through the mess of my consciousness. My shoulder pangs too, the result of a tumble I took down a shallow ravine while avoiding disloyal imperial soldiers two days ago.

Ignoring all those niggling discomforts, I swipe my hand over my face in an attempt to sharpen my focus. The horse I'll have to swap sometime tomorrow to make sure it doesn't die on its feet lets out a faint snort and paws the ground again, its head turned to the west.

I ease closer to the edge of the grove, staying low. As I rest my hand on one of the trunks near the open fields beyond, a flash of light catches my eyes.

What the fuck was that?

The stark brightness fades, but I catch the distant glimmer of campfires and torches. A trace of woodsmoke reaches my nose. The moonlight falls across the peaks of army tents and roaming figures in dark uniforms.

My gut clenches. I thought I'd gotten away from Lavira fast enough that I should stay well ahead of Valerisse's forces. Apparently they started to head south around the same time I did.

This development doesn't need to affect me. I can clamber back onto my horse, strain my gift for long enough to vanish into the distance cloaked in darkness, and get enough of a lead that these marching soldiers will never catch up with me again. That would be the smart thing to do.

But as Bastien wouldn't hesitate to remark, my wits haven't generally been my most lauded quality. And as I study the camp a little longer, another flash of light, this one tinged yellow, catches my attention.

It darted by so quickly I couldn't make out any shape of it, just a streak against the darkness. Are Valerisse's soldiers practicing some odd magic they're planning to use against Aurelia and her allies?

Resolve wraps around my innards, drowning out wits and pains alike. If the traitorous pricks are up to something unexpected, I need to find out what it is.

At least then I won't go back to my woman—my *wife*—totally empty-handed.

I waver between riding over for the ease of a quick getaway and going on foot for better stealth. It's easier to conceal just my form than a horse's as well, and I can't count on the animal recognizing the need for silence.

After a matter of seconds, urgency propels me onward on my own.

I creep across the lumpy terrain, the small swells making me feel as if I'm a giant tramping over hills that only come up to my knees. The grass whispers against my trousers, but otherwise I make no sound. I pull a layer of shadows around me to help my dark clothing blend into the night.

A sharper ache wakes up inside my skull. I grit my teeth and keep going.

I'm maybe halfway across the distance to the camp when another glowing shape flickers into being over the tents. This one has a greenish tint. I think I make out wings and a rounded head before it fades back into the moonlight.

What in the realms are these assholes conjuring?

As the voices of the soldiers on watch become audible, I spot a patch of wiry bushes up ahead. Swallowing a relieved sigh, I duck down behind them and release most of the shadows I've been dragging with me.

My headache isn't impressed, but at least it isn't going to get much worse for the time being.

I've only been poised there for a minute or two before an immense swatch of bluish light soars overhead. Its vast shape looks almost like… a whale?

My confusion lasts only as long as it takes for the enemy soldiers to react.

"Fuck," one of them mutters. I strain my ears to pick up the rest of his words. "Jurnus too? I don't like this."

His companion speaks in a derisive tone. "So the gods are

putting on a light show. Do they really think they can intimidate those who walk with Sabrelle's favor? They can't touch us."

"Why are they sending omens?" one of the others grumbles. "Don't they want what's best for the empire?"

"Maybe they're testing our mettle, making sure we're totally committed before we face the false empress and her army."

The last voice doesn't sound fully convinced. A smile tugs at my lips.

Look at my beloved, shepherding even the gods to her cause. If she could have seen this…

She needs to know the other gods are already campaigning for her cause just as Sabrelle is trying to impose her will on Vivencia.

A flood of orange butterflies streaks through the camp, waking up a few of the soldiers with started yelps.

One of the sentries tsks his tongue. "Not everyone's passing the test."

"They'd better get their act together once the tribune joins us."

"Yeah, she isn't going to have any patience for fools."

A chuckle rings out. "I doubt even the gods would dare to challenge her when she has Sabrelle's blessing. Don't worry about them. We're going to crush anyone who tries to get between us and that throne, so we can see a proper ruler put on it. Hit them with all our might, fast and hard, and we'll plow straight through those deluded idiots."

That's their intended strategy, is it? I guess it fits Sabrelle's reputation for brutal strength, but I'd gotten the impression she didn't object to a more refined strategy once in a while.

The trouble is, from what I know about Aurelia's situation and the size of Valerisse's forces, plowing straight through the soldiers Axius managed to assemble might work just fine.

I scan the camp for several minutes longer, until my weary eyeballs feel like they might fall out of my head. As I pull back from the bushes, my foot comes down on a brittle twig.

Crack.

A few heads swivel my way. "Who's there?" one of the sentries hollers.

Shit. I yank a thicker swath of darkness around me and wince as pain lances through my temples.

A couple of the soldiers step cautiously toward me. I can't stay hidden if they walk straight into me.

Breathing as shallowly as I can, I set one foot back, and then another, glancing down to make sure I'm not about to set off any more natural tripwires. Even the mild impacts of my feet rattle through my skull.

Just hold on—another few steps, another few minutes…

The nearest sentry reaches the bushes, shakes his head, and returns to the camp. I continue easing backward, a little faster as I leave the tents farther behind.

I don't completely release the shadows until I'm back in the shelter of the grove of trees.

I stagger and catch myself on a trunk. The bark scrapes my palm.

The ache in my head swells, my stomach lurches, and I vomit the meager dinner I gulped down hours ago into the brush.

Not quite done, I tell myself through the haze in my head. Have to move. Have to get home.

Have to make it to *her*.

I untie the horse and haul myself onto its back. Leaning my head against its mane, I clench my hands and drag a thin cloak of shadow around us.

Just a little farther. Just out of their view.

Great God help me, keep me conscious.

The paling of the imperial guard's face at the palace gate reveals just how awful I must look.

"P-prince Raul?" she stammers. "I mean, Your Highness. Are you all right? Do I need to call a medic?"

I don't think there's any cure for the aches and pains of overusing one's magic—and besides, those hurts have faded over the past day once I reached safer territory.

The only salve I need is the woman within these walls.

I shake my head. "Someone should see to the horse. It's exhausted. I just need to rest."

I don't, of course. I walk straight to the shuttered bedroom near my own, open up the wall, and weave through the hidden passages to Aurelia's apartment.

I rode through the night again. Dawn light is only just streaking across the gardens outside. When I emerge into the empress's chambers with a faint hiss of the secret panel, Aurelia is sleeping, her face pressed against the pillow and far too tensed for someone supposedly in the deepest form of relaxation.

As always, there's the stubborn ex-emperor standing guard by the door. I catch Marc's gaze, bracing for some caustic comment, but after his initial stare, his mottled face actually… brightens.

"I told her you'd make it," he says, sounding almost as dazed as I feel. "She'll want to be woken up for this."

It isn't as if I need to ask his permission. All the same, a companionable warmth lights in my chest with the knowledge that I had it anyway.

We don't need to fight anymore. Not when we're both so dedicated to the woman sleeping here.

Not when we have so many greater enemies to conquer.

I step to the bed, every particle in me clamoring to gather my wife in my arms, but looking down at my scabbed and dirt-streaked hands hovering over the pristine covers makes me balk.

Scars still mark my knuckles from where I bashed my fists against my bedroom wall so many times—but they've become faint with time. I've no longer needed to flail out ineffectually against the empire's horrors.

The woman lying before me showed me a better way.

Before I can push myself onward, Aurelia stirs. Her eyelids flutter open. She gazes at me for one dreamy second as if she isn't sure she's woken up yet.

Then she flings back the bedspread and throws herself at me.

I catch her in my arms and hug her close. Her wild but sweet scent fills my nose, flooding away all the stenches of the road. Her body with its mix of softness and strength melds perfectly against my taller frame.

Our mouths collide, and I lose myself in the heady pleasure of kissing her. Of confirming she is mine and I am hers.

I'll do whatever she needs from me—but gods willing, let me never have to leave her side again.

When our lips part, her voice spills out in a murmured rush. "When I heard—I was so worried— Did Valerisse find out you'd come?"

"No. I discovered her soldiers looting the governor's house before I could get in there. Saw the men they were stringing up and heard the talk about marching, and I knew I had to get back."

No need to mention the close calls. But everything else I witnessed—

"Your plans have been working," I hurtle on. "The other gods—they've been regaling Valerisse's military camps with omens, trying to unsettle them. Prospira, Jurnus, Inganne—maybe more I didn't see. They're on your side. And I heard the soldiers talking—"

"Hey." Aurelia touches my face, her dark blue eyes capturing my soul. "You can tell us everything in a proper briefing later. Right now… I just want to celebrate that you made it back to me."

I can't hold back my grin. "Sabrelle herself couldn't keep me away. But… I'm not in the best condition for any major celebrating." I cast a critical glance down at my travel-soiled clothes. "I can't remember the last time I had a bath."

A mischievous light glints in Aurelia's gaze. "We can take care of that right now." She glances over at Marc. "If my maids come early, tell them I asked not to be disturbed yet."

He nods, his penetrating gaze clinging to her like it so often does these days. But he doesn't raise any protest when she takes my hand and walks me to her bathing room.

My empress sets the water running into the marble tub, a dollop of soap frothing it, and reaches for my shirt. I'm not about to let her do all the work. We yank the stained fabric off together.

"Couldn't wait to get me undressed, huh?" I tease automatically.

Aurelia's hands still by my waist. She looks up at me, enough anguish surfacing in her expression to drown my playful inclinations.

"You've done so much for me," she says, her voice gone raw. "Let me look after you a little?"

My heart skips a beat and then pounds harder, but there's nothing unpleasant about the heady thumping. It's a different sort of thrill than the carnal sort I'm most used to provoking… but I wouldn't trade it for anything.

Aurelia has two other men she can turn to for anything she needs—three now, going by the more affectionate vibe I've picked up on between her and Marc since his marriage ceremony for us. I've never thought of myself as having all that much extended value to a lady even without competition.

But it mattered so much to her that I returned. That I'm here with her, alive and well—the simple fact of it, even if I had no news to share, even if all I do with her in this moment is give in to her bathing me.

And that's why I'd run all across the continent, through enemy armies and under burning skies, in an instant if she asked it of me again.

So much love wells up inside me I can barely breathe. This *isn't* going to be only a bath, no matter what she'd be satisfied with.

I kick off my shoes while she loosens the ties on my trousers. After shedding pants and drawers, I'm stripped of everything but the ring that binds my heart to hers, but you'd have to cut that off my finger to remove it.

I step into the rising water of the bath before any more stink of the road can drift off me.

As I slide deeper into the soothing heat, the bubbles tickle my nose. Enchanted currents ripple against my skin, whisking the dirt and sweat down a pipe.

Aurelia grabs more of the soap.

"I can—" I begin.

She stops me with a firm look. "Let me."

The trace of a plea in her tone halts my voice. I tip my head back while she lathers my hair and then rinses it. The strokes of her fingers over my scalp send a different sort of heat coursing over my skin.

By the time she's continued her ministrations down my chest, my cock is standing at attention. Desire smolders low in my belly. I consider her nightgown—simple by imperial standards, and no doubt she has plenty of the things—and grasp her by the waist.

"What—?" she manages to gasp before I'm lifting her over the edge of the tub. She isn't the tiniest of women, but she's no challenge for my strength.

I settle her on top of me, her legs splayed around my waist, and we both groan as my cock rubs against her sex.

Aurelia glowers at me even as pleasure warms her expression. "You were supposed to be—"

"I let you take care of me. I've spent too many days away from you, Shepherdess. I'll be damned if I'm not going to have you as close as I can get now."

I roll my hips beneath hers, and her breath breaks.

She bows her head, her mouth crashing into mine. I swivel one palm against her breast through the wet silk while grasping her thigh with the other.

I know this woman's body so well it only takes a moment to line her up perfectly. Then I'm plunging into the most giddying place I've ever known.

Aurelia's slick channel squeezes my cock, and I almost explode just like that. Holding back the surge of my impending release, I rock up into her.

I'd heighten her pleasure with my gift, but I'm afraid reaching for the shadows again after the recent strain will throw off my regular aptitude for this act. I want to savor every moment of our reunion fully.

She wants an attentive lover, not one half unconscious with pain.

The water sloshes around us as we buck together. Every inch of her dampened skin glides so perfectly against mine. Bliss flares with each desperate caress, each urgent kiss.

She must have needed this too. I've only had to test my restraint for a short span of delicious torment before one flick of my thumb over her clit has her arching over me, shuddering with her release.

The sensation flings me over the edge with her. I come hard, burrowing my face against the crook of her neck with a scrape of my teeth.

Aurelia relaxes over me and touches my jaw to guide me into a gentler kiss. She stays there with her head tipped close as her breaths even out.

"Welcome home," she murmurs.

A smile stretches my lips. I pull her even closer, reveling in the understanding that no matter whether my family gets off their asses, no matter what treacherous soldiers threaten this palace, that's exactly where I am.

And where I'm going to stay, even if it kills me.

Chapter Forty-Five

Aurelia

The joy of Raul's return buoys me through my maids' fussing over my hair and dress. When I reach the dining room for breakfast, the sight of Axius brings all my other concerns rushing to the front of my mind.

I murmur a quick word to a page to ensure the high commander is sitting next to me at the main table. The grizzled man moves to join me with an evaluating gaze. He must be able to guess I made the request because I need to talk to him.

I wait until the servers have laid out our first course of delicate pastries topped with frothed eggs. "That specially trained squad we discussed sending on a mission. Did you end up dispatching them without us discussing it?"

An expression even more somber than usual shadows Axius's face. "No. The last couple of them I was able to reach arrived just as the pox struck. Several of them fell ill… The woman who acted as captain of the squad in the past was hit particularly hard and passed away before you'd created your cure. The others will still be willing to serve—I should have raised the matter sooner."

"We've all had a lot on our minds in the past few days." My stomach knots at the thought of one more skilled ally cut down in Sabrelle's campaign, simply because she was willing to help me.

Everyone I turn to, I'm only drawing into deeper danger.

But how much danger will they face under Valerisse and whoever she'll set on the throne if I give up?

Despite the melancholy news, Axius's answer does kindle a little reason for hope. Raul said he saw omens from various other godlen appearing to the enemy soldiers, trying to divert them. If those weren't illusions conjured by our side, then they must have come from the godlen themselves.

Have I proven myself to enough of the gods for them to overcome the warmonger in their midst? From what Raul described, even Jurnus is supporting me, despite my failure to distribute the enchanted mirrors.

But Valerisse's forces are still marching on us. What will it take to actually stop her?

"Let me think on how to best use them, and we'll incorporate that into our strategy discussion today," I tell Axius, and bite into the crisp pastry. Even if my stomach is rebelling, I need to keep my strength.

My gaze drifts across the room and comes to rest on the end of the table where my princes are currently seated. Raul has just walked over, scrubbed clean thanks to my own efforts and dressed for court rather than stealthy travels.

All three of his foster brothers spring up at the sight of him. Lorenzo catches Raul in a quick but emphatic embrace, Bastien claps him on the shoulder with the widest grin I've ever seen from the prince of Cotea, and Neven's face lights with eagerness, bringing back the puppyish impression the youngest prince has mostly shed over the past year.

As I watch them, affection wells up around my heart. We are a family, in so many more ways than just our romantic entanglements.

Just as I'm about to drag my gaze away before anyone finds my intent interest suspicious, a glow flares around my lovers.

I freeze in place, but no one around me reacts to the pinkish sheen hazing the three princes' silhouettes. Even Axius takes in my stiffened posture, glances over, and then looks back at me with obvious confusion.

Am I the only one who can see it?

Then it's an omen meant just for me.

The rosy glow thickens, streaming around my three lovers like the ribbons we used in our marriage ceremony. More light unfurls here and there in the shape of actual roses.

Then the imagery fades away, leaving an ache in my throat and a stutter in my pulse.

An omen like that could only have been sent by Ardone, the godlen of love. Her color, her symbols.

I haven't made an appeal to her yet. Is she inviting me to?

It hadn't seemed as though the assistance of a godlen mainly focused on beauty and desire would be all that useful in a war, so I hadn't given her much thought—but I did commit to courting all of their favor.

We're going to need an awful lot of love of one sort or another between the citizens of this continent if we're going to end this war without thousands of soldiers slaughtered. If we're to have any hope of going forward after in cooperation with the other royal families.

The other royal families those princes represent.

The idea comes to me, as clear as the divine light the godlen cast over my lovers, without any need to draw on my gift. What better way could there be to honor all Ardone stands for in this world?

Picturing the possibilities, a joyful flutter passes through my chest, but a quiver of nerves chases after it. To make such a statement, to declare so publicly…

But that's what will show Ardone how committed I am to the love I've found. My small confession about Marc in front of the court was hardly a gesture on the same level as the traveling palaces being erected nearby or the canals filled in across Cotea.

It's a message I want everyone to hear, even if I hadn't been sure I was ever going to risk speaking it.

My throat has totally choked up. I manage to force down enough of the breakfast not to provoke any concerned remarks from my neighbors, but my pulse is thrumming with anxious anticipation.

I know this approach is right. I know I can present my new commitments the right way.

And if I fail… then maybe I wasn't up to the task of saving the empire anyway.

I go straight from the dining hall to seek out Pierus. The imperial cleric has connections to all the temples in and around Vivencia.

He brightens at my approach as if looking forward to whatever new quest I might set him on. I'm not sure he'll appreciate my purpose all that much once he's seen where it leads… but I'm not getting into that part yet.

"What can I do for you today, Your Imperial Highness?" he asks.

I set my hand against my godlen mark. "I wish to make a statement in Ardone's honor in the main city square as soon as possible. The palace staff can pass word through the city— can you ensure as many clerics and devouts of Ardone as can leave off their duties will gather there to witness and support it?"

Curiosity flickers in the cleric's pale eyes. "Certainly. Do you think you'd be ready by the twelfth bell?"

I nod again. "Yes, that will do nicely."

It'll give me a few hours to pull the arrangements together—but not so much time I might lose my nerve.

As I ascend the stone steps at one end of the vast city square where I presented myself before at two emperors' funerals, Marc dares to lean close to me with a murmur. "Are you sure about this?"

Knowing all he does, he must be able to guess what I'm planning. His tone sounds only concerned, not upset.

I can't blame him for being worried about the consequences when I am too. But the godlen reward boldness on their behalf.

Perhaps I've held back for too long already.

I shoot him a quick smile. "It's time."

If not now, I may not ever get another chance. And making my love real before as much of the world as can witness it suddenly feels more important than I can say.

If Valerisse cuts *me* down, let it at least be with my people knowing who I was.

The court nobles who joined us scatter the steps around me. I signaled Lorenzo before we left, and he sidles over with Bastien and Raul nearby. A matching concern to Marc's is etched in his rich brown face, but when our eyes meet, I catch a giddy glimmer there too.

Two clerics in pink robes—including Pomia, who married me to Marclinus—and several devouts from their temples stand poised along the lower steps. Beyond the line of guards at the base, a swarm of at least a couple thousand citizens watches. A babble that's a mix of excitement and apprehension warbles through the air.

Banners of pink silk hastily grabbed from the palace storerooms sway in the warm breeze around the steps. A sweet floral scent wafts from the rose bushes set along the edges of our stage and farther out amid the crowd.

Palace staff are handing out drinks of the rose-laced juice usually brought out for Ardonalia, the official festival of the godlen of love, and the palace musicians wait off to the side ready to take up their instruments.

Whatever my people make of my announcement, I want to treat it as a celebration, not a confession.

I raise my hand, and the crowd falls silent. With deliberate emphasis, I tap my fingers to forehead, heart, and gut before squeezing my hand against the godlen mark on my sternum.

Ardone, if you're watching over me now, may you let all the families this declaration concerns see what comes to pass, by whatever method suits you. Let my love be known far and wide.

I get no sense of whether the godlen agrees, but I didn't expect to. The calm I've cultivated inside me holds me steady.

"Devoted people of Dariu," I call out. "We've faced much to fear in recent months, and our greatest challenge is soon ahead of us. There's been increasing talk of war and combat. But before I face that challenge head on, I wanted us all to remember what matters most: love and compassion."

I motion to the clerics and devouts. "Those who've dedicated their lives to our treasured godlen of love are here to sanctify the words I say to you today. I've spent time in fear myself, uncertain of whether I should be open about what's in my heart. No more. What's most important is you knowing how much I care and how much that caring can be a strength."

Another devout moves into view near the bottom of the steps—one dressed in the simple white tunic and trousers of those dedicated to Elox. I think I recognize him as one of the senior medics from the palace. No doubt some of his colleagues have come to witness my proclamation as well.

I return my hand to my chest. "I can't express how much love I still hold for my husband." At least, the half of him who proved worthy of my affection in the end. "But Ardone blessed me with a heart that can encompass so much more devotion, within Dariu's borders and beyond. In recent weeks, I've found happiness and dedication with the guard who's protected me from so many threats and with three of our visiting princes from the outer territories."

As a startled muttering passes through the crowd, I beckon my three princes right over to me. I squeeze Lorenzo's hand, then Bastien's, then Raul's for all those watching to see.

My mouth has gone dry, but my voice remains steady. "Prince Lorenzo of Rione, Prince Bastien of Cotea, and Prince Raul of Lavira have sworn to stand by me and Dariu through all that lies ahead for the empire, and I will stand with them as well. The fondness we share reflects how well all the countries of the empire can come together and tackle whatever problems we may face. Before Ardone, I declare that my heart belongs to them alongside my late husband. We will bring the empire to a brighter future together!"

The murmurs rise, but to my relief, Cleric Pomia steps forward with what might be a glimmer of tears shining in her eyes. She smiles so brightly the worst of my anxiety melts away.

She turns toward the crowd with a swirl of her pink robes. "I have seen the divine touch on the empress! Ardone honors this love as Her Imperial Highness honors our godlen by announcing it. How lucky are we to have a ruler with such a capacity for devotion!"

I don't know what holy indication she saw, but her approval sets my spirits soaring.

As the uneasy sounds falter, I lift my voice higher to get to the rest of my declaration. "There are all sorts of love, are there not? I love all of you and my court as well, as every ruler should love the people they serve, wishing that you might live only the most joyful of lives. I will not drag you into violence on my behalf, unlike those who try to threaten the rightful imperial ascension."

I point toward the distant city gates. "In two days' time, the princes and I will join our army marching well beyond Vivencia's walls, to meet the traitors before they can wreak any havoc here. Any of you who wish to lend your support will have my immense gratitude, but I won't ask it of you. It's my job to protect your lives here and those of all Darium citizens across the empire. I will fight for you fiercely, with all my heart, to defend all you love too."

As my last words ring out through the air, the tension in the crowd shifts. Several cheers rise up with an initial smattering of applause. More and more whoops and shouts of appreciation carry across the square.

In that moment, with so many hands and voices raised in support, I can almost believe we're ready to bowl over Valerisse and her invaders right now.

Then the medic I noticed barges in front of me, his mouth twisting.

He jabs his forefinger toward me. "No! No more of this. Your reign must end here!"

Chapter Forty-Six

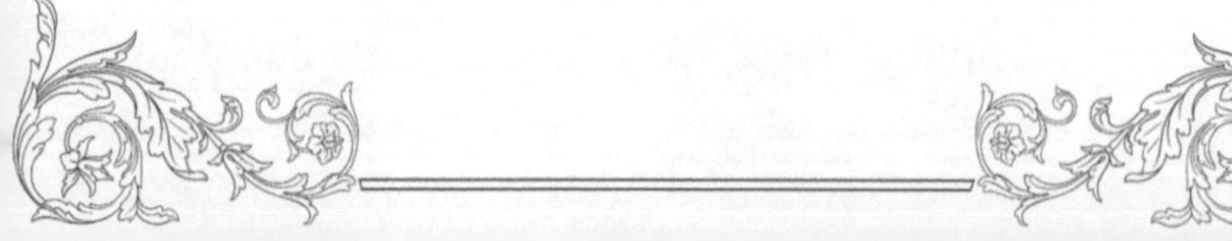

Aurelia

At the medic's words, a chill sweeps through me. My jaw goes slack for a second before I attempt to compose myself.

My guards are already hustling forward, two of them grabbing the devout by the arms. He struggles against their grasp, his eyes flashing. "The empress tarnishes Elox's name. She calls him her chosen godlen, and yet she'll give us no peace!"

Is that what he's taken offense to about me? He thinks I should roll over and let Valerisse trample me, my daughter, and the empire I've given so much to save?

As my teeth set on edge, crimson light flickers around the man. A glowing image of a stallion rears over him before vanishing in a blink of an eye.

He has Sabrelle's support too. Of course he does—she's

found a way to twist even the ideals of the godlen most opposite her to her ends.

"That's enough," one of my guards snaps. More soldiers are closing in to drag my critic away.

And the entire crowd is gaping, the celebratory atmosphere I managed to create disintegrating.

"Wait!" I step toward the medic, ignoring the lurch of my heart and Marc's grunt of protest.

My people need to see that I *am* still in favor of peace wherever I can have it. That I won't shout down complaints without giving them due thought.

I tap my bodice over my godlen brand. "I follow the teachings of our godlen of healing and peace as closely as I'm able. Elox has never called for an absence of all violence. One of his greatest teachings is that sometimes blood must be spilled to clear the ground for peace."

A principle that helped keep me strong while I schemed to murder not one but two emperors.

The medic screws up his face as if he's considering spitting at me. "You'll bring only ruin. You've placed yourself above it all, no matter what words you speak. Nothing touches you, and you think that's made you divine, higher than the rest of us who'll suffer."

His accusations sound like a bunch of vague blather, but my mind locks on to the comment about nothing touching me. What does he think has tried to "touch" me?

We knew someone at the palace must have been rousing members of staff against me. Is he upset that I've escaped those attacks?

Perhaps we've found the traitor who riled up the other staff against me. Hiding among us in plain sight all this time...

I don't wish the crowd to hear about the threats I've faced

and to wonder how many more I can endure after all, so I keep that suspicion to myself.

"I promise you, none of that is true," I say. "It's the enemies of the empire who are threatening us with ruin. I've never struck out against anyone. I meditate with Elox every day, and I know—"

"You pervert his cause! You twist his ideals! You—"

One of the soldiers clutching the medic's arm slaps a hand over his mouth. "The ravings of a lunatic," she hollers for the benefit of the crowd.

Or one whose mind is addled by another godlen's influence.

I swallow thickly, groping for the right words to set this spectacle back on the right course. My sense of certainty escapes me.

What if he isn't totally mad? Can I really say I've set the empire on a more peaceful course with all my schemes?

I lift my hands skyward in a silent plea to Elox. An omen from him now would settle all this conflict.

For a few strained thuds of my heart, nothing comes. Then a pale glow forms around me, shimmering off my skin.

I'd almost believe it really is my godlen signaling his approval… except it doesn't hold the same unearthly warmth I've felt from Elox's touch before.

My gaze twitches sideways. Lorenzo meets my eyes, his face set with concentration.

He's conjuring this illusion for me, to "prove" I'm worthy before the crowd by whatever means necessary.

We really are facing all our challenges together, aren't we?

I tamp down a pained laugh. The crowd is gasping in awe. Even the medic has stopped struggling, his eyes wide with his startled stare.

Let's end this.

I extend my arms toward our audience. "Please, revel in the peace we have and all those you love!"

A renewed wave of cheers breaks out.

The soldiers escort the medic away, presumably to lock him up in the palace cells alongside the junior staff he roped into his plot, and my personal guards close in around me.

Marc's voice comes out tight. "We should get you back to the palace."

For once, I don't mind him giving the orders.

My three princes accompany me in the imperial carriage for the short drive. Even though my gut is still tangled about our last moments in the square, I reach toward the opposite bench to squeeze Lorenzo's hand. "Thank you."

He smiles crookedly and makes a sign that amounts to, *I'm here for you.*

Raul huffs. "Is there no depth Sabrelle won't stoop to? Can't she admit when she's wrong? What fucking good is might if you throw it around like a club, battering everyone in sight?"

Bastien's face is drawn. "She's been the primary godlen of the most powerful country in the continent for centuries. I suppose even the divinities aren't exempt from ego."

"She'd better get over it soon."

Or we'll do what? It isn't as if we can literally go face to face with her, only the hordes of supporters she keeps flinging at me.

Bastien turns to me. Some of the tension fades from his expression with the brightening of his dark green eyes. "You really told them. You—they all know now."

Yes. The enormity of the announcement I made before the medic's interruption washes over me again in a giddy wave. "I'm sorry I didn't warn you what I intended. I didn't want any of you trying to argue me out of doing it."

Where he's sitting next to me, Raul hooks his arm

around mine. "You were amazing. Not that I think we should start getting you off in front of the entire court, but… it'll be pretty incredible not having to pretend I see you as nothing but my empress."

His remark brings a mix of joy and nervousness squirming through my chest. The common people accepted my confession well enough, but they see me as a figure nearly as high above them as the gods. The court only just swallowed the idea that I've dallied with a guard.

Well, at least the princes are about as close to my station as anyone can get. And my earlier point about Marclinus's many indiscretions will hopefully stick in their minds enough to stop them from muttering too openly about the number of partners I've accumulated.

I smile at all of my lovers, shoving my nerves down to wriggle in my gut. "I wish I could have brought our love out into the light sooner."

Lorenzo brings my hand to his lips. *"I'd have stood beside you in secret my whole life if that's how it needed to be, Rell."*

That's all the conversation we have time for before the carriage jerks to a halt by the main palace entrance. As I step out before the looming marble structure, the worries I tried to suppress come crawling up again.

"I should go to the temple," I say. "Give myself over to a more intensive meditation with my godlen. I don't want Elox to think I value the illusion of his support over the genuine article."

Please, let him not be offended by Lorenzo's hasty deception. He wouldn't have wanted one of his disciples to wrench me off course, would he?

Perhaps I haven't given him enough consideration these past several weeks while I've courted the favor of his fellow godlen.

None of my husbands, not even Marc, protests that we

have more important matters to see to. Perhaps they recognize the importance of this task to my confidence.

"Do you want company?" Bastien asks.

I shake my head. "No, I'll focus better on my own. I'll see you soon."

And then, because I now dare to even with nobles departing from their own carriages farther down the drive, I lean in to give him a quick kiss.

The prince of Cotea's pale skin flushes from neck to cheeks. A little of my giddiness returns, enough to carry me through the palace halls to the temple doorway.

As Marc peers into the domed space, he frowns. "Now that one devout has come at you, I'm not sure we should hang back even in here."

"He only threw words at me. I escaped unharmed." In any outward fashion, anyway. "I have faith that the gods will watch over me."

He backs down, though his frown doesn't budge.

I kneel on the now-familiar silk cushion beneath Elox's placid statue and close my eyes.

My godlen didn't lend his support during the confrontation I just faced. Did I offend him in some way before today?

I tip my head to the light that streams through the stained-glass panes above. *Elox, I welcome your guidance as I always do. If you feel I've gone astray or that I've failed to do your principles justice, please let me see.*

As my heart thuds on, the shapes on my eyelids barely budge. A sense of hopelessness has started to well inside me when my mind drifts into a dream-like vision.

The whole of the empire stretches before me like it does on the map table in the strategy room. I hold my arms toward it as I did to the audience in the city square, and gentle white light washes across every town and river, forest and mountain.

The vision dwindles as quickly as it rose up. I blink and peer up at Elox's statue.

Is he saying that I'm on the right path to spreading peace as we always imagined? Or is he telling me I need to do *more* to make it happen?

Why has he gone so distant when I need him most?

A cleared throat breaks through my uneasy contemplation. When I glance toward the doorway, Axius has joined my guards.

He stays where he is, but I'm not sure there's anything more I can glean from this place.

I get to my feet and hurry over. "What is it?"

The high commander grimaces. "I apologize for interrupting your worship, Your Imperial Highness. We've had a new communication through your... most direct means."

The mirror. My breath snags in my throat. "Valerisse again?"

What new threats could she throw at me?

Axius dismisses my suggestion with a twitch of his head. "It seems she wasn't able to take control over every artifact you put in place. Although I don't know what the message is."

He doesn't feel comfortable saying more when staff or members of the court might be near enough to overhear. I can appreciate his discretion, even as the suspense gnaws at me all the way to the mirror room.

Lorenzo is already in the office waiting for me, a cautious smile lighting his face. My heart skips a beat. "Your mother?"

He nods and beckons me into the mirror room. *"I haven't spoken with her yet, but Axius summoned me."*

I suppose it's unsurprising that Valerisse's reach couldn't

extend to stealing back the relic I gifted to Queen Anahi. I'm not sure how quickly the tribune could communicate with any soldiers who might still be loyal to her all the way in Rione.

Small blessings.

As we position ourselves before the mirror, the queen of Rione studies both me and her son with an oddly tentative air. Remembering the news I've now made public, I let myself twine my fingers with Lorenzo's in front of her. He glances down with a jolt of shock and then smiles far more brilliantly than before, adjusting his grip on my hand.

When I return my attention to the queen, she's outright staring, but a trace of a smile has touched her own lips.

"An image came to me not long ago," she says. "Of you standing with my son—and two of the other princes the empire has taken in?—and declaring what he means to you. It felt so real… It was, wasn't it?"

Even if Elox has eased back, Ardone must have spread the pronouncement of my love. A heady shiver passes through my chest.

I squeeze Lorenzo's hand. "It was. I thought, with the relationship I'm hoping to form with Rione and the other conquered countries, that I should be open about the smaller relationships that will help us build those first bridges. Although they don't feel all that small to us."

"No. I can imagine they don't." She pauses. "I've also gotten wind that your enemy is on the move."

I lift my chin. "That's true. We expect to have to engage her forces in a matter of days."

"And woe betide us all if she strikes you down," Queen Anahi says, sounding as if she actually means it. She dips her head to me. "Let us begin our relationship of cooperation in earnest now, Your Imperial Highness. I've already sent all the soldiers we can offer to the boats to set sail on your word. They'll reach you as quickly as they're able."

My lungs tighten. I can't imagine Rione's squadrons alone will be enough to turn the tide.

I don't know if I can promise them anything but a slaughter.

But she's putting her trust in me. I have to accept it—and ensure I prove her right.

"Send them," I say, with all the determination I can summon. "Let us put down the usurper and usher in the future every country of the empire deserves."

CHAPTER FORTY-SEVEN

Bastien

High Commander Axius reins his horse to a stop at the crest of the low hill. The rest of our small party draws to a stop around him.

We peer down over a sprawl of fields and shrubland that stretches at least a couple of miles before rolling into small slopes farther north. The mild early-spring breeze carries the faint scent of the newly blooming wildflowers that dot the landscape.

It's a far more peaceful scene than it should be, given our purpose here.

Axius glances around at us—Aurelia, her guards, my foster brothers, and a handful of other military officers he holds in highest esteem. "This is the only route it'd make sense for Tribune Valerisse to take when approaching Vivencia. The hillier areas to the west and the river marshes to the east would slow them down too much and make them vulnerable to ambush."

Gazing over the open terrain, Aurelia nods slowly. "And there aren't any settlements near this particular stretch of terrain?"

"The nearest town—other than the one we passed an hour ago coming here—is on the other side of those hills to the north. There aren't even many farms in this region as the soil doesn't take crops well."

"All right." The empress appears to gather herself. "This does appear to be the best place to make our stand. Good visibility, some higher ground to position ourselves on, minimal collateral damage."

She can't quite stifle her grimace at those last words. The woman I love hates the thought of innocents being harmed in this war more than just about anything.

Which is why I'd rather be marching with her than any other leader I can think of.

"We don't have much time left to prepare," Captain Evando remarks.

Axius's mouth twists tighter. "We don't. Based on our latest reports from the limited means we have, her army will make it to this point in a few days."

We're only three hours' brisk riding from the capital, but it'll take much longer for the main mass of our soldiers to make it out this way, just as Valerisse's force has to travel at marching pace.

Marc clears his throat. "I'd imagine we should give the infantry their orders and send them on their way almost immediately, then."

He manages to make the statement sound more like a suggestion than a command, no matter how tempted the former emperor might be to give the latter. One of the many ways the man I once hated has transformed himself before my eyes.

How different might the empire have become if it'd always been Marc acting as imperial heir and then emperor —if Linus had never existed?

He was still a prick in his own ways, if not quite as horrific as his twin. And I'd rather not picture any alternate world where he was able to win enough loyalty from Aurelia that she never strayed into my and my fellow foster princes' arms.

The life I'm living right now… impending war be damned, it's a more fulfilling one than I dared to picture even a few months ago.

As I'm reminded of by the grunt of agreement from Axius and the sweep of his gaze toward me, Lorenzo, Raul, and Neven in our little cluster off to the side. "They're already well-organized and prepared to set out. Do Your Highnesses have anything to add?"

I restrain the smile that tugs at my lips. Aurelia has made it amply clear that she considers the four of us generals of sorts in this conflict.

There's a prickling in my one lung after the exertion of the ride and a knot in my gut at the thought of the violence no doubt ahead of us, but I wouldn't give up the chance to fight for the woman I love and the dazzling future she's imagining for anything.

"Nothing obvious occurs to me," I say. As much as I want to help Aurelia every way I can, military strategy is hardly my forte.

All of us dismount to stretch our legs briefly while the true military officers further discuss strategy amongst themselves. Aurelia ambles over to join our royal cluster, her brow knit.

"I've been thinking of more ways we might skew the

odds in our favor in the coming battle," she says quietly. "I've found a rather large range of uses I can put my gift to. I may be able to create a potion that would weaken the soldiers—mentally or physically. Or perhaps even better, make them lose their nerve so they'll outright desert."

Raul makes a dismissive sound. "Why spare them from justice after they marched against you?"

"It's hard to say how much they should be blamed for following a godlen's urging." Aurelia aims a small smile at Neven. "Not even we have been impervious to Sabrelle's influence. If I can prove that I'm the stronger ruler, surely both she and those she's set against me will back down?"

Neven shifts on his feet with a frown at the intended battlefield. "Sabrelle hasn't felt all that reasonable to me."

Aurelia squares her shoulders. "We'll just have to see. I'll do whatever needs doing. I just—I don't want my reign to begin on a bloodier note than I can help, if I can help it."

The thought of the upcoming bloodshed has been weighing on her more with each passing day. It shows in the slant of her mouth and the tension carried in her jaw.

I wish I could kiss all that strain away. I *could* kiss her now in front of all these witnesses, and no one would be shocked, but I'm not such an idiot I'd assume it'd actually solve anything.

Our biggest problem isn't even how much blood is shed but stopping most of it from being on our side.

Lorenzo brushes his fingers over the back of Aurelia's hand, a subtle caress that's still more than any of us would have dared before she claimed us as her partners. *"If you made a potion like that, how would you get the enemy soldiers to drink it?"*

Aurelia tilts her head to one side, her gaze going distant. "That's part of what I've been mulling over. I could concoct a formula that would be absorbed through the skin—but I'm not sure how far we could distribute it catapulting vials into the soldiers' ranks."

An image comes to me almost as vivid as a divine vision, with a tightening of my gut. "We could work together on that."

Her attention jerks to me. "What do you mean?"

I wave my hand toward the sky with its puffs of drifting clouds. "We should be able to combine our gifts without much trouble. Perhaps I could summon rain and we could imbue it with your concoction to pour down over Valerisse's army."

Aurelia stares at me in silence for long enough that embarrassed heat starts to creep up the back of my neck with the suspicion my idea sounded absurd. Then she reaches to squeeze my forearm. "Are you sure you'd want to attempt it? A collaboration that immense... You didn't want me to attempt any collaborations at all."

Oh. She's simply recalling my earlier cautions.

I offer a crooked smile. "I'm not saying I like the idea of losing another piece of myself or seeing you harmed. But if that's the only way we can win this—or the only way we win without more casualties than you can forgive yourself for—then... then I suppose an empress gets to decide how she's going to reign despite anyone else's misgivings."

Aurelia's answering smile is so bright it lights me up from inside. "We'll do whatever we can, then."

Raul lets out a disgruntled sound. "If there's any other way to distribute it *without* taking that step, maybe we should try to find it?"

Have I become the incautious one between us? I rub my face. "You're right. I might be able to cast an already-brewed potion into the wind and rain it down without any merging of gifts. We should attempt that first."

I just don't know how much time we'll have to weigh the logistics and risks in the moment.

As if in answer to my suggestion, the breeze gusts over us with a little more force, stirring wisps along Aurelia's upswept hair.

Neven makes a puzzled sound. "What's that?"

As I glance over, a delicate shape comes flitting through the air, so small and thin it's only visible when it's within ten feet of us. It looks almost like a butterfly, but there's a shiny yet papery quality to its wings that makes me doubt it's anything alive.

It swoops down and lands on my shoulder.

The others gape as I pluck the unexpected arrival off my jacket. It is an insect constructed out of paper, coated with a bit of wax presumably to fend off bad weather.

When I turn the figure over, it unfolds into a flatter page. There are no words, only a simple illustration of a cloud of actual butterflies descending on a castle.

Raul's forehead furrows. "Who in the realms sent that, and why?"

My breath has caught. A giddy tremor runs through my nerves. "Who else would send a note specifically for me? It must be from my father. He has a devout on staff who can send messages across long distances with his magic."

Lorenzo blinks. *"And he's warning you about a horde of butterflies?"*

I can't hold back a short laugh at my foster brother's bewildered tone. "No. I think he felt that writing anything specific would be too risky if intercepted. It'd have to pass by whoever Valerisse has left in Cotea to keep an eye on my family. It's a symbolic message. The best I can guess, knowing him and the situation we're in... He's saying he'll send people. As many as he can. They're the butterflies. Aurelia— the empire—that's the castle."

Did my past arguments finally win him over, or did he have his own vision showing Aurelia's claiming of me and that convinced him?

I suppose it doesn't matter either way, only that we have the additional support. And he wanted me to know so we could make use of the fact.

Aurelia presses a finger to her lips, already thinking through the possibilities. "They'll be approaching from behind. How will he stop Valerisse's allies from realizing?"

"Maybe they'll bowl right over the pricks," Raul says, sounding very satisfied with the thought.

"They won't be able to bowl over the whole army. If Valerisse realizes they're coming, she might be able to dispatch them all before the main battle even begins." Her fingers flex at her sides. "We have those illusionists... I wonder if they have enough power between them to conceal a small army."

Lorenzo frowns. *"That would be a massive undertaking. It's drained me just hiding myself for a few days at a time on the road."*

A flicker of disappointment crosses Aurelia's face, but the news has buoyed my spirits. I can't let hers falter.

I grip her arm in turn. "It's all coming together. Your whole country was founded by a small group who managed to overcome a much larger enemy. We'll find a way."

Aurelia's pensiveness doesn't lift. My father's offer is what she hoped for, but she has no way to coordinate with him— or Lavira or Goric, if they're summoning their resources on her behalf too. So many more people she wants to protect from the worst harm that could befall them.

Can I really say our ambition won't leave us all dead by the end of the week?

Even back at the palace in the midst of the evening's court gathering, the disturbing question lingers in the back of my head. Cards and darts aren't enough to distract me from the sense of impending doom.

Of course, that might be partly because I'm a little afraid of doom finding me right here. Every time one of the Darium nobles glances at me, every murmur that passes between them around me, I can't help wondering if they're sizing me up and finding me unworthy of their empress. Deciding that they're better off rid of me if I've wheedled my way so far into her life—or her for letting me in.

So, even though Raul and Lorenzo are sticking close to her, I meander through the room, always at a distance. Seeking the answers I haven't been able to give her yet.

It isn't only nobles among us tonight. Axius suggested that any of the military officers who wanted to should join us for tonight's revels, to enjoy a little leisure before many of them march off tomorrow. A couple of captains are currently awing their distinguished audience with their darts skill. Others have found themselves caught up in intensely curious conversations with nobles who must be equally nervous about what's to come.

Not the most relaxing of leisure escapes, but maybe they're enjoying getting to be in a position of authority with the nobles for once.

Captain Evando has joined us even though he's going to be remaining at the palace—something it's clear he isn't pleased about, but Aurelia has insisted that he hold the last line of defense if any of the enemy threaten the city. He sips his glass of wine slowly and watches the court from a spot by the wall.

Until Neven ventures over. He says something with a wave of his hand that looks a little aggressive to me, but the corner of Evando's mouth ticks upward.

I pause to watch the two of them—my youngest foster brother who I've had to accept isn't a kid anymore; the captain who, now that I'm thinking about it, only has a year or two on me as best as I can judge.

Neven's eyes flash and his cheeks flush. He prods Evando's chest in a way that looks awfully familiar—and that Evando doesn't pull away from.

The captain simply laughs and grasps Neven's shoulder with a squeeze that lasts a bit longer than seems merely friendly.

Whatever he says next, Neven appears to mellow out. He nods, a smile playing with his lips.

When he walks onward, I amble over beside him. "Your taste has shifted from musicians to the military, has it?"

The prince of Goric stiffens and spins toward me with a narrowing of his eyes. "If you're going to make a fuss—"

Guilt jabs through my stomach. I hold up my hands before he can go on. "No, nothing like that. I was only… making conversation. And trying to keep up with your life. Evando seems like a decent enough fellow."

"More decent than previous musicians?" Neven mutters.

I wince. "I might have been overly disapproving of that situation. It's your life. You should live it as you see fit. If you're happy, then who am I to judge?"

Especially when my own love life has hardly been fit for public consumption until very recently.

Neven's shoulders come down. He bumps one against mine. "It's not as if I'm settling down any time soon. But… it's nice to have good company when you can find it, isn't it? Of all types, not just brotherly."

His voice has gone a tad wry.

I have to smile. "I can't argue with you there."

And maybe I shouldn't be depriving myself of the non-brotherly company I've earned now that I don't have to.

My heart thumps faster, but I let myself weave through the crowded room toward the spot where Aurelia is cradling Coraya in her arms. She murmurs something to our daughter, who babbles cheerfully in return, drawing a laugh from the nobles clustered around them. Her wooden toy hisses with the beads jostling together inside it.

At the sight of me approaching, a gleam more pleased than I've seen from her recently comes into my lover's—my *wife's*, I have to remind myself—eyes. She beckons me closer and adjusts Coraya against her bosom. "Prince Bastien, I think our imperial heir needs a change of scenery. How would you feel about entertaining her for a spell?"

The nobles glance over at me. My pulse outright stutters.

Will they realize I'm acting as more than just a substitute fatherly figure—that Coraya truly is *my* daughter, not Marclinus's? Is it really safe to get this close to her?

I can't deny the affection in Aurelia's gaze. If I'm being honest, the desire to hold my daughter here before everyone, to finally be a real part of her life, overwhelms my fears too.

I accept our little girl carefully, bracing her against my chest so she can gaze at the room around us in her wide-eyed way. Coraya hiccups and then giggles, gripping the front of my shirt with her tiny fingers while she waves her toy with her other hand.

She's so wonderfully, gorgeously alive. And so wonderfully, miraculously mine.

But no one else appears to suspect a thing. The nobles return to their conversations, focusing on the empress in their midst. Raul shoots me a quick smirk, but he smirks a lot, so no one would find that unusual.

And I hold and cluck my tongue at my daughter, accepted as part of the empress's inner circle. As if I truly belong here.

We really succeeded. We won this victory, however long it'll last before Valerisse might smash it to pieces.

Coraya looks like she could be Marclinus's daughter, and that's the story we've presented. So that's all anyone sees.

As I grin down at my daughter, a deeper well of joy rises up inside me—and brings with it a flare of inspiration that stops me in my tracks.

Maybe the answers I've been searching for are right here in the family we've created.

Chapter Forty-Eight

Aurelia

As I gaze down into the dark, stone-lined pit, my fingers curl into the sleeves of my dress as if trying to pull my body away. The frenetic thump of my pulse urges me past my hesitation.

I glance up at the Kosmelian cleric who led us to this isolated room in the temple. "I'm ready."

He looks even more hesitant than I feel. "Are you sure, Your Imperial Highness? We wouldn't normally expect— The meditation hollow is typically only used by myself and our devouts— You can commune with Kosmel in the main worship chamber far more comfortably."

My smile tightens. Every inch of my skin prickles with the awareness of my guards, my princes, and Axius watching. I have faith in my husbands, but will the others look at me differently if I lower myself into the shadows this way? See me as tarnished?

But Kosmel *is* the patron of shadowy places and tarnished souls.

"I can't commune with him anywhere near as closely there," I say. "It's important that he see how committed I am to honoring his will."

The trickster godlen is the last divinity of the nine—the only one I haven't made a direct appeal to yet. Maybe some part of me hoped I wouldn't need to when he's such a significant figure to my home country. Surely he'd feel some sympathy to my struggles.

I can't take his support for granted, though. We set off to confront Valerisse's forces tomorrow. Every detail of every strategy could make a difference in how many survive, in the fate of the entire continent.

This is no time for my courage to fail.

The cleric dips his head in acceptance, hands me the offering pouch I requested, and eases to the side. A narrow spiral path runs along the wall of the pit, leading down to its base some twenty feet below.

The stone floor is shrouded in shadow... but I can make out traces of movement within the darkness.

A creeping sensation runs through my nerves. My limbs balk, every instinct reminding me of the maladies rats can carry, of the fragile balance of my health that I've needed to consider since my sacrifice.

I will trust Elox and Kosmel to see me through this appeal.

I ease down the path with careful steps, setting my hand on the wall as soon as I'm low enough. My guards hover overhead as if they think they might have to wrench me back out.

No enemies wait for me below. Only the rustling of furry bodies brushing together and the tiny clicks of their claws.

My other hand clutches the pouch. My nerves jump at

the thought that the rodents might leap at it rather than waiting for me to bestow my gift voluntarily.

The rats continue their scurrying across the floor of the pit. As I descend farther and my eyes adjust to the waning light, I make out even darker patches between the lowest stones: holes that lead to the tunnels they live in that weave through the entire temple.

My breath snags at the base of my throat. I hold it through my last several steps to the bottom, my heart pounding so hard it dizzies me. A musky smell that's thick but not entirely unpleasant fills my nose.

As I place one foot and then the other right on the floor, the rats adjust their course to make room without seeming to pay much attention to me. There have to be at least a dozen of them scampering across the rough stones at any given moment, some slipping away into the holes while others emerge.

I lower myself to sit cross-legged in the center of the pit. A few of the furry bodies brush against my legs through my skirt, and I suppress a flinch.

They're only animals. Sometimes harboring disease, yes, but also clever and determined and capable of affection. Hardly horrifying.

Swallowing hard, I loosen the mouth of the pouch and spread the bits of cheese, bread, and nuts across my lap.

At once, a few of the rats leap onto my skirt. In a matter of seconds, the scurrying bodies have become a flurry of motion, wriggling across my legs to snatch a morsel and darting off again.

My jaw has clenched, and my arms have gone rigid at my sides. Closing my eyes, I will myself to relax with all the self-control I can summon.

I lift my hand to tap it through the gesture of the divinities. Then I extend my thoughts beyond my body.

Kosmel, I come before you now to show my faith in you. So many could die on my behalf in the battle ahead. If any trick could see us safely through the danger, I'll take it. Please, show me what slyness you would have me carry out in your honor. I put my life and those of my subjects in your hands as the first leader of Accasy did all those centuries ago.

I give myself over to the darkness and the movements of Kosmel's sacred animal all around me.

Let the rats eat their fill. Let the shadows wrap around me. The darkness holds answers too.

An image wavers up in my mind: a mass of soldiers in the Darium uniforms of white bones on black fabric. Other companies march toward them from either side in green and blue… and then, as they draw near, their clothes ripple into a matching black and white as if they're all part of the same swarm.

My mouth goes dry. The image echoes the comment Bastien made to me last night after we left the hall of entertainments. *"What if we could hide our allies in plain sight?"*

Sabrelle has used that tactic against me enough times, hasn't she? Transforming people I thought were colleagues or loyal servants into my enemies under my nose.

Do we have enough gifts between us—can those talents be stretched far enough—?

The pictures flowing through my head waver with my doubts. I straighten my spine against them and inhale deeply.

I will honor Kosmel by trusting his tricks. It's the best offering I can make to him.

The vision of the horde of soldiers expands in my mind —and just for an instant, a smoky wave seems to wash over them, wiping away all the colors and the skeletal designs, toppling them so they sprawl out in a sea of pure Kosmelian gray.

Then the image wisps away. I find myself blinking in the darkness, my pulse racing through my veins.

What was that last part supposed to mean? Or was the godlen simply confirming that he would feel honored if I follow his suggested tactic?

I close my eyes again and let my mind drift, but no further impressions come to me. The rats have settled down after their furor for the food, trotting past me to carry out their own business, though a light weight on my calf tells me one has decided my lap makes a good bed.

With an odd mix of amusement and revulsion, I nudge the little creature off onto the floor. It scuttles away with no sign of offense. I draw myself back to my feet, brushing a few lingering crumbs from my gown.

The climb out of the pit feels much faster than the descent. My party and the cleric all watch me intently as I take the last few steps to the surface. I spot a couple of devouts peering from a nearby doorway.

"I've seen Kosmel's advice, and I will heed it," I tell the cleric. "Thank you for giving me the space to reach out to him."

"Of course, Your Imperial Highness. Should you ever need anything else, you only have to ask."

I hold the message I received in as we hurry to our horses. Only once we've left the temple well behind in the city streets do I start giving my orders.

"High Commander, the illusionary specialists and the gifted dedicats we meant to pair them with will need to set out as soon as I give them their instructions. Kosmel reassured me that completely concealing our military allies shouldn't be necessary. We merely need to convince Valerisse's forces that the soldiers from the outer territories are merely more Darium troops coming to join them—make them look as if they have the right uniforms."

A rough chuckle tumbles out of him. "Still an immense task, but adjusting the appearance of their clothing should be significantly less immense than erasing them from view altogether. You think we'll be able to deceive the tribune for long enough for them to get within striking distance?"

"Kosmel will be watching over our trick. I believe he will see it through." I pause. "We'll need to send at least a couple of pairs to Goric and on a cautious route to Lavira as well, in case the other kingdoms are sending their own soldiers."

If Rione and Cotea were swayed, there's a decent chance the others were too. I can't leave them to be slaughtered.

Of course, if we stretch our resources too thin unnecessarily, we *all* might be slaughtered.

The uncertainty pinches my gut, but I set my chin. I took a chance reaching out to the outer territories for their aid in the first place. I owe it to them to trust them to come through for me when we need it most.

Not that long ago, I thought the biggest leap I'd ever make was crossing the continent to marry into the imperial family. I thought the only person whose life I'd be risking for my plans was my own.

I never could have imagined the precarious territory I've found myself venturing into now, but my plans haven't changed. If I want to see the empire's people free and safe, I have to keep going.

Everyone who's agreed to come with me has accepted those risks for themselves too. I can't let myself forget that.

As if influenced by my thoughts, Bastien speaks in a low tone. "I could ride ahead toward Cotea and prepare them for the strategy. Whichever officers my father has sent with the troops might listen to me faster than Darium representatives."

Conflicting jabs of anxiety pierce through me: the fear of seeing him leave clashing with my worries about our schemes going wrong. But it isn't just the Cotean soldiers we need to think of.

I shake my head. "I need you here for everything we're going to attempt. At some point… I have to trust that my allies will cooperate without special persuasion."

Or we're most likely doomed regardless.

We don't have to ride far. Knowing we'd be sending them off soon, Axius assembled the illusionary experts and the associates who've volunteered to attempt to merge gifts with them in one of the military camps set up around the city walls—the one closest to the Kosmelian temple.

The high commander nudges his stallion to a gallop to arrive a little ahead of the rest of us. The camp is mostly empty now as the main force has moved north, but several tents and a few covered wagons remain. When I rein my horse to a stop at the edge, our hastily assembled company has gathered in front of me.

Most of my companions dismount, but I stay in the saddle where I can see everyone's faces. Along with the eleven illusionary experts are familiar faces like Baronissa Hivette's, whose gift for transmitting images we're hoping will extend the distance and breadth of her partner's mirages, and Calvus the harpist, whose gift for projecting and intensifying sound seems to be able to combine with illusions in similar ways.

They could have stayed in the palace and hoped to remain far from any fighting, but they're here. I'm not going to let any of them down.

"We have a divine mandate for our plan, delivered by Kosmel in all his impressive trickery," I announce. "We're going to hide the foreign soldiers right before our enemies' eyes, making them believe the newcomers are more Darium troops on their side. We'll send you with as many actual uniforms as you can carry to help bolster the illusion, but most of the deception will depend on you. High

Commander Axius will give you further instructions on who will head to which region and how to best make your approach."

Everyone nods, the soldiers with a spark in their eyes that makes me think they've been eager to finally put their skills to full use. Hivette squares her shoulders, nervous but determined.

Gods, I hate to think how her wife will worry while she's off on this perilous quest.

Because I'd feel like a villain not to, I add one more remark. "Remember what we told you about the possible consequences of combining gifts. Don't push your magic until you're coming within view of any of Valerisse's forces. And if you've had second thoughts about attempting it at all, please let us know. I wouldn't order you to risk another sacrifice."

Not a single person budges from their cluster. If anything, their expressions turn more defiant.

Calvus offers a hard grin. "The traitors aren't getting away with this. I'm looking forward to finding out how far I can stretch my talents to protect the empire."

A murmuring of approval follows his words.

After the preparation Axius has already given them, it takes less than an hour before all pairs are ready to ride out. I stay at the camp to see them off. As the stable hands who've come out with their steeds start distributing the horses, Calvus ambles over to where I'm standing with the princes.

He offers me a respectful bow. "Never thought I'd see a time when even a musician could help win a war, but I'm glad for the chance, Your Imperial Highness."

My lips twitch upward at his wry tone. "I'm grateful for your willingness to attempt it. We'll miss your music until you return."

"You'll have plenty of other good company in the

meantime." His gaze darts over the princes, and Neven's posture tenses.

He and the harpist had some kind of relationship for several weeks during last year's coronation tour. Are there lingering hard feelings?

Calvus simply arches his eyebrows at me. "You've hoarded all the other princes. I suppose I'm lucky I got to dally with one while I did."

A sound of protest escapes Neven. "You shouldn't talk to the empress like that. She never— Anything *I* did—"

The harpist raises his hands in surrender, his expression softening as he meets his former lover's gaze. "It was more a compliment than a complaint. I think the 'wild princess of Accasy' has been good for all of us in different ways— including you. It's been a relief to see you in a better temper these last few months."

Neven hesitates, and his stance relaxes slightly. He aims a trace of a smile at me. "She's definitely got a knack for leading the way."

Calvus bobs his head to me again. "Let that talent lead us all the way to victory."

I watch him ride off with the others and try to ignore the sinking sensation in my stomach. It remains heavy through the short trek back to the palace.

I stride into the front hall already girding myself for the final meetings and preparations ahead—and a small crowd of nobles hustles in to meet me.

Bianca steps forward at the head of the bunch. Most of the noblewomen who've joined our combat training sessions, including Hivette's wife Damina, follow her alongside perhaps fifteen of the court noblemen.

Bianca holds her head high. "We're not letting you go out to fight those would-be usurpers alone, Your Imperial

Highness. Tomorrow morning, we're all setting out with you to do battle however we best can."

A sharper pang radiates through my chest, but a simultaneous swell of affection dulls the worst of the pain. "I'll be honored to fight alongside you."

By all that's holy, let our efforts be enough.

Chapter Forty-Nine

Lorenzo

Raul grabs another patch of shadow, which solidifies into a thin ribbon in his grasp. "One more go?"

I nod, readying myself.

Raul flings the shadow ribbon like a whip, and I cast my gift alongside his. As I picture the shadow seeming to stretch longer and wider, it shifts before my eyes.

But not just as an illusion. Raul threw it toward the posts we set up as targets near the wall of the training room, aiming for only the one in the middle. The expanded swath smacks into two others on either side as well—and knocks them over.

We've accomplished the combined effect several times before, but seeing it in action still brings a breathless laugh to my throat. When we work our gifts together, my illusions can turn real—at least, when the illusion I'm conjuring is playing off what my foster brother is already wielding.

I grin at Raul as he lets the shadows dissipate. With matching enthusiasm, he bumps his shoulder against mine. "I wonder just how much shadow we could master if we really stretched ourselves?"

Aurelia's voice carries from the other side of the room. "We're not finding that out today. We won't be finding it out *at all* unless the battle depends on it."

I turn to meet her firm stare. The worry I can sense behind her deep blue eyes brings an ache into my chest.

She could see everything she's worked for fall to ruin in the next few days, but she's still doing her best to keep us safe. Still trying to ensure no one sacrifices more than they have to for her mission.

I can't even imagine how much that battle is going to wrench at her no matter its final outcome. My wife isn't made for war, even if she's willing to grit her teeth and push through it.

I make a gesture of acquiescence alongside Raul's huff of mock-disappointment. "We'll play nicely," he promises in a teasing tone.

We've been careful to only experiment with relatively small effects, partly to avoid any harmful consequences of merging gifts and partly so we don't exhaust ourselves before we face the enemy.

Aurelia has needed to make similar considerations in different ways. She returns to the form she was moving through with the Sabrelle-blessed sword, weaving the blade through a series of parries, feints, and stabs that looks graceful after all her practice. She's moving slowly, though, rather than risking more strain to her muscles and her recently healed arm.

Captain Evando frowns where he's standing a few paces away to evaluate her process. "If all goes well, *you* shouldn't need to use that sword at all."

"But that's not something we should count on." Aurelia lets out a ragged sigh and lowers the weapon. "Sabrelle will see that I haven't forsaken her, even if she has me. I'm willing to honor the might and skills she champions, even if not exactly the way she'd prefer."

"If she can't tell that already, she's an idiot," Raul mutters, and then flicks his fingers through a hasty gesture of the divinities as if afraid his insult will make more trouble for our empress if he doesn't atone.

Aurelia rolls her shoulders. "I think that's enough training for today. It's getting late, and I need to check on my brews."

She slides the sword into the scabbard on the thick leather belt strapped around her waist—the same one she'll wear when we ride out tomorrow.

Raul and I head to Aurelia's chambers alongside her and her guards. After her announcement of our role in her life, no one dares to make a remark when we follow her right into her bedroom.

Marc stations himself by the door as usual. He doesn't seem to have been able to shake his sense of himself as her guard first—or maybe he really is concerned that he'll need to defend that doorway on her behalf.

Over near the desk, a couple of cauldrons are bubbling. An acrid herbal scent laces the air. Aurelia's cat perches on a nearby trunk, eyeing them with apparent suspicion.

Bastien glances up from where he's sprawled in a nearby armchair, a thick text open on his lap. "Do we have any dried osserfew? It seems as if that can be a key ingredient in certain paralytic potions."

As she rests her sword on her vanity, Aurelia nods. "I've got a bag of it with my other supplies."

Bastien glances back at the book, worrying at his lower lip. He's been trying to contribute to Aurelia's preparations however he can, but I don't think there are many medicinal substances she'd be unfamiliar with.

Our empress moves to each of the cauldrons, sniffing and pausing to tap into her gift. She turns off the burner under both, giving one a stir and adding a sprinkling of pale powder to the other. "As soon as they're cooled, we can bottle them."

The saddlebag lying nearby is already stuffed with all sorts of ingredients. She wants to be ready to craft a concoction in the moment if the need arises.

I don't want to think about how much *she* might sacrifice if she calls on any of us to enhance her magic with our own. I'm not sure any effort would feel like too far to her if she thinks it could turn the tide from tragedy to victory.

Even at her own expense.

One of the nursemaids has been waiting in Aurelia's apartment as well. When Aurelia walks over to her, the servant gets up from her chair and holds out Coraya, who's dozing.

Aurelia slides her arms around her daughter and tucks her close, dipping her head as if in an attempt to completely encompass the baby. The ache in my chest spreads up to my throat.

We've come so far, created so much of a family, and yet it feels as if we're still on the brink of disaster, barely a bit of stable ground beneath our feet.

But I suppose completely overturning the course of a centuries-old empire could never be easy.

All the same, a pulse of determination pushes through the ache inside me.

The battle we're charging into tomorrow could be the worst horror of Aurelia's life. I want her to remember how far she's come to get to this point—and how much she's gained along the way. All the joys we've found in this life together that she can draw strength from no matter what else comes.

Aurelia cuddles Coraya for a few minutes longer and presses a kiss to the baby's forehead. She hands her daughter back to the nursemaid, who bows and leaves the room.

Before our empress can suggest more preparations, I go to her and grasp her fingers. With my other hand, I make a quick sign in the air. *Come with me?*

Despite the stress tightening her expression, a hint of a smile touches her lips. "Where?"

I motion to the hidden panel in the walls and extend my illusionary voice so my foster brothers will hear my explanation as well. *"A little walk, just the two of us. For old time's sake."*

Marc's posture pulls straighter. "She shouldn't be going off without any guards at all—"

I wave off his objection. *"No one will even see her. We won't be gone for long."*

As I meet his steely gaze, I aim a few more words only at him. *"She needs this."*

The former emperor's jaw works, but he backs down—mostly. "If she isn't back here in an hour, we're raising the alarm."

I shrug in acceptance of his demand and tug Aurelia with me. Bastien's and Raul's gazes follow us, Raul's mouth tensing, but they let us go.

We are a family, but we also know that sometimes we can each bring our wife something special on our own.

As I guide Aurelia into the secret passages, keeping my fingers twined with hers, she stays silent and allows me my secret. I lead her to the unused bedroom that's our most frequent entry and exit point. Before we step out into the hall, I project an illusion around us that should hide us from the view of any passers-by.

Tension hangs over the entire palace. Even though it's relatively early in the night, few nobles are ambling through the halls. No music spills from the hall of entertainments. The occasional voices I catch are low with strain.

We slip out into the back gardens. As we venture beyond the glow of the lanterns along the palace façade, I loosen my grip on my gift a little. It's easier to conceal forms and movement in the darkness, as Raul well knows.

Only a little chill has entered the night air. I tuck Aurelia closer to me all the same, looping my arm around her waist.

We skirt the orchards until we reach one particular tree. As the silver-sheened leaves come into view, I feel Aurelia's understanding in her intake of breath.

She tips her head close to kiss my cheek. "Where we first started down this path together."

"I thought if there was any night to enjoy a twilight pumello, it'd be this one."

I step away from her just far enough to snap off one of the gleaming white fruits that hang amid the wizened branches. Twilight pumellos produce their delicacy all year round, but only a handful across the year, which is part of the reason they're so treasured.

Another part is the incredible flavor. I hold the supple, apple-sized treat to Aurelia's lips so she can take the first bite. She offers me a sly smile that sends a jolt of desire straight to my groin before digging her teeth in.

It was by this tree where I first dared to kiss her. Where she first accepted my affections, for however short a time *she* dared back then.

When I take a bite of my own, the mix of caramel sweetness and lemony sharpness brings those memories even more vividly to the forefront of my mind. I chew slowly and then draw Aurelia to me so I can kiss her again.

Our mouths meld together, provoking a soft sound in

her throat that has me hard in an instant. I have the sudden wild impulse to take her right against this tree amid its glimmering leaves—but I could hardly enjoy it knowing the guards on the grounds might stumble on us or while concentrating on creating an illusion to hide us.

And Aurelia, as always, is thinking beyond just the most immediate pleasures. After our lips part, she touches my cheek and smiles like there's nothing beyond this night. "We should bring back a few for the rest of my husbands. A treat like this ought to be shared with the whole family."

I can't argue. Her natural generosity is just one of the many reasons I fell in love with this woman against all practicality.

I kiss her again, long and hard, and turn to snap off three more of the colorless fruits. There'll only be a few left when we're done, but the empress can take whatever she wants from the palace.

And what does it really matter if the yield is diminished? This may be the last chance any of us have to taste something so sweet.

Chapter Fifty

Aurelia

As Lorenzo and I emerge into my bedroom, Raul lets out a guffaw. "That *was* a short diversion. What—?"

His gaze catches on the glistening white fruits cradled in my arms, and he cuts off his words with a low whistle of awe.

"I wanted to share the bounty." I walk over to hand one of the pumellos to Raul and another to Bastien.

Marc pushes off the door and stalks over to join us. His face is unreadable, but his tone sounds more wry than critical. "Pillaging my pumellos, are you?"

I arch an eyebrow at him. "I believe they're *my* pumellos now. I did bring one for you."

"Well, I suppose now that it's already picked…"

He accepts the pale fruit and turns it in his hand as if examining the tender skin for flaws.

Raul and Bastien have already bitten into theirs.

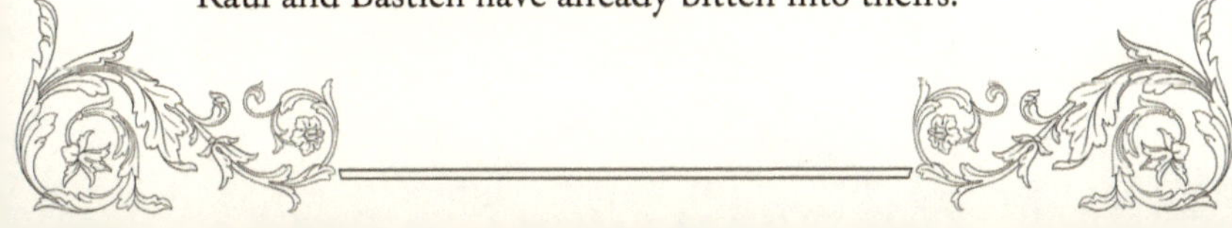

"Fuck," Raul mumbles around his mouthful.

Bastien closes his eyes with a worshipful expression that makes my offering worthwhile all on its own.

Lorenzo ambles up beside me, taking another bite of the fruit we've been sharing and holding it out to me for a turn. As I sink my teeth into the soft flesh, the incredible tart sweetness is amplified by my memories of the first pumello we ate together, more than a year ago.

Back then, I thought I was only seeking allies to help me survive until I could be married. I assumed my life would revolve around Marclinus and nudging the empire toward a better path in what subtle ways I could manage.

I never imagined I'd find myself with not one but four husbands, all of whom I've given my heart to fully. That I'd end up ruling the empire rather than dabbling from the sidelines.

That I'd be leading the charge against a horde of traitors in order to save not just my position but all our lives.

The last thought brings a bitter tang into my mouth that offsets the sweetness. I swallow hard and turn back to Lorenzo.

He strokes my cheek before taking the fruit from me. There's so much affection in his deep brown eyes that it buoys me out of the gloom.

Tonight, we're not yet at war. Tonight, we can celebrate what we have rather than mourning what we might lose.

Marc finally bites into his own pumello. He stares down at the faintly pinkish flesh as he chews, his eyes widening slightly. With his next bite, he savors it even more slowly.

His gaze lifts to meet mine. "You know... I don't think I've ever actually eaten one before. We've had the tree my whole life—I assumed I must have—but Linus did tend to claim the special feasts. I can't recall ever tasting this flavor."

The startled delight in his tone brings a smile to my lips. "I'm glad you had the opportunity now."

A short laugh tumbles out of him. "You do have a habit of yanking me into new territory. You're the real treasure in this room."

He sets the pumello aside and traces his fingers up my jaw to draw me into a kiss. My pulse hiccups with the brush of his lips against mine, the matching sweetness mingling.

We've kissed in front of my other lovers before, but only when Bastien commanded the former emperor. My princes have never had to watch our intimacy unprompted—not since the days when Linus would force his attentions on me in front of the court.

Marc must catch my hesitation. His posture tenses, and he moves to draw back.

I catch the front of his jacket before he can and press my mouth to his hard, pouring all the devotion that's grown between us into the act.

He might have been the last of my husbands to find his way into my heart even though he was the first to claim the role, but I don't want him to feel that I place him lower than them in some hierarchy of love. I wouldn't be here without him any more than I'd be here without them.

I can no longer imagine my life without all of them by my side.

Whatever worries I might have had about the princes' reactions vanish the moment we break from the kiss. Lorenzo is beaming as if he couldn't have pictured a better progression to our evening, and a sly glint has lit in Bastien's eyes. Raul's mouth has formed a familiar smirk.

The gleam of gold on their hands reminds me that there's one other way I should confirm my devotion before we leave tomorrow. I slip away from them to my vanity and reach into the back of one drawer.

When I turn back to Marc, I'm clutching the fourth gold ring he had fashioned. "I believe this is yours. You've gone too long without it."

The smolder that lights in the former emperor's eyes sets my body aflame in turn. He holds out his hand and lets me fit the slim gold band around his forefinger.

The words I've never spoken directly to him spill from my tongue so easily now. "I swear before all the gods to love and honor you from now until my last breath leaves me."

A strangled sound escapes Marc, and then he's kissing me again, so hard my head spins.

My princes give us our moment, but Raul has never been the patient sort. As Marc teases his fingers along my jaw and tilts my face for another kiss, the prince of Lavira steps forward to slide his arm around my waist. "Well, if we're getting started on the full festivities… We'd better all satisfy our wife to the best of our abilities, hadn't we?"

When I glance toward him, he grazes his thumb across my lips, provoking a tingle of heat. His gaze flicks across his foster brothers. "No slacking tonight, any of you."

While Bastien snorts at the warning, Raul claims my mouth. A heady tingle spreads through the rest of my body. It condenses in my sex with a throb of need.

"So damned beautiful," Bastien murmurs, kissing the side of my neck from behind. He teases his fingers over my hair to free the upswept strands from their pins. A magic-conjured breeze ripples beneath my dress to lick at my skin.

I turn to capture his lips next. The prince of Cotea kisses me as if he could bring me to life with just the passion of his embrace.

Then he takes charge of our whole company in the way Bastien does best. "We don't want to keep our empress from her sleep too long. Let's get her out of this dress and thoroughly satisfied without any further delay."

As Raul gets to work on the lacings, I tug at Bastien's shirt. "I shouldn't be the only one getting stripped down."

He grins. "No, your eyes should be satisfied too, shouldn't they, Star?"

He motions to the others and hauls his own shirt over his head, rumpling his auburn hair into an even more endearing state. Marc gives another halting laugh before pulling off his guard jacket and the shirt beneath.

Lorenzo sheds both shirt and trousers without remark and takes over the loosening of my gown when Raul pauses to toss aside his tunic. Marc glances around at the other men, and a shadow crosses his face.

"I'm sorry," he says, abrupt but quiet.

He's looking at the dull pink shape of the imperial crest branded on Bastien's chest just below his godlen mark. The brand all three of the princes bear, that Marclinus ordered me to sear into their skin.

We all go still, the fraught memory sweeping over us all.

"Was it your idea?" I have to ask, the words snagging before I can propel them from my throat.

Marc shakes his head. "Linus proposed it—and pushed for us to go through with it, when he was caught up in his jealousies… which I suppose were both valid and utterly unfair. But I agreed. I oversaw the branding. He wanted me to be the one observing your reactions."

His gaze shifts to me. "You never let how much you cared show even then. Even when I made you…"

He can't seem to go on.

I take his hand in mine, twining our fingers. "I cared so much it gave me strength. Better a brand than seeing the men I love executed because I failed to hide that love."

Maybe that's what Sabrelle understands the least about me. Love has never been part of her domain. But every act of violence I've committed, every torment I've endured to gain the power I have, it's been for love—for my country, for the people who've suffered, for my friends and family and the men I can now call my husbands.

Raul folds his arms over his chest in an arrogant pose. "Give us a little credit too. We're the ones who got burned."

Marc's expression stutters. "Of course. I meant the apology mainly to you. I—"

Raul claps him on the shoulder with a chuckle. "You're going to have to put up with a lot more hassling if you're sticking around, my no-longer-imperial foster brother. This one isn't that hard to forgive. It's her crest now. None of us mind being marked with that."

Bastien cocks his head, the glint in his eyes brightening. "Perhaps Marc needs one of his own. I'm sure he wouldn't want to be left out."

Marc's jaw works. "It would be reasonable compensation."

Lorenzo waves the discussion aside with a roll of his eyes. *"We're long past it now. And the two of you already scarred him in a much more obvious way. Let's not get so caught up in the past that we neglect our woman right now."*

He trails his lips along my jaw and tugs my dress down at the same time, and all the other men's gazes snap back to me.

Raul's voice drops to a seductive purr. "I'm sorry, Shepherdess. We shouldn't have gotten diverted from the real goal."

He drags the gown past my waist so the silk puddles around my feet. Then he pulls my drawers after the dress and nudges up my chemise so he can bring his mouth to the place I need it most.

With the first swipe of Raul's tongue over my sex, I gasp. Marc lets out a growl as if unwilling to be outdone and drinks in my next whimpers with an emphatic kiss.

He draws back just far enough for Bastien and Lorenzo

to strip off my chemise. As my first husband dives back in, his foster brothers turn their attentions to my breasts. Bastien laps his hot tongue over one nipple while Lorenzo teases the other between his nimble musician's fingers.

I stroke my hands down Marc's chest and over Lorenzo's shoulders, rake my fingers through Bastien's hair and grip Raul's dark strands until they pull free from his short ponytail.

The prince of Lavira sucks deeper, his teeth grazing my clit. He delves his tongue inside me to provoke a more potent jolt of pleasure. A moment later, a wider object—smooth but firm—eases between my folds to stretch my opening.

The mass of solidified shadow fills me with a perfect pressure. Raul pulses it in time with the movements of his mouth, and the thicker rush of sensation propels a moan from my lips.

Bastien evidently believes I deserve more. He sucks down the tip of my breast with a shock of bliss and then lifts his head to steal my lips from Marc. Then he nudges Raul with a rasp in his demanding voice. "Fill her properly. Take her to those heights you're always bragging about."

His foster brother chuckles between my legs, the vibration sending a new thrill through my sensitive flesh, but he follows his orders. Raul straightens up, removing his drawers as he does.

He raises me against his massive frame, the muscles in his arms flexing as he grips my thighs as easily as if my body was made of air. A cool pressure against my ass and back suggests he's manipulating the shadows again, this time to help support me.

He settles me over his cock, and all other sensations fade away. There's only the proportionately massive length of him sliding between my folds and stretching my channel so perfectly I must have been made for him.

Another whimper spills out of me. I tip my head against his shoulder with a flick of my tongue across his tawny skin, and Raul groans in approval.

When he's filled me to the brim, the delicious burn radiates from my core all the way to my toes. A gentle hand caresses my backside. Warmed oil slicks across my back entrance with a carefully probing finger.

Bastien kisses my shoulder and continues his ministrations as he casts a glance toward Marc. "Do you think you can handle lifting her to even higher pleasures?"

Marc's voice comes out strained. "I— Aurelia?"

He's asking me for permission. Confirming that I want him in every way I want my princes.

Raul holds me against him, remaining still while the other men play their parts. I can't help pressing my hips against him in an attempt to take him even deeper, to summon even more stimulation.

"Yes, please," I whisper.

Bastien clicks his tongue. "What are you waiting for, then?"

With a ragged breath, Marc comes up behind me. His hand replaces Bastien's at my ass, testing me. He brushes his lips against my back—one shoulder blade and then the other, more kisses down my spine—as his slacks rustle.

When he presses into my other opening, a needy whine creeps from my throat. It's so much—I'm so full—and somehow I want even more.

Marc wraps one arm around my torso so he can stroke my breast while he eases out and then plunges in again more forcefully. Raul drops his head to claim my mouth once more, adjusts my position between us, and matches the other man's rhythm rather than setting his own.

A strange warmth blooms in my chest that's a very different satisfaction than the sort I know my lovers have set out to offer me. They're all collaborating in this effort, all focused on me and my pleasure, without concern for any of those past offenses that linger in our shared past.

I don't pick up on a shred of doubt about this relationship from any of them. We've all embraced it as fully as Raul and Marc are literally embracing me between them.

They *are* lifting me high, sending me soaring. With each joint thrust, I'm spinning even farther in a haze of ecstasy.

Lorenzo trails his hand between me and Raul from my chest to my hips. He strums my clit just as the other two men surge into me, and my nerves crackle with the power of my first release.

I moan and clutch at them, my muscles clamping with the impact. Marc's breath hitches as he pumps into me faster. His head bows against my shoulder, his forehead damp with sweat, and I dig my fingers into his tarnished curls.

The tug against his scalp tosses him over the edge with me. Cursing against my skin between wild kisses, he rocks to a stop.

He hugs me tight with a mumbled "Love you" that cracks open my heart. I turn my head to meet one more kiss before he withdraws.

Raul's shaft remains rigid inside me. He nuzzles the side of my face, his voice gone husky. "Shall I offer you even more of a ride, Empress?"

All I can emit is a wordless noise of assent, but my most experienced lover recognizes it for what it is. He grins against my cheek and whirls us toward the bed. "Let's give you a different angle."

As he sprawls out on his back with me over top of him, never detaching our bodies, the other men follow us. With a smirk of his own, Bastien beckons Lorenzo. "She shouldn't have to go without. You can take over where our ex-emperor left off."

I hum in agreement, and Lorenzo clambers into position behind me, all eagerness. His hands skim along my sides and over my ass before he slides inside.

"Any way I can have you is a blessing, always," he murmurs in the most heated of tones.

Watching from the sidelines now, Marc simply smiles with no sign of offense at being replaced. He flicks his gaze toward Bastien, and his smile grows. "You take good care of our wife, brother."

The compliment sounds completely genuine. Bastien blinks, and his smile softens in return.

Marc certainly isn't wrong.

I lean forward, finding my balance between the two lovers inside me, and tilt toward the prince of Cotea. "And he should be rewarded for that."

I free Bastien's erection from his drawers one-handed. He touches my face with the tenderest of caresses before leaning back on his hands. When my mouth closes around his cock, his head sags. A choked groan reverberates from his chest.

Raul squeezes my ass. "That's our incredible woman."

As the prince of Lavira thrusts up into me, Lorenzo presses deeper too. *"And proving more incredible by the day."* His illusionary voice wavers with his fraying control. *"Love you so much, Rell."*

I bob my head over Bastien in time with the surges of pleasure, swirling my tongue around his rigid length and soaking in his salty, musky flavor.

There's nothing left but the five of us, the blaze of bliss roaring up inside me again, the hitches of breath and the echoing groans.

When I shatter apart the second time, pouring my cry over Bastien's cock, the rest of my lovers come with me. The hot spurt of Bastien's cum hits my mouth alongside Raul's last desperate pumps and Lorenzo's swaying to a stop over me.

Once we've untangled ourselves, I slump into the covers totally sated. Every worry has been washed from my mind, if only for the next few minutes.

I grope for Marc to tuck himself closer too and find myself encircled by all four of my husbands. As sleep hazes my mind, it occurs to me that this is the first time we've all shared this bed together.

I don't think there's anything I wouldn't give to ensure it isn't the last.

Chapter Fifty-One

Aurelia

Valerisse's army arrives like floodwaters creeping over the northern slopes, a sea of black dotted with fragments of white.

Flanked by Axius and my princes, I watch them come. One of the camp servants presses a steaming mug into my hands, but the richly bitter beverage barely rouses my spirits.

All around me, thumps and clinks sound amid the numerous troops we've been able to assemble from all across Dariu. The few dozen nobles who traveled alongside me have set up camp farther along the hill, wanting to leave me most closely protected by fully trained soldiers. Several Rionian squadrons caught up with us last night in their sky-blue uniforms and have settled in at our right flank.

The mass of my army still looks so small compared to our enemy.

By the time Valerisse's force has come to a halt a mile distant across the fields, I think it must be twice our size. And I'm not sure I'm seeing all of it or if even more soldiers remain concealed by the low hillocks behind them.

There's been no signal to indicate that any of the disguised troops we were hoping would fall in with Valerisse's have reached her army yet. The soldiers before me are all her loyal followers, ready to cut me down because she and her godlen claim I'm not fit to be empress.

As I stare at them, a tremor of doubt winds through my thoughts.

Am I proving them right? Am I sending thousands of the men and women I'm supposed to guide to prosperity to their deaths instead, for my own hubris?

How does this war set the empire right?

A glance at my gathered soldiers, standing in formation or stirring from their campfires and tents at the news that the enemy has arrived, sends an ache lancing through my gut.

I never wanted this. The plan I made with my parents and sister in hushed conversations in my palace back home only relied on me. I risked my life to bring down Emperor Tarquin. I let my lovers risk theirs too so we could survive Linus's madness, and even that compromise wrenched at me.

I'm a wild princess from a backwater country most of these people have never ventured to and never will. Who in the realms am I to order them to lay down their lives so I can hold the throne?

Lorenzo notices my reaction and shoots me a quick, warm smile. Among my many guards, Kassun draws himself straighter with a nod to me as if confirming he'll defend me to the end. All through the troops, soldiers dart gazes my way… and their expressions look brighter after.

I breathe deep against the swell of my nerves. These people *want* me on the throne. They believe in me and my way of ruling—one different from the imperial figures before and certainly far from anything Valerisse is offering.

They're fighting not just for me but for themselves, for the empire *they* wish to live in. If I surrendered now, I might be saving them from death, but not from whatever miseries the tribune and her godlen would inflict next. I'd be letting my supporters down in a much worse way.

I know all that. I wouldn't be standing here if I didn't. It's just harder to remember with the likely instrument of our destruction laid out in front of me.

I tap my fingers down my front, extending my prayers to all eight of the godlen I've appealed to over the past several weeks. *Elox and Inganne, Estera and Prospira, Creaden and Jurnus, Ardone and Kosmel, please stand with me and my people against this gravest of threats. Guide us well and see us through. If I'm alive to do it, I'll continue to honor you every way you deserve.*

The plea feels desperate even to me. May the divinities recognize why the circumstances call for it.

From where he's set up a temporary shrine not far away, Cleric Pierus catches my gesture. He echoes it, holding my gaze. "The gods are with you."

Let's hope that's true.

Across the fields, Valerisse's army appears to be settling in rather than preparing for an immediate attack. As evening begins to fall, fires spark amid the masses of bodies.

They're going to take a break, eat and rest after their long trek. Why not, when they can see they have us well out-numbered?

They can't imagine we would dare to force the confrontation when it'd put us at the disadvantage of giving up the slightly higher ground as well.

One figure on horseback breaks away from the sea of

uniforms. It streaks across the fields toward us, waving a white flag of parlay.

My throat tight, I go forward with my closest associates and my guards to meet the messenger.

The rider draws to a halt several feet away from me where I stop at the base of the hill. His eyes glint beneath his helm in the waning light. "Princess Aurelia of Accasy, Tribune Valerisse offers one more opportunity for surrender. Have your people lay down their arms, and no blood needs to be shed here."

That's it. No real terms to negotiate, just, "Give up or you'll be slaughtered."

Never mind that I'd imagine Valerisse will slit my throat even if I fold now, but it's possible she'll simply exile me to Accasy as if I was never much of a threat to begin with.

My resolve has hardened into an impenetrable shell around the soft heart she'd mock. My reply comes firm and steady. "I am Your Imperial Highness Empress Aurelia as ordained by the gods, and I will not bow to a traitor. If she means to defy divine will, I must stand against her for the empire's sake."

The soldier doesn't appear ruffled by my reminder of the treason he's a party to. He tips his head. "So be it."

Then he rides off without another word.

As we stride back up the hill, Axius falls in next to me. "They'll most likely attack at first light in the morning—once they're rested but hoping to catch us before we're quite roused. We should sleep in shifts and have everyone alert well before dawn."

I nod, though the squirming of tension in my stomach suggests I'm not likely to get much sleep at all. "Pass on the orders."

By my tent, the same dun canvas as the others so it

doesn't stand out as a target, I check the jugs that hold my two prepared concoctions and the bundled ingredients in case I need to invent another. Three cauldrons are already filled with water, ready to be set to a boil as soon as I might need to brew something new.

My pulse thumps at a shaky rhythm, spiked with adrenaline. I lie down on my sleeping pallet and close my eyes, but my thoughts spin on in the darkness.

When the call goes up throughout camp for everyone to ready themselves, I can't remember whether I ever drifted off. The pounding of my heart draws me to my feet and out into last dregs of the night.

Bastien appears near my tent, his auburn hair turned starker red by the wavering firelight. He has his bow slung over his shoulder alongside a quiver of arrows, but that's not the main way he'll be fighting today.

I tap the top of the larger jug. "As soon as they start moving, we'll need the rain."

His face tenses in momentary concentration. "There's a damp patch of cloud not too far to the west. I can bring it here in a matter of minutes. I'll start nudging it this way so it's even closer."

Marc steps up at my other side, his gaze on the distant slopes. "I've tried to sense their greatest weakness, but at the moment it's nothing we could exploit without leaving ourselves open far more."

I touch his arm. "We expected that. Don't strain your gift —try again if it looks like the situation may have shifted enough to allow better possibilities."

His mouth twists. "I've never wished more that I made a greater sacrifice. If my gift could—"

His words are cut off by a louder holler. "They're coming!"

Goosebumps dapple my arms. I spin toward the enemy

encampment, but there still isn't even a faint haze of dawn touching the sky. I can't see anything other than the tiny flares of campfires and torches.

They're striking out even earlier than Axius predicted. Maybe Valerisse has soldiers with gifts for helping their colleagues navigate the darkness.

All across our camp, my soldiers scramble with even greater urgency, tossing on helms and brandishing their weapons. The officers bark orders to assemble them into their formations.

I wrench the cork out of the jug and glance at Bastien. "As soon as you can."

He signals his agreement, his face turned sallow and his eyes distant as he urges the wind against those far-off clouds.

I adjust the reinforced vest I'm wearing beneath my simple dress—a birthday gift from Raul that's protected me before—and strap my sword belt around my waist. The hasty thudding of soldiers' feet all around me echoes my racing pulse.

Bending, I quickly light the camp stoves beneath my waiting cauldrons. The more prepared I am, the more likely we'll make it through this onslaught.

Axius calls for us to douse the larger campfires—to lessen what light we're giving the enemy, I presume. But even as the flames flicker out with hisses of water, a few gray smudges of daylight creep up from the horizon.

Valerisse's force has already crossed half the distance between our camps. If we hadn't risen early in anticipation of a dawn strike, her soldiers would have caught us still scrambling.

As it is, the dark clouds to the west roll in much slower than my straining nerves can take comfort in. I bite back the urge to tell Bastien to work faster.

He can see the coming threat as well as I can. The rain

won't do anything for us if he's too drained to carry out the rest of the plan.

Our archers shoot a flurry of arrows toward the approaching army, but most rattle against the shields the soldiers raise. The officers by our catapults yell for the larger projectiles to be launched.

One boulder smashes into the middle of the enemy ranks, toppling at least a few of our opponents. Another whips into their midst, and another—those stopped and broken into dust by someone's gift as they descend.

The other princes hurl their gifts into the fray. Raul digs into the shadows that still cloak the landscape, and the front line of marching soldiers topples as if felled by a trip wire. As their colleagues halt to yank them back to their feet, Neven heaves a specially rigged catapult with his enhanced strength to send a whole volley of granite blocks down on their heads.

More of the enemy soldiers stumble and collapse, and flickering lights spark around them. Illusions I know are Lorenzo's whip between the skeletal uniforms and whirl around them, distracting and disorienting them.

Thunder rumbles overhead, the most welcome sound I've ever heard. Marc dashes to the jug and hefts it up to wait for Bastien's signal.

At the beckoning gesture of the prince's hand, the former emperor splashes the liquid out into the air. Rather than falling to the ground at his feet, a gust of wind whisks the potion up toward the clouds.

Grinning at the initial success, Marc tosses the rest of the contents out for Bastien's summoned wind to catch. My concoction streams up to meet the incoming rain.

Bastien managed to keep the clouds only over Valerisse's army, still a couple hundred paces distant from our first ranks. The atmosphere is hardly overflowing with moisture, but the heavy drizzle patters down tinged with purple. A bitter scent reaches my nose.

I brewed the potion as concentrated as I could make it so that it could reach as many as possible when combined with the water of the rain and still sink quickly into the soldiers' skin. The sedative is a sister to the one I brewed to "kill" the rebel in my confirmation rite for Sabrelle, although that one needed blood drawn to fully knock out a man.

The mingled drops hit armor and uniforms. They must be trickling through the gaps in helms and mail, soaking through fabric to flesh.

All at once, shouts go up through Valerisse's army. Someone must have recognized the potential threat. An invisible force smacks through the falling rain and sends it flying toward us instead.

We were ready for that response. Gifted soldiers on our side form barriers of their own. The drops splatter across the conjured walls and dribble to the grass to soak into the earth instead.

Bastien grimaces, his shoulders relaxing only slightly. "I already blew it all across the field. I don't think they deflected much."

But how much of the diluted potion soaked in far enough to have an effect on our targets?

Raul swings his arms again, tripping more rows of soldiers with his ropes of solidified shadow. Beyond them, a few others are staggering, hands pressed to their heads as if trying to steady themselves.

Here and there throughout the mass of uniformed figures, more and more start to sway. A few dozen outright collapse. Others slump against their colleagues.

My spirits lift with the rising dawn. The strategies we planned are wearing the enemy down. Maybe we can overcome Valerisse's army before our blades even clash, without needing to fling bodies into battle or risk unexpected sacrifices after all.

Another volley of our arrows shrieks through the air, with Bastien joining in now. This time, the enemy soldiers aren't quite as sharp about jerking up their shields.

As forms crumple through the front ranks, Raul whips out rippling lashes of shadow all through the mass of bodies. In the midst of their stumbles and yelps of alarm, Lorenzo casts another wave of dizzying illusions.

The catapults groan with more flung boulders. Their dust showers the enemy army, but a few of the massive rocks hit their marks unshattered.

Supernatural energy warbles through the air from the gifts various other soldiers on our side are bringing to bear— lurching the ground beneath our opponents' feet, speeding the arrows faster, cracking the joints of armor and the buckles of belts.

There's still so many of our attackers, surging over the far-off slopes to fill the fields between with their mass of black and white. Have we felled a third of their number?

We're closing the gap. As long as we keep going—as long as we don't falter—

I glance at my other jug, that one of a potion meant to confuse the mind, but I'm not sure there's any point in attempting to rain it down on the enemy when they're aware of that trick now. Maybe later, after they've been distracted by other gambits.

Bastien follows my gaze. I make a quick gesture to indicate he should focus on using his talents in other ways.

He smiles tightly. With the launch of his next arrow, a sudden wave of wind roars across the fields.

The soldiers who were already wavering crash into one another. Several of the formations have fallen into total chaos. I catch sight of officers riding amongst them, hollering orders I can't make out—of a figure that must be Valerisse with a plume in her helm so richly purple it might very well be illegal for anyone not of the imperial line to wear it.

She raises her arm, the bronze band gleaming around her bicep.

A flash of ruddy light washes over her army. The soldiers gather themselves with renewed determination.

Raul grasps at the thinning shadows, and Lorenzo hurls out a deluge of illusionary images. Arrows rain down through the fading drizzle.

From somewhere in the enemy ranks, a barrage of magic-driven energy hurtles toward us.

The brutal wave sweeps across a vast span of terrain like a lightning storm brought to earth, sparks crackling. It surges up the hill so fast it shrieks through the air.

Soldiers farther down the hillside cry out in pain. My guards leap in closer around me, whipping out their own gifts to shield me in their various ways.

Even so, the impact wallops me hard enough to send me staggering backward. My ears ring. I stumble onto my ass.

For a few moments, my head reels. I gulp for breath.

Grunts and groans carry from all sides. Still dazed, I shove myself upright on shaking legs.

As far as I can tell, I'm unharmed other than the pained stutter of my heart and the ache that's woken up in my recently broken arm, but all around me…

Hundreds of our soldiers lie limp across the hillside. Even Axius has crumpled to the ground nearby, blinking blearily as blood trickles from a cut on his forehead.

Just beyond him, Cleric Pierus sprawls face down in the dirt next to his toppled shrine. The blast has seared his robes red and black.

The back of his head has been smashed right off.

Dear gods… Of all the people…

He'll never come back home to his wife.

I wrench my gaze to Raul, who sways where he's fallen to a crouch. His bulging arms hang slack at his sides despite the straining of his jaw as if he's willing them to move.

Are they paralyzed? Completely ruined?

Next to him, Lorenzo has toppled to his hands and knees. His eyes rove wildly, focusing for only an instant before they flick onward. His head bobs as if he's lost all sense of balance.

In front of me, one of my guards cries out. "Kassun!"

The chill that was swelling inside me pierces right through my heart.

The skeptical man who once muttered derisive remarks about me, the guard I won over through combat and confidence who's since defended me with every shred of his courage, has crumpled where the surge of magic hit him while he shielded me.

Blood gushes from a gouge in Kassun's chest too massive for anyone to hope to survive. His eyes have already clouded over.

For me. He died so that I wouldn't.

He'll never again laugh as he spars with his fellow soldiers —or with me—in the training room. Never again make a pretty maid giggle in the halls.

Tears sear my eyes. It's too much.

"What's happening?" Bastien demands in a hard voice that can't quite disguise its edge of panic. "Aurelia? Fuck!"

He swipes at his own eyes where he's braced by the jugs —both of which are now shattered, the contents of the second spilling across the ground. The prince's bow lies snapped amid the shards.

The skin of Bastien's face is reddened, his gaze vague as if he can't see anything at all. What did that deluge of hostile magic do to him?

Valerisse lets out a whoop of victory, and her army rushes toward us. The bottom of my stomach drops as if I've been hollowed out from the inside.

We're bleeding now, all across this hill. So many have died for me… and in a matter of minutes, I might very well follow them.

Chapter Fifty-Two

Marc

I heave myself off my knees, my arm aching where I yanked it up to shield my face from the worst of the magical blast—as if a few more scars would really make difference on my already mottled features. My other hand stings where I scraped it on a rock embedded in the earth. My ears throb with the sudden shifts in pressure.

Bodies lie strewn across our hillside. Some are still stirring, staggering to their feet, but… Great God help us. Did Valerisse plow over half our entire army in one fell swoop?

A sickly sensation twists through my abdomen like creeping vines. I've never fought in a position of such disadvantage before. I've never led the charge against anything other than ragtag bands of rebels, easily crushed.

These are our own imperial soldiers we're battling, chosen

for their strengths and trained to greater might. Their leader has ridden into more battles than I ever have.

I knew all that going into this standoff. It isn't as if I could have missed the vast sprawl of Valerisse's forces swarming the terrain ahead of us. But in the first exhilarating phase of the clash, it didn't seem to matter. I could feel our strength rippling through our ranks, potent enough to overcome any foe.

Apparently that impression was as much an illusion as anything Lorenzo could conjure. We're battered and broken now—fuck, is that Axius struggling to even sit up?—limping to meet the next charge.

My gaze snaps to Aurelia. I didn't focus on her closely in my first glance after the onslaught of magic, only making sure she wasn't injured before I got my own bearings.

Now, I take in the grayed cast of her face, the color leeched from beneath her tanned skin. The whites of her eyes gleam with a panicked glint I've seen before... in my opponents before I ran them through.

She's still standing, but her posture is starting to slump. Only the set of her jaw holds firm against the horrors around us.

My formidable wife with all her stubbornness and sweetness mixed together... Can her determination withstand even this?

Does it matter, if determination isn't enough to get us through the next ten minutes?

I yank my attention back to the incoming army, to our diminished forces shooting out arrows and tightening ranks at the base of the hill as the remaining officers holler. Valerisse kicks her stallion faster, her sword and armband flashing in the strengthening sunlight.

I haven't reached to my gift, but as I watch her, a vision

unfolds before my eyes. I see myself on horseback, pushing through the enemy soldiers with a prize held high by strings from my hand. The uniformed figures fall back at the sight of whatever my prize is, but my focus is all on Valerisse.

In the haze of the vision, she smiles, triumph dancing in her dark eyes. She holds out her hand to accept my offering—

And I whip out my sword to plunge it into her neck.

As she crumples, I lift my other hand alongside the first in a pose of victory. "It's over! I am your emperor, returned! Sabrelle has blessed me above all others on this day!"

My spirits soar at the cheer that rises from the mass of soldiers around me—and I look up at the "prize" I'm holding.

Those aren't strings. They're strands of hair. Strands of Aurelia's thick brown hair, twisted between my fingers above her severed head. Her lovely face has gone blotchy and vacant as gore drips from her ragged neck.

The image smacks me back to reality with a lurch of my stomach. I look to Aurelia again, and the vision surges after me.

Cut down that guard who's the fastest at blocking and that one who's deftest with her sword before either can react. Slice the empress's head right off her body, grab the horse tied by a tent just below…

My gut outright heaves. I double over, sputtering as the little breakfast I forced down surges up my throat. Red tinges the edges of my sight.

Sabrelle. The vision wasn't brought by my gift but as a divine missive, although it amounts to the same thing.

The godlen of war is showing me how I can win this battle—for myself, no one else. How I could end the conflict and reclaim the throne I lost.

I can almost hear her murmuring in my ear. *It would only*

be a small sacrifice, wouldn't it? Giving up one woman who's already betrayed you a dozen times over?

Deep down at the bottom of the heart I'm still getting used to feeling, a twinge of temptation tugs at me. To take this chance, to prove Linus wrong, to do my father proud—to rule the empire as I was always meant to.

Aurelia's voice breaks through the turmoil in my head. "Marc, are you wounded?"

The question rings with both resolve and concern, as if she'd cross oceans to heal me if that's what it takes.

I straighten up and meet her eyes. The fierceness has come back into her stance and her expression.

For me. For the man who betrayed *her* over and over in so many ways, who she opened her heart to anyway.

Near my other side, Raul is shoving himself upright, swaying with his arms too limp to help his balance. He peers at me, his teeth baring in a feral grin. "We'll pay them back for everything. Come on, brother."

There's no wariness or animosity in his gaze. All of that has fallen away between us.

Something in me cracks open with an even sharper pang than when Aurelia encouraged me to reveal myself to Axius. It was such a relief to speak to him as who I truly am... but even that wasn't really myself, was it?

The high commander still thinks of me as Marclinus, as the sum of everything my twin did as well as me. Like everyone did the entire time I was imperial heir and emperor.

But Aurelia and my foster brothers... They see *me*. Just Marc, just my own faults—and everything I've done to make up for them. They want to stand beside me and have me standing with them as I am.

I've heard Aurelia call us a family before, but somehow it never quite hit me until this moment.

What could Sabrelle offer me that's anything close to this feeling?

The clamor of the battle rushes back through my awareness, reminding me that I'd better get to work if I want to make sure the godlen of war and her dupes don't steal that family from me.

I swipe my hand across my mouth and stare out at the enemy army, tapping into my gift properly this time.

Where are they weakest—how can we break through their onslaught with what we still have…?

A vision that's all my own swims up: our people attacking the barrage with all our might, battling so fiercely we draw all the enemy's focus—until they're battered from behind and squashed between us.

My pulse stutters. We don't have enough numbers to send even a small regiment to skirt the battlefield and attempt to carry out that strategy on our own. But my gift has never shown me what's outright impossible before.

Is it only wishful thinking, or should I trust that the pieces will fall into place?

Just for a moment, my throat chokes up at the thought that I might be calling for our doom. But what else will we face if we *don't* give this battle our all right now?

If it's doom one way or the other, we might as well take as many of the enemy down with us while we can.

"Hit them with everything we've got!" I shout. "Hard and fast—don't give them a moment to breathe."

A few officers' heads tick my way, probably puzzled to be getting orders from a supposed imperial guard. That's fine, because Aurelia trusts my judgment.

She raises the Sabrelle-blessed sword she's drawn so it flashes in the morning sunlight. "We rally now and strike back with all our strength! Don't hold back. Every weapon, every gift, every bit of strength—now is the time to use it!"

Axius teeters to his feet but manages to echo her commands with a hoarse call of his own. "Soldiers, heed your empress!"

Despite the near-catastrophe we faced, despite the bodies still slumped among us, a ripple of dogged energy washes through our forces. The arrows fly with renewed speed. The catapults hurl projectile after projectile. Someone takes the initiative to set the sacks of rocks aflame and launches them into the midst of the enemy in streaks of fire.

The front line of Valerisse's army crashes into ours with a chorus of grunts and gurgles, but I don't think I've ever seen Darium soldiers fight as valiantly as those on our side down the hill. Propelled by the shift in the atmosphere, they stab and slash with the vigor of twice as many.

They'll do that to defend the ruler who's won their loyalty over and over again, far more legitimately than I ever did.

The longing grips me to run down among them and add my own blade to the fray. But my duty, as both guard and husband, is to stay here as the final line of defense if they should reach Aurelia.

Instead, I jab my sword toward the sky like she did. "For the true empress! For Empress Aurelia!"

Raul picks up the chant, and Bastien where he's braced against a nearby tent, and Neven back by the huge catapult he's manning. It flows across the hillside through all the soldiers, Darium and Rionian, who haven't yet reached the thick of the battle, louder with every iteration, vibrating with fervor.

"For the true empress! For Empress Aurelia!"

Let none of us forget why we're here, why we had the chance to fight for a better world at all.

Aurelia grasps my arm, the urgency in her gaze silencing my own hollers. "Marc, I need you to work with me. It's going to take more than any regular tactic to hold them back."

I don't know exactly what she means yet, but the answer falls from my lips automatically. "Whatever you need."

No doubts remain, no room for hesitation. I'll follow this woman to the ends of the earth.

And beneath it, if it turns out my gift has actually paved the way to our destruction.

Chapter Fifty-Three

Aurelia

The clang of blades and grunts of pain spur me faster. I yank Marc over to my collection of potion ingredients by the cauldrons already bubbling.

"If we can combine our gifts, we might be able to give our people the edge they need," I say, squeezing his hand. "Let's see what kind of potion would be most effective to weaken the enemy. Something that I can actually brew before they overwhelm us."

Marc sucks in a breath, but the worry that shadows his face is only for me. "If the gods decide we're asking too much —you shouldn't risk yourself."

I meet his gray gaze steadily, the ache of my grief welling up in my throat. "I'm already risking myself just being here. I might have died minutes ago—like Kassun, like Pierus." My voice catches, and I pause to gather myself. "I'm only trying to find the path that means fewer of our people follow them. Please. No one else's gift can guide mine like yours might."

He swallows with a bob of his throat. "All right. You focus on the 'patient' when you're devising a cure, don't you? We'll aim our gifts at Valerisse's forces together."

His agreement doesn't settle my nerves. If anything, my pulse thuds faster. I don't know what the consequences of our appeal might be.

I do know I won't like the consequences if we don't give this battle our all.

Beyond Marc, Raul bumps his shoulder against Lorenzo's. His arms still dangle limp at his sides, but his voice is clear enough. "Focus on me, brother. We're going to collaborate, just a little differently than we did before. I need you to be my arms. Are you with me?"

His warm but firm cadence appears to penetrate Lorenzo's daze of shock. The prince of Rione blinks hard and gives his head a little shake. He still sways with apparent dizziness, but he steps closer to Raul so they can support each other.

The larger man casts his gaze toward me as if asking my permission. I nod, ignoring the lump that's choking me.

None of us is going to surrender without pulling out every tactic we can.

I twine my fingers with Marc's, but I don't bother setting a rhythm. For all the wretchedness we've put each other through, we know one another as well as any two humans can.

Our hearts are already in sync. I trust that our gifts will follow our lead.

We stare out over the fields now churning with fighting men. An arrow whistles toward me only to be smacked aside by one of my other guard's gifts. The host of them has shifted to follow me to my new position.

If they can buy us enough time to see this gambit through…

I let my attention slide over the thousands of uniformed bodies surging across the grassy terrain. I need to cure this moment of their violence. Neutralize the contagion of their hostility. Heal my country of the havoc they've been wreaking.

A tingle spreads over my skin from where my hand and Marc's are joined.

Please, I think to Elox, *let me see the best way to stop them. A way that's fast and true. For the safety of all the realms. For the peace I'll bring. Please.*

A pinching sensation pricks at my gut. A chill washes over me that some part of my innards might be dissolving with this massive act of magic, but I hold firm, repeating my plea, concentrating on my intent.

Marc sucks in a sharp breath—and then I see it.

An array of herbs and powders flickers before my eyes. All of them must go into the cauldron—this one first, then that. Ten minutes for them to properly steep once they're at a boil.

We have time. We *must* have enough time.

I release Marc to snatch at my stockpile. My hands tremble with the leaves I scatter across the frothing water, the bits of root and flecks of crystalline mineral that follow it.

My first husband watches from behind me, silent until I've stirred and stepped back from the mixture.

"Do you know what it'll do?" he asks.

I open my mouth and close it again. I didn't ask that specifically. My intent was so broad.

I glance at him. "Do *you*?"

A thin smile curves Marc's lips. "I think Elox may be trying to make a point about the value of peacemaking. You should at least be glad that I don't get the impression it's going to burn anyone's skin off or dissolve their organs."

"Ah." A strangled laugh lurches out of me. "Well, I suppose that's good news."

"How are we going to get it onto them, though?"

A shout amid the fray draws my attention. New tendrils of shadow are whipping through the enemy ranks, lashing at ankles and tangling feet.

Raul smirks where he's poised next to Lorenzo, keeping up a low murmur to steady his foster brother's focus. Lorenzo is still blinking more than usual, but he maneuvers the shadows that stretch across Raul's hands without hesitation.

I spin toward Bastien. The prince of Cotea hasn't let go of the tent post he's using to ground himself, his dark green eyes as vacant and bloodshot as they were when I first looked him over. His head twitches as he attempts to follow the battle by sound alone.

I step closer. "Bastien, do you have enough energy to use your gift again?"

He lets out a raw chuckle. "As well as I can."

I grip his shoulder. "We'll work it together. I'll be your eyes, like Lorenzo is being Raul's hands right now. And when this is over, I'll see that the medics get you *your* eyes back."

"As long as we get to the point where you can ask them to try, I don't even care about the outcome." He rests his palm over my knuckles. "Let me know when and what, and we'll make it happen."

I stir the potion again, wishing every minute didn't feel like an eternity. The gasps and thuds of falling bodies jolt through my nerves. At the corner of my eye, Kassun's slumped body haunts me.

I tried to let him go. If he'd let me take him off duty a week ago…

Would I have died in that case, without him adding to my defense? Would he really have preferred that outcome?

I swallow hard and keep stirring.

When I peer down at the pot and my gift tells me it's ready, a gasp of my own rushes out of me. "Now. We need to fling this concoction over as much of Valerisse's army as we can."

Hot as it is, it'll be a stinging sort of rain, but I can't help that.

Bastien links his arm with mine. The clouds overhead start to churn, but their moisture is already dispelled.

This rainfall will be only my brew.

The prince of Cotea takes a slow breath. "Look where you want the wind to go. Think about the healing you're trying to do. That seems like the best way to merge our gifts."

I stare down at the cauldron, imagining the air whipping down and scooping up the greenish liquid. Picturing the serene glow that's appeared to me in visions before spreading across the fields with its patter.

A gust warbles past me and plunges into the cauldron. With a lurch of my heart, I flick my gaze toward the soldiers I want to aim the contents at.

A flurry of pale green flings from the cauldron up into the air and streams over the heads of our allies. I will it farther, faster, not even entirely sure how much I'm controlling it now and how much Bastien is simply directing it through impressions he's getting from me.

It streaks out against the lightening blue of the sky—and splatters across the center of Valerisse's army.

I don't know how many soldiers the droplets hit, how many got enough of the spray for the effects to take hold. The uniformed figures barely flinch at the impact.

Then a man in their midst lets out a bellowing laugh. He

swings his arms around another man braced next to him, engulfing his colleague in an insistent hug.

Before my eyes, more guffaws and giggles break out through the army. Someone starts singing a hopeful children's tune. Friendly voices carry through the clatter of the fighting.

It isn't a huge number of them, but they're disrupting the soldiers nearby: with embraces and eager chattering and tugging them into playful dances. Even though my stomach remains balled tight, a small smile tugs at my lips.

Elox is making a point indeed—perhaps with a little inspiration from Inganne. The desire for peace and joy can be just as much an obstacle to an enemy as a blade or a boulder can.

And no doubt this approach is more effective than any other I could have taken. If the soldiers my potion struck crumpled with wounds or poisoning, their fellows would push forward with even more desire to strike me down. If I'd turned them hostile to their colleagues, it'd be easier for those colleagues to fight back.

Instead, they're being faced with the men and women they've been preparing alongside for weeks offering affection rather than violence. Reminding them of what they might be giving up in their lives back home if they see this battle through to the bitter end.

Will it be enough?

Raul and Lorenzo's joint effort keeps tripping up the soldiers along the front lines, but the mass of Valerisse's army is still cutting down our own people all along the base of the hill. More gifts blare and blast on both sides. Our ranks look far too thin.

We haven't turned the tide yet. Maybe with just a little more...

I turn to Marc, meaning to suggest that we try again or

that I brew another batch, and see that he's squinting at the distant hills. My gaze ticks to follow his.

More soldiers are approaching, one mass to the northwest and another, larger one to the northeast. Their uniforms glower with the same black base and white bones as the enemy we're already engaged with.

My legs wobble—and a blaze of ruddy light streaks across the sky.

Not one of Sabrelle's omens. It's a red dove, the symbol our illusionists promised they'd show us when they were approaching.

My pulse hitches.

"Fight on!" I holler to our soldiers. "Don't let them gain one inch of ground. Show them the might of those loyal to the empire!"

I doubt my army has any idea why I'm suddenly energized. Valerisse glances toward the oncoming troops and turns back with a smile I can make out between the cheek guards of her helm even across the distance. Whatever other soldiers have noticed the new arrivals, they must also assume it's allies joining the fray late. No sentries have warned them.

Our trickery is working as planned.

The arriving troops must be exhausted from the pace they'll have set, but at the sight of the battle underway, they surge forward even faster. They sweep across the field from both sides, rushing toward our enemy's flanks.

At the last moment, just as the forerunners raise their blades, the illusionary teams drop their magic. Uniforms flicker to pale Cotean green, Lavirian red, Gorician brown— and the familiar dark green of my home country.

Even Accasy made it in time.

As more clashes of blades ring out across the landscape, I thrust my sword toward the sky once more. "Our allies are here! All of the empire unites against the traitors!"

The conquered countries weren't able to pull together enough troops to overwhelm Valerisse's force, but our numbers look nearly equal now—and the newcomers have taken her people by surprise. Dozens of soldiers topple in the first onslaught from behind.

My supporters on the hillside rally all over again. Determined shouts resonate all around me.

For the first time, victory is truly in reach.

We aren't the only ones to realize that. I catch flickers of fear crossing the faces of the nearest enemy soldiers. Those on the far edges of the battle wheel around, shifting and scrambling as they attempt to defend themselves from the other side.

Valerisse's horse rears. She glares straight at me with narrowed eyes, claps her hand against her blessed armband, and leans low as if to speak to someone beyond my view.

I'm already bracing myself when a roar of power reverberates through the soldiers.

The unseen force knocks aside even Valerisse's people, opening up a passage through their ranks, framed by invisible walls. As her horse springs forward along the narrow path, the effect veers up the hillside.

My soldiers dodge the swath of magic and swing swords and spears only to have them bounce off the protective surface. Arrows patter off the top.

A few of my guards leap in front of the surge of magic only to be knocked to the side. Their own gifts crackle and sizzle off the racing force.

One of them manages to hurl up a barrier right in front of me with a hum of magic that trembles into my flesh. Sparks flare between the opposing walls.

But I don't think Valerisse intended this effort to fell me on its own. She's galloping toward me, looking absolutely intent on delivering the killing blow herself.

I hold my sword out defensively, my legs shifting into the stance Captain Evando has coached me in for months. The weapon feels heavier than usual in my hands—maybe because the godlen who blessed it is much more invested in the woman closing on me.

A ruddy glow lights all around Valerisse's form. She slows her horse as it climbs the slope and dismounts about ten paces away from me.

The path behind her contracts and vanishes, encasing us in a smaller but still impenetrable bubble. I'm not sure how much my guards' efforts are protecting me anymore. Marc bangs against an invisible surface a few feet away while Raul and Lorenzo ram it with a mass of condensed shadow from the other side.

The magical barrier doesn't so much as creak. I suppose the dedicats who've conjured it dispersed the rest to concentrate on solidifying the shield around the tribune and me.

Valerisse stalks toward me, violet feathers bobbing in her helm, her mouth set in a grimace, her eyes gleaming with triumph. The athletic grace of her strides speaks of total arrogance.

She assumes I'll be easy pickings. That she can make a spectacle of cutting me down, and nothing else in this battle will matter.

She might not be wrong.

When she stops, only five paces away now, and lifts her voice, I realize she has an amplification charm by her throat. It projects her words far and wide.

"So-called empress, did you think you could win by begging for favors from all the countries beneath us? Don't you know that real strength can't come from shaky alliances, only from what *you* can do for yourself?"

Her words couldn't have pricked deeper if they came

from divine inspiration. My chest constricts with the thought of the loyalties that lead to the deaths all around me.

I've fought so little of this war in any way she'd actually consider fighting. My allies have taken the worst of the blows.

That doesn't mean I haven't earned my throne, though.

"You have no idea how much strength it's taken for me to get to this moment," I retort.

She scoffs. "Sitting pampered in your palace in Accasy and then more of the same here in Dariu—and you think you can talk about struggle? The Darium empire was built through combat and domination. You would never have lasted a day during the founding."

A quiver tickles across my throat. When I speak, my voice resonates as loud as hers.

"It isn't the time of the founding any longer. We've left the Great Retribution far behind. We can be more than survivors grappling with each other to come out on top. As a tribune, I'm surprised *you* don't know how much strength there is in bringing people together for a common cause."

At the corner of my eye, I see Bastien standing shoulder to shoulder with Lorenzo now. Is it their gifts working together, air and illusion, to project my voice like hers?

Can she not see how much strength there is in what we're accomplishing right now?

She doesn't want to.

Valerisse rolls her eyes. "We march into battle with all the blessings of our godlen of war, the godlen who gave the imperial family their sacred charge. Sabrelle will see you fall."

I raise my voice even louder. "The empire answers to all the godlen, and I have their blessings. I'm guided by all of them for the good of all the empire's people. Let them show they stand with me as I have honored them, even as Sabrelle turns her back on the rest of our divine guardians!"

Sheens of light flicker within the barrier: orange and green, blue and pink, yellow and gray and a wash of deep purple that wavers all around me as if Creaden himself has wrapped me in his approval.

Then white. The pure, soothing white of my chosen godlen washes over me from above like a stream of warm sunlight.

Elox may not have offered an open show of his support before, but he's here now. He's facing this challenge with me.

Gasps that are all astonishment and awe rather than pain reach my ears from the soldiers surrounding us. Valerisse's face hardens into a mask of resentment.

She takes another step forward, her sword lowered but her fingers clenched around the hilt. Her words take on a sneering lilt. "Show you can earn Sabrelle's favor, then, as you've failed to so many times before. Are you actually going to fight, or only hide up here behind your guards and soldiers? Let's see what might the 'empress' can bring to bear!"

My limbs quiver with the urge to answer her challenge, to launch myself forward with a swing of this sword—but that's exactly what she wants. She's goading me, knowing that if it comes to a regular skirmish, she has years if not decades of experience over me. She wants to show my failure in combat before all the soldiers assembled on both sides.

Every particle in me longs to demonstrate the strength I do possess, the respect I've more than earned.

Valerisse and her godlen have backed me into a corner too many times. I came here, I did battle with her, but it's been as much on my terms as I could make it.

If only she'd step close enough for me to use the addling potion in my ring... But I doubt I could touch her before she ran me through with that sword.

A chill trickles through me despite the support the gods showed me. I won them over, but can I really win this fight?

What if my methods aren't enough? Should I take my chances while I have them and attack Valerisse? With the blessed sword, I might be able to snatch Sabrelle's favor from her...

Even as that doubt grips me, I feel the gazes of the people all around us. The soldiers still standing who marched here on my behalf, the princes who threw in their lots with me over their own families, the man who was once emperor and now hails me as his empress.

They followed me because they believe in *me*, in all the ways I'm different from the rulers before. Great God save me, *I* believe in me too.

I've trusted in my own methods to see me through so much struggle before. I will not let my principles be compromised any further.

I'm not a warrior. I'm not a killer—never willingly.

The woman in front of me is, though. Perhaps in her tactics against me, she's revealing what would get under her skin.

I let my own sword dip as if I no longer see her as a threat. Drawing on the well of calm I've cultivated inside me, I meet her eyes with all the serenity I can exude. "Why should I fight you when you know I've already triumphed? Eight godlen support me, while you can only call on one. You talk about strength, but the only kind *you* know is lashing out with fists and blades."

Valerisse's eyes narrow. "That's how strength is enforced, which you'd know if—"

I interrupt her before she can launch into a longer criticism. "You can't offer the empire the joy of play and making art or the kind of creativity that can transform people's understanding. You can't offer my people the wisdom of history and philosophy to recognize what a healthy society needs. You can't offer them a willing ear to listen or the means to connect and collaborate across all the borders from north to south."

A flush creeps over Valerisse's face. "None of that matters," she snaps. "We'll sort out the rest once we see a true ruler on the throne."

Unruffled, I continue. "A true ruler would be thinking about how the empire's citizens will find abundance of all sorts, not how to shed their blood. A true ruler would wish to raise our people up rather than tearing down what others would build for them."

Marc continues banging on one side of the barrier while Raul is throwing his shoulder against the other side. The rest of my guards are pummeling the invisible shell around me as well. A tremor wobbles through the air.

From the tightening of Valerisse's jaw, I think she can feel it too. She's running out of time.

Because even trapped in here, I'm not alone. I have so many people on my side.

I'll be the empress they deserve.

Her lips pull back as if in a snarl. "I'll raise the empire up properly, on conquest and victory. You haven't built anything."

I have to hold back a snort at the thought of the very literal palaces I'm having constructed in Vivencia while we speak. "I offer them love that can cross status and borders. I offer them the cleverness to see through any battle by their own terms, no matter how great their opponent."

"Why are you talking as if you've defeated me? I could run you through right now."

I gaze back at her, softening my voice. "No, you couldn't. Because I'm bringing peace, and my godlen and I won't let anyone shatter it. Nothing you say or do can touch me. And everyone, even your own soldiers, is seeing that right now."

A harsher tremor ripples through the air. Sparks flicker where my protectors are striking the barrier, as if it's on the verge of disintegrating.

Valerisse lets out a wordless growl of frustration and hurls herself at me.

The sunlight flares off her blade and her helm. I step back instinctively. My gaze falls across her armor.

I don't know whether it's simply a natural keenness of sight, a lingering effect of merging my gift with Marc's magic, or some touch of divine magic. Whatever the case, my attention catches on a shift in the armored plates over Valerisse's chest.

There's a small spot just beneath her breast where one slat has broken away in the fighting. It must have been bashed by a spear point or a swipe of a sword. All that lies beneath is a scrap of fabric.

My arm moves as if of its own accord, through weeks of practice and a sense of certainty I can't totally explain. I whip my sword into position to meet the tribune's rush, not striking out, just bracing for impact.

Valerisse is hurtling forward too swiftly to adjust course even if it'd occur to her that she should. She slams straight into my weapon, and the blade pierces through that tiny opening and into her flesh.

The impact shoves me farther backward. The blade slices through sinew and muscle to clink into the plates of steel against her back. Blood spurts over me.

And Valerisse's sword keeps swinging at my neck.

The last part I can only attribute to Evando's training and Lorenzo's insistence that we focus on defensive skills. I twist to the side and roll away from the tribune's toppling body and her vicious strike.

The blade glances off my upper arm, only carving the thinnest of stinging lines in my skin. I hit the ground shoulder first and roll further.

Valerisse slumps over against the grass, her body already limp as the life blood pulses out of her.

The magical barrier surrounding us cracks. Marc rushes in to wrench me farther away, the princes at his heels.

I hug him tight just for a moment, my lips brushing his cheek, and then ease away.

All the soldiers have paused in their fighting, watching the confrontation just as Valerisse wanted it. Before their eyes, I flip her body onto its back with my foot and yank the Sabrelle-blessed sword from her chest.

Staring down at her slack corpse and the blood-drenched ground beneath her, picturing all the other bodies strewn across the hillside and field, a sudden rush of anger crackles through my veins.

I point my sword to the sky, blood dripping down its blade, and shout to the heavens. "Sabrelle, I've conquered your champion. I fought my way, and I won. If you still deny me my rightful place, then it's *you* who've betrayed me."

I will not cower. I will not beg. She can accept me or not, but I will remain.

It wouldn't surprise me if the clouds still streaking across the sky rumbled with her disapproval. But after a few strained breaths, all that comes is a beam of scarlet shining down on me from above, glowing over me as if the godlen is aiming a spotlight at me.

Heat washes over my skin that's forceful but not quite hostile. I have the vague impression that she's grudgingly embracing me and telling me I'd better not fuck up after all of this.

She lets me radiate her approval for several thuds of my heart before all to see, and then the light fades away.

My breath rushes out of me. I stiffen my spine against the urge to slump with exhaustion.

All across the field, Valerisse's soldiers lower their weapons. They gaze around them, left adrift, all the furor of justice-seeking wrenched from their grasps.

There's no one left to call them anything but traitors.

As I watch them, I can't summon any fury toward them. They were following their godlen and a woman who'd always led them well against a stranger who, I can admit, didn't fit the typical empress mold.

And now they have to live with the knowledge of their treason. How can we welcome them back into the fold with that fact tarnishing everything else they think and do? How will they accept the new terms I mean to offer the conquered countries after they've just clashed with their armies as enemies on the battlefield?

An image floats up from the back of my mind: the last piece of the vision that came to me in Kosmel's rat pit. The wave washing over the imperial uniforms and turning them a neutral gray—neither all good nor all evil.

I turn toward the one cauldron that's still bubbling, reaching toward my gift. "There's one more potion I need to make. Get the medics and anyone else with healing gifts seeing to the worst-injured! Let's save every life we can."

My husbands gather around me as I paw through my ingredients, chasing the fragments my gift presents to me.

"What are you making?" Raul asks. "It's done."

"It is. I need to make sure it doesn't continue later. Guilt and resentment can corrode the spirit so easily." I toss in another bundle of herbs. "We're going to wash all the treachery from their minds and let them start anew."

By the time I'm finished brewing, one of the medics has made her way to Bastien. When his vision clears at her attentions, a shuddery sigh slips out of him.

I motion him closer. "Let's make it rain one more time."

He lifts the potion I've concocted up to meet a new clot of heavy clouds. The messengers I sent out while I brewed have urged the armies from the outer territories farther back.

The sudden deluge courses down over only Valerisse's forces, laced with a chemical to turn their memories of the past few months into nothing but a dream.

All across the fields, the expressions turn from horrified or frightened to vague confusion.

As they drop their weapons, I walk down the hill to meet them.

"You've been through a trying time," I say. "But now you can come home."

Chapter Fifty-Four

Aurelia

As I compose myself with the broad purple tent set up for my use, a growing warble of voices filters through the fabric walls from the gathered civilians. Most of them sound excited, or at least curious, don't they?

Bianca peeks inside and steps in at my beckons. With a click of her tongue, she re-pins one lock of my hair. "Your maids were a little sloppy."

"I sent them off while they were still trying to fuss. I needed a moment alone." I smile at my friend so she doesn't think her presence is unwelcome. "I've had it now."

Bianca smiles back and smooths her hands over her ornate gown. The vicerine looks as polished as always—even with the pale nick on the left side of her jaw.

An arrow grazed her in the middle of the battle a week

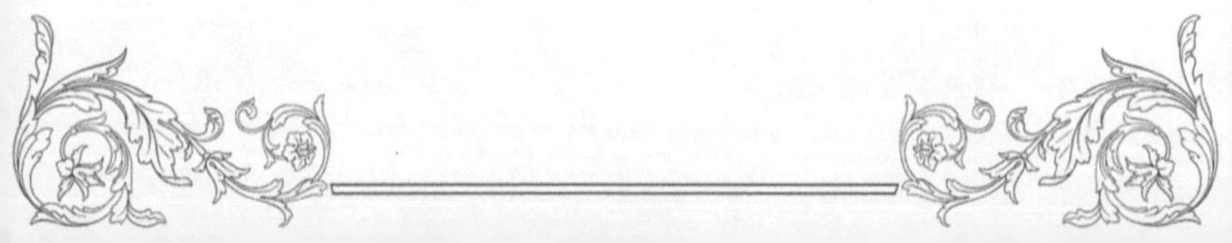

ago—it came inches close to stealing my closest friend from me along with so many others.

"It's a big thing you're doing today, but I think they're ready for it," she says. "We've all been ready for a change for a while, even if not all of us realized it."

I can't hold back a wry chuckle. "They'd better be ready for it, because I'm going ahead either way."

The vicerine's gaze slides to the tent door. "I'm not sure *she* deserves the honor you're giving her."

I don't need to ask who she's talking about. "It'll help the rest go down easier. Reinforce the sense of peace. And I'm not going to say anything untrue."

"Well, I've learned to trust your strategies." She pats my arm. "Go lead the way, and we'll find out what the future holds."

Lorenzo ducks past the flaps and makes a quick gesture to me. *Everything's in place.*

I square my shoulders and move to join him. "Let's reshape the empire."

Beyond the tent stands a tall platform that was constructed yesterday for our purposes. I climb the steps with Lorenzo beside me and my guards at my heels.

My other husbands are waiting for me on the smooth wooden surface above. Raul, Bastien, and Marc fall in to flank me, Marc in the new uniform I had commissioned for him that elevates him beyond the rank of guard. We haven't settled on a definite title for him yet, though I'm partial to Imperial Protector.

As I move across the platform, a soft twinge passes through my belly. The medics who inspected me after the battle were startled to discover that a small chunk of my liver had vanished. My repayment for the magic I worked with Marc and then Bastien, I suppose.

I'm lucky it was an organ that can adapt to such a loss.

The gods looked kindly on me. I'm the only one among us who extended my gift so far I evoked another sacrifice.

Before me, on the sprawling plains that stretch beyond this side of Dariu's capital, thousands of citizens from both the city and the surrounding countryside have gathered to hear my announcements. Many of the curious gazes linger on the marble coffin placed at the front of the platform.

I fasten my amplification charm to the bodice of my dress and nod to the cleric and devouts in Sabrellian red who've been waiting off to the side. They ease a little closer.

Clearing my throat, I lift my hands toward my audience. "Greetings, my people of Dariu—and wherever else you may hail from. It's wonderful to see so many of you gathered here today to welcome in what I hope will be a long-lasting time of peace and prosperity for all of us."

Those words are enough to provoke an initial cheer. Most of my audience are Darium, but a few soldiers from the outer territories have lingered since the battle last week, perhaps to report back to their respective royal families.

I step forward so I'm right at the coffin and cast a solemn glance down at it before lifting my gaze to the masses again. "First today, we must recognize the sacrifice of Tribune Valerisse. Her methods may have been misguided, but there's no denying that she was dedicated to protecting the empire. I wish we could have worked together rather than being at odds. I'm grateful that her commitment allowed me to demonstrate my own."

At my beckoning, the Sabrellian cleric and his devouts surround the coffin.

I tap my fingers through the gesture of the divinities. "I give the tribune's body over to the representatives of the godlen she served so avidly, to be offered a hero's entombment. Before the gods, I thank Sabrelle for sending such a worthy challenger, who pushed me to expand my own might and understanding. May our godlen of war continue to ensure all our rulers are worthy of this realm."

As the last words fall from my lips, the sunlight wavers at the edge of my vision. I get a fleeting glimpse of a circlet of glowing red descending toward me, as if to rest on my head atop the crown I'm already wearing.

My heart skips a beat. Sabrelle appeared to recognize my victory on the field the other day, but I haven't been sure the godlen had completely set aside her animosity. It seems my act of honoring has earned even more good will than I hoped.

Or perhaps, just like the people they watch over, our deities sometimes need a little time to fully adjust their thinking when they realize they've been wrong.

No gasps or murmurs follow the omen. I don't think it appeared to anyone else. It was an acknowledgment just for me.

The red-clothed devouts heft the coffin between them. Their cleric leads the procession off the platform and to a waiting cart behind a crimson carriage.

Sabrelle's blessed armband goes with them, hidden in a locked compartment within Valerisse's final resting place. I suspect it's best for all of us if it's never unearthed again—and possibly the godlen agrees with me on that point now.

I sweep my arm toward a marble tower poised off to the side of the platform, this one only ten feet tall—but it's just the beginning. "To all the other heroes who fell on the battlefield, I'm erecting a memorial in their honor. This obelisk is only the peak of it. The full structure will be three times as tall, to stand in the center of Vivencia's main square, with the name of every man and woman we lost carved into it."

The dove-pale stone with its ruddy veins feels like an appropriate material to represent the final compromise between pacifism and violence. I can't stop my gaze from flicking over the smooth surface as if I could read the names from here.

I wish I could do more for Kassun, Pierus, and the others who gave up so much to see me survive.

My throat tightens. I clench my hands against the pang of loss.

But maybe the best thing I can offer them is to carry out all the good I hoped to do for the empire as soon as possible.

I pull my posture straighter to address the crowd again. "The trials we've faced over the past few months have also brought one very important fact to light. In Dariu's time of need, all of the outer kingdoms risked life and limb to come to our aid and support the imperial family. Rione, Cotea, Lavira, Goric, and Accasy sent all the soldiers they could despite the threats they'd faced from Valerisse's forces. Let us hear a cheer for them!"

As the chorus of whoops and eager shouts ripples through the crowd, I check to confirm that the expected tables have been set up around the edges of the gathering. Dozens of palace staff wait to dispense the goods we've carried out here.

I spread my arms in a gesture of munificence. "After seeing the other countries of the empire prove their allegiance so emphatically, we are going forward from today with a new mandate of peace and friendship between us. From this day onward, the royal families of each kingdom will govern their own territories, collaborating with me, my daughter, and future emperors and empresses to come to ensure all of the empire thrives!"

The cheers that meet that proclamation sound more hesitant, but I press on before any doubts can set in. "The princes of those realms will remain here in Dariu as confirmation of our collaboration—and as my devoted companions. Their families have sent a bounty of gratitude for all of you to enjoy! Let us all now partake of their generosity."

I point out the sets of tables one by one. "Please feast on the delicacies each kingdom has provided: rye crisps with coconut jam from Rione, the finest ale from Cotea, stuffed figs and cheese croquettes from Lavira, cured mutton from Goric, and roasted lacquernuts with sips of creekvine wine from Accasy. While you eat, some of Rione's best musicians will delight our ears while a delegation from Cotea shows off their newest innovative tools that we'll soon all make use of."

As the crowd shifts to investigate the offerings, the air hums with enthusiastic chatter. No one shouts in protest about my declaration—no one questions my right to make it.

I've seen them through a civil war and shown them just how strong the empire still is, without the need for tyranny.

Affection for these people and all the others throughout the empire swells in my chest, softening the ache left by all the other funerals we've needed to hold for our fallen soldiers on both sides of the conflict.

They fought for what they believed in, for a better empire. I'm going to see that everyone still living gets that, whether it happens the way some expected or not.

My husbands ease closer around me, Marc resting his hand on the back of my elbow, Raul taking my hand. Bastien gazes out across the plain and then shoots a grin at me.

"They've already started on the dancing. You deserve to be part of this celebration too, Signal Star. Come on."

As ever, I'm more than happy to follow his orders. We descend the steps to the fringe of the crowd and form a circle of our own amid the merriment.

Hours later, when we return to my apartment after the reveling, I reach for my door without thinking. I'm about to withdraw my hand and fish for the key when the deadbolt slides aside as if by magic.

Not as if. That *was* magic. I stare at the door for a few seconds, my mouth gone dry, and then try the knob.

It turns smooth as butter. The door swings open to beckon me in.

A startled laugh snags in my throat.

Raul lets out a soft whoop of encouragement. "It seems the palace recognizes just how well you fill the role of empress too."

The oldest enchantments in this building are meant to respond only to imperial blood. I wasn't sure how we'd handle Coraya's lack of that once she was old enough.

It seems I don't need to worry about it after all. The stones and wood have embraced my rule too.

That magic came from the gods originally. I suppose it's following their lead. They're all on my side now.

My guards are gaping too. When I glance at them, one drops into a deeper bow. "Good night, Your Imperial Majesty."

No trace of resentment shows on Marc's face. He takes my elbow to lead me inside. "As it always should be."

Chapter Fifty-Five

Three years later

Aurelia

Queen Anahi and her family arrive for the Unity Festival first. The elegant carriages crafted from the same sleek but sturdy wood as Rione's famous ships roll through the imperial estate's gates and over to the white-washed palace that overlooks the orchard.

As the queen of Rione once greeted me on arriving at her home, I wait to welcome her with my husbands, my guards, and a bustle of staff around me. Even though we've conducted this festival twice before—and hosted other visits in between—my pulse kicks to a faster pace.

Anahi accepts the footman's hand to help her down from

the vehicle and bobs her head to me—a little lower than is really necessary when we're theoretically on equal ground now. Old habits die hard… but they are fading faster than I dared to hope.

I dip my own head in return. "I hope your journey was smooth and swift."

The queen smiles at me more warmly than she offered on our first meeting. "It was, and made all the more enjoyable by anticipation of the festivities to come."

Lorenzo steps forward, and his mother squeezes him in a quick but emphatic hug. He clasps his father's hand before his sister grabs him in an embrace of her own.

When the crown princess draws back, she clicks her tongue at her brother. "You need to come visit us again soon, Lore. A Rionian shouldn't go too long without being on the sea."

He grins back at her and flicks his hand in a gesture of agreement.

We've barely seen the Rionian party into their traveling palace before a page informs me that the Cotea convoy has been spotted. I hustle over to their accommodations, where the walls and windows boast various adjustments the avid innovators have made during their visits.

King Stanislas reunites with his son a little more stiffly than Lorenzo's family, but Bastien beams as they shake hands and ducks down to murmur to his little niece and nephew.

Neven joins us only just as the Gorician carriages pull through the gates, his cheeks a little flushed and his neck sporting a faint blotch that he jerks up his collar to hide.

Raul raises his eyebrows at his younger foster brother. "'Sparring' with your captain again, were you?"

Neven mock-scowls at him, but the gleam of his eyes reveals his good humor. After three years together, he and Evando haven't yet gotten bored of their playfully antagonistic relationship. In fact, they enjoy it so much they moved into shared quarters in the palace last summer, to no one's surprise.

Queen Dafina fusses over her son until Neven's blush has darkened, and then we're rushing over to welcome the Lavirians, who certainly won't appreciate a lapse in hospitality. Queen Benvida descends from her carriage with a bearing so regal it's almost imperial. When her gaze flicks over my gown, I'm glad I let my maids truss me up in one of my most ornate.

I wouldn't want the queen of Lavira to feel I'm failing to give her visit the proper respect.

As servants dart around bringing immediate refreshments, Raul teases his mother about whether she'll have any room for dinner. She tuts at him with obvious affection. "Knowing the kinds of feasts the imperial chefs whip up, you can be sure I come ready to indulge."

By the time the last line of carriages rattles over the cobblestones into the palace grounds, I only have Marc left beside me out of my husbands. But I can't resent the princes' time with their families when my heart is lifting at the thought of seeing my own.

As the Accasian procession draws up to the rugged stone palace built in my former country's honor, Marc lifts my hand to press a kiss to my knuckles. "Take all the time you need."

I maintain some standard of imperial decorum, clasping Father and Mother and then my sister in quicker hugs than I might have otherwise, blinking firmly at the happy tears that try to form in my eyes. I can't stop a wide grin from stretching across my face as I personally escort them into their temporary home.

My two-year-old nephew gasps and claps his hands at the dark wooden interior, as if this is the first time he's seen this replica of Accasian architecture before. He was barely more than a baby the last time he came, so as far as he's concerned, it probably is.

Father watches his second grandchild with a fond gleam in his eyes before taking in the halls and the room I lead him and Mother to with undisguised awe of his own. He beckons me inside, and my guards hang back beyond the door.

In the privacy of the royal chambers, I squeeze my parents as tightly as I wanted to before. Father kisses the top of my head and then gazes at me with so much admiration a glow lights in my chest.

"You've really done it," he says quietly. "Year after year, you're building something new here—and I don't mean the palaces."

I grip his hands. "I couldn't have done it without you."

He makes a soft scoffing sound. "I didn't believe in you enough when you were finding your way. I was so nervous… I should have trusted that you'd carve a path somehow or other."

A lump rises in my throat. "I had plenty of doubts too. What matters is that we're here now, setting our own courses and bringing our people with us."

The new festival I founded is celebrated all throughout this half of the continent, but I think nowhere quite as energetically as in Vivencia's central square. The city folk and visitors from across the country flock around the refreshment tables and the musicians, pausing here and there to peer up at the monument that towers in the center of the space.

Even while I stand on the imperial platform at one end of the square, too far away to decipher any of the names carved into the mottled marble, a fresh pang reverberates through my heart when I look at it. For all I've built, I still mourn the lives we lost in winning our peace. Too many of them.

Never again.

The highlight of the Unity Festival in Vivencia are the demonstration tents set up along the edges, dedicated to our allied countries. Every year, the royal families bring with them the latest examples of their most valued crafts and trades. Darium nobles and merchants decide on new purchases for the year, and the representatives of the outer territories strike their own deals with each other.

And it's not just the other countries bringing their people and goods to us. I spot a young man talking with one of the Goricians while motioning to the marble display model of a temple. From his eager gestures and the way his face has lit up, I suspect he's going to find himself an apprenticeship with the master stoneworkers before he leaves the square today.

Over by the Accasian tents, a girl of maybe twelve is exclaiming over the newest line of horses one of our breeders has been cultivating. Perhaps in a few years, she'll be following my footsteps backward to the country of my birth.

How funny is it that by releasing the conquered countries from the empire's oppression, we've become so much closer knit than we ever were when we theoretically lived as one.

Over recent months, I've made tentative diplomatic overtures to the countries on the other side of the Seafell Channel. Perhaps at the next Unity Festival, the kingdoms of Silana or Icar or Bryfeen will trust us enough to send their own representatives.

Someday the entire continent might be unified again, through bonds of friendship rather than domination.

Lorenzo takes up his vielle and joins the melody the court musicians are playing, and more of the civilians take to dancing. Coraya prances around me, swishing my skirt as if it's her dancing partner.

I scoop up my daughter and spin her around, reveling in her delighted laugh. She squirms around to reach for Raul, who doesn't hesitate to oblige her unspoken demand. As he swings her onto his shoulders, she giggles and digs her hands into his hair for balance.

"Now dance, Papa Raul," she orders him.

As the prince of Lavira bobs her through a rough jig, Bastien comes up beside me. He dips his head to kiss my cheek.

I revel in that sensation too—not just the brush of his lips but the total comfort he shows and I feel at showing such affection before all our people.

In the wake of the civil war and all the changes that've followed, the empire's citizens have barely blinked at my ongoing relationship with the four men they don't know are confirmed as my husbands. We've discussed carrying out a public marriage ceremony in a few more years, once we're absolutely certain it won't harm my position as empress.

But Coraya has been calling all of her fathers "Papa" along with their names for the past year, and I haven't heard a single suspicious word about that fact either. Possibly because for whatever reason, it started with Raul, and the entire court is aware he couldn't possibly be her birth father.

When he sets her down, she runs to Bastien next and tugs on his hand with a cajoling gaze. The prince of Cotea laughs, but he's never been able to resist our daughter.

"Only for a minute," he tells her. "We don't use our gifts frivolously."

"Much," Marc murmurs, easing closer behind me, but his tone is only amused. He sets his hand on the small of my back. We watch together as Bastien summons a cushion of air to lift Coraya a foot off the ground, as if she's flying.

The sight of a familiar face amid the nobles around us draws my attention away from my daughter momentarily. I raise my hand to beckon Bianca over. "You made it in time!"

My friend pats her looping hair and aims a wry smile at me. "You know, I do appreciate being mistress of my own estate, but it gets rather boring being there for long. A little peace here and there is plenty. Who could want that over the drama of court life?"

I laugh. "Fair enough."

Thankfully, ever since the estate and associated title I gifted her gave her the freedom to divorce Ennius, very little of that drama has involved her. I can tell she prefers watching from the sidelines.

Bianca leans closer to me. "Which is not to say I'm not awfully grateful for the fact that I can count on quite a bit of peace even when I'm here."

I tap my elbow against hers. "Then I'm grateful I could provide you with it."

Lorenzo leaves off his playing while the court musicians carry on and extends his hand to me in a request for a dance. Bianca gives me a little shove toward my lover, and I let him tug me into step with him.

I take a turn with the prince of Rione, and then with Marc, and then Raul, and then Bastien. All around us, my court and the visiting royals make merry to the music as well. The kings and queens, crown princess and princes and their spouses, whirl in each other's arms.

Axius moves more stiffly but no less enthusiastically with his wife. Baronissas Damina and Hivette match each other's movements perfectly. Off by the edge of the platform, I catch sight of Neven's pale head ducked next to Evando's slightly darker one.

Bianca doesn't bother with entertaining even the pretense of enjoying physical advances anymore, but she looks nothing but pleased to gambol between us hand in hand with Coraya, who's giggling all the while. The obligation-free role of honorary aunt suits her perfectly.

When I sink into the throne set up in the middle of the platform, my daughter races over to scramble onto my lap. I cuddle her against my chest while I gaze out over the mass of people I've somehow brought together.

With only darkness showing beyond the windows, I kiss Coraya's forehead goodnight and cross the hall to my apartment opposite hers. All three of my princes and Marc follow me in without hesitation.

They still keep their own rooms in the palace—I granted Marc one apart from the guard dormitories once he became known as my consort—but they rarely sleep there. I had my bed expanded not long after the war was over, and a couple of broad sofas arranged so there's plenty of opportunity to share the room without feeling crowded.

Marc shrugs off his fancy guard jacket and tosses it over the back of a chair, his gaze gone distant. "Those new irrigation techniques the Cotean agricultural representative talked about have a lot of potential. Maybe you should see if they can send a few people to give training sessions in the Darium farmlands."

I pick up the journal I left on my vanity. "Good idea. I'll make a note of that for our meetings tomorrow."

Raul glowers at both of us. "And then you'll cut out the governing talk, because our wife has had a busy day and she deserves a break from politics."

Marc narrows his eyes at the other man, though a smile lingers on his lips. "The work of leading an empire can never be completely set aside."

Raul snorts through a smile of his own. "Then lead it in your head for a little while, Your No-Longer-Imperial Majesty. And get that no-longer-imperial ass into bed."

We do all end up in the bed, in our usual full formation with me tucked in the middle and my four lovers taking the sides, head, and foot of the vast mattress. Sprite curls up on the pillow in the corner that's become permanently hers.

Next to me, Bastien teases his fingers over my hair. His expression turns pensive. "You requested more mirewort from the medics this morning."

I hum in agreement. "My supply is getting low."

His fingers trail across my shoulder. "I know you're still establishing yourself and ensuring the transition is going smoothly… but do you think someday you'll want to give Coraya a sibling or two?"

The other men go still around me. By my head, Marc lets out a disgruntled sound. "Going for another without giving anyone else a chance?"

Bastien rolls his eyes good-naturedly. "I wasn't thinking it'd have to be *me* doing the deed."

Raul's bark of a laugh sounds a little strained. "Well, we know it won't be me."

I peer down at him where he's sprawled by the footboard and nudge his arm with my toes. "You know any children I have will be yours too, no matter how they come into being."

His eyes soften. He takes my foot in his hands to massage the arch. "Never doubted it. And I'm not going to regret my sacrifice when the gift I got for it ensured you stayed alive."

Lorenzo dips his head to give my neck a provocative nip. His breath spills hot across my skin alongside his illusionary voice in my head. *"Do you think— Do we need to worry about what the court and everyone else will make of it?"*

His caress brings a giddy hitch into my voice. "It's not as if they won't realize any other children I have must be one of yours. They can't imagine 'Marclinus' has returned from the grave. I doubt *which* of you it is will matter much to them."

Marc strokes his fingers across my temple. "As long as you don't give any indication of removing Coraya as your heir, I can't imagine anyone raising a fuss about it." He pauses. "*Are* you considering it, then?"

I think of Coraya nestled in my arms on the throne, of watching her frolic with her fathers. The answer wells up inside me. "I think motherhood is something I wouldn't mind experiencing more of. When the time is right."

Raul arches an eyebrow. "Then it'll only be a matter of who gets the next turn."

Bastien, having already had his, stretches his arms in an unusually languid pose. "Perhaps we should leave this one to the fates. Find out whose seed is stronger."

I wrinkle my nose at him. "We're not going to make a competition out of getting me pregnant."

He grins. "I don't know. It sounds like a much more enjoyable trial than any other we've been through."

I can't hold back a guffaw. "All right, I'll give you that."

I lean back into Lorenzo's embrace, tuck one hand around Marc's wrist and the other by Bastien's neck, and rest my feet against Raul's solid chest where he's continuing his massage. "One more dream to add to the list for after I'm finished seeing my greatest one through. Any other child I have is going to be born into a world we can be proud of."

"You know," Raul says in an unusually soft tone, "for the first time, I'm actually looking forward to everything the future could bring."

A deeper warmth washes over me, full of affection for the men around me and the knowledge of theirs for me—and hope, shining like the signal star Bastien likes to call me.

A smile stretches my lips. "So am I."

The Gods of the Abandoned Realms

THE ALL-GIVER (the Great God, the One) - overseer of all existence, creator of the godlen

THE GODLEN OF THE SKY

Estera - wisdom, knowledge, and education

Inganne - creativity, play, childhood, and dreams

Kosmel - luck, trickery, and rebellion

THE GODLEN OF THE EARTH

Creaden - royalty, leadership, justice, and construction

Prospira - fertility, wealth, harvest, and parenthood

Sabrelle - warfare, sports, and hunting

THE GODLEN OF THE SEA

Ardone - love, beauty, and bodily pleasures

Elox - health, medicine, and peace

Jurnus - communication, travel, and weather

About the Author

Eva Chase lives in Canada with her family. She loves stories both swoony and supernatural, and strong women and the men who appreciate them.

Along with the Royal Spares series, she is the author of the Rites of Possession series, the Shadowblood Souls series, the Heart of a Monster series, the Gang of Ghouls series, the Bound to the Fae series, the Flirting with Monsters series, the Cursed Studies trilogy, the Royals of Villain Academy series, the Moriarty's Men series, the Looking Glass Curse trilogy, the Their Dark Valkyrie series, the Witch's Consorts series, the Dragon Shifter's Mates series, the Demons of Fame series, and the Legends Reborn trilogy.

Connect with Eva online:
www.evachase.com
eva@evachase.com